The End
of
Camelot

by

Diana Rubino

The New York Saga, Book Three

This is a work of fiction. Names, characters, places, and incidents are either the product of the author's imagination or are used fictitiously, and any resemblance to actual persons living or dead, business establishments, events, or locales, is entirely coincidental.

The End of Camelot

COPYRIGHT © 2015 by Diana Rubino

Cover Art by *Diana Carlile*

The Wild Rose Press, Inc.
PO Box 708
Adams Basin, NY 14410-0708
Visit us at www.thewildrosepress.com

Publishing History
First Vintage Rose Edition, 2015
Print ISBN 978-1-62830-842-6
Digital ISBN 978-1-62830-843-3

The New York Saga, Book Three
Published in the United States of America

It was New Year's Eve, they were alone, and he was harmless. So far. So she took the necessary two paces over to him and placed the honey ball between his custom-made choppers.

He closed his eyes, and she watched him savoring the sweetness. She didn't dare say another word as she ran her index finger over a glob of cream on the cannoli plate, raised it to her lips and licked. "Mmmm," she voiced, wishing she hadn't.

Their eyes met and locked. Faster than lightning, they came together like magnets. Their lips met, sweet and sticky and hot. She didn't want him to stop, but her inner voice screamed how wrong it was—*It's forbidden!*—echoing the nuns in Saint Gustina's. She shooed it away like an annoying fly. *Leave me alone. I'm not a kid anymore.* Her arms circled his neck, and his hands slid down to the curve of her back. Dare she move in closer, pelvis to pelvis, an unthinkable act three seconds ago? Her body was betraying her, betraying Jack, taking on a will of its own as she crushed herself to him. The kiss intensified. She tasted cannoli, and her fogged mind told her he'd been sampling them all day. She breathed in his cologne, so foreign it repelled her, so new it aroused her even further. Her tiara slipped off her head. She caught it just as he pulled away.

He held her at arm's length as in a tango. "Oh, *cara mia*," he growled—and if he said another word in Italian, she knew she'd explode. A passion long dormant stirred inside her.

Dedication

To my husband Chris

Acknowledgments

My thanks go out to:

Melvin Lee Ewing for the expertise on sniper techniques and hardware;

My cousin Paul W. Rubino for the advice on firearms and police procedure;

Angela Rosati for the Italian opera advice, Napolitan dialect, and for reading the manuscript;

Rosalia Bengardino for Campobello di Mazara;

Vince Pilgrim for the facts about cameras and television production;

Linda Unger for the fashion details;

Janet Adams for reading the manuscript, for all your support, and for believing in me;

My gifted editor Nan Swanson and The Wild Rose Press for believing in me. I'm so grateful to all of you.

Edgar Allan Poe for teaching me about irony. *In pace requiescat.*

Prologue

Washington, D.C., September, 1959

Vikki McGlory aimed her Smith & Wesson .38 and fired at the metal target. "Bull's eye." She kissed the gun's warm barrel. A smudged red lip print bloomed against the steel gray metal.

The gun now empty, she didn't bother to reload. That was enough target practice for one day. She slipped the weapon into its customary place, the leather holster hidden in the center pocket of her crocodile tote.

She headed back to work. But, God, she hated her job. Trying to follow her grandmother's footsteps into politics had been a huge mistake. Vikki longed to get back to her painting and costume designing, to the sunny studio waiting for her on Fire Island. Only one thing kept her here: NBS's star reporter, the free-spirited, captivating, and eligible Jack Ward. She never missed his newscasts and had devoured his autobiography in one sitting. He didn't know she existed, but she planned to fix that. She'd already decided he was the man she was going to marry.

****

Christmas Eve, 1960
Larchmont, New York

Vikki trembled as her two heroes met in front of the twinkling tree. "Dad, this is Jack Ward. Jack, this is my father."

"How do you do, Mr. McGlory." Jack offered his hand.

"Billy to you," he insisted with a wink, as he returned the firm handshake. "It's great to have you join us for the holidays."

The evening raced by in a swirl of introductions, delicious food, fine wine, and a live orchestra. Billy threw fabulous parties, and this one was no exception. Late that night, Jack walked Vikki to her room in the family wing of the mansion. Through her champagne-heightened haze of happiness, she heard him promise to love her always. He kissed her goodnight, and as his kiss deepened, she responded willingly. Her dreams were coming true. But they weren't married yet, and if there was one thing her dad had taught her, it was that she was a prize worth waiting for.

The next morning, Jack drew her into the library, dropped to one knee, and slid a diamond solitaire on her finger.

They exchanged vows the day after John F. Kennedy took the Oath of Office. So began the fairy-tale life she'd always dreamed of. And she called it Camelot.

Chapter One

April 2, 1963

In one day, Benzo Battolini became the world's most sought-after hit man for one simple reason: he'd just been hired to assassinate the president of the United States.

But that wasn't till November. Now, he crouched behind a clump of trees at the water's edge, stalking his current hit. His witness, a CIA operative, squatted next to him, nibbling on a chicken wing. Battolini wished they didn't have to work in pairs like this. He was a loner, on and off the job.

But it was a chance to show off, although this hit was gravy: the subject spent more time on his fishing boat than on dry land, so the getaway would be even easier. Conditions were perfect: no crowds, no obstructions, no wind. The hardest part was the waiting around.

So they waited. And waited.

He drained the last drop of Kool-Aid from his flask and sang every Jimmy Roselli song ever written. He was dying for a puff of a Camel and a shot of Jim Beam, but smoking or boozing on the job was out—an old Army rule that stuck.

Another hour dragged by.

The CIA operative didn't say much. Battolini

wasn't the chatty type either, so after a brief exchange about Cuba, sniper rifles, and the best cathouses in their native New Orleans, they clammed up and waited some more.

Finally, the boat glided into view. The target proudly held up his catch of the day while a crony snapped pictures with a Brownie.

Battolini peered through the 10x scope of "Scarlett," his Winchester 70, and steadied her barrel on a log. He took a deep breath, exhaled, and during the lull, counted to three. He squeezed Scarlett's trigger. The man's head exploded like a hand grenade.

A primal surge shot through Battolini and he let out a satisfied grunt, as if sexually sated.

"Bull's-eye!" The CIA operative clapped him on the back. "I wish I was as good a shot as you."

"Keep practicin', Lee, and you just might be."

With Scarlett wrapped in a blanket and tucked under his arm, Battolini strolled back to his car, Lee Harvey Oswald at his heels. A smirk spread Battolini's lips. "After November, I'll be cruisin' around in my own yacht," he muttered. Too bad about having to take out JFK, though. He had nothing against the guy personally—but business was business.

****

November 1, 1963

"This job might be a challenge," Battolini commented to his fellow assassin Vero as they cleaned their rifles. "They been beefin' up security at JFK's latest appearances. I never seen so many Secret Service agents around a president."

"Yeah, they went whole hog at the Four Seasons fundraiser last night." Vero spoke with a cigarette dangling from his lips. "The limo ducked into a garage, so he didn't even step outside, and three Secret Service men stayed at the front entrance the whole time. You know who else was there? Jack Ward."

"That nosy bastard reporter from NBS?" Battolini ran a hand over his chin stubble. "Come to think of it, I seen him at every JFK rally and news conference since we got our orders. He either got demoted to the White House Press Corps or he's onto us."

"Maybe he oughta get taken out." Vero sucked on his cigarette.

"I ain't no boss, but I wouldn't mind gettin' him outta my hair." Battolini attached his telescopic sight to Scarlett and peered through her with one eye closed. "He's such an arrogant son of a bitch, I reckon a lotta people want him six feet under."

"Then wait till one of them calls you, so you'll get paid fer it." Vero tossed his cigarette butt on the ground and crushed it with his heel.

They snickered.

"Ward actually thinks we don't notice him lurkin' around?" Battolini shook his head. "He's on TV more than Gleason, fer Chrissakes."

"Hey, I'm goin' to Miami a few days early, to rest up before the hit." Vero lit another cigarette. "Wanna join me?"

"Yeah, why not? It's the twenty-first, sneakin' up on us fast." Battolini glanced at the calendar. "The boys are makin' arrangements with the Miami cops. Then we can scout the motorcade route and figger out all the picayune details. Ya know, this is the first presidential assassination that won't be done at close range with a handgun."

"Shur ain't easy to get near the president, not like in the old days. Times they are a-changin'," Vero commented.

The phone rang and Battolini went to answer it. "Marc Antony here…Yep…Oh, yeah?…Is that right?" he drawled smoothly. "That sonofabitch…Yes, sir, Cassius is right here."

Vero gave Battolini a "What's up?" gesture. Battolini exchanged a few more words with the caller and hung up.

Vero held his rifle up like a coveted award. "So who's the son of whose bitch?"

"They just changed the date and place on us. Now it's Dallas on the twenty-second," Battolini replied in his usual unruffled manner. "I was aimin' to take a speedboat to Cuba on Thursday from Miami, right after the hit. Fidel's throwin' a shindig that night. Now we have to hightail it to Dallas on Friday. Screws up all my plans."

"Well, sometimes life just throws ya a curve, don't it?" Vero said. "How's the saying go, 'I was plannin' the future when the present hit me in the face' or some such?"

"Yep, sometimes it just hits you in the face. Or, in our business, in the back of the head, heh, heh." Battolini stretched and grabbed his car keys. "Hey, let's go for ice cream."

"Ice cream?" Vero laughed. "You're like a little kid sometimes, you know that?"

"So?" Battolini headed for the door. "Come on, let's go. I'm dyin' for a vanilla cone with them colored bugs all over it." His mouth started to water.

They got into Battolini's car. He drove down the

strip and past the city limits sign.

"Hey, slow down, will ya?" Vero warned. "Whatcha doin', seventy? I don't wanna die in a car accident tonight."

"Trust me. You won't."

Battolini smirked as Vero peered around at their surroundings growing darker and less familiar. "Hey, uh—where we goin', Ben? There ain't no ice cream places around here."

Battolini slowed down, turned onto a dirt road, and stopped. He whipped out his Colt Cobra and aimed it at Vero's head. "Get out. Now."

"What?"

"Get out," Battolini repeated patiently, like a suggestion.

"Ben, what—what'd I do?" Vero threw the car door open, scrambled out, and broke into a run.

Battolini shook his head. Who did this sorry idjit think he was messing with anyways? He got out, squeezed the trigger, and watched Vero's skull shatter. The body keeled over with that satisfying thump Battolini always enjoyed hearing.

"Nice shot. Hope I do that good on 'The Big D' day. Ask what you can do for your country, heh, heh." He blew on the end of the smoking Colt's barrel.

Battolini didn't kill for fun. He'd learned over the phone from his handler that Vero had blabbed to some French Quarter hooker about being hired to assassinate the president. Now, just as JFK was heading south for more politickin', rumor had it that the media was onto the plot. That must be why that nosy reporter Jack Ward was scoutin' all the JFK events with his eagle eye. Now that Vero got his, that bigmouthed hooker was next—and if Jack Ward knew too much, he'd have to go, too, before all hell broke loose.

Battolini drove back into town and raced up his street, blowing his horn. He shouted out the open window, "Hey, wait! Hold your horses!"

The Good Humor truck pulled over.

****

November 21, 1963
The Dallas Hilton

He pulled the curtain aside and glanced down at the pool area. It was warm for November, and he could see Ward down there doing his expert breast stroke.

"You love water so much, I'll give you water, Jack, old boy," he muttered, turning away from the window.

At midnight, he snapped on a pair of surgical gloves and rapped on Ward's door. It opened, and the popular reporter, draped in a satin robe, flashed his trademark Pepsodent smile, like he was on the air. "Oh—hello," Ward chirped.

"It's goodbye, you vulture." He slammed Ward's head against the wall and smothered him with a chloroform-soaked rag.

Ward struggled for all of three seconds before sliding to the floor in a crumpled heap.

After turning on the water full force, he stripped Ward's body, hauled it into the filling tub, and held the head under until the breathing stopped.

He felt for a pulse. None.

A feeling of raw power surged through him. Watching this bastard die was better than hot sweaty sex.

He drained the tub, washed the chloroform off Ward's face, and filled the tub again. For good measure he tossed in a cake of soap.

A half-empty bottle of Scotch stood on the bar. He took his time polishing it off while he did some snooping. He didn't want Jack Ward's credit cards or fancy jewelry. But the stacked blonde in the wallet photo, her hair draped over her bare knockers, sent another raw surge to his loins. He flipped it over and read, *To my loving husband, yours forever, Vikki,* in neat script. "I could screw you into the floor right now, bitch," he growled, sliding the photo out of the wallet and leering at it. "Now that you're a widow, maybe I will." He slid the photo into his own wallet.

He finished off the Scotch and placed the empty bottle on the edge of the tub without giving the submerged corpse another glance.

Did Ward actually believe he could thwart a presidential assassination? Who the hell did that two-bit reporter think he was anyway? The Man from U.N.C.L.E.?

Glancing around, he noticed the portable tape recorder still running. Ward must've been dictating into it before he answered the door. Holy smokes! The entire murder was on that tape!

He yanked the reel off the machine, looking forward to playing it over and over, reliving his triumph again and again.

On his way out, he saw something else he could use, lying on the floor next to Ward's robe. He slid it into his shirt pocket, closed the door, and strolled down the hallway, whistling Dixie.

Chapter Two

November 22, 1963
Larchmont, New York

Vikki entered her foyer and dropped her shopping bags on the floor. As she locked the door and kicked off her alligator pumps, the phone rang. She answered it in the kitchen, so she could raid the pastry box while she chatted.

"Vikki, it's Linc Benjamin." His ragged voice came over the line. "I have terrible news. Jack is dead."

"What?" She couldn't have heard right. "What did you say?"

"Jack was found in the bathtub of his hotel room this morning—"

She dropped the phone and slid down against the wall. Her glasses fell off her face. The room spun. Sunlight glared. She smelled the new coat of wax on the kitchen floor.

"Vikki? Vikki?" came faintly from the dangling receiver. She crawled over and grasped it. He would tell her it was a mistake, they had the wrong man, or it was another of Jack's practical jokes.

"My Jack?" she whispered.

"Vikki, I'm so sorry," he sobbed.

"Linc—no, please. Tell me it wasn't Jack. Are you sure? There must be a mistake. Not Jack." Her heart thudded like a hammer. A stabbing pain pierced her chest. She held the receiver away from her ear.

"Vikki, are you there?" His voice came through the earpiece. "If you want, I'll be right over. I can tell you everything when I get there, or right now, whatever you want."

"Now!" she demanded.

"The Dallas police found him drowned in his hotel bathtub—"

"Dallas? What was he doing in Dallas? He's supposed to be in Chicago doing a story on the FBI," she screeched, beyond rational thought. No, this had to be a mistake!

"I don't know, Vikki. The maid found him. The Dallas police tried to call you all morning, but you weren't home, so they called here, at the network. Do you want me to come over and—"

"Wait!" She squeezed her eyes shut. "Now—where is he now?"

"Parkland Hospital. They're going to bring the bod—er, bring him back to New York after the autopsy." His voice broke again. "God, Vikki, I'm so sorry. I feel like I lost my brother."

She went blank, too stunned to think. Her hands shook so much she could hardly hold the phone.

"Vikki, do you want me to come over—"

"No." She released the receiver. It swung away and banged against the wall. She curled up on the floor as the ticking clock echoed the thudding of her heart.

She wept in unbearable grief, shutting her eyes tight, her head cradled in her arms. A jumble of thoughts rendered her helpless.

"Please, God," she prayed, "Let it be a mistake and

Jack will come walking through the door."

The doorbell rang. "Jack?" She forced her eyes open.

"Vikki!"

Her head throbbed with each pound on the door.

"Vikki! Are you okay? Can you hear me?"

The voice was her father's, and as much as she wanted him with her, holding her, rocking her, the present was too much to bear. She wanted one last visit to the past with Jack, happy and alive and free from harm.

But the raw truth seared her soul: *The past is gone, and so is your beloved Jack!*

Too weak to walk, she crawled to the door, reached up, and unlocked it.

Her father rushed in and knelt beside her. "Vikki, honey?"

She collapsed into his arms, heaving gut-wrenching sobs.

"It's okay, I'm here," he crooned, like he was singing the songs he wrote for her.

"Dad, Jack—" She couldn't bring herself to say it yet. The words were too ugly, too real.

"Yeah, I know. He got shot. When I looked in the sidelight and saw you lying on the floor, I thought you were hurt."

She gulped. "I answered the phone and it was..." That seemed like a hundred years ago already.

He helped her up, and she forced herself to gulp enough air to stay conscious while he said, "I'll turn on the TV and see what the news says about the shooting—"

"No, he wasn't shot! They found him in the tub—"

"Vikki, here, let me get you on the couch. Come on, babe, that's it." He helped her off with her coat. "Now, what are you saying?"

"Dad—Jack…"

"I know." He nodded. "JFK was shot in the head. The governor of Texas was shot, too."

"No! My Jack! They found him—" Sobs burst from the depths of her soul.

"Huh? What…Your Jack?"

Unable to speak any further, she nodded.

"Something happened to him?" He sat her down on the couch.

She drew in a ragged breath, and he grasped her hands.

"Oh, God. Oh, Jesus Christ, Vikki." He held her and stroked her hair as she sobbed, her tears staining his scarf. "Okay, Dad's here, I'll stay with you. I'm sorry, I thought you were talking about President Kennedy. He just got shot."

"President Kennedy?" She shook her head in disbelief. "No. Jack's friend from the network called, and—" She couldn't go on.

"Don't talk. I'll get you a brandy or something." He glanced over at her liquor cabinet.

She didn't even want him leaving her for a few seconds. He hung her phone up, and it started ringing instantly. She heard spurts of conversation. His voice sounded like an echo in a marble tomb. He finally stopped talking and came back with a brandy bottle, a snifter, and her eyeglasses. "I found your glasses on the floor." He took her into his arms and rocked her back and forth. "You'll be okay, you're strong, you're my girl," he murmured, and she wished he'd sing to her.

Instead he explained that President Kennedy had been shot on the motorcade route in Dallas.

Dallas?

She finished off the brandy, curled up, and cried herself to sleep. When she awoke, it was dark out. Her father sat by her side, hunched forward, staring at the television. "Jesus, I can't believe it, I can't believe it," he kept repeating, shaking his head.

Another flood of horror assaulted her.

President Kennedy is dead, too.

She stared blankly at the screen, a glowing gray blur without her glasses.

Walter Cronkite's voice quavered as he fought tears. "The president of the United States…is dead. President John F. Kennedy…is dead. The president was pronounced dead at one-thirty Eastern time, twelve-thirty Dallas time." Like a lesson, they had to repeat it again and again to the disbelieving public until it sank in.

She put on her glasses and watched images, filmed earlier that day, of the open limousine gliding through downtown Dallas, a tanned and beaming president and a radiant Mrs. Kennedy waving to the adoring crowd.

She knew exactly what Jackie was going through now.

As of 1:30 Eastern time, 12:30 Dallas time, the fairy tale was over for both of them.

Chapter Three

Mrs. Ward and Mrs. Kennedy both buried their husbands on Monday, November 25. Vikki didn't watch any of the television coverage; she'd been too busy with her own Jack's wake, funeral procession, and last goodbye at the gravesite. Thank God the reporters and hangers-on went to the nation's capital and left her alone.

Only later did she hear about some Dallas strip club owner killing Lee Harvey Oswald on live television. "I know that guy from someplace," Billy commented, studying the *New York Times* front page.

How her father knew a shady character like Jack Ruby, she didn't want to ask.

****

Through a blur of tears she stared at the photo of Lyndon Johnson taking the oath of office on Air Force One, a dazed Jackie Kennedy at his side, still wearing her blood-spattered suit. With the entire world gawking at her, the now-former First Lady stood brave and strong.

"Give me strength like Jackie, please, Jesus, get me through this!" she prayed.

She called on that strength when the Dallas Police ruled Jack's death an accidental drowning and closed the case.

****

One day slid into the next. She staggered through each hour, her body a numb column. Billy stayed with her, and they spent hours at the piano together. All she could choke down were animal crackers and cream soda, and he finally called his cook over to whip up her favorite Italian feast. The garlic and gravy aromas teased her appetite, and she ate some of it with a few sips of Chianti Classico. She later threw it all up. No, she wasn't ready to hold down a meal.

But she attended 5:30 mass every day, received communion, and walked home.

On the days when she could think straight, she asked the same question over and over: How could Jack have drowned in a bathtub?

Unable to go near their bed, she slept in the guest room, but only in spurts, between nightmares and cold sweats. Visions haunted her: Jack laughing and full of life, then flashes of his face drained in death.

Again the question badgered her: How could Jack have drowned in a bathtub?

Praying kept her sane, along with her father's company and his music. Her ninety-year-old Grandma Vita came over, and they sewed together. And for a little while each day, she escaped into the world of cartoons and game shows.

Her hair grew unruly and her nail polish chipped, but she didn't care. She had no interest in laundry or ironing, either. She wore wrinkled blouses; she went without her girdle.

She didn't give a damn what she looked like anymore.

Another question plagued her: What was Jack doing in Dallas when he'd told her he was going to

Chicago?

Now that the police had made it clear they were done, she had to get the answers herself.

She started with a call to the president of NBS. He was out of town, so she left a message.

Later that day, as she and Billy played gin rummy, NBS delivered Jack's personal belongings. "Please stack the boxes in the study at the end of the hall and close the door after you," she instructed the courier. With Jack's scent still lingering there, and his favorite pipe propped on the ashtray like he'd be back any minute, she couldn't bear to set foot in that room.

Linc Benjamin called at least twice a day. "Vikki, is there anything I can do?" he begged once again.

About to say, "No, thanks, there's nothing," one more time, she stopped. "Actually, Linc, there is something. Can you come over tonight after work?"

****

For the first time since Jack's funeral, she starched and ironed a blouse and arranged a hairdo. She forced herself to pull on a girdle and nylons. Applying lipstick was a chore. But she couldn't let Jack's best friend see her looking like a frump.

Her father was at a meeting in the city, so she was alone when Linc arrived.

She handed him a dry martini, and made an even drier one for herself. "Linc, NBS delivered three boxes of Jack's things. They're in his study, and I'd appreciate it if you could go through them for me. I need to find some information."

He swallowed, and fidgeted with his tie clip. "If you want me to. But I'd feel—you know, like an intruder, snooping through his personal stuff."

"You won't be snooping. I know he wouldn't mind you doing this. Please?" Her voice broke. "For me?"

"Are you looking for something in particular?"

"Well, yes, the fountain pen I gave him when he won his second Emmy. But something else has been bothering me." She swallowed and took a breath. "I need to see if he wrote any notes about why he went to Dallas. He doodled all the time, everywhere, on his arm, on the walls when he talked on the phone…maybe you'll find something in there, on a pad, on a matchbook, anything."

"Why don't we both go in there together and—"

"No, Linc, I can't. He—his presence lingers in there. I can't face it." Her eyes filled with tears.

"Sure, Vikki. I'll bring the stuff out here." He got up and jangled his pocket change. "Uh—where's his study?"

She sensed his anxiety to get out of there and leave her alone. "End of the hall. Three cardboard boxes." She raised her chin in the direction of Jack's sanctuary. "I can't go in there. I hardly set foot in there while he was alive, but now…"

As Linc did an abrupt turn and headed down the hall, she sank into her recliner. She'd given away Jack's matching chair. With the cushion conformed to his body, it had been too agonizing to look at.

Linc returned and placed one box on the floor, brushed his hands together, and went back to get the others.

Cracking her knuckles one at a time, she peeked through the opening at a pile of composition books with the black-and-white cloud-pattern covers. A Dallas business directory stood upright. "Why Dallas?" she wondered out loud, as if the book would give her the answers she so desperately needed. She flipped through it but found none of Jack's scribblings.

Linc came back with the second box and placed it beside the first. "Jack's leather briefcase is in here." He pointed, then headed to the study for the third carton.

Why hadn't Jack taken his briefcase to Dallas?

Linc returned with the last box. He opened one of the composition books. "Jack was always writing in these notebooks, even during a broadcast, on the commercial breaks." He released a weary sigh and polished his glasses on a handkerchief. Then he slowly turned the pages, each one covered with Jack's scrawl. "His notes for his interviews with the astronauts. Yeah, here's a bio sketch of John Glenn, directions to Cape Canaveral…"

Vikki's thoughts drifted back to Jack's take on the space program.

Even that was too tame for him. "Kid stuff," he'd scoffed, watching Alan Shepard skyrocket into space and back to earth. "Let's see him cover a race riot in Alabama."

She forced herself back to the present. "Nothing to do with Dallas, though," she said.

Linc shook his head.

"I need to go through each notebook with a fine-tooth comb if I'm going to find any useful information," she said, mostly to herself. "I can't overlook the tiniest detail." Knowing how painful this was going to be, she shuddered. She'd have to force herself. "What else is in there?"

"Pens, stapler, that globe paperweight UNICEF gave him." He shuffled through the contents. "Just all the stuff they scooped out of his desk drawers."

Pens? She leaned over and scanned the items lying at the bottom of the box: odds and ends, just like he'd said. To be sure, she tipped the box toward her and rifled through it. Her glasses slid down her nose, and she pushed them back up. "It's not here."

"What isn't?"

"Jack's fountain pen, the one I gave him when he won the Emmy last year. I had Cartier engrave 'Emmy Award Winner' and the date into the barrel. It was eighteen-karat rose-and-yellow gold."

"Yeah, I remember seeing him with that." He nodded with a hint of a smile. "It was pretty flashy."

"It was a work of art. The police didn't return it with the personal items he had on him in Dallas, and it's not here, either." She rummaged some more, although she knew she wouldn't find it.

"You're assuming he had it with him in Dallas," Linc said.

"He always had it with him. He even wore it clipped to his robe when he was walking around the house. He never let it out of his sight."

"Is it in his car maybe?" he asked.

Unable to inhale the car's leather-and-pipe-tobacco aroma, she'd given her father that job. Billy certainly would've retrieved the pen, along with the loose change and driving gloves he'd cleaned out of Jack's Ferrari. "No. He never kept anything valuable in the car."

"Maybe it's in the briefcase." Linc reached over and popped the locks. He shook his head as he swept his eyes over the contents. "Nothing but a *Wall Street Journal* and a *LIFE* magazine from last August seventeenth."

She glanced at the cover, featuring a close-up of the glammed-up Marilyn Monroe, who'd died—under mysterious circumstances—two weeks before this issue came out. "Try the last box, Linc."

He pulled the flaps apart and took out a Burberry raincoat, emptying the pockets of a cab receipt and a half-used roll of Certs. "Nothing written on?" she asked as he folded the coat with the precision of a tailor and laid it on the sofa.

"Nothing." He looked at her and flinched. "Vikki—can I keep this roll of Certs?"

"Certs?" What an absurd request.

"To remember him by. He always sucked on Certs. It's something personal of his. I don't want anything valuable—just this." He closed his fingers around it like it was a gold nugget.

"Of course you can. I'm sorry, I should've offered you a pair of his cuff links or something, but I let his parents take all his personal items, even his Emmys. All I've got left are the clothes in his closet, and his books—"

"That's okay, this is more of a memento of Jack than anything. Funny how something so worthless could mean this much to me." His voice wavered as he struggled to hold back tears.

"I understand." She nodded.

He quickly returned to the briefcase and closed it up. "That's it, Vikki. I'm sorry. Don't see that pen anywhere."

A violent anger welled up inside her. She clenched her fists. "Some bastard is walking around with Jack's cherished pen." The knife in her heart twisted, deepening the open wound.

"They returned his wedding ring, his Rolex, his keys, his suitcase, even his half-smoked pipe, but not a pen? Who would want it?" One thing she didn't want to tell Linc was that a topless photo of herself was missing from Jack's wallet. Who'd swiped that? One of the detectives maybe? Or the killer himself, to get his jollies? Knowing something so intimate was missing made her tremble with mortification.

"The pen could've just gotten lost," Linc said. "Things do get lost, you know."

"Or stolen."

"I'll have everybody at the network do a thorough search for it. I realize how much sentimental value it's got to you." He reached for his drink, took a swig, and chomped down on the olive. "You should look through these notebooks alone. I don't want to intrude."

"Please, Linc, just do it for me; I can't put it off any longer." She waved a shaky hand through the air.

He drained his drink. "Okay, anything for you." He picked up another composition book, opened the cover, and began reading.

"Oh, Jack, what happened to you in Dallas?" she asked out loud, and Linc looked up at her. "Sorry, just talking to him."

His face was pained as he nodded. "I've been doing that a lot myself these days."

Too impatient to sit and watch Linc, she made herself take the next book on the pile, an appointment diary. She hoped to make some sense of the code words he used in his notes.

On the inside cover was printed a list of the traditional gifts for wedding anniversaries, and a guide for interpreting siren alerts in the National Civil

Defense Code. The first page of Jack's notes listed appointment dates and places. The name CASSIUS in bold block letters headed up some illegible scrawl. It was the next page that startled her—along with Cassius's name and whereabouts on certain dates was also written "119K." She knew this particular code because she'd had to type a memo for Jack once. Coming across "119K" she'd asked him what it meant, and he'd replied casually, "Oh, that's Jack Kennedy. I use that code because JFK was elected by 119,450 votes over Nixon." Cryptic enough, she supposed.

But who was this Cassius? Castro? A senator or congressman? The name was written several times on that page next to 119K. The next page was headed "Diamond" followed by a few scribbled paragraphs.

"Cassius, Tape XV" headed the following page, filled with more notes about Cassius and 119K. She knew Jack had constantly dictated into his tape recorder, but she wasn't sure where he kept the tapes. They hadn't turned up yet. If they weren't in these boxes, they might be in his study or his closet—she hoped.

"Did you find any reel-to-reel tapes?" she asked Linc as he read another of Jack's notebooks, his lips moving.

"Hm? No, no tapes. Sorry, I was caught up in this. The notes on his interview with McCarthy. That was one profound interview. It says here that the interview itself is on Tape XXI, if you ever find it. 'Repent, commie-bashing heathen!' Jack wrote in the margin." Linc let out a sad laugh.

"Jack thought politics was too much like religion." She turned to a page covered with a sketch of Niagara

Falls. He'd drawn a barrel at the top. "He always wanted to go over Niagara Falls in a barrel," she mused, and once again, her thoughts drifted. "Jack lived every moment like it was his last."

But a bit too cocky, sporting the sparkle in his eye and the casual toss of his head.

A bit too reckless on his motorcycle, in his speedboat, and in his plane, which he took on short hops when he didn't feel like driving.

But that's what thrilled her about him; cheating death was his idea of a good time. "I'm too young to play it safe," he'd say every time he strapped on a helmet or laced up a parachute.

She recounted her many pleadings with Jack not to be so reckless all the time—just once in a while. "Jack, please be careful," she'd warned so often. She joked that if she got a half-dollar for each time she said it, she'd earn more than he did. But once he became NBS's top investigative reporter, they upped their ante at every contract renewal. His "No, thanks, I'm quitting to sail around the world," was always countered with another hefty salary increase.

So he stuck with NBS, schmoozing with senators and astronauts and movie stars. Then came the Emmys and superstardom.

She opened another book to the first page, headed "Missile Crisis." Jack had attended the press conference following JFK's televised speech about the missiles in Cuba, with the U.S. on the brink of World War Three. "Bay of Pigs Fiasco" headed the next page, with another tape number.

She didn't want to tell Linc about the Cassius and JFK scribblings yet. She put the diary aside and took a sip of her drink.

"The first thing I need to do is find out what he was doing in Dallas," she said, making some mental notes of her own. She was finally starting to think rationally again. That blinding shroud of grief receded enough for her to think straight at least once a day.

"I was out of town most of that week, so I didn't know where he was supposed to be." Linc rubbed his temples. "His going to Dallas must've been a last-minute assignment."

"Or maybe not," she countered.

He stopped rubbing and looked up at her with tired eyes. "Why not?"

"I think he planned that trip way in advance, Linc. As reckless as Jack was, he never did anything on impulse."

Linc shrugged. "Maybe he just wanted to see the presidential motorcade."

"Why in Dallas? If he wanted a glimpse of Jack Kennedy, he could've got on the shuttle to D.C. anytime. Why go to Dallas?" She shuddered as her fingers clenched the sofa arm. "Linc, I have a terrible feeling something was going on. He didn't go to Dallas on a lark. He knew something was going to happen there, and it all went terribly wrong for him. I feel it. I just feel it."

"Women's intuition, huh?" Linc gave her a shaky smile. "Hey, isn't your aunt or stepmother or somebody in your family psychic?"

"I never put any stock in the supernatural and am not about to start now. My faith in God is enough. That other mumbo-jumbo borders on blasphemy." *How did this bizarre family trait originate anyway? Some remote*

25

ancestor from the scorched hills of Sicily or famine-ravaged Ireland? "My aunt Tessie reads Tarot cards and carries on an ongoing dialogue with notable dead people. And my step-grandmother, Jadwiga, had a Ouija board tell her who killed my grandfather's cousin, which got my great-grandfather Caputo off a murder rap. But that happened around the turn of the century; it's all legend now."

"Sounds very intriguing. You and your forebears have a heritage worthy of the history books."

"Oh, I don't know about that. It might make a good television series, though." She felt herself blushing, as she always did when anyone praised her family's accomplishments. "I used to wish I'd come from an ordinary family with no famous names or faces. My father couldn't even take me to the park without getting hounded for autographs. The nuns at school always asked me for Dad's autograph. They loved his Broadway musicals, and it always embarrassed me when we sang his songs in music class. But Dad doesn't crave the spotlight the way Jack did." She let out a spent sigh.

"I always said Jack could've been the next Clark Gable," Linc mused. He yanked his glasses off and dabbed at his eyes with his tie. "I'm sorry, Vikki."

"No, it's okay to cry. Please—don't think you have to hold back for me. I'm handling it, really. I'll never stop grieving, but just the fact that I got dressed and had you come over, I feel like I'm getting back into the real world now. Although I do have my moments. Like when a song comes on the radio, or—" She didn't need to go on. His nod told her he knew.

"Look, Vikki, I'll do everything I can to help you,

in every way, you know that. But why do you think Jack knew something was going to happen in Dallas, something that went wrong?"

She adjusted her glasses and looked straight at him. "Linc, I'm going to tell you something, but you must keep it to yourself, for your own protection. I can trust you, can't I?"

"Of course." He folded his hands and leaned forward. "I got to be a top NBS executive by knowing when to open my mouth, but especially when to keep it shut."

"You met my godfather at Jack's funeral, right?"

"Oh, yeah. The one who dresses like Bugsy Siegel. He's a character, all right." Linc's lips twisted as he struggled to keep a straight face.

"Well, later that night, he told me he'd heard that the assassination was planned way ahead of time. Lee Harvey Oswald didn't get up that day and decide to shoot the president. It was very carefully plotted, by more than one person, with more than one assassin. Oswald may not even have been on the Book Depository's sixth floor at the time of the shooting. Like he said when they caught him, 'I'm just a patsy.' And Ruby killing Oswald two days later adds further suspicion."

"Yes, but—" He polished his glasses again. "Oswald's dead. Ruby's not talking. How did your godfather come to these conclusions?"

"He has acquaintances who are likely to know about this kind of thing. Besides that, he knows Jack Ruby." She waited for his reaction.

Linc's eyes bugged out. "What?" When he put his glasses back on, he looked even more startled. "How?"

"From Chicago. They were both—you could say 'associated'—with Al Capone in the old days," she explained.

His jaw dropped. "You mean—your godfather's in the Mafia?"

"We don't like to call it the Mafia. But he's been involved in organized crime most of his life. He's not the boss he once was. But he's got his sources and connections down there in South Florida, and word has it that there's more to the assassination than the public's been told. But my godfather doesn't happen to know all the facts. He doesn't know who was behind the shooting, who set the whole thing up. Not yet, anyway."

"Not yet?" His voice rose. "You mean he's investigating it?"

"No, this is just what's going around. All he heard was that Oswald didn't act alone, and Ruby didn't kill Oswald out of pity for Mrs. Kennedy. Oswald and Ruby knew each other, and they both had the same connections. The whole thing's complicated. The world might never know what really happened or who was behind the whole thing."

Linc stared at the floor. His ears twitched. "So it was a conspiracy."

"Linc, don't repeat any of this," she warned him. "I don't want word to get around NBS that Jack Ward's widow said the assassination of John F. Kennedy may be an inside job. That'll start a war for sure."

"Of course. I'd never betray your confidence. I just—it came as a surprise, that's all." He held up his right hand. "I swear on all my departed loved ones' graves, I won't breathe a word to anyone." He didn't have to get that dramatic, but he made his point. "So what's it got to do with Jack?"

"I've been thinking about all this—I can't think about anything else—" She took a ragged breath. "I have a feeling Jack's trip to Dallas coincided with the president's visit on purpose. Jack knew about the assassination ahead of time."

"But—but—how?" came out in a hoarse whisper.

"I don't know yet. But I need to know just what happened to Jack that day. The police closed the case, so I intend to find out myself." Determination steadied her voice.

"I need a refill." As Linc went to fix another drink, she asked herself once again, *What was he doing in Dallas?*

Now she took that question further: *What was he doing in Dallas the day John F. Kennedy was assassinated—possibly by a conspiracy?*

Linc came back with two refills and started playing Twenty Questions, like the seasoned journalist he was. Did her godfather know any other mobsters? Why did Ruby shoot Oswald on live television? Where were the other gunmen at Dealey Plaza, and how did they get away when Oswald got caught?

"Linc, my godfather only told me what he heard," she said. "He's sixty-eight and not inclined to spend his golden years probing the assassination of John F. Kennedy."

"But if what you said is true, this is the biggest murder mystery in U.S. history!" He threw his arms up and let them fall to his sides.

"Put the martini down, Linc. You've had enough. So if it is, maybe someday the truth will come out."

"I just can't help wondering what it would be like to know a secret like that, to never tell another soul, to take it to our graves with us," Linc rambled. "Keep the world wondering for centuries to come."

"Just let it stay a secret. I only told you this because I think Jack might have been involved with the wrong people and got himself killed." There—she said the word she'd been dreading to even think. She took a gulp of her martini. "If only he *could*'ve drowned—if only it *were* an accident."

"Killed? Oh, no, Vikki. Who would've—it's just too horrible to think about." He shuddered.

"Linc, Jack surfed fifty-foot waves the way you walk across a room. He swam the English Channel. He was an expert swimmer. He loved the water. And he drowns in a bathtub? It's just not feasible, especially after seeing all this." She gestured toward the diary, but it was too late. Maybe she should've munched some pretzels before those two martinis.

"All what?" He reached for the diary, but she slammed her hand over it.

"Just some notes Jack wrote here that refer to JFK. It got me wondering if there's a connection."

"A connection to what?" He thrust his head forward like a pigeon. "The conspiracy?"

She hadn't planned to tell Linc about her suspicions. But after seeing Jack's notes, she couldn't keep it bottled up inside. As Jack's best friend, maybe Linc could find out a few things.

"Look, in several of these notebooks he wrote the name Cassius next to JFK's code name. He's got other code names and places and dates in here, too. It looks like Jack had a few run-ins with this Cassius person and was mixed up in the whole thing."

"Oh, God, Vikki, you don't think Jack was—was actually in on the assassination!"

"No, of course not." She waved a dismissive hand. "Jack idolized President Kennedy. It looks like he was investigating the possibility of a conspiracy. And I'm wondering if Jack's death had something to do with the conspiracy, too."

Linc whistled through his teeth, staring intently into his martini glass.

"He died on the same day and in the same city as President Kennedy. That was no coincidence, Linc. I'll bet my life on it."

He drained his drink with a large gulp. "Come on, Vikki, it had to be an accident. Who would want to harm Jack? The world is far worse without him."

"To get him out of the way. If he was onto them— oh, God, I can't even imagine! Jack's ki—death might've had something to do with this Cassius. This name is all over the notebooks here."

"It just doesn't seem possible," Linc insisted.

"We're going to start at the beginning, Linc." She sat up straight. "Can you find out when Jack's plane reservation to Dallas was made? I need to know if this assignment was planned in advance or NBS sent him down there at the last minute, or if NBS sent him at all or it was his own idea. He left that Wednesday night. He told me he was going to Chicago to do a story on the FBI and couldn't talk about it till he got home."

"Well, I don't know anything about that. But I can find out about the plane reservations." Linc reached for the phone. "I'll call NBS Travel. There's always somebody there late." As he dialed, she went into the kitchen and popped a handful of Milk Duds into her mouth, washing them down with a swig of cream soda.

After a lengthy conversation that included a lot of holding on, he hung up and leaned against the sofa, rubbing his temples, his lips drawn into a tight line.

"So, when did he make the reservation?" she asked him.

"He didn't." Linc spread his hands and shrugged. "He flew his own plane out of Idlewild that morning. Landed in Fort Worth."

She blinked in surprise. "He flew his own plane down there? Why?"

"I don't know. For some reason, Jack wanted to fly down there himself. He wasn't on any commercial flight. We can check with the president of the network, Art Gordon. Maybe Jack told him something about the trip."

"I'm a step ahead of you." She narrowed her eyes. "I have a call in to Gordon already. He's out of town."

"Well, he should know why Jack went to Texas." He glanced at the bar and back to his empty glass, as if debating whether to have another drink.

She walked over to the coffee table. "Then he should know why Jack felt it necessary to fly his own plane there and lie to his wife about it," she added, ripping open a bag of M&Ms and pouring them into her favorite Wedgwood candy dish.

"If Gordon does know anything about Jack's trip, he should have told you already." He went for the M&Ms.

"Maybe not. I didn't ask." She grabbed another handful.

"Well, you want to finish going through his things,

or just work on what you found already? Maybe you'll find more information, or some other names. You want me to keep looking?" he offered, chomping on the candy.

"We can call it a night. I need to sit and think some more. I haven't had a complete, rational thought since…that day. My mind is just starting to function now."

He squeezed her arm. "All right, call me if you need anything."

"Yes, I will, Linc. Thanks." She walked him to the foyer. "When I get to the bottom of Jack's trip down there, that should tell us a lot more."

"I'll find out whatever I can, too." He grabbed his coat off the tree and shrugged into it. "Call me if you need anything at all, day or night."

After seeing him out, she wished she'd asked him to box up Jack's things again. Now they were scattered all over, and another stab of grief tore her heart apart. But she couldn't continue relying on other people. She knelt before the belongings and began placing them back in the boxes, all except the notebooks with Cassius and 119K written all over them.

Then she packed a bag, unable to spend another night in the place she'd called Camelot.

****

As she walked down the stairs, her valise in tow, she couldn't get something out of her mind: Jack's tapes. Bracing herself against another wave of grief, she stood at the threshold of his study. She entered the room, closed her eyes, and inhaled the lingering aroma of his pipe. Its smoky sweetness gave her a strange comfort. She approached the built-in, floor-to-ceiling bookshelves. Copies of his memoir took up the entire top shelf, *So Far So Good—Jack Ward* boldly heralded on each spine in a parade of self-pride and optimism.

"Where are those tapes, Jack?" she asked out loud, scanning the rows of volumes. As if he guided her, she spotted them on the next shelf down. She wheeled the ladder over, climbed up, and retrieved one of the leather cases that looked like three volumes stuck together. She flipped it open, and inside were several reel-to-reel tapes, labeled with Roman numerals.

She brought them into the living room, took the first one out, and cued it up on her recorder with an empty take-up reel.

Inhaling deeply, she squeezed her eyes shut as she hit the Play button.

Chapter Four

"Take as much time as you need, babe." Her father headed down the walk, leaving her alone. "I'll wait in the car."

"Thanks, Dad, I'll be right out." Vikki took one last look around the home where she'd spent the happiest days of her life.

The spacious Tudor was her dream house, with every luxurious appointment a young bride could want—fireplaces, hardwood floors, matching drapes and upholstery. A kitchen loaded with gleaming appliances, five bedrooms, three baths, and a fenced-in backyard with an in-ground pool. A porch swing for summer nights under the stars. Their own little Camelot, just like Jack and Jackie.

She picked up her valise and recited the play's last line, "Don't let it be forgot, that once there was a spot, for one brief shining moment, that was known as Camelot," wondering if Jackie said that when she left the White House for the last time.

****

"Let's hear it again, and this time I'll jot down the key words." Billy rewound his tape machine and pulled a writing pad off his shelf. His studio equipment played Jack's tapes much more clearly than her portable Emerson. She now recognized the other voice on Tape XV, which she'd found among another pile of reels in

Jack's desk drawer. "That's Herbert Whitefield, one of the network's VPs. Jack always joked that Whitefield was afraid Jack would become *his* boss someday."

"Yeah, I can tell. Let's listen again." Billy pushed the Play button, and Jack's voice came through the hundred-watt speakers, filling the studio with an eeriness that frightened and pained her at the same time.

A series of clicks, then:

Chicago, March third, nineteen-sixty-three. Now it's more than a hunch—I'm convinced someone's going to assassinate the president before this year is out.

I'm doing a story on the head of the Chicago FBI office I've worked with before and know pretty well, Phil Randolph. Randolph replaced Guy Banister, who's now in New Orleans. Anyway, this story centers on Randolph's investigation of some Soviet dissidents who had connections to Castro, and the vendetta they have going on with JFK. Randolph told me that during the transition from Banister to him, Banister told him about the CIA's Cuban activities in New Orleans, which JFK opposed. Banister was relocating down there to get involved in it. Banister was very anti-Castro. But before we got working on the story, Randolph wanted to show off his fancy line of questioning and his crack investigative techniques, so he let me sit in on an interview he was about to do with a young ex-Marine who's an FBI informer. I'm not going to say his name here, for obvious reasons. I'll just call him Cubby, because he reminded me of the kid on the Mickey Mouse Club show. Cubby works part time in Nagle's Bar in New Orleans, owned by an associate of mob boss Carlos Marcello. Cubby heard a conversation in

Nagle's Bar between three men who were looking at a gun catalog. One of them, whom the others called Cassius, said that looked like a good gun to get the president with.

I had a feeling Cubby knew more, so the day after the interview, I looked him up and appealed to his sense of patriotism as an ex-Marine. I was as persuasive as possible, pulled out all the broadcaster's tricks. It worked, because he agreed to meet me on his own turf, in New Orleans. That's when he told me a few things he'd told Randolph, but Randolph had laughed him out of his office and out of the FBI altogether. But after what Cubby told me, I wasn't laughing.

So I flew to New Orleans to meet him. He wouldn't let me interview him on tape, so I'll paraphrase what he said. The day he was in Nagle's Bar, he heard three guys babbling over a gun catalog, one of them saying this would be a good one to the get the president with. Cubby couldn't tell if they were rifles or handguns; he couldn't see the catalog close up. A few minutes later, Tony Marcello came in to service the pinball machine. Tony said, 'There's a price on JFK's head. When he comes south, he's dead,' and said to one of the guys looking at the magazine, 'Hope you're up to it, Cassius,' or words to that effect.

I think I know who this Cassius is now. I went to several back-to-back JFK functions in the last few months, and noticed one particular character in attendance. I can't put my finger on it, but he just didn't seem to fit in, looked real uncomfortable all dressed up.

I got a list of all the events' attendees, and everybody's on the up-and-up. Except this one guy whose name isn't on the list. Logical deduction and a gut hunch tells me he's Cassius. Cubby gave me a pretty good description of the guy, and if it isn't the same guy I've been spotting at these things, he's got a twin brother.

The next thing I have to do is follow the trail south.

I can see why the FBI laughed it off—they hear stories like this all day long. But if they won't take it seriously, I will.

A series of clicks, then:

Washington D.C., March twenty-seventh, sixty-three. His voice was barely above a whisper. *I'm here at the Sidwell Friends School, where JFK is scheduled to give a speech to the kids. And I'll be damned if Cassius isn't lurking in the back of the room, in a beat-up painter's cap and overalls, trying to look like a janitor. Too bad he forgot to leave the diamond pinkie ring home. His shifty eyes are casing the joint, but I don't think he's seen me yet. He's yanking at his collar and shuffling from one foot to the other.*

We're still waiting; the prez is five minutes late now. It's usually Jackie who shows up fashionably late; I've always known him to be on time. Looking around here and at the other rallies and events, I'm wondering what makes this Cassius guy think he can get a handgun by the S.S.—they always search everybody these days—it'd be hard to even get within firing range. The day McKinley was shot, the S.S. didn't get a chance to screen the crowd, and they'd allowed people to have handkerchiefs because it was a hot day—well, Czolgosz took that opportunity to wrap his hankie around his revolver, and that was the end of McKinley. Ah-ha, here's the prez.

The roar of the crowd intensified, followed by a

burst of applause. Kennedy started speaking, applause bursting out after every other sentence.

Cassius is slipping out, Jack said, when the President's speech ended. *And so am I.*

"Who the hell is Cassius?" Vikki implored her dead husband's voice as the machine clicked off and on again.

Los Angeles, April twenty-ninth. I was at a party at RR's house. We started discussing the Cuban Missile Crisis, and eventually it got around to the last three bungled plots to kill Castro. A few guests and I got into a heated discussion, and one of them, a banker named Nichols, told me he picked up a woman on the side of the road in Beaumont, Texas. She introduced herself as Darla and told him she was making a drug run from Miami to Houston with two Italian male companions. Darla had gotten too high, so the guys abandoned her at a roadside bar. She got kicked out of the bar, so she tried to hitch a ride. She was grazed by a car and slightly injured. Soon after, Nichols picked her up from the roadside. As he drove her to the hospital, she told Nichols her Italian cohorts had said that on the way back to Miami they were going to wait for JFK to show up; he was scheduled to appear there, and he'd be killed that day. When Nichols reported Darla's prediction to the police, they laughed him out of there.

The Off and On buttons clicked, followed by a rustling of the mike, and Jack's voice, in an agitated tone:

November sixteenth, JFK campaign speech, Atlanta. This is the twelfth event where I've seen Cassius lurking around. This is no coincidence. I have to get hard evidence, and I think I know where to get it.

They changed JFK's November twenty-first Miami campaign stop to Dallas/Fort Worth on the twenty-second practically overnight, and that looks suspicious. I know a certain official there who isn't above a little bribery. I'll see if anything is being planned in Dallas/Fort Worth to necessitate that sudden change of venue.

A knock sounded. *Come in,* Jack said, followed by an opening and closing of a door and some footsteps. *Oh, hi, Herb. I was just dictating some notes here.*

How was your trip? You okay? asked Whitefield, along with the scraping of a chair.

The bastard almost got me. Sure scared the bejeezus out of the bell captain and everybody else there.

You think it was them? Whitefield's voice, now closer to the mike.

I don't know who it was; I didn't see who did it. It was a sniper shot. It sounded like it came from the hotel roof, when I was getting out of the cab. It was dark and raining, and I'd just ducked back into the cab to grab my briefcase, so that's probably why he missed. Then I went into the lobby, and that was the end of it. Never saw him. It couldn't have been Cassius; if it was, he'd have got me.

Next time they'll blow your thick skull to bits. What the hell's the matter with you, Jack?

I'm not afraid of some half-ass hit man. Jack's tone was resolute. *We have a better chance of getting nuked these days.*

Whitefield said, *Never mind getting nuked. I want you to get the hell off this wild goose chase and go back to covering the damn news. They know you're on their trail, and you don't mess with these guys.*

Jack replied, *Don't you think I'd love to personally turn Cassius in to the Feds right now? Then they wouldn't think it was such a joke. But I'm still not a hundred percent sure what his role is, if he's the ringleader or what.*

Listen to me for a minute, Jack. Whitefield's voice rose. *Suppose, just suppose—wouldn't it be something if we kept this whole thing to ourselves and got the whole assassination on film? From two different angles, you with one camera, me with another? You know how big that would be? We'd have the only professional footage of the whole thing—the crime of the century—to be broadcast around the world. NBS'll conquer the world of broadcast journalism. We'll become filthy rich and practically run the television industry. Think what that would mean for the network.*

Jack said, *Ha! For the network? For you, maybe. For being on the spot and filming the whole thing and being there to scoop it all as it happens. I know you inside and out, Herb. Who are you kidding? Sorry if I'm stepping on your toes, friend, but I'm going my own way on this. I want to blow the lid off it in a special report that breaks into regular programming in prime time, preferably Sunday night, when the country's glued to the Ed Sullivan Show. History'll be changed for the better. Imagine—one reporter saving the life of the president of the United States from assassination, especially in a plot this complicated. The network will still benefit, and besides, when I scoop this story, another Emmy is in the bag, maybe even a Pulitzer, the Nobel Peace Prize. Imagine, three Emmys in a row! Maybe I'll become* your *boss, old buddy.*

Very funny, Jack, was Whitefield's reply, but he didn't sound amused.

A sound like a slamming of a door followed, then Jack snickered into the microphone.

Herb may want to film the whole thing, but I'm staying in front of the cameras. Jack chuckled again, in that mildly amused, dismissive way of his. The tape ran out.

"RR was his code name for Desi Arnaz," Vikki said. "RR, as in Ricky Ricardo. Some of the stars out there liked Jack and invited him to their parties when he was on the coast."

"Well, that explains—uh, 'splains—why they'd be talking about the Missile Crisis." Billy stopped writing. "Let's sum this up here. Looks like Jack was on this Cassius guy's tail to stop him assassinating JFK, and this Herb veep didn't want him to blow the story apart on television and reap all the glory." He looked at Vikki and slid the pencil behind his ear, reaching for a cigarette. "Smoke?"

"No. Who shot at Jack at that hotel? I wonder if it was Cassius. It looks like Jack tailed Cassius all the way to Dallas on the twenty-first. And then—" She couldn't finish the thought. She glanced at the stack of tapes, none of which had told her anything; they were either interviews with public officials or entertainers or Jack's own thoughts on issues like the U.S. involvement in Vietnam. Nothing to tell her what happened in Dallas on November twenty-second. She knew he had more tapes stashed away, and she had to find them. "Get rid of these tapes. I don't want any reminders."

"I'll put them in the safe." Billy rewound the tape.

Putting the cigarette in his mouth, he tossed the reels back into the cigar box and took it out of the studio.

She cracked her knuckles one by one and read over her father's transcript, Jack's voice echoing through her mind. "I'll find you, you bastard, whoever you are," she said reverently, like a vow. "If I have to die doing it."

****

An hour later, she was still sitting in her father's studio, but she'd moved over to the piano bench, idly plucking the keys, thinking. Maybe this FBI informer, Cubby, could tell her more if she played upon his sympathy as a grieving widow—she hoped.

She got on the phone and asked Information for the FBI office in Chicago as she scanned her father's notes once again. She asked for Jack's friend Phil Randolph.

After the usual bureaucratic shunting around, she said a quick "Thanks be to God" when Randolph finally came on the line.

"Mr. Randolph, I'm Jack Ward's widow, and you let him watch an interview you did with a young informer…"

He hemmed and hawed, making it apparent he was reluctant to tell her anything. She was ready to start begging when he breathed a deep sigh into the phone and told her the young informer, whose real name was Gary Heitmann, had been murdered a week after the Kennedy assassination. "And he died in the most bizarre way," Randolph added, with typical detachment in his voice, "with a karate blow to the neck."

"My God, who could've done that?" was all she could say. She was too stunned to come up with anything thoughtful or sympathetic.

"If we knew that, we'd be able to find out a lot

more," was his veiled reply. She knew right then she wasn't going to get any more information out of the FBI.

That night, she dozed in front of the television. She got up and tried to sleep in her bed, but the kaleidoscopic images whirling through her mind made sleep impossible. She drew a bath, poured some Calgon into the tub, lit a candle, and sank into the warm fragrant water.

"Come on, relax," she urged her rigid, tense body, inhaling deeply. Taking baths had always been her favorite way to relax; she'd fallen asleep in the bath many times, waking up in cold water, shriveled like a prune. She remembered how many times she'd tried to lure Jack into their oversized tub with a glass of wine so they could unwind together after a long day. But Jack never took baths. A quick shower was more his style.

At that second, something gave her such a start she felt like she'd been hit by lightning.

She sat upright, the water sloshing over the edges of the tub. Now she knew for certain Jack didn't drown in a bathtub. And it wasn't because he'd swum the Channel or sailed around the world. It was a much simpler, glaringly obvious reason.

Jack never took baths!

The gray of dawn strained through the curtains as she dried off, got dressed, and grabbed the phone to call the Dallas police.

She finished her last cigarette and crumpled the pack as they jerked her around from receptionist to desk sergeant and back on hold again. She decided that if she got any more of a runaround she'd be on a plane to Dallas, as much as she dreaded going there. Like

Jackie, she'd always hold Dallas responsible for her husband's death. "I want the world to see what Dallas did to my husband," the First Lady had said when they'd asked why she wouldn't change out of the pink suit splattered with her husband's blood.

"Mrs. Ward?" A pleasant drawl came on the line after forty-eight seconds: she'd been watching the clock. "This is Lieutenant Frye."

"Yes, Lieutenant, we talked the day of my husband's death. You know—the case that was never solved? One of your detectives had been handling the case, and—"

"Mrs. Ward, we closed that case because we have nothing more to go on."

"Well, you do now. I've got his own voice on tape saying he was shot at by someone named Cassius, whom he followed to Dallas on November twenty-first. He could not have drowned in a bathtub for one reason—he never *ever* took baths. Is that enough for you?" She tried not to shriek, but couldn't hold back.

"Listen up, Mrs. W—"

"No, *you* listen up, sir. I want this investigation reopened. I'll make a copy of this tape and send it to you, or I'll bring it personally. Is that what it takes? I'm—"

"Now, little lady, let me git a word in sideways here." His tone became condescending, but instead of giving him more hell, she busied herself opening a new cigarette pack and kept quiet. "He could've said anything to anyone about being followed, stalked, by anyone. That is not evidence. We can't reopen a homicide case with a tape recording. He could've said Castro was out to git him, or Satan, or anybody. The

ME's report showed that he died by drowning, whether he took baths or not. He couldn't have died any other way."

"So that's your final word?" She struggled to keep her voice from shaking.

"I'm afraid we can't do anything further on this case, ma'am."

"You mean you *won't*. But *I* will. Watch me." Now she knew why the Dallas police were being held partly responsible for JFK's death.

She strode out of the house and up the street, breathing in the frosty air. It stung her lungs and cooled her boiling blood. The sky was the gunmetal gray of an early winter dawn. She quickened her pace to work off her rage. The bakery wasn't open yet, but she knew Mr. Valore was inside, starting the doughnuts. She rapped on his door, and he let her in. The sweetness of the dough's aroma calmed her as she watched him fill a box with pastries and tie it with string. "Oh, don't tie it up. I'm going to eat some on the way home."

And eat some she did. She felt all the warmth of her Nonna's kitchen right there on the sidewalk as she bit into a cruller.

By the time she got back to the house, she had fogged-up glasses, a shirt drenched in cold sweat, and a plan of action. She knew Jack's soul couldn't rest until she brought his killer to justice.

One more thing was growing in her mind—a way to carry out Jack's work. He'd wanted to expose the JFK assassination plot. Maybe she could do that for him too. But first things first.

Cracking her knuckles, she put coffee on. As she stuffed another cruller into her mouth, her stomach grumbled for the first time since she couldn't remember when. Her stomach and pastries went way back.

The sweep of slippers across the floor jarred her back to reality.

"Morning, babe. Any word from the honcho at NBS about Jack's trip to Texas?" Billy stood in the kitchen doorway patting himself down for a cigarette pack.

"No, he didn't call back yet."

"Give him till noon, then try again. These guys are pretty busy in the mornings." He shook a cigarette from her pack on the table.

"I just talked to the Dallas police about reopening the case with that new information from the tapes." She got some cups down from the cabinet.

"What'd they say?"

"Not enough evidence to reopen it. I'm wondering if they're hiding something." She watched the coffeepot.

"Nah, I doubt it. Cops'll be cops." He took the spoons she handed him. "They're just doing what they're best at, sliding their thumbs in and outta their butts."

"I have questions even they can't answer. Jack tells me he's going to Chicago and instead he goes to where the president of the United States falls victim to an assassination plot. That's what has me stumped. Not why he flew his own plane there. Why he had to lie to me about where he was going."

"I wouldn't call it lying. He was just trying to protect you, if he really was involved in the plot." Billy poured them each a cup of coffee and opened the paper, taking out the entertainment section.

"I never heard him mention Dallas, ever." She chewed on her cruller, stirring sugar into her coffee.

"Just talk to the network president and see what he has to say for himself."

"I also need to look for an apartment." Vikki sipped and swallowed. "I was thinking maybe the West Side Highway. I like the views from there."

"The views? Of what, Weehawken? You can stay here as long as you want, babe, you know that. There's no hurry to leave here. We love having you back in your old room." Billy added a precise measure of anisette to his coffee with a shot glass, a ritual she'd watched him perform since she was in her highchair.

"I love being here, too, Dad." But she had mixed emotions about returning to the house she'd grown up in, sleeping in the same room they'd kept like a shrine, with the matching ruffled curtains and bedspread, the Elvis posters, the pink princess phone. It was hard to return to that room after all that had happened, but thoughts of her childhood home comforted her at the same time. "I don't want to impose on you and Greta, so I don't want to stay much longer. But I know what I have to do, and that's get to the bottom of what happened to Jack that day. If the cops won't, I will."

"I hate to burst your bubble, babe, but that won't be easy—or safe." He slurped his spiked coffee.

"Nothing worth having is easy. But I'm going to do this if I have to die doing it. I have the strangest feeling, Dad—I can sense him urging me to find out the truth, so he can rest easy. I don't think he even knows what really happened. He would've done the same for me. I'm going to find out who killed Jack if it's the last thing I do." *And it very well may be,* she mouthed

48

silently. She lit a cigarette off his and poured more coffee. "I'm going to call the detective NBS uses all the time. He digs up more dirt than Louis Leakey."

Billy nodded. "Not a bad idea. Use my phone in there. We won't bother you. Greta's not even up yet."

She went into her father's studio and phoned NBS.

When she reached Linc, she asked him, "Linc, what's the name of that detective the network uses to dig up dirt on everybody? Carl somebody? You know, the guy with the plastic hair."

"Oh, no, not that obnoxious bastard."

"That's just what I need, Linc," she insisted.

He blew out a stream of air. "All right, hold the wire." She heard some shuffling, and he came back on the line. "Carlton F. Frost of CFF Investigations, on West Fifty-Fourth Street." He gave her the number. "So how are you doing?"

"In the last twenty-four hours, I've gotten two dead ends, or more accurately, two brushoffs—one from the FBI and one from the Dallas police."

"What'd you call the FBI for?" he asked.

"Jack had interviewed an FBI informer who knew something about the JFK plot, and—" The words stuck in her throat, which had gone dry.

"You okay?"

"He was murdered," she forced herself to say. "With a karate blow."

The silence at the other end made her think he'd hung up. "Linc?"

"Yeah. I'm still here. Jesus Christ, that's downright bizarre."

"Now are you convinced Jack was involved in something sinister?" she prodded.

"Just make sure you stay safe."

"I'm not worried about myself. Jack's watching over me." She wouldn't have said this to just anybody. But she knew Linc would understand.

"Okay, but just be careful. And let me know how it goes with Frost."

"I will, and thanks." She hung up and dialed Carlton Frost's number.

Frost wasn't in, but his secretary took the message, which Vikki emphasized was urgent. "It's beyond urgent," she reiterated. "I want him to investigate a brutal murder."

The secretary's reply of "Yes, ma'am, of course," reassured her, but Frost was in such demand, with such a heavy caseload, he only picked the plums. Vikki hoped this would be juicy enough for his jaded taste buds.

She returned to the kitchen, dragged on her cigarette, and tried to think up other ways to get to the bottom of this, just in case Frost didn't come through.

"You talk to the gumshoe?" her father asked, now scanning the stock quotes.

"He wasn't in. I left what I hoped was enough of a teaser so he'll get back to me. But he's such a sleaze, he—" Something in her mind clicked, and she snapped her fingers. "I know who else might be able to help me."

Billy lowered the paper. His eyes lit up. "Of course. Why didn't I think of it? What gave you the idea? Any remote chance it had to do with the mention of sleazes?" He gave her an encouraging wink, and she darted across the kitchen.

Not another word had to be said. She was already

on the phone.

****

Rosario Ingovito was her godfather and Billy's best friend, an exemplary citizen to the outside world, but she knew better. After her dad had divorced himself from the rackets in 1933, Rosie stayed on, but the older he got, the lower he slid in the ranks. He still enjoyed sticking his thumb in a few pies: number running, off-track betting, small-time stuff.

Vikki loved to hear the stories about their nefarious shenanigans back in the day—the bootlegging operations, the speakeasies, the raids.

During Prohibition, they'd owned one of New York's most modernized speakeasies. The closets had electrical wiring that, when connected to two coat hooks, allowed a current to open a false panel to the hidden booze. The bartender had a buzzer that could make the shelves collapse and let the bottles fall into the sewer through a trapdoor.

She wouldn't have believed it, coming from anyone else's mouth, but her dad didn't dream up stories. He dreamed up songs, which catapulted him to Broadway superstardom and his own orchestra, but spin tall tales? Never. He provided the proof when he dragged out the yellowed newspaper clippings, and she devoured them over and over. It read like pulp fiction.

Nobody ever leaves the mob alive, but her father had managed to escape somehow, and she'd always wondered how he did it. He refused to tell her, however. "I wrote it all down in a journal," he'd always say, "and after I croak, you'll see it."

She fondled the diamond cross around her neck and prayed, "Please, Jesus, let me find out the truth about what happened to Jack, not for me, but for him. No matter what it takes."

Her stepmother, Greta, came into the kitchen, greeted Vikki with a peck on the cheek and Billy with a slip of the tongue. It went on and on, so she looked away. Greta was the only mother Vikki had ever known; she didn't have any memory of her birth mother, who'd died when Vikki was an infant. "Pru's life was snatched away from all of us," her father always said as Vikki studied the only photo her mother ever sat for, her wedding portrait. Having inherited her father's tall solid stature and fair coloring, Vikki wondered if she really was the offspring of the slight, delicate Prudence Muller. But her dad had told her more than she wanted to know about her accidental conception in the bathtub and their rush to the altar three months later.

"How's the book going?" she asked her stepmother, a popular author of true crime stories. Maybe she could give Vikki a few hints about catching a killer.

"Not too bad. I finished the first draft about three this morning. You want some cereal and fruit, Vikki, or you just having dessert?" Greta always tried to get her to eat right, but she was too much like her father that way. They both needed three things to kick-start the day: a cigarette, a pastry box, and a cup of coffee—or four, after a rough night: a shot of anisette.

"This is okay." She grabbed another cruller. "I'm not really hungry anyway. It's just something to do till Rosie calls back."

This made Greta look up from her Cream of Wheat and cast a sideways glance at Billy. "What about

Rosie?" Affable and generous as Rosie was, he wasn't on Greta's "A" list, because he still dabbled in the rackets.

"Vikki called him a couple minutes ago and left a message to call back. We're gonna ask him somethin'," Billy offered. She was grateful to her father for including himself in this.

But she knew better. "Okay, Dad, we've got some 'splainin' to do now."

"Yeah, Billy, are you going to tell me what it is, or do I have to cajole it out of you?" Greta abandoned her bowl and sidled up to him, slowly running her hands down his torso.

"You wanna tell her, babe?" Billy asked Vikki, easing Greta away.

Vikki broke off half of one more cruller. "You won't like it."

"If it involves him, I know I won't. Why didn't you ask him whatever it is when he was here for Jack's funeral?" Greta went back to her cereal.

"Greta, the question has been haunting me—how could Jack have drowned? And in a bathtub? He didn't take baths." Vikki dunked the half-cruller into her coffee. "I confirmed my doubts when I read his notebooks and heard the tape. He wrote 'Cassius' several times next to JFK's code name in the notes, and he mentions Cassius on the tape. I think Jack followed this guy to Dallas and there's a link to the JFK shooting. Rosie might be able to help, because of…what he's heard about the JFK assassination being a conspiracy."

Greta turned to her husband with that look that always made him either cave in or crawl out of the room. But this time he wasn't even looking at her; he was busy clearing away his dishes, something else she'd trained him to do.

"Billy!"

He turned and ran his long piano fingers through his silvering but still abundant chestnut hair. "Look, Greta, it looks suspicious, especially after what we heard on that tape. And if our hunches are correct, some cocksucker is out there walking the streets while my son-in-law is lying murdered in his grave. Vikki wants to find out what really happened to him. And if Rosie can't help, nobody can."

"I already got all I could out of the Dallas cops, Greta." Vikki refilled her coffee cup and added a heap of sugar. "I don't like the way they spoke to me, either, very patronizing. I know I'm not Jackie Kennedy, but I deserve better than having the case slammed shut in my face. So I'm going to do their job for them."

Billy added, "They were too busy with the chaos in Dealey Plaza and chasing Oswald down, and by the time they found Jack's body, the killer was long gone, if there was one. Now we know there might've been assassins all over Dallas. And one of them might've killed Jack."

"But why Rosie?" Greta insisted.

"I also called a private detective." Vikki stirred her coffee, the spoon hitting the cup with rhythmic clinks. "But he wasn't in. So, in the meantime, I think Rosie might be able to get to the bottom of it."

"Well, if anybody knows the bottom, it's him." Greta lit a cigarette and blew out the smoke in a huff. "You're skating on thin ice here, Billy, and letting your daughter do this?" Greta always looked older when she was mad, and now she was good and riled. As she narrowed her eyes, the wrinkles around them stood out. Her lips puckered, bringing out the lines there.

"I'm not 'letting' her do nothing." He splayed his hands. "She's old enough. I can't stop her. Hey, look, if some asshole whacked me and disappeared, wouldn't you search high and low to try to find out who did it?"

Greta slid him her smartass look, angling her chin and looking down her nose, about to deliver a zinger. "Yeah, so I could send him a thank-you note."

"And if he had a schlong as big as his bank account, you'd sink your claws into him," Billy countered with a smirk.

This kind of banter went on all the time. Vikki had grown up on it. But she preferred the Lucy brand of comedy.

As she sipped her coffee, the phone rang. She held her breath.

Billy snatched it up. "Hey, Rosie." He gave Vikki a reassuring nod.

After a cryptic conversation—they never had any other kind—Billy hung up and gave her a hug. "He invited us down to his place to discuss the whole thing. Said we can come down now, start the Christmas holiday early, if we want. He has a few ideas."

"Like what?" she asked.

"He didn't tell me. We don't talk about stuff like that on the phone, you know that. The FBI might still be on his tail after that last mix-up." He slid back into his chair.

That "last mix-up" involved a high-class prostitution ring her godfather had somehow gotten caught up in. But after five years they gave up. She knew the FBI kept their mob surveillance to a minimum; either they didn't have the resources to curtail the huge organization or they looked the other way. There was no love lost between J. Edgar Hoover and the mob-hating Kennedys.

Billy turned to his wife. "Wanna spend the holidays in the fun and sun, Gret?"

She shook her head. "No, thanks. I'll head to the Tyrolean slopes, if it's all the same to you. Leave me out of your shady schemes."

Vikki hid a secret smile, glad Greta wouldn't be joining them. She'd only be a distraction. Whenever they went to Rosie's Florida estate together, all Greta wanted them to do was swim and water ski and sunbathe. But this wasn't a vacation. This was business.

****

The phone rang just after Billy hung up from making plane reservations. "For you, babe." His hand covered the mouthpiece. "The top brass from NBS. His secretary's connecting him."

She took the phone and a curt voice told her to hold for Mr. Gordon. After a few rings, the cordial Mr. Gordon was greeting her by name and offering condolences, like he was reading from a sympathy card.

"Thank you, Mr. Gordon. Now. I'd like to know why my husband flew his plane to Fort Worth on that day instead of taking a commercial flight to Chicago, like he told me."

"He did go to Chicago, on the morning of the eighteenth," he reported. "Then he told me he was going to Tampa and Miami Beach to cover President Kennedy's campaign visits, and on to Fort Worth in his own plane on the morning of the twenty-second for another Kennedy speech at the Chamber of Commerce. I'm sorry, Mrs. Ward. You have a slight mix-up there in the dates."

"Wait a minute." She shut her eyes. "The Chamber of Commerce? Why send NBS's top reporter to a speech at the Chamber of Commerce?"

"He *told* us he was going; he didn't ask. We gave Jack free rein. He flew his plane into Fort Worth, and, tragically, he never got back, so it's still there at the airport. I'm sorry, Mrs. Ward. We all held Jack in the highest regard here, and we miss him terribly—"

"Right, okay, thank you." She didn't want to sit through another eulogy.

So Jack had lied to her. Why? If all he'd planned to do was cover Kennedy's speech at a Chamber of Commerce…

But he had no intention of going to the Fort Worth Chamber of Commerce. He'd fooled even the television station, leaving his plane in Fort Worth and heading straight for Dallas—and his death.

"Oh, why, Jack, why?" she implored her departed husband's spirit.

Chapter Five

"Dad." Vikki rapped her knuckles on his bedroom door. "We have to leave for the airport in a half hour."

"Okay."

A half hour later she knocked again. "Dad, we have to leave in ten minutes."

"Okay, I'm comin'."

Ten minutes later, "Dad, we're going to miss the flight."

"I'll catch tonight's flight," he answered from behind the closed door. "You go on ahead."

By the sound of things, he and Greta were taking their time saying goodbye and celebrating the new year early.

I hope I'm that energetic when I get old, she thought as she got into the airport limo alone.

****

"Sorry, sis, but you're not on Mr. Ingovito's guest list. I can't let you through the gate." The guard peered through her car window and eyeballed her like she was a Playboy centerfold.

Who's this lawn ornament calling "sis"? She could've flung an equally demeaning zinger right back, but opted for the high road. "I beg your pardon, but I am Victoria McGlory Ward, Mr. Ingovito's goddaughter, and I am expected here." She sat at the gate to Rosie's estate, bone weary and dying for a

Zombie with a hunk of pineapple and a little paper umbrella.

"At what time?" He glanced at his watch—a cheap designer knockoff.

She revved the engine of her rented Chrysler Imperial. "Any time I want. But he is expecting me. Now."

"I'll phone up to the main house to see if he's available to take callers." His eyes lingered on her.

"You do that." By now, her blood was bubbling. Who was he to detain her at the gate when all her life she'd waltzed in as the guards bowed to her? He was a new hire; he hadn't been here at Easter. She certainly would've remembered the ovoid face, the olive oil complexion, that porcelain crown job clamping a cigarillo in place, and the way he smoothed down his hair with the pinkie-ringed hand brandishing buffed nails.

Most of all, she would've remembered that careful enunciation covering up his Flatbush accent. *What's Rosie grooming him for?*

He hung up the phone and turned to her. "You're right, he was expecting you. Okay, you can go troo, uh, through now." No apology, just a flash of his dentist's handiwork, minus the customary gold tooth.

She cracked her knuckles and floored the Imperial, hoping she kicked up enough gravel to put a dent in that slick pompadour.

****

He stood staring after her. *She's Mr. Ingovito's goddaughter? Madonne, what a dish. And frisky, too.* He knew she wasn't really steamed—she was just playing with him. She wasn't like all the other dames, who tittered like schoolgirls around him. *Certo*, she was gonna be more fun than the Trifecta at Hialeah, even when he didn't win—all the fun was in the race.

They just don't breed them like that down here. She made him homesick for Brooklyn.

"I hope you'll be stayin' a while," he almost sang, watching her car roar up the gravel drive.

****

The butler escorted her to the veranda, where Rosie sat nursing something clear on the rocks. He stood and held his arms out to her. She stepped into his embrace and a new flood of tears burst out.

"It's okay, doll, it'll be okay."

He brought her head down to his shoulder and held her tight. His scent of Old Spice and DiNobili cigars blanketed her.

When she calmed down, they sat together and looked out over the lagoon where his yacht, *La Comare*, was sunning herself in her slip.

Life in the tropics was kind to Rosie. He hardly looked like a nearly-septuagenarian grandfather. He sported a full head of boot-polish-black hair, maintained a healthy regimen with his third wife and his Danish mistress, still dallied with his two ex-wives—who happened to be sisters—and held court to an assortment of grandkids and *paisans*.

"You hungry, doll?"

"No." She gazed at the water glinting in the sun, such a contrast from what she'd left behind. She turned back to Rosie and took the cigarette he offered her from a gold case. He lit it with a gold lighter. "Who's that dolt at the gate? Is he the organ grinder at your feast-day block parties?"

"That's Al. Does a great job around here." He stretched his legs and yawned.

"Just Al?" She let an amused grin curve her lips. "Not Bruiso or Rockhead or something equally descriptive?"

"Aldobrandi Gambaloto Emiliano Raimondino Po. They shortened the last name from Postrettanno when him and his family got to Ellis Island. We just call him Al. Don't need a nickname."

"After a few more run-ins like the one at the gate, I'll come up with a few." She sat back in the lounge chair and took a deep breath of the humid air.

"I like 'em that way. Intimidates people. I see he didn't do that to you, though." He chuckled.

"So what part of Sicily is mourning his absence?" She took a drag of her cigarette.

"Campobello di Mazara, in Trapani. The family come to New York when he was a kid. But speaks beauty-full Sicilian."

"Well, his English didn't knock my socks off." She flicked an ash into the pedestal ashtray between them.

"He's just tryin' a better himself." Rosie lit a cigar with his gold lighter. "He had a few hard knocks. But he's a devoted worker. Got me to the hospital when I had that heart attack. If he wasn't there, I'd be sittin' on the right hand side of the Father right now. Or maybe the left hand side."

"So that's why you gave him a job?" She took another drag.

"Nah, he already had the job." He waved away a fly. "He was working at Hialeah when I met him. He loves racehorses and wants to breed his own someday."

"Does he know he needs another horse for that? Or

does he think he can put himself out to stud?"

"I told him about the birds and the bees, but I think he taught himself about the horses." Rosie looked at her and winked. "Glad to see you two are off to such a good start."

"Oh, he just rubbed me the wrong way, not wanting to let me in 'troo da gate.' " That accent made her smile. It was so…*back home*.

"I gotta be careful, doll." He chomped on his cigar. "Lotta crime these days."

That brought a bitter laugh to her lips. "Speaking of crimes, I brought those notebooks and tapes…"

****

No event, however tragic, precluded the five-course Italian meal. So, when Billy arrived later that night, they all sat down at Rosie's table and chowed down on manicotti and garlic sausage and meatballs in gravy and honey ham and fruit tarts and cannolis and cappuccino like it was Saint Anthony's feast day.

Grateful her appetite was back, Vikki stopped after the second cannoli and opened the button on the side of her slacks.

"Okay, Rosie, what'cha got?" Billy asked over Chivas Regal and cigars. He and Rosie hunched over their shot glasses like she'd seen them do her entire life. Too keyed up to drink, she sat and puffed away on her cigarette.

"I kinda suspected when I heard what happened, but now word's just as good as official that Oswald didn't do the deed alone like they want the world to believe." Rosie puffed on his stogie.

"But it was his rifle they found on the floor there, wasn't it?" Billy asked.

"Like he said when they brung him in, he was a patsy. Besides the sixth-floor perch, there was another assassin behind a fence in Dealey Plaza there, and one more in the Dal-Tex building next to the Book Depository, in your classic triangle, to hit the target from all angles. One of 'em used Oswald's rifle they got from his garage." Ice cubes clinked in his glass as he lifted it to his lips.

It seemed wrong to refer to the slain president as a target. But they were talking facts here, cold hard facts.

"So who was it? And can we connect this to Jack?" Vikki tried not to fidget so much, but she couldn't sit still. She lit another cigarette to keep her hands busy.

"I'm not high up enough to find out exactly who these gunmen work for, but if I was a gamblin' man, I'd bet my worldly goods on Carlos Marcello or Santo Trafficante." Rosie poured himself a refill.

"What do you have to go on?" Billy held his glass out and Rosie refilled it.

"The day after JFK's killing, right before I come up to New York to Jack's funeral, I was talkin' to a friend a mine in Miami, one of Trafficante's button boys. He said Trafficante told a Cuban exile leader named Alemán that he was out to get blood vengeance against the Kennedys and that JFK would be killed before the election of sixty-four." Rosie took a sip. Ice cubes clinked again. "Now, I heard bits an' pieces before that about Trafficante and Marcello wantin' to take JFK out. Trafficante's real close to Marcello down there in New Orleans, where Oswald come from. And ya know Trafficante's the Florida boss here. Anybody wit' two ears knows both them guys hate the Kennedys, even more than the Russkies. 'Specially Bobby."

"It's ironic, isn't it? One of the most beloved presidents in history, hated by a few who hated him enough for…enough to do this." Vikki wiped away tears for Jackie. "And tragic."

"That's what happens when the wrong people hate ya." Rosie shook his head. "That's why it couldn' a been Oswald alone. The shooting of JFK like that, with three gunmen—it wasn't a bunch of amateurs. There was some high-level power behind it. They want the world to believe it was only one gunman, and…" He shifted in his seat. "See here, now what happens, they get Oswald to be their fall guy. Then Ruby shoots Oswald. When I knew Ruby from Chicago, we called 'im Sparky, 'cause he had a short fuse in the old days. He hooked up wit' the Trafficante gang when he moved to Dallas, and is still on the fringes there. Why'd he kill Oswald? To protect Mrs. Kennedy from havin' a face a trial, he says. Nah—it's too pat. They don' go whackin' guys to be nice to widows. Too many pieces of this puzzle might never come together, but Oswald didn't jus' take a cheap crappy rifle and plug the president 'cause he didn't like 'im. Nah, too simple. From what I heard so far, there's more to it than Oswald and Ruby. A lot more. There's a whole cast of characters. We just gotta find a trail that can lead to your Jack."

Vikki's head spun, hearing all this.

"You want a drink, babe?" Billy squeezed her hand.

"No. I wish we'd discussed this before the three-hour meal." She felt it rising, although she should've been glad to hear about this possible link—that meant she was one step closer to finding out just what had happened in the bathtub at the Dallas Hilton.

Rosie continued, "I have a few ideas rollin' aroun' up here." He tapped his noggin. "One is, I thought we'd pay my old buddy Sparky a visit in the slammer, but it'll take some strings pullin' to see him anytime before his trial. For now, we know your Jack prob'ly had somethin' to do with this Cassius, since he mentioned Cassius a lot. I'll ask aroun' to see if anybody knows this guy. Then maybe Sparky can tell us somethin' that can lead us to what happened to Jack."

"How long should it take to get to see Ruby?" She lit a cigarette with the one she'd just finished. She spat it out, realizing she'd lit the filter.

"Prob'ly not till after his trial. I hope it'll be a 'speedy' one as our trusty Constitution decrees." Rosie added ice to his glass with tongs.

"Rosie, I want an active role here." She leaned forward. "So when we track this Cassius down, I want to meet him."

She caught her father's cocked brow. "We're not casting one of my Broadway musicals, babe."

She rolled her eyes. "I know that, Dad. But this is my mission. Greta pulled me aside yesterday and asked me if I was sure I wanted to do this. I know she's still kind of scared, having lived through all the Prohibition mob stuff and all, but you know what? I'm not afraid. I know Jack's looking after me from up there."

"He might be, but we're dealing with some dangerous characters down here," Rosie warned.

"I can take care of myself if it gets dangerous. I can handle a piece, too, Rosie. Hell, you're the one who bought me my first twenty-two. I knocked down more clay pigeons than anybody else at the range, remember?" She smiled at the memory.

He chuckled. "Yeah. Little Annie Oakley here. But the front lines ain't no place for a lady."

"Yes, it is." she insisted. "I can talk to your contacts—I can be pretty persuasive. One thing I learned as a political science major was how to sweet-talk. Men find it easy to open up to a pretty young woman—especially one who can match their wits, unbeknownst to them."

Rosie wrinkled his nose and screwed up his mouth. "Are you followin' her here, Billy? 'Cause she lost me halfway between the political science and the sweet-talkin'."

"Yeah." Billy nodded. "She means she can tell 'em what they wanna hear, like good politicians do—and if necessary, act dumb. But that's the key word. 'Act.' "

Rosie fiddled with his pinkie ring. "I'm sure you can sweet-talk like the best of 'em, doll, but I know some people who were expert interrogators during the war. They can ask the right questions. That's if we can find these suspects. But meanwhile, I want to enjoy the holidays with you and kiddo here."

An overwhelming rush of love warmed her. After thirty years her dad was still "kiddo" to him. Just like she was his "Annie," after her middle name, Anna. But their private joke was that it also stood for Annie Oakley.

"If we hit a trail that leads to the mob rather than some Cuban nationals or something like that, at least we know how to deal with them." Billy stubbed out his cigarette and folded his arms.

"I'm hopin' it was the mob, 'cause if Castro or some fanatic commie group was behind the JFK shooting, we could be on the brink of World War Three right now." Rosie flicked a cigar ash into the Italy-shaped ashtray.

"Christ only knows how LBJ would stand up to the Soviets." Billy lit another cigarette. "But who the hell needs another world war?"

She knew her father didn't want the U.S. in another world war—nobody did. She was old enough to remember the ration coupons, the shortages, the air raids…and the "date which will live in infamy," in the words of Franklin Roosevelt.

She could still see her father and stepmother clinging to each other in despair on that cold December morning, assuring her that the Japs wouldn't get anywhere near them in New York. "God forbid," she thought out loud. But horrible things still happened here. The president was murdered before the entire world, and no one could get over it.

"I appreciate all your help, Rosie," Vikki said, "but whoever we track down, I want to talk to them myself."

"We'll see," and she knew that was his way of saying, "back off." She should've known he was going to try to take over, act like the honcho he once was. He was enjoying this, too. It disturbed her. But she kept her mouth shut about it. For now.

"Tomorra I'll get on the horn to a certain party who has contacts in Dallas, so we can get in and visit Sparky, and in the meantime I'll talk to a few connections who have sources who might be able to tell me somethin' about this Cassius." Rosie took a drag on his stogie. "Miami's the best place for me to start, 'cause I know more people there. Then New Orleans. There's a lot of pro- and anti-Castro groups in both places. I heard Oswald was one of 'em."

"Pro or anti?" she asked.

"Both. He went whichever way suited him at the time. Or whichever way they told him to go. Apparently was pro at the time of the JFK shootin', though. They set it up to make it look like he was getting revenge for the times JFK tried to kill Castro. Like things ain't confusin' enough as it is."

"Anyone care for another top-off of your tipple?" Billy asked.

Rosie declined, but now Vikki was ready. "I'll take one, Dad."

This time he poured them each a shot of anisette. "*Salut.*"

Rosie said, "I know I said take one step at a time, but I just want you to know ahead of time, if we do track down Jack's killer, we're also gonna—carry it out."

Rosie and Billy exchanged glances that needed no words, no gestures. She knew that look; she'd seen it in their eyes every time they heard some mob figure got whacked. "I don't even want to think about that now." She removed her glasses, rubbed her eyes, cracked her knuckles, and knocked back her shot.

"Business is business, Annie." Rosie gave her a resolute nod. "You see what happened to President Kennedy, that was business. We catch this motherf—er, that's business, too. We don't start nothin' we can't finish."

They'd told her many times, in detail too graphic for her stomach, about how hit men impaled their victims on meat hooks or hacked off their genitals or employed any number of torturous methods on those who'd held out, or finked, or cheated in one of their casinos.

She couldn't imagine holding a person's fate in her hands. The reality of it made her shudder.

"I just want to find Jack's killer, Rosie. Who knows? He may be dead already, for all we know."

"It wouldn't surprise me." Rosie ran his hand over his silver hair. "After something like this, they start droppin' like flies."

****

She always had a blast at Rosie's, going everywhere in his chauffeured limo, shopping till her feet ached, or lounging on his yacht, drenched in coconut oil. But this visit just wasn't the same. Nothing was the same anymore. She wasn't the same person she'd been on the last visit, playing tennis and water skiing and skinny-dipping in the pool at midnight with Jack. Christmas was less than two weeks away, and she trembled thinking about it. It would be more bearable here in Florida's warmth than at home with falling snow and jingling sleigh bells. But the calendar was a painful reminder that the anniversary was approaching…that magical morning when Jack slipped the ring on her finger. She even remembered the time, 10:15. How could she get through this? "Let me be strong, like Jackie," she prayed.

She spent her time poring through Jack's notebooks for more leads buried in his cryptic scribblings. But she didn't see any more Roman names, just monikers and initials: R.R., who she knew was Desi Arnaz, and L.L., whoever that was. She didn't pay them any attention. First things first, and first she had to find out who this Cassius was.

The next day dawned chilly, and the Florida sun

hid behind a shroud of dark clouds. It rained. And rained.

Rosie made some calls from his den, on his private phone line, behind a closed door.

But nothing satisfying came out of it. "I talked to a few guys I know who run numbers and other stuff from Miami, who have connections to Trafficante," he told her when he came out. "One of 'em, Joe Peanuts—he used to be a peanut vendor at Yankee Stadium—he had to deliver somethin' to Santo, and heard Santo swear vengeance against the Kennedys. But this time it wasn't the same ol' braggadocio. Santo was talkin' real serious, with a calendar and a map of Miami out, and was sittin' down. He only sits down when he's talkin' serious. That's the way you can tell Santo really means what he says, when he's sittin' down. I asked Peanuts if Santo said anything about a Cassius, or anything about Dallas, and he said no. Santo planned to get JFK in Miami."

Braggadocio or not, all it meant to her was another dead end.

But she didn't let it shatter her. Somehow, she knew she was going to find this murderer, who was as much a coward as Jack was a hero.

The next day Rosie came to breakfast chewing on a toothpick. "I got good news. I just talked to a friend who can get us into the Dallas County Jail to talk to Jack Ruby—after his trial in February."

She recoiled as if stung. That's what she wanted, but it scared her just the same.

But it was a step closer to the truth.

****

She attempted some semblance of a routine. She

went to mass every day, dropped to her knees on the padded kneeler, with her head resting on her hands, and inhaled the sweet incense. But churches in South Florida weren't the same as back home, and a chill went through to her bones when she stepped back outside. They couldn't do anything outdoors, so she and Billy sat at the piano or played cards. She started drinking before dinnertime, something she hadn't done since college. "Please don't let me turn into a lush," she prayed. So instead of hitting the sauce, she drowned her sorrows in milk with double shots of Bosco.

****

After mass Monday morning, she went up to her room. As a kid, she'd decorated it with matching pink lace bedspread and curtains, a pink canopy over the bed. Overlooking the rose garden was her balcony, where she'd always fantasized about Prince Charming climbing up and whisking her away. Now, she couldn't even go near it; it was too painful a reminder of the night Jack did just that: climbed up, swept her into his arms, and made love to her right there under the stars.

Fighting tears, she went to her phone and called Linc.

"So, how are you passing your time down there?" he asked.

"I'm bored out of my skull. It's miserable out, but I suppose I'd be more miserable at home." She glanced out the window at the overcast sky. "We're having a good enough time, but I'm going stir crazy. I need to get something going here on this situation. That detective never called me back, and I can't wait for my godfather to make his—never mind. I can't talk about it over the phone. I'll see you when I get back after New

Year's."

"All right, Vikki. Merry Christmas."

Although she'd done this just yesterday, she phoned Carlton Frost once again, to make sure he knew she was in Florida and had the number.

The secretary gave her regrets once again. "He's out of the office, but as soon as—oh, you're in luck, he just walked in."

Vikki's heart stopped. She held her breath. When Frost came on the line, she didn't know if she was more annoyed he'd ignored her or grateful that she finally got him. But his repeated apologies convinced her he really was busy. "You have all my attention for the two minutes I have to spare."

When she placed the receiver back in its cradle, she had a commitment from Carlton Frost, who was more than happy to fly down to Palm Beach the next day, all expenses paid, for a consultation she couldn't discuss over the phone. "I can use a day in the Sunshine State," he'd added upon agreeing, but as she assured him this job would be worth his while, she informed him of the current climate, and even if it were ninety and cloudless, they wouldn't be meeting under a beach umbrella. She only hoped he could dig up some evidence leading to Jack's murder the way he dug up dirt on his other unwitting subjects.

****

"Che brutto giorno, no?" Aldobrandi Gambaloto Emiliano Raimondino Po commented, flashing a Mack-the-Knife smile, as Vikki drove through the gate in the rain. Too shaky and preoccupied to swap Italian banter about the weather, she returned, *"Si, molto brutto!"* Yeah, an ugly day, all right.

"But I've seen uglier," she sighed as she exited her godfather's estate.

She glanced at Al in her rearview mirror. He grinned wider than before and chuckled out loud. *Is he laughing at me or with me?*

She couldn't give him another thought; her nerves were on edge about this upcoming meeting with Frost. She gripped the wheel to keep her hands from shaking.

****

Al watched her car disappear around the corner. He knew she was just simmering under that layer of ice. Standing there, he fantasized about chipping away at it, and, just like when he watched the horses tear down the track, his blood started to race.

****

She headed for her meeting with Carlton Frost at The Suncloud, a quiet out-of-the-way restaurant for discreet deals and trysts. It was a place to go and not be seen.

Frost worked for NBS on an as-needed basis, which kept him in four-leaf clovers. He was their pipeline to public figures who had private lives NBS felt it was their divine right to know about. He also did background investigations and general poking around. Overbearing and pushy as hell, he got into his share of fistfights with celebrities and irate philandering husbands. He'd have made a great investigative reporter but probably made more dough running his infamous agency. In simple terms, he was a whore. Just the guy she needed to hunt down the evidence—or the bastard who'd last seen her husband alive.

She detested his type, with a two-by-four on his shoulder, or more to the point, clanging brass balls. But for Jack's sake she could put up with him for a lunch hour, and would gladly cough up a five-figure check if he did his job.

She sat nursing a nonalcoholic piña colada when he sauntered in looking like he'd just bought his clothes at the Palm Beach airport—a baby blue double-breasted suit, a necktie embossed with little sailboats, and white loafers. A white snap-brim fedora with a red band. A gold I.D. bracelet. Dark sunglasses, even on a day like this. A signet ring caught the light when he waved to her. He looked like *Miami Living*'s Pimp of the Month.

He swept the hat and shades off, raised her hand to his lips, and kissed her fingers, then took ownership of the booth opposite her. "I must say, Mrs. Ward, I was hoping we'd meet again under happier circumstances. Let me offer my sincerest condolences. Jack was a great asset to NBS, a powerful presence in the world of broadcast journalism, and an all-around great guy." He nodded. Wow, what a performance. Thorough enough for someone who'd only met him in passing at awards dinners. Forget journalist. Frost was a politician who'd missed the boat to D.C.

"Thank you." Now she wished her drink had a jigger of rum in it.

He continued nodding and repeating "great guy" till the waitress came over and took his vodka rocks order. "So how may I be of service?"

Knowing she'd be paying handsomely for his discretion, she came right out with the bottom line: "I believe Jack might have been murdered, and I need you to either find some evidence I can take to the police to reopen the case or find his killer."

He stroked his chin. "My specialty is philandering

husbands, cuckolding wives, bandits, and con artists, but I can give it my best shot. I've dealt with the real pond scum before."

"I hesitate to say 'present company excepted.' But I called you instead of anyone else because of your reputation." She had this guy figured for one whose masculinity thrived on flattery, so she gave him some.

"I'll take that as a compliment, then." He glanced around for the arrival of his vodka rocks.

"I don't think you're capable of being insulted, Carl. Just find whatever—or whoever—you can."

"I'll do my best, Mrs. Ward." He slipped a spiral notebook and fountain pen from his pocket. "Now, can you give me a little background information?"

She handed him photocopies of Jack's notes and a copy of the Cassius tape. "Jack was tailing a guy from New Orleans who calls himself Cassius…"

Three vodka rocks and a swordfish steak later, he had all the information he needed, along with a ten-thousand-dollar retainer.

As long as she was paying him a king's ransom, she gave him the name of her Park Avenue hairdresser. "Make the appointment soon, because he gets booked up fast. Movie stars wait to get to this guy."

"So I'll be adding this to your bill, I presume." He raised a brow and his hair went up with it.

"If you pull this job off, you can go to Milan and buy a whole new wardrobe and add it to my bill." The check came and she tossed her charge plate on top of it. "Maybe you ought to anyway," she couldn't help adding. He might've been her type when she was young and dumb, but after Jack, it would take a Roman god to spark her interest.

****

Vikki hadn't heard anything about Mrs. Kennedy. How was she coping with her widowhood? Did she relive that horrible scene over and over, or did she remember anything at all? Vikki hoped she'd blacked it all out.

"How traumatic that must've been for Jackie," she said to Rosie once again. They hardly talked about anything else. "Why couldn't those bastards have killed him some other way, instead of in a public place, sitting next to his wife? Why punish her?"

That made Rosie laugh. He leaned forward and stubbed out his cigar. "You kiddin'? They deliberately did it that way, in public. To show Bobby he messes around, he's next. Them guys got ice runnin' through their veins. Like I said, business is business. Ya know, when I heard how it was done, even before I talked to anybody, I had it figured for a mob hit."

"How?"

"Coupla reasons." He stuck out a thick index finger. "First, they killed him in public. That's an old tradition. The victim's seen as a mortal enemy, so he gets gunned down in front of the world. Second"—he held up two fingers—"Oswald's your typical scapegoat. The lone nut who's set up to look like a follower of Castro, so they make out like he's gettin' back at JFK for his anti-Castro policies and JFK's attempts to whack Castro." He added his thumb to his two outstretched fingers. "Third, and this is the most typical of all—this goes back to the old Sicilian ways—they catch the suspected assassin, then blow him away before he has a chance to talk. It's also a warning to other big-mouths out there who might talk. The whole thing reeks of the mob."

"So Jack might have been involved in the mob." A pang of fear shook her voice. She hugged herself, freezing cold all of a sudden.

"We don't know that for sure. It looks like he mighta just got tangled in their web, whether he wanted to or not."

She lit one cigarette with another. "I'm beginning to think I didn't know Jack at all."

"I learned a long time ago you never really know nobody. But don't worry. We'll find this bastard. Meanwhile, enjoy Christmas. You see the presents I got under the tree for you and Dad and the kids there?" He waved in the direction of the family room.

"It's very generous of you, Rosie, but I don't know how I can face Christmas." The clocks ticked down to the minute Jack slid the ring on her finger. She hoped to be unconscious at that time.

"It'll be just fine. You're stronger than you think." He leaned forward and patted her hand. "If it's warm enough, we'll take the boat out. Have Al take us around the bay."

"Al can pilot a boat?" She blinked in surprise.

"Yeah, he's good at lotsa things. He's a big opera buff, just like you. Has a voice to make angels cry. Does a mean Mario Cavaradossi." He closed his eyes and swayed to an imaginary aria.

She brightened with interest. "Opera, huh? I'll have to talk to Al about that. But I have too much on my mind to think about anything remotely connected with entertainment right now."

With Christmas three days away, she hadn't done any shopping. Celebrating the holiday in any way just didn't seem right. But she couldn't stiff her father and godfather, whose home was hers. So she freshened her lipstick and excused herself. "I'll be back later. I have to put a few things under the tree myself."

Al, at the gate, gave her a polite wave. Maybe Rosie had chewed him out for that "sis" routine on the first day. She used the minimum of effort to nod back. She didn't want to socialize or exchange pleasantries with anyone, even about opera, one of her passions. Her need to find Jack's killer was her only passion right now—now she knew passion could be more painful than grief. Praying—and hoping—kept the pain from consuming her.

"Just till I find out what happened to Jack. Once I find out, it'll all be different. I'll be able to live again, and Jack's soul can rest," she assured herself as the gates opened and she drove through. She glanced at Al and heard his amused snicker. So he'd seen her muttering to herself, as she'd done since she was a lonely kid. Normally she would've spent several minutes explaining herself away. But right now she didn't care.

****

Once again he stared after her, baffled. He had to find out what made her tick. If only he could get near her without getting gelded.

****

After Vikki sent him out for M&Ms and Bosco for the third time, with orders through the maid, Al couldn't wait any longer—he had to tell Mr. Ingovito what was on his mind.

"Uh, *Goombah*—" He halted in the doorway to Rosie's den but wouldn't go any further until invited.

"Your goddaughter—am I doing something wrong? I think she hates me."

Rosie chuckled and tossed his racing form aside. "Nah—come on in, get us a coupla cigars, sit down. She's goin' through a hard time right now. She's just been made a widow."

"Oh, *Madonne*—I didn't know." Al went over to the humidor and took out two Cuban cigars.

"You know Jack Ward, the newscaster. Found drowned in a hotel bathtub. That was her husband."

A shock went through him like he'd been prodded. "Jesus, I'm sorry." He automatically blessed himself. "I used to see Jack Ward on TV all the time—he wasn't just a newscaster, he was a TV personality." He sat across from his boss.

Rosie nodded. "Yeah. Terrible thing to have happen."

"Well, now I know that's why she's—I mean, she never talks to me, just—" Al waved his hands around. "I thought I was doing something wrong, upset her, or got her the wrong kind of potato chips or something."

"Not at all." Rosie leaned forward and lit his cigar off Al's lighter. "But right now she's goin' through a lot, like you are."

Letting all this sink in, Al puffed on his cigar, savoring it like fine wine. "I try to talk to her, even to make small talk about the weather, but she's always— how you say—preoccupied. I want to ask her if she's mad at me, maybe I done something wrong, but can't get the chance."

"She's the life of the party when she's in her right mind, but you just caught her at the worst time." Rosie gave him a narrow-eyed grin. "You, eh, like her type?

Tall leggy blondes? I thought you went for genuine Italian broads, you know, four foot eleven, the bun and the beauty mark."

"Me?" He stuck out his bottom lip. "Nah. I always went for blondes. But real blondes, not the kind you find down here, the bleached ones with black roots. But Vikki is an interesting dame—woman. I saw her shooting pool, playing poker—" He nodded with admiration. "You made a good choice for a goddaughter."

"Yeah, smart, too. Got a master's degree." Pride brightened Rosie's eyes. "You can talk to her. She won't bite your head off."

"Oh—" Al shook his head and tapped his cigar on a marble ashtray. "She wouldn't be interested in me. What could I talk to her about?"

"Opera, for starters. That alone'll keep you going for a few weeks." Rosie gave him an encouraging grin.

"Yeah?" He sat upright. "None of the women I ever met knew *The Barber of Seville* from the local barbershop quartet."

"And she dances up a storm," Rosie added.

"No kidding." It took all Al's willpower not to shut his eyes and picture them on a dance floor…

"Don't be afraid of her, just 'cause she went to college and all that. She's lonely right now. And mournin' her husband."

"Jesus, I'm so sorry," Al whispered. The conversation had already dredged up his own grief. He didn't want to cry in front of his boss, but his soul ached for her. He wished he could comfort her somehow, say a novena, give her a tender kiss on the hand—anything.

"Yeah…" Rosie puffed on his cigar. "She's in shock, still. But talk to her. She could use somebody her own age to gab with."

He waved that idea away. "I don't think she wants nothing to do with me. I'm nobody."

"Don't be so sure about that. She asked me some questions about you." Rosie cuffed him on the chin. "When she come in that first day, she wanted to know how you got the job here and all. She was just miffed 'cause you wouldn't let her in the gate."

"Oh, that—I'm sorry, but you told me if they weren't on the guest list—"

"Hey." Rosie held up a hand. "You were doin' your job, and I told her that. She's okay with it now. But you can talk to her. She don't bite."

"It's kind of—how you say—" Al spread his fingers. "Intimidating. She's educated, she's smart, her father's here, you're here—doesn't make me feel all that big."

"Believe me, both me and her dad would love to see her enjoy the holidays. You kids talk to each other, dance, have a good time here. New Year's Eve's comin' up. You got plans?" Rosie gave him a gentle rib-jab.

He shrugged. "Nothin' special."

"Can you work that night? On the boat? Help the cook whip up a nice dinner, then take the boat out? I'll hire a band, throw a party—you come aboard, say, three or four o'clock. After eleven-thirty, you're a guest. And I'll pay double." Rosie flicked his ash.

Al nodded. This was something to look forward to. "*Benissimo*."

"When we're on the boat, ask her to dance. She

needs that, to take her mind off all this what she's been through. It's a good idea you come up with."

"Well, it wasn't really my idea. I was just thinking she hated me." Al shrugged and pinched out his cigar, saving it for later.

"She don't hate you." Rosie gave Al a smile he'd never seen before. Al tried to remember the word he'd learned that would describe it perfectly—yeah. Enigmatic. That was it. Something hid behind that smile.

Rosie's brow furrowed. "You know, I'm thinkin'…" But he trailed off, drumming his fingers on the arm of the chair.

Al tensed. "What?"

"You heard you can get more flies with honey?"

Al nodded.

"She loves *strufoli*."

"Oh, so do I!" His mouth began to water. "The more soaked with honey, the better."

"Go think up a menu for New Year's Eve. We'll have about twenty guests. I'll make sure the other cooks can help out. But keep room for lotsa desserts. She loves sweets."

Al gave him a knowing smile. "I noticed. How about anisette cookies?"

"Whatever you come up with. I'll trust ya. Bake up a storm if ya want." Rosie waved his hand through the air. A stream of smoke followed in an arc.

"You got it, *Goombah*." Al stood, gave a little salute, and turned to leave.

"And, uh—" Rosie stopped Al as he reached the doorway. "There's another thing you both like, even better than sweets and opera."

He turned. "What's that?"

"Guns."

"Mama mia! Pensiamo lo stesso!" Do we think alike! He left the room convinced they were made for each other. In three ways, at least.

****

It was a struggle, but she refused all booze during the holiday, opting instead to swallow a few sleeping pills at night so she'd be coherent during the day. Rosie honored her request to cover all the clocks in the house so she wouldn't know when it was 10:15 a.m., the minute she and Jack became engaged. She even saw Al covering a few of the clocks. Did he wonder why he'd been ordered to do that? she asked herself, even though she really didn't care what he thought.

Her half-siblings, Thomas and Theresa, came down, and, combined with Rosie's family, they had the traditional Italian Christmas. On Christmas Eve, after the feast of fried eel dredged in flour and fried in olive oil, baccala and male crabs, baked mussels in tomato sauce—and stuffed with scrambled eggs, parsley, garlic, and Romano cheese—and a pincushion fish Rosie always called "la ritz" in dialect, they gathered around the tree to open their presents. Rosie gave her a mahogany jewelry box with a blue Tiffany's box in each drawer. Opening each box, she gasped in wonder at a purple sapphire pendant, a pink topaz bracelet, a ruby necklace, a diamond-and-emerald choker, a three-strand pearl necklace, and a diamond tiara.

She smiled over the tiara. Where would she ever wear something like that? Jackie had never even worn one. Or had she?

Her father's gift to her was much more practical: a

shiny new .25 caliber Bauer automatic pistol fitted into a box designed to look like Dickens' *A Christmas Carol*. "Thanks, Dad. I was going to buy another piece." She had to admit, it felt custom made to fit her hand.

"Of course that's not all." He proceeded to stack box upon box in front of her, which took her close to a half hour to open: an assortment of dresses, jackets, skirts, blouses, hats, and purses, all by Givenchy, her favorite designer as well as Jackie's. Tucked into one of the purses was a gift certificate to Enzo Arnolfo, a shoe store on Fifth Avenue. "I draw the line at shoes," he said. "For a fella, that's as hard as buying unmentionables."

By the end of the evening, so much gift wrap and bows and ribbons lay strewn around they had to wade through it all to cross the room.

Rosie invited his staff to join the family for a toast. Al entered first, in a midnight blue suit looking like it was painted on by Da Vinci. She hadn't realized she was staring until her father tapped her on the shoulder. "Babe, you with us?"

"Mm? Oh—sorry."

"Time for the prayer and the toast." He handed her a champagne flute.

Rosie stood. "My gratitude goes to the Almighty One for my family here, my faithful helpers, and especially to Al, who saved my life when I had my heart attack. If it wasn't for him, none of us would be together here tonight. Al—may God and all His saints bestow his blessings upon you and yours. Amen."

Al looked embarrassed, if that was possible. His eyes darted around the room, and he motioned for Rosie to go on.

He spoke the toast in Italian: "*Auguro che quest'anno che viene sara il migliore per ogn' uno di noi, e che ci porta ottimo salute, felicita, amore e prosperita. Salut.* May this coming year be the best any of us have ever had, brimming with health, happiness, love, and prosperity. Cheers," he repeated in English.

They clinked glasses and drank to the prospect of better times to come. To her surprise, Al came up to her, touched his glass to hers, and handed her a small box. "Just a little something, not much, but hey, it's Christmas." His shoulder lifted in a slight shrug. His eyes burned into her. She tried not to stammer. He exuded a raw sexuality that aroused something primitive in her. Or maybe it was just the racy scent of his cologne.

"Oh, that's so nice of you—" She nearly dropped the box, flustered beyond words, in any language. "I—didn't think you were going to, I mean—"

"It's okay. You can open it later if you want."

"No, of course I'll open it now." She searched for somewhere to put the champagne flute, but gift wrap and ribbons covered every surface.

"Here, I got it." As he took the glass, his fingers brushed hers, and she tingled. She tried not to fumble with the wrapping, but this was mortifying. He hardly knew her! Was he sucking up? Somehow she didn't think he had to—with anyone—ever.

"Godiva Chocolates. Oh, you really know my weakness," she gushed as she opened the box.

"I learned you have a sweet tooth," he said. "But I thought you deserved something a little better than M&Ms tonight."

A chocolate oyster shell opened to reveal a perfect round white chocolate pearl.

"It's—it's so beautiful I don't want to eat it!" she stammered, still too worked up, too hot and bothered, to say anything sensible.

"You can." He nodded. "They make a lot of those. Sorry to say, but it's not one of a kind."

Memories flooded her, torturing her. She fought a torrent of tears. "Thank you, Al, that was very thoughtful of you. Merry Christmas."

"Merry Christmas to you, too. Just trying to make the holiday special for everybody. It only comes once a year, so…"

So he really was a softie under that suit of armor. Head-turning handsome at first glance, up close his features were rather ordinary, blending in symphony to create a striking overall picture. Guilt berated her for the times she'd snapped at him, or just plain ignored him. "Look—I'm not always so cold and aloof—I'm going through a very difficult time right now. It's hell, in fact."

He nodded his understanding. "So am I. But like all things, it'll pass with time, and time will sweep it away into the past." He handed her back her champagne flute, excused himself, and left her knee deep in torn-up gift wrap, wondering what kind of hell he was going through, and how he stayed so composed, so professional, through it all.

She needed to ask Rosie what demons Al was fighting—oh, hell. Why use a middle man? She could ask him herself. Another thing—weren't oysters and chocolate aphrodisiacs? Would he know something like that? If so, was the gift a hint? Standing there, she now knew what a hot flash felt like.

But he wasn't around much after that. He had the week off, so he only showed up briefly the day after Christmas to run a few quick errands. One other thing he had time for: when she entered her room the day before New Year's Eve, she found a beautiful bouquet of white roses on her dresser, and as she inhaled their sweet fragrance, she tore open the card: "I hope the new year will be a new beginning, for both of us. Al."

Hmm…that could be taken more ways than one, depending on how deeply she read between the lines.

But come on! He's a servant buttering up the boss's goddaughter.

Then she started to analyze the syntax of what he'd written: Had he put that comma in there deliberately, or just to break up the sentence? "A new beginning, for both of us" didn't quite mean the same as "A new beginning for both of us."

Oh, what does he know about English punctuation? He's from Sicily, for God's sakes!

So what *did* he mean?

She stopped berating herself, dashed off a thank-you note, and started trying on her new fashions. Just for laughs, she slipped the diamond tiara on. Right then she decided to wear it New Year's Eve. Why the hell not?

She was still the princess around here. *But the fairy tale is over.*

Chapter Six

Carlton Frost explored the French Quarter on foot. "Hoo-wee." He whistled out loud and ogled the scenery like a bumpkin, wondering why he'd never come here before. Every door of every bar and restaurant gaped open. Jazz music and laughter poured out into the crowded streets. What a swinging place. Made New York look like a tomb.

He strolled down St. Peters Street, marveling at the Creole architecture—the cast iron balconies, the arched openings of the facades. He deserved a drink, so he wandered into Pat O'Brien's to soak up the atmosphere—and maybe soak up some spirits at the same time. Why not? He had Vikki Ward's twenty-five Gs *and* his fee from the bigwig at NBS who wanted the exact same information. Once more, NBS was handing him four-leaf clovers. But this time he was getting paid twice for the same job, including expenses. So which of them was paying for this Slow Comfortable Screw in the curvy hurricane glass? Hell, he'd have two, charge one to each of them.

Mrs. Ward wanted him to find evidence or the killer, and he'd have to be thicker than a five-dollar malt not to figure out the obvious choice there. The hell with evidence. This was his lottery ticket.

With a warm belly and a jaunty spring in his step, he next headed for the network affiliate's offices downtown. He smoothed his hair and whipped out his card as he asked for the crime reporter, Nathan Sorensen.

Sorensen made him wait longer than he was accustomed, which miffed him. He went into the lobby and spat on the floor. But he knew the pace here in the south, so he put up with it and spent his waiting time guessing what size bra the secretary wore. The reporter finally showed up. After the customary handshake, Frost asked, "May I go through the archives for an important but confidential—for now—case I'm trying to crack?"

Sorensen answered all his questions: who was who in this town, the good cops, the bad cops—and between them they figured Hilario Vero was the "Cassius" in Ward's notes and tapes, whose bullet he'd been lucky enough to dodge, giving him another six months to live.

"What was left of Hilario Vero was found in the Slidell woods with a bullet in the head," Sorensen informed him. "Hauntingly similar to the president's wound…"

"Hey, you never know," Frost's tone carried a hint of doom. "Might've been the same killer."

"Or may have been one of his partners. You know about the Triumvirate?"

"No, who's that?" Frost lit a cigarette.

"When Murder Inc. folded, the Triumvirate started, right here in New Orleans." A boasting tone crept into Sorensen's voice. "They mostly do high-powered political hits. Sometimes our government hires them, sometimes foreign governments. There are always three of them, but they're not always the same guys. They have a rather high turnover—for certain reasons."

"So Cassius was one of this Triumvirate?" Frost probed, blowing out smoke.

"What I know about them is that they've always had names that go together. One's Marc Antony, one's Brutus, and one's Cassius. Julius Caesar's assassins." Sorensen raised a brow and gave him a half smirk. "Get it?"

"Oh, yeah, I get it." So there were three of these bastards running around. "They might've got JFK?" He puffed away, his pulse racing.

"Maybe. Maybe not. That's not for us to ask. And don't do too much asking. Especially around here. Trust me on that." Sorensen turned on a heel and slunk out. Alone at last, Frost dug his way through the archives. The shelves stuffed with files and film cans loomed up over his head, but he zeroed in on what he was looking for. He plowed through the archives for an hour, then sweet-talked the secretary into letting him borrow an office with a phone. He flipped through the Yellow Pages for P.I.s. Why not just go to the first one listed? Banister, Guy, at 544 Camp Street.

****

Frost knocked.

"Enter!"

The dumpy brick building was a throwback to the post-Civil War era, holding its own under the scrutiny of a bronze Benjamin Franklin from the square across the street. But when Frost entered Guy Banister's office, he stepped right into a Raymond Chandler dime novel—caged fan swirling musty air around, rusty file cabinet drawers, all open and bulging with files, a chipped-up old desk strewn with papers, more junk spilling out of wire baskets, a black candlestick phone, a half-empty whiskey bottle, and behind the desk had to be none other than Guy Banister, P.I., perusing the *Times-Picayune*, a cigarette dangling out the side of his mouth, a torn-off tissue bit stuck where he'd nicked his chin shaving.

If this wasn't Guy Banister, it was Philip Marlowe come to life. Frost strode up to Banister and thrust out his hand for a hearty shake. "Carlton Frost, CFF Investigations, on Manhattan's West Side," he rattled off his intro. "I'm cracking a juicy case here, and you were the first one recommended to me." He poured on the flattery. "Care to talk turkey over some good Creole cookin'?"

"Who's cookin' Creole? You?" Banister narrowed his eyes and his lips in a doubtful sneer.

"Not me. I'm only passing through. How does dinner at Antoine's sound? We can have dinner, cocktails, shoot the breeze—the tab's on me, of course. I can steer some lucrative contracts your way. I've collected quite a string of connections." He wiggled his brows for emphasis.

Either Banister was gullible enough to swallow that or he just figured free meals at Antoine's didn't come waltzing into his dive every day. He tossed his paper aside and rose to his full height, dwarfing Frost in his elevator shoes. "Why not? It's a slow week."

They walked down Camp Street and headed for the French Quarter and Antoine's, where Frost, ever the optimist if not opportunist, had already made dinner reservations. Creole didn't turn him on, but when in Rome, he did as the Romans did. And, cripes, was the menu pricey—Rome-style pricey. Banister would've had to be an idiot to pass up a free meal here.

After Frost gave his name to the maitre d', a hostess seated them at a cozy table. Over martinis, he told Banister about the case. For good measure, he dropped a few names of local politicians he'd looked up.

"I learned that Hilario Vero was probably Cassius, but his corpse turned up in the woods a few weeks before the Kennedy hit." Frost chomped on his olive. "Shot in the head."

"Somehow I don't think he'll be missed—he hasn't been yet." Banister took the menu from the waiter and browsed it. "Ya know, they created Oysters Rockefeller and *pompano en papillote* here."

So between the Oysters Rockefeller and *pompano en papillote*, Frost realized he didn't need to repeat this performance with any more P.I.s in the Yellow Pages. He had an ally here. As well as an open invitation. "Call me if you need anything else," Banister offered.

"Hey, you're one of the most cooperative dicks I've ever come across," Frost admitted. "You're real open and unassuming." *Almost naïve*, he added to himself. Frost always knew opposites attracted.

Then again, some guys just turned real chummy with a belly full of Oysters Rockefeller and *pompano en papillote*.

✳ ✳ ✳ ✳

Hilario Vero. What a name. If Frost hadn't been from Queens, he'd have thought the guy made it up. Cassius was dramatic enough. But it fit the bill if he was one of the Triumvirate.

Now for the fun part. Frost knew he had to find that hooker Vero had blabbed to about being in on the plot. Vero's next of kin, an aunt in Old Gretna, was listed in the archives in an article about Vero's last crime, rigging a poker game. Vero lived with her, the article said. So Frost headed to Old Gretna, a genteel, non-touristy part of town.

Muriel Vero opened her door with a big grin and a handshake that damn near crushed his knuckles. She had to be one of those washed-up glamour girls of the '40s. He pictured her looking *va-va-va voom* in a tight sweater and with great gams during WWII, when she likely held down a Rosie the Riveter job.

"Big Daddy's, that's where Hilario used to go to meet women, all the time. His last girlfriend worked there…" Muriel sucked on a cigarillo as she mused.

Well, hot diggity. That's all Frost had to hear. "*Merci beaucoup*, Aunt Muriel. You're still an attractive woman." He pitched the compliment, tipped an imaginary hat, and headed for the door, ready to hightail it over to Big Daddy's on business, courtesy of Jack Ward's fat-checkbooked widow.

He remembered passing by Big Daddy's when he first got to town, taking in the view through the open door, planning to return when he got skin-starved.

Aunt Muriel chased him halfway down the walk. "Oh, wait, you can't go see her—"

Frost turned to face her. "Why not?"

"She's dead. She was found shot. They ruled it a suicide." She panted to catch her breath.

His eyes popped. "When?"

"November. Two days before Kennedy, in fact."

While Frost stood there open-mouthed, Aunt Muriel explained, "Kandi was her name…" *It figured.* She made it a point to spell it. "Such a nice girl, too."

Yeah, nicer than whoever whacked her.

"Well, thanks, Aunt Muriel. You've been a great help." He gave her arm a squeeze.

She even showed him a picture of her nephew with Kandi, a bubble blonde. But Frost didn't look twice. Why bother? She was dead now.

****

Frost decided to take some time off for himself— enough working for other people.

But this was one damn lonely city for a single fella, he realized after forty-eight hours of dining, drinking, walking, and sleeping alone.

He took Banister up on his invitation. Back to the Camp Street office he went to dig up more dirt and ease his longing for human companionship. The hooker he'd rented last night hadn't even wanted to chat. After her "wham, bam," he didn't bother with a "thank you, ma'am."

Frost lured Banister over to the Can-Can Cabaret, where he'd landed last night after the wham-bam. Sitting in the smoky room with a sax wailing behind them and a stage full of jiggling boobies within grabbing distance, Frost hoped this case would drag on for a while. Damn, he was getting to like the Big Easy.

"Hilario Vero, the first Cassius, was dead before JFK was killed, so I need to find out who his replacement was." Frost offered Banister a cigarette, which he refused. "I got my own brand," he said.

Frost went on, "The Triumvirate always keeps three members intact. So I need to know who could've stepped in at short notice. If he was blown away, who could the replacement have been? How do they recruit assassins anyway? With a promise of a good salary and easy advancement and a gold watch on retirement?"

Banister shook his head. At that moment, Frost considered slipping him a few of the bucks he'd made off Vikki Ward and the chump from the network, even though the checks hadn't cleared yet.

"These guys would never hit Kennedy. They might kill some dictator for the CIA or some foreign CEO who doesn't want to go along with a big merger, but they wouldn't do anything on U.S. soil." Banister tossed the menu aside. "They don't want the FBI breathing down their neck. I think you've been fed a bunch of bull corn, bub. Local legends. If something like that was going on here, I would sure hear about it. Why would The Triumvirate shit on their own doorstep?"

"I don't know, but they shat on it this time." Frost spotted a waitress and snapped his fingers.

"Look, Carlton—it is Carlton, isn't it?" Banister leaned forward and stared Frost in the eye.

Not one for eye contact, it unnerved him. "Carl to you," he corrected in a cordial tone.

"Carl—I don't think it's a good idea for you to get involved in this." Banister spoke in a near-whisper. "Do you know who you're messing with here? Do you realize one of the biggest Mafia chiefs in the world, Carlos Marcello, lives only a few miles away? He so much as looks at you sideways, your head blows up."

Frost rolled his eyes, having heard this song before. "I'm from the beautiful borough of Queens, bro. One of my clients was Joe Bananas a few years ago."

Banister didn't seem to recognize the name, so Frost continued, "This is unmarked territory to me, but I really dig it here. I feel like I belong. I'm even thinking of moving here permanently, or at least getting a second apartment. I can get used to this twenty-four-hour-a-day nightlife. So I might stick around. The only way to do that is to make enough scratch. And if this job pans out, I'll be set for life. So I'm not going to throw in the towel now."

As they ordered drinks, Banister looked troubled. He blinked, frowned, and fiddled with a ring on his middle finger. *Hell, could everything I've found out so far be bull corn?* Uh-uh. He was a good judge of character—he knew when somebody was snowing him. This plot was a thick one. All the more reason to dig deeper and find out just what Jack Ward was doing in Dallas, destined to meet JFK at the pearly gates that day. Now his own curiosity had the better of him.

Their drinks arrived, and Frost took a gulp. "Wouldn't it be nice never to have to work again, Guy?" Frost urged, swirling his vodka rocks in his hand. "Land a one-shot deal with such a big payoff you're set for life?"

"I never thought of it; it was never within my reach." Banister sipped at his bourbon. "Figgered I'd always be a workin' stiff."

"Eh—that's for the birds." Frost shot his cuffs and his gold Tiffany cuff links twinkled. He couldn't let his Rolex slip out without pushing his sleeve up. "The finer things in life —that's what life's all about. Maybe if you hooked up with the right partner, combine your talents, share your leads—two brains are better than one, and four balls are better than two. You know what I'm getting at, Guy?"

Banister shook a cigarette from a pack. Frost whipped out his gold lighter. "Allow me."

"You want to go in business together? You've been

here, what, two days?" Banister blew a stream of smoke toward the whirring ceiling fan.

"Just think it over, Guy." He pulled his persuasive tone from his bag of tricks. "I have some high-power clients. NBS for one. They have resources to burn. I make obscene amounts of money off them, to put it bluntly."

Banister nodded.

Frost snapped his fingers at the passing waitress and signaled for another round. "Think about it, pal. Meanwhile, I'm not splitting till I crack this case." He didn't tell Banister, but he planned to return to the network affiliate, sweet talk the crime reporter, and get the name of the most reliable homicide detective in New Orleans. "I may make piles of dough, but I earn it."

"I see that." Banister's eyes roved up and down Frost's suit with a mixture of admiration and envy.

"I know it's not dinnertime, but let's get some grub. My inner clock took a hike when I hit this town, and I like it that way. I might even ditch the Rolex." Frost gave his new pal a toothy grin.

They went to Alex Patout's, and he made sure Banister saw the fifty he tossed on the table after dinner, not waiting for change.

****

"You know who the local hit men are, even if you don't have the evidence to put them away. Any of the bad boys gone up in the world lately? Come into unexplained bucks?" Frost, in his new Armani suit and Gucci loafers, grilled Detective Daryl Cecil in a small room at Police Headquarters, Frost's card propped up against a coffee mug on the table between them.

Cecil tossed his doughnut wrapper into the metal waste can. "Yeah, I'd like to nail this guy Rino Tieri. He's been nothing but trouble since he came back from Korea. He's the prime suspect in half a dozen of my cold cases, all long-range rifle work. But we can't get no hard evidence. My one witness disappeared off the face of the earth the day before I was due to bring him before the grand jury." He rattled off a couple more names and resumes of local hoods, but Frost had already fixated on Tieri. If Frost was the head of the Triumvirate looking for a replacement Cassius, that's sure as hell who he'd audition.

"Hm. It could take me months to investigate all these guys. No way is my client going to pay me to stay here that long." He stood and stuck out his hand. They shook. "Thanks for your help, but I might stick around to take in some more of the nightlife. Later, bro."

"Now that I helped you, it'd be nice for you to help us. How 'bout making a donation to the new Widows and Orphans Home we just opened here?" the detective asked.

"Hey, why not?" Frost pulled out his wallet and placed a few hundreds on the table like playing cards. He didn't mind giving back a little. Besides, he had a thing for widows.

He went back to his hotel and called an old buddy of his at the Pentagon, General P.J. Walther, who owed him a favor he'd never called in—he still hadn't paid Frost for the revealing photos of his cuckolding now-ex-wife.

"Hey, Pete, tell me what you got on a Rino Tieri, served in Korea, got discharged in fifty-nine, and we'll wipe the slate clean." One less dirty slate in his collection.

He headed back out again and picked up a few kitschy souvenirs—a T-shirt, a paperweight, and some brass tokens from nineteenth century brothels—what a good idea. *Why'd they phase out something so convenient?*

****

Frost returned to his hotel and retrieved the waiting message from General Walther. He got right on the horn, and his army buddy rattled off a few facts: Rino Tieri was a marksman with sniper training; when stationed in Korea, he got a less than honorable military discharge after he almost killed a staff sergeant who welched on some poker game debts he owed Tieri.

This was a thorough enough profile: crack shot, poker player, violent temper. He had his man; he'd bet on it. And as long as he was betting…

He went to the concierge. "Where can I get some action? As a high roller, that is."

This week's game was in a back room of the grand old Hotel Entremont. Frost swaggered in, shot the breeze with some of the players, and dropped Tieri's name. "I heard he won a few chips here the night Kennedy got shot."

"Yeah, he's been bettin' a hell of a lot recently, but he's not here tonight," one of the gamblers replied without looking up from his hand or blinking.

"No, Tieri wasn't around that week; he was out of town," the dealer corrected him.

After another hand, Frost cashed in his chips and walked away with what he'd come here for—the dirt on Tieri and a pocket full of poker winnings.

****

His first stop the next morning was to a drugstore for some spray for his breath and Odor Eaters for his feet. From the phone booth in back, he called Banister's office. It was New Year's Eve, but everybody seemed to be open for business today. Hell, every day was New Year's Eve in this town.

"Hey, Guy, Carl here. Any chance I can borrow your typewriter for a sec? I won't bother you. I'm a fast typist, use all the right fingers on the home keys, don't hunt and peck."

Banister gave him the okay. "Anything else I can do to help? It's a slow day."

"Yeah." Frost ran his finger up and down the phone wire. "In fact, there is. I'm cooking something up, and I might need you for backup. I want you to hold something for me in your office safe for a few days. This is big. Just say yes; it'll be the best decision you ever made, pal o'mine."

"Sure, Carl," Banister replied, with none of last night's waffling. "It sounds like something I can't pass up. Who knows when another opportunity will come by? What you got?"

"I'll tell you when I get there, but meantime, can you find out where a Rino Tieri hangs out?"

"Uh—yeah, I'll have that by the time you get here," Banister said. "But I got a few odds and ends to take care of here. Give me an hour. No, make that two."

Frost strode up Camp Street, the wind nearly whipping his hat off. The more he thought about this whole thing, the more steamed he got, and he started to sweat in his new suit. Damn those gunmen, getting all that dough when Frost worked all his life and still wasn't sure he could retire at forty. If this job didn't pan out, he'd have at least another ten years of toil ahead of him. Oh, if only he could hit the big time! The more he walked these festive streets, booze and jazz swirling all around him, the more he longed for a life of leisure…here in the lazy south where he could lounge on an ivy-covered verandah and sip mint juleps all the damn day, gazing out over trees dripping with Spanish moss.

Hell, those sleazy gunmen bastards didn't deserve to have it all. The wrong damn people were rich. He deserved a piece of the American dream. And damned if he wasn't going to grab it.

As he walked, taking a detour around Lafayette Square so he could think more, he fixated on one thing: blackmail. Blackmail was the only way to go on a job like this, chasing after this variety of scum. After this, he'd be living the good life, hopping from bar to cathouse to bar. Oh, and he'd have to buy his gold-digging wife off, but that was a mere bag o' shells.

By the time he turned back onto Camp Street, he knew he had this Cassius guy by the balls. Blackmail wasn't one of his strong points, but in this case it was easy because he had the guy cold.

Ah, to live in The City That Care Forgot. He'd already made up his mind he wanted to live—and die— here in the Vieux Carre.

Chapter Seven

By the time New Year's Eve rolled around, Vikki was sleeping nights without popping pills or a vodka bottle by her bed. As she dressed for Rosie's yacht shindig, the intercom squawked: "Victoria, telephone call for you."

She picked up.

"Vik—er, Mrs. Ward, Carlton Frost reporting."

"I wasn't expecting to hear from you so soon," she admitted.

"Why not? Because it's New Year's Eve, or because I took less than six months to get you results?"

She gulped. "Results? What did you get?" Her breath caught in her throat. Her heart tripped.

"I tracked down your Cassius."

"How?" she gasped, stumbling over to the bed. Her knees wouldn't hold her up.

"I caught him because he boffed some loudmouthed hooker, but that's a moot point because he brought about his own destruction. He's dead now. And guess what. So's she. Couldn't keep it shut at either end."

Linc had been on the money, all right. Frost was a weasel. No wonder the network's ratings shot up when they got him to dig up dirt.

"I mean—*how* did you find him? What led up to it?" She tried to stay calm with deep breaths.

He snickered. "I know it's not printed on my business cards, but my official slogan is 'Ask me no questions, I'll tell you no lies.' "

"Well, is he connected with Jack's murder?" Her hands shook.

"Could be. I have a few more odds and ends to check out before I can tell you anything else."

"When do you think that'll be?" Her fist clenched around the receiver.

"I'm hoping to start the new year off with a bang. 'Nuff said."

Relief washed over her like a warm shower. "Okay, I won't ask any more questions. Oh, God, Carlton, if this pans out, I won't know how to thank you!" If he'd been there, she'd have signed over another ten grand check, she was so grateful.

"When I wrap it up here, then we'll see how you can thank me." It sounded like he was fishing for a bonus. But she'd hand over all her worldly goods if he could deliver Jack's killer. It would be the next best thing to bringing her husband back.

"Then I hope we'll talk soon. I'm going back to New York on the second, so call me at my father's after that," she told him.

"Right-o." He rang off, always in a hurry. But she didn't mind his abruptness; once he had a job to do, he didn't waste time on cordialities.

She had gripped the receiver so tightly she had to pry her fingers off it.

"Jack, I believe this guy'll find out. He knows what he's doing." She spoke to his spirit, still unable to display a photo of him. Hearing his voice on tape was torture enough; she couldn't bring herself to look at those laughing eyes or that catchy smile. His image was as clear in her mind as if he stood before her in the flesh anyway.

She crowned herself with her new tiara and went downstairs.

She found her father and Rosie shooting pool in the game room. A maid emptied ashtrays as the butler restocked the bar.

"Dad, Rosie, I have some great news…"

****

Frost entered Banister's dime-novel office with the fleshed-out scheme that would plunge them both in clover.

Banister, on the phone, cut the conversation when Frost came in.

"Perfect timing, just finished my call." He hung up. "That guy Tieri you're looking for lives in the Garden District." He gave Frost a piece of paper with the address. "I cleaned up the typewriter for you." He pointed to an ancient Underwood that looked like its next stop should be the Smithsonian.

"Good deal." Frost gave him a thumbs-up. "Got some paper and a few carbons?"

He settled in at the old clacker and typed up everything he'd figured out about Hilario Vero being the original Cassius, Rino Tieri being his replacement, and their roles in the JFK assassination. He put the two carbon copies aside and slid the original into a plain letter-size envelope.

"Here's what you do, Guy." He handed Banister the envelope. "You put this envelope in your safe, and if anything happens to me, you take this straight to the FBI."

"What the hell is this, Carl?" Banister didn't make a move to touch it.

"My insurance. See ya later, pal—I mean, partner." He turned on a heel and split.

On the crowded street, he checked his watch. Eleven-thirty. Nineteen-sixty-three would be history in just over twelve hours, and as he'd told Ward's widow, he planned to ride it out with a bang.

After all, he was in the Big Easy.

****

"My detective found Cassius in New Orleans," Vikki spilled her news to her father and Rosie.

Rosie scowled, but Billy displayed an encouraging grin. "So what'd he say after that?" Billy rested his cue stick on his shoulder.

"He doesn't know anything else yet. He's going to get back to me when he does."

"For your sake, and for Jack's, I hope he comes up with somethin,' Annie." Rosie's voice rumbled like an engine, soothing her as much as when her father sang. "Jus' don't give him any more money," he warned. "Not till he comes up with some results. Flesh-and-blood results. You also gotta be careful this guy ain't a fink. You never know who you're dealin' with in something like this."

"If Frost was a fink, he'd have been dead a long time ago." She went for a ceramic donkey on the bar. She pulled the ear down, and a cigarette slid out of the butt. "He's legit. I mean, not legit that way, but—" She lit the cig and blew out a stream of smoke as Rosie nodded.

"Okay, let's enjoy New Year's. We're having dinner on the boat, so we can board whenever ya's want." Rosie chalked the tip of his cue stick.

"Al will be at the helm?" That fell out of her mouth as she wondered what spurred her interest.

"Nah, I got another guy, Tony Barbaro, to be the captain. Tonight Al's in the galley." He took a shot at the 15 ball but missed.

"He cooks, too?" She couldn't keep the surprise out of her voice.

"Yup. The best veal *parmigiana* this side of Calabria." Rosie held his fingers to his lips and kissed them. "*Delicioso.*"

There was only one thing she *hadn't* heard this guy could do.

****

When she came into the galley looking to satisfy her sweet tooth, there was Al filling cannolis, singing "'O Sole Mio." She halted in her tracks. They stared at each other for a stunned moment.

"Oh, sorry—I didn't know you'd be in here so early." She started to turn on a heel and leave him to his performing arts.

"Wait!" He held out a hand speckled with powdered sugar. "What can I get for you?" Now he sounded like he should—a servant. He smiled, and a twinge of something forbidden spread through her lower anatomy. He sported a floppy chef's hat, which on other guys looked cartoonish, but it gave him a continental flair; it must've been the way it was angled, like a beret.

"I just came in here for a—" Now, what the hell had she come in here for? She swept her eyes around, and her gaze landed on a plate of *strufoli*, drizzled with honey and sprinkled with colored confection dots.

"*Strufoli*?" He read her mind.

"The display is too perfect to disturb." Her mouth watered at the sight of the little fried dough balls piled in a perfect pyramid.

"Just don't take them from the bottom." He went back to his cannoli filling, his gaze lingering on her. Like those classical portraits, his eyes followed her across the room as she plucked a honey ball from the top of the pile and halted with it halfway to her mouth. She didn't want to eat it in front of him. She didn't want him to see her smacking her lips and licking her fingers and grabbing for another one, which was all the fun of eating these things—but not in front of a servant, especially him.

"You want one?" she offered, though she knew she shouldn't. It was a breach of protocol, but who paid attention to protocol around here? Certainly not Rosie. His staff was like his extended family, and they all called him *Goombah* in the most affectionate way.

"Sure." But what he did next unnerved her. He opened his mouth, waiting for her to pop in the one she was holding.

Dare I engage in such an intimate act? I hardly know this guy! But it was New Year's Eve, they were alone, and he was harmless. So far. So she took the necessary two paces over to him and placed the honey ball between his custom-made choppers.

He closed his eyes, and she watched him savoring the sweetness. She didn't dare say another word as she ran her index finger over a glob of cream on the cannoli plate, raised it to her lips and licked. "Mmmm," she voiced, wishing she hadn't.

Their eyes met and locked. Faster than lightning,

they came together like magnets. Their lips met, sweet and sticky and hot. She didn't want him to stop, but her inner voice screamed how wrong it was—*It's forbidden!*—echoing the nuns in Saint Gustina's. She shooed it away like an annoying fly. *Leave me alone. I'm not a kid anymore.* Her arms circled his neck, and his hands slid down to the curve of her back. Dare she move in closer, pelvis to pelvis, an unthinkable act three seconds ago? Her body was betraying her, betraying Jack, taking on a will of its own as she crushed herself to him. The kiss intensified. She tasted cannoli, and her fogged mind told her he'd been sampling them all day. She breathed in his cologne, so foreign it repelled her, so new it aroused her even further. Her tiara slipped off her head. She caught it just as he pulled away.

He held her at arm's length as in a tango. "Oh, *cara mia*," he growled—and if he said another word in Italian, she knew she'd explode. A passion long dormant stirred inside her.

She pulled her glasses off; they were so steamed up she couldn't see through them. "Stop," was the only word she could say, and that didn't carry much conviction. It sounded more like an invitation, which he accepted. His lips found hers once more, and they drank each other in, two starved, deprived primates discovering something beyond delight—raw need.

It ended too soon for her. "If that's the appetizer, I'd like to see the main dish." She didn't know what made her blurt that out,

He didn't hesitate. "Now?"

"Uh—no. I didn't mean it that way. I meant— It was a compliment. What I really mean is, I don't want to be your—" Still in a fog, she couldn't even form a word that he'd take seriously. *Who the hell are you kiddin'?* was what she expected him to say.

"What? Convenience? You aren't," he purred. "It's New Year's Eve, we're two people intensely attracted to each other, and the moment was perfect. Can you deny that?"

She didn't know what she had the strength to deny at this point. With her knees still wobbling, she looked away and focused on the huge gravy pot simmering over a low flame. Not the only thing simmering around here, she realized, forcing her breath to even out.

"No, but I don't know if you're aware of my situation. I'm a widow. A recent widow. I shouldn't be doing this. It's forbidden," she echoed the nuns. "It's very disrespectful to my husband's memory, and I'm ashamed of myself."

"Your godfather told me you're a widow. I'm very sorry." His timing for the condolence could've been better. But what else could he have said? "Are you really ashamed of yourself? Do you think you're being so disrespectful?"

"Of course," she shot back. "He's not gone two months yet."

"Don't, Vikki." He traced his finger along her jawline. She tingled all over. "You have to forgive yourself. You're human. We all are."

"This must never happen again." But did she really mean that? God, it had been so long since she'd been kissed that way.

"It won't if you don't want it to." It sounded like a dare. "I've had my share of grief." His eyes grew darker.

"I wanted to ask you—if you don't mind sharing." She adjusted the tiara back on her head. "What was that hell you said you were going through? You don't have to tell me if you don't want to."

He took a step back and cleared his throat. "It's not the happiest thing to talk about on New Year's Eve, but—my father was shot to death in front of me by a mobster when I was a kid. I learned to survive without him, but—seeing something like that when you're that young makes you grow up seeing the world a little different, you know?" He took a deep breath and released it. "Besides that—my mama's terminally ill. That I learned how to handle better, because it's not so sudden, you know? I'm—how you say—doing all my grieving now. Once she's gone it'll be a blessing."

She shook her head, stunned. Sympathy for him tore at her heart. "I'm so sorry, Al." And here she was feeling so alone.

"Thank you. When Rosie told me about your husband's death, I was overcome with pain for you. You're much too young to be a widow." His voice soothed her.

Her muscles relaxed. "The police ruled it a drowning and closed the case. But I think he was murdered, and I want his death avenged." Holy mackerel, did she just say all that? What possessed her to blurt this all out to him? Her attempt to cover it up came out as a string of disjointed stammerings. She tensed up again.

"I understand your outrage." His eyes, dark and penetrating, pierced through her, as if reading her soul. Was he one of those servants who listened at keyholes and already knew all this? Or was he so perceptive all he needed was one detail to work up an entire conclusion?

"I expect you to *state zitte* about what I just told you," she warned with as much authority as she could muster as she leaned into him. *"Capisce?"* came out less forcefully than she'd have liked.

"I'll never tell another living soul," he promised, and she believed him. "I hope you're looking into it."

"Yes, I—have someone investigating it." They hardly needed words at this point. Should she say more?

He nodded, one step ahead of her, it seemed. "Mr. Ingovito might be able to help."

"Rosie's trying, but he's not the big shot he was in the thirties." Their connection strengthened. "But just for tonight, I need freedom from tragedy and pain and want to enjoy the short time I have here," she said.

"You will."

She took that as a prediction. "Are you going to be…around tonight?" Again she surprised herself; she became this presumptuous only when well smashed. But wasn't she? Booze wasn't the world's only intoxicant, she'd learned from her few trips around the block.

"My shift ends at eleven thirty." He glanced at the wall clock. "I'm not piloting the yacht tonight. Mr. Ingovito told me to consider myself a guest."

Her heart leapt. Only two and a half hours away!

"Will you dance with me at the yacht party?" He began to hum a song she couldn't place.

He sure made his advances in advance. "I'll be happy to. Just look for me." Her tone was throatier than she wanted it to be.

"I won't have to." His wink melted her from the neck down.

Somehow she forced herself out of there, never having gotten that honey ball.

Chapter Eight

Frost counted seven gongs of distant church bells. This horrific year had five remaining hours. He planned to complete his task, then head out to Bourbon Street for some serious celebrating—and not just because it was New Year's.

He chased away a tinge of remorse for lying to Vikki Ward on the phone. She'd sounded so happy about his findings. But, hell, she wasn't paying him enough to feel any more than a tinge.

After donning new duds and spraying his hair into place, he headed out the hotel's revolving door and jumped on the Charles Street streetcar to the Garden District. A short stroll brought him to the address Banister had given him for Rino Tieri, aka Cassius.

The stately antebellum mansion stood among ancient oaks, a prime piece of real estate. Assassins sure made good dough. He bristled with envy.

He scoured the grounds and peeked into the garage. Only one car, a Caddoo, of course, was nestled in there. So the odds were in his favor that the king was alone in his castle.

He rang the bell, and Westminster chimes bonged somewhere inside. As footsteps approached, he got out his Colt and pulled back the hammer. He wanted to be ready for anything, although he hoped to hell this would work out the way he'd planned.

The door opened. A lean, tanned bruiser stood there, his silk shirt open to the navel, sleeves rolled up, a gold crucifix on a rope chain adorning his hairy chest.

"Yeah?"

"Mr. Rino Tieri?" If it wasn't, he'd eat his hat.

"Yeah? What you want?"

He stepped closer to the infamous Cassius. "Happy new year, pal." With a move Cassius didn't even see, Frost delivered a leg sweep and hit the guy in the ankle with his foot, knocking him off his feet. He pistol-whipped him around the head, ignoring the sickening crack of bone and the spurts of blood staining his Burberry trench coat. What the hell, he could buy another one.

He cocked his gun and aimed between Cassius's eyes as he slid one of the carbons out of his coat pocket. He tossed it onto the floor next to the prone figure instinctively clutching his crotch.

"Read it. Now," Frost demanded. "And no funny stuff, or the originals of these are on their way to the cops and the FBI."

He stood tapping his foot and checking his watch as Cassius wiped the blood from his eyes and groped for the letter. Frost pushed it closer to him with his toe. "Read it. Now. And one peep out of you, and you get it." He took in the decor while he waited, and decided the place was typical of a wop who'd just made a wad of dough in the rackets. Shiny wallpaper that looked like wedding gift wrap covered two walls. The other two were mirrored. Rows of wine bottles lay on a rack. A dripping chandelier glittered above his head. A French Quarter whorehouse wasn't much tackier.

Still lying on his side, Cassius unfolded the letter

and read it. He tossed it aside and looked up through now swollen eyes. "Yeah? So what?" he rasped.

"I want a cool million wired into this account by January second." With a smirk, Frost tossed a business card on top of the letter. It listed his offshore bank and account number in neat script. "I think I got a full house here, loser."

Cassius's hands shot out in front of him, as if to ward off a blow. "No!" He jerked his feet forward. Frost stumbled back. His aim wavered. He got a tighter grip on his pistol.

"No what?"

Phut! Phut! Two silenced gunshots went off as Cassius jerked backward. Blood spurted from his head and splattered the walls. Frost spun around to face a bruiser in the doorway, the band of his fedora gleaming in the chandelier's glow. Frost knew if he lifted his gun, this breath was his last.

"Royal flush," the bruiser recited with a theatrical flair. Frost recoiled at the sight of a silenced .44 pointing at his heart.

"Who are you?" Frost held his hands up. Dammit, this was not going as planned! He didn't want to share his ill-gotten gain with anybody, least of all this prick, wearing what looked like Rod Steiger's wardrobe castoffs from *Capone*.

"Shaddup! Never mind who I am," the bruiser spat at Frost and glanced over to the side. "Guy, take his shooter."

Frost's jaw dropped when Guy Banister moseyed into the entry hall, as if on cue, and snatched his gun from him. Frost bolted, but stumbled over Tieri's corpse. He went down with a thud, cracking his head on the pine floor. Through his blurred vision, he saw the carved legs of a grand piano. "They got me. I'll be a son of a bitch," he muttered, more pissed at himself than at the clever bastards who'd double-crossed him.

Banister grabbed Frost's hands and yanked them behind his back. Rope cut into his wrists, burning his flesh. He howled in pain. "Ow, watch it, huh, asshole?"

"Why couldn't you just leave town when I gave you the chance?" Banister drawled. "I liked you, you sorry sumbitch."

"Who's your dago pal, Banister?" Frost snapped, determined to have the last word, the final insult.

Banister's dago pal stepped forward and ground his heel into Frost's head like a cockroach. "My name's Benzo. But my business associates call me Marc Antony. Guy, you can scram. I'm gon' watch Mr. Frost end the old year a couple hours early. But first he's gon' tell me everything he knows, aint'cha, Mr. Frost?"

"Go to hell, ya slimy greaseball!" Frost hissed between clenched teeth.

Marc Antony kicked him. Frost wailed in agony, spat out blood and a few teeth. "I wmfth umfmpth."

"Wrong answer." Marc Antony yanked Frost's left shoe and sock off, and stuffed the sock into Frost's mouth.

Marc Antony knelt before him. Frost's final agony came from a cutthroat razor slicing his throat.

****

New Orleans was the last place Benzo Battolini wanted to return to. But if he ignored the order from his handler, he'd be the one with a sock in his mouth and a slashed throat. The order was to take out a nosy New York gumshoe who'd gotten too close to Cassius for comfort. So he had to kill Cassius—and Brutus, too, if necessary. The fewer in the know, the better. Guy Banister had also handed over Frost's "insurance," now smoldering in the ashcan behind the shabby office on Camp Street.

After the job was done, Benzo had to hightail it out of town. His estranged wife ran a cathouse here; all he had to do was breathe the air and she'd track him down. Not that he wouldn't mind sampling some more of the wares at her highfalutin' establishment, which she ran from their Metairie mansion. They'd started the business together—he brought in some knockout gals to work there and customers to pay for them—but her bossy ways got the best of her. She started treating him like a flunky, never letting him see the books, cutting him off from the merchandise—which he'd recruited himself! Then she had the *coglioni* to call *his* livelihood "immoral"—that's when he calmly packed a bag and moseyed out. "*Au 'voir*, vamp." He knew she'd figure he was off on one of his jaunts. But he never came back, and couldn't stay now if he wanted to. She'd tried to track him down once, but not because she craved his affection—she wanted to hit him up for child support. *Well, kiss mah grits*, was his answer to that. She was the one who'd wanted the kid anyway.

He longed to stay in his beloved birthplace instead of living on the lam. He missed the town's leisurely pace, the booze, the cathouses, the jazz. But after November 22nd, it was far too dangerous. He didn't trust anybody, least of all the mob or the government. It wasn't enough he'd pulled off the crime of the century; they'd wanted him to kill his fellow assassins. He didn't dare refuse. But he couldn't help wondering: Is my hide next?

So he did his business. Now he had to scram before anybody spotted him.

But he got one more call from his handler that night.

"You want me to what?" He cradled the receiver as he tossed his clothes back in his valise. "Ah, shee-it."

But he couldn't refuse.

So he had one more hit to do—and on New Year's morning, Guy Banister lay on his floor with a bullet in his body.

Chapter Nine

Billy noticed Vikki's agitated state as she entered the yacht's lounge that night. "C'mon, we're takin' a stroll." He walked her out onto the promenade deck, where she confessed.

"I'm ashamed of myself, but I'm growing very attracted to Al," she confided to her father.

"Babe, finding another man attractive isn't a cardinal sin. You won't rot in hell." He cupped her cheek. "I need to tell you something." He paused, searching for the right words. "When your mother died, I forced myself to stay away from women, thinking I'd be cheating on her. But one year to the day after her death, Greta came to me and let it all out—she'd been in love with me for fifteen years, and it was about time I stopped living like a monk, and—" He took a breath. "Well, you can guess what happened next."

"You married her." Vikki nodded.

"Well, yeah, but—I mean—in the next two minutes."

She looked away into the blackness of the ocean. "Okay, I get the picture, Dad." She chuckled. "The topic seems to drift that way so often now that I'm older. So you regret waiting a year?"

His eyes widened. "Hell, yeah! It was torture. I was a pretty sharp-lookin' fella, a dead ringer for Gary Cooper, if I don't mind saying so, and the bearcats never stopped chasing me. After all, I was playing nightclubs, forming my orchestra—I drank to keep my mind off—" He cleared his throat. "Off other things. But when Greta showed up and the moment of truth arrived, instead of feeling proud of myself for my year of self-inflicted celibacy, I felt your mom applauding me, urging me to get on with my life, saying, 'What the hell took you so long, Snuggles?' She called me that since the first day we met."

"You would've stayed that way if Greta hadn't come to you?" She faced him and leaned on the rail.

He shrugged. "As long as I could stand it. I got to the point where I was enjoying the suffering, like a martyr. But Greta made me realize that your mother wouldn't hold something over anyone, least of all me. Even when we were married, she had her life, I had mine. But I was never unfaithful to her, not once," he declared with a solemn shake of his head. "When Greta came along and told me she'd waited for me all those years, I knew it was okay, and your mother gave us her blessing from above."

"This is hardly a year, Dad. Jack's only been gone five weeks." She gazed out into the ocean again.

"I knew Jack, and you knew Jack, and we both know what kind of person he was. He was a free spirit. He never held you back from doing anything you wanted. But he's gone, Vikki, and you're here to carry on." He squeezed her hand. "You like this guy? For Christ sakes dance with him. It's New Year's Eve. You don't think Jack's up there dancing with some chippie right now? Hell, for all you know he might be in that great ballroom in the sky cutting in on Jack Kennedy to kick up his heels with Marilyn Monroe."

She let out a sad laugh, nodding. "Oh, yeah. That's my Jack. He met Marilyn once, you know. At some Hollywood premiere."

Billy shook two cigarettes from a pack and captured one with his lips. "What else did he admit to?"

"Nothing." She shrugged. "He said she had big hips."

"Smoke?"

"No, thanks." She rested her elbows on the rail.

He lit his cigarette and flipped the match overboard. "Just remember what I said. We're not shooting for sainthood here."

She gripped the rail. "I'm still at odds with my feelings."

"Just don't fight your heart, babe." He blew out a stream of smoke. The wind swept it away. "I'm gonna do a few numbers with the band later. Anything you'd like to hear?"

"I love the way you play 'Stardust.' And I plan to dance to it tonight."

****

They went back in. Her eyes swept across the lounge, searching for Al. As the band struck up a cha-cha, she heard a loud woman's laugh. She turned around, and there was Al, twirling Rosie's maid across the floor like Fred Astaire.

"He didn't waste any time," Vikki muttered at the amusing sight. Rosie's maid was old enough for her father.

"I'll dance you over to him so he'll take the hint and cut in." Billy eased Vikki onto the dance floor.

"No!" She stepped back. "I don't want to make it obvious. Let Carmen have fun, Dad. She works hard enough."

Vikki and Billy finished the dance and approached the band. "I'll sit in on a few numbers with you cats." As Billy approached the piano, she reminded him to play "Stardust."

She glanced over at the clock. Ten minutes till midnight. She ducked into the ladies' room to touch up her lipstick and perfume. When she came out, Al walked directly toward her, arms extended. Without a word they glided onto the dance floor together. Her father started playing his promised "Stardust" and she closed her eyes, breathing in Al's mingled scents of cologne and creme de menthe. The crowd started counting off the seconds, and at the bursts of "Happy New Year!" the band broke into "Auld Lang Syne." She swept her glasses off, Al lowered his lips to hers, and everything converged into a blur. Her arms wound around him. She wept, for her loss, for fear of the future, of the unknown, of this man whose mouth claimed hers. This time she didn't ask Jack to forgive her. She hoped he *was* tripping the light fantastic with Marilyn right now.

****

They said goodnight at the end of the driveway. "If you want me to come in with you, just say the word. I won't consider it forward." They stood well within kissing distance.

She liked *his* *f*orwardness, unnerving as it was. "No. This is as far as we go." She wrapped her mink stole more tightly around her.

"I understand."

"Do you really?" she challenged. "You really know what I'm going through right now?"

He stroked her cheek and ran his thumb over her bottom lip. "Of course. I'm no stranger to grief. It knows me pretty good by now. It watched me grow up."

She shivered at his touch, fighting arousal. "Then tell me this, Al. Would you deny yourself the company of women for a long time afterward if you found yourself widowed?"

"No." He shook his head. "I wouldn't. But that's who I am. I'm weaker than you are, *cara mia*."

Well, not every guy was like her father.

"The pain never goes away," he said softly. "But I'm human—and so are you."

She nodded. "I'm not arguing with you about that, but I'm too tired to make any major decisions right now. We'll talk again." She was more turned on than tired, but didn't dare admit that.

"*Buona notte, cara mia*." His lips brushed hers. Although he offered to drive her, she walked up Rosie's quarter-mile gravel drive, inhaling the bracing air as it enveloped her with its cold comfort.

When she got to her room, she glanced at the phone. Plucking the tiara off, she wondered if Carlton Frost was on the job.

****

"So you're leaving tomorrow." Al stood in her doorway with a bag of her clean laundry. "You visit here a lot?"

"Just holidays, mostly. But maybe things will be different now." She left that hanging in the air. "Will you be staying on here permanently?"

"I don't know. I like the tropics, but I love horse country. I'd like to move out west and be a cowboy."

His tone rang earnest and sincere.

A *cowboy*?

She tried not to smile, picturing him in a ten-gallon Stetson and hand-tooled leather boots with spurs. But then, he'd look good dressed as The Poor Soul.

"I'll see you next time, then, I hope." *Kiss me,* her eyes pleaded. She raised her chin ever so slightly.

He didn't disappoint. "Till then, *cara mia.*" He lowered his mouth to hers. She dropped the bundle on the floor, not caring if her pink pettipants were half spilled out of the bag.

****

"Al's takin' you and Dad to the airport," Rosie told Vikki as his butler carried her valise down the stairs and placed it in the limo's trunk. "Where is your old man anyway?"

"Probably still packing." They reached the limo. "You know the way he waits till the last minute to do everything."

"Well, you have a safe trip, and you come back at Easter time, ya hear it?" He pinched her cheek.

"Of course, Rosie." They embraced, cheek-kissed, and embraced again.

"I'll be in touch." He gave her a wave. "Meanwhile, pray to Saint Anthony. He's the one for when you want to find something—or somebody."

As the limo's engine hummed, she longed for another stolen moment with Al. He got out of the driver's seat and opened the back door for her as a Corvair pulled up alongside them. A woman with a lipstick red beehive sat behind the wheel, slitty eyes focused on Al.

"Al, where you going?" she demanded. "We're

s'posed to go to lunch."

He slapped the side of his head. "Oh, *managgia*, I forgot. All right, I'll meet you there. I just gotta do this run to the airport."

Vikki realized she was staring. The woman glanced over with a smug smirk she'd probably perfected when she got her first pair of Mary Janes.

"Hello, sweetie pie." Her voice dripped with Crystallose. "I'm Mona. Al's fiancée."

Vikki managed a hello to the signorina, but had nothing more to say as the butler finished loading the limo's trunk. As the Corvair took off, Vikki slid into the limo's back seat and started fiddling with the radio dials. Billy got in next to her. His knitted brow told her he knew something was up. She didn't respond.

No one tried to make conversation. She changed stations until Beethoven's thundering Fifth Symphony filled the air. If anybody wanted to talk over that, they'd need a megaphone.

So Al's a creep. Grow up, she kept telling herself as the limo pulled up to the curb at the airline terminal.

Without exchanging a glance or a goodbye with Al, she stalked away to the ticket counter.

"Okay, what was that all about?" Billy asked as they walked to the gate.

"That was his fiancée who pulled up in the Corvair." Her voice cracked with bitterness.

"Oh." He shrugged. "In ten years she'll be a *mamadella* and you'll still be a knockout. Or maybe five years, if she keeps that hairdo."

"It doesn't matter now, does it?" She handed the attendant her boarding pass.

"There are many *scungili* in the sea, babe." He

gave her a playful nudge.

"I know. But until now I thought he was a cut above *scungili*." Another of Jack's practical jokes maybe?

****

As they walked in the door and dropped their bags in the entry hall, the phone started ringing. Billy answered it in the kitchen and gave it to her. "It's for you, babe. CFF Investigations."

Carlton Frost! Her heart hammered.

After a brief conversation, Vikki hung up the phone, stunned. "Oh, God, no."

Billy rushed up to her. "What? What's the matter now?"

She shut her eyes and gasped for breath. Leaning on the counter, she shook her head in disbelief.

"What the hell happened on the phone there?" Billy rolled a cigarette between his fingers. "What is it?"

"The detective I hired—he's dead." Shaking, she stumbled to a kitchen chair.

"Holy Moses." Billy let out a low whistle.

"He got killed on New Year's Eve, in New Orleans." Her mouth dry, she swallowed a lump.

"Killed how?" He got her a glass of water.

"Murdered. Brutally." She hugged her knees, unable to stop shaking.

He sat next to her and stroked her hair. "Did they catch the murderer?"

"No, nothing about that." A sob escaped her throat. She gulped the water. The cold hurt her teeth.

He gave her a clean handkerchief, and she wiped her tears. "I didn't even know I was crying."

"Well, what did the messenger say?" He tossed the unlit cigarette on the table.

"It was Carlton Frost's partner. He's taking over Frost's caseload, but I told him to drop the case. His murder had something to do with the job I hired him for, I just know it. I'd told Frost everything—how I thought Jack had been murdered, the names in the notebooks and on the tape—" She took a ragged breath. "He was determined to get to the bottom of it. Not because he was such a proponent of justice, but because I was paying him twenty-five thousand dollars." The aroma of percolating coffee made bile rise to her throat.

"His life in exchange for twenty-five Gs." Billy got two cups from the cabinet. "What is it with some people and dough anyway?"

"Oh, God, I feel terrible. He had a wife, and he must've had kids—" She buried her face in her hands.

"Don't start blaming yourself now, babe." He put the cups down. "These guys know the risks."

"He called me at Rosie's and told me he'd found Cassius but wouldn't say how. If it wasn't for me—"

"We don't even know who killed him. Whoever it was, it wasn't you, and it wasn't your fault," Billy assured her.

She stood and walked through the cold empty house, cracking her knuckles. The ever-thrifty Greta had turned the heat down to one degree above pipe-freezing temperature. She chased gooseflesh from her arms. But she would've shivered if it had been ninety in there. "What a horrible thing to have happen. Even for him." She walked back to the kitchen, where Billy sifted through his mail, tossing most of it into the garbage.

"Let's light a fire, get your mind off it. We'll call Pizza Roma and order a couple pies. And have some of that Valpolicella Rosie gave us for Christmas." He stood and cupped her cold face with his hands.

"I don't want to eat or drink, Dad. All I can do is wonder how long it'll be before Frost's death gets traced back to me."

"It won't." Her father's promise rang in her ears. "As long as I'm alive, you're safe."

Oh, how she wanted to believe that. She left the kitchen and started piling logs in the fireplace to keep busy. He sat on the couch with the *New York Times*. "Dad—you still have all your guns, right?"

"Do seagulls shit in seashells on the seashore?" He gave her a confident grin. "You want one to keep under your pillow, I'll give you Greta's Bernardelli Automatic to carry around the house, till you practice a little with your new Bauer and get used to it. It's nice and light, too."

She prided herself on her ability to handle firearms, something her father had made sure she could do when other girls her age played with Kewpie dolls. "I have mixed feelings about the new Bauer. I'm kind of afraid of it. I don't want to pack a rod walking around the house. I just want to make sure we can defend ourselves."

"Babe, you're talkin' to an old pro here." He tossed his head. "Well, an ex old pro."

"So are these guys," she reminded him.

"Yeah, well, I bet I got at least thirty years on them, and I forgot things they ain't even learned yet." His voice carried a cocky lilt. "That's if there is anybody out there. You don't know anything yet. Now, let's light a fire and order a pepperoni pie." He lit the logs, and she held her hands out to the warm glow.

What a way to start the new year, she told herself, turning her wedding band around and around. A 1963 calendar stood propped up on her father's desk, still open to December. She tore it into bits and flung it into the fire.

****

As Vikki and Billy feasted on their pizza and Valpolicella, Linc showed up. Billy sat him down and served him up a slice.

"Can you give me Mrs. Frost's phone number, Linc?" Vikki poured him a glass of wine. "I want to go over there and offer my condolences."

"The funeral's tomorrow at some church in Queens, if you want to go." He chomped on his pizza.

"No, I'd rather call on her personally." She took a slow sip of wine. "I feel responsible for Frost's death, but I know full well it's the nature of the business."

Linc patted her shoulder. "No, don't you go feeling guilty, Vikki. Frost was the type of guy who was asking for it sooner or later. He lived on the edge like nobody I ever kn—" He stopped himself and blushed to his roots.

"It's okay. Jack was like that, too. We all know it." She gripped the stem of her wine glass.

"Some of us are lucky and live to a ripe old age, and some don't make it," Billy said. "It's all a crap shoot. You can quit smoking and go out and get hit by a cigarette truck."

"Frost looked for trouble, but in a different way from Jack. Jack knew how to have fun. Frost was a ruthless bounty hunter." Linc wiped his mouth with a napkin.

"I'm beginning to wonder if Jack was, too." Vikki refilled Linc's glass.

"Let's play a few hands of poker, get your mind off all this." Billy cleared the dishes and dumped them in the sink. If Greta had been home, he'd have been up to his elbows in suds already.

Linc had never played poker in his life, so Vikki found it therapeutic teaching him the game. With Perry Como crooning on the hi-fi, good company, her favorite wine, and the warmth of the crackling fire, she welcomed the temporary break from reality.

****

Carlton Frost's widow greeted Vikki at the door, she stepped inside, and they embraced.

Yet another young widow, and all eerily connected to the same plot.

As her hostess served tea, Vikki offered her condolences—in this case, it was empathy. "I'm so sorry, Catherine…"

"I know, Vikki. I can truly say I know what you're going through, now." Catherine's teacup wobbled in her trembling hand.

"Did Carl tell you why I hired him?" Vikki asked.

Catherine shook her head. "Not all the details. He was in too much of a hurry."

So Vikki explained. "…and I need to find out who killed Jack. What has me baffled is that final trip to Dallas. He told me he was going to Chicago. I'm beginning to think Jack had another side to him that he just didn't show me."

"All ambitious, success-driven guys do." Catherine placed her cup in the saucer with a clink. "I know there's a lot Carl never told me. I just didn't ask. I really didn't want to know. I didn't want to know what he *did* tell me. But you know how pillow talk goes. Sometimes he just had to get certain things off his chest."

Vikki circled her cold fingers around the warm teacup. "Jack always told me where he was going. Until—that final time."

"You were lucky." Catherine looked into her eyes. "I hardly ever knew where Carl was. He'd call and say he was okay, and that was it. I knew he was in danger most of the time. But I never had the guts to follow him, or try to find out what or who he was involved with. I don't know if Carl's partner told you, but another man was found dead at the scene, a few feet away from Carl's body. They identified him as Rino Tieri, a professional hit man with mob connections."

"Cassius!" Vikki choked on the name.

"Who?" Catherine sat forward.

"That had to be Cassius." Vikki caught her breath. "Carlton was after him—that's the name in Jack's notebooks and on his tape, the man he thought was after Kennedy." Oh, God, they both got killed together. She couldn't think straight. Who could have killed Frost *and* Cassius?

"Are you sure your husband was involved with the Kennedy assassination plot?" Catherine asked.

"Yes, Jack had Cassius all over his notes, next to JFK." Vikki rambled on, running her words together, and she still couldn't talk as fast as her mind whirred. "Carlton trailed Cassius to New Orleans, where Jack had interviewed an FBI informer who later got murdered—"

"Wait! Stop!" Catherine covered her eyes with her

hand. "I don't want to hear any more. I never wanted to know what Carl was doing or who he was after, and I always vowed that if he was killed on the job, I wouldn't want to know the details, because I knew it would be like this—connected to the underworld. And I don't want anything to do with them, or them to have anything to do with me." She poured a short stream of rum into her tea, took a sip, and dabbed at her lipstick with a napkin.

"I'm sorry." Vikki wet her lips. "I won't tell you, then. But I want justice for Jack, and it's more than I can say for the authorities that should be handling it. But to them, the case is closed. So it's up to me to find out. And that's what I'm going to do," she declared for the umpteenth time.

"But these are professional assassins you're dealing with." Catherine's warning died in the folds of the drapes.

"I know they're professional assassins. But they don't know who *they're* dealing with." Vikki spoke with conviction. And with a Bauer in her purse.

"Vikki, I'm an average American housewife. I didn't go to college, I started having kids at nineteen— all I wanted was the American dream in the suburbs. Unfortunately, my husband couldn't settle for something so mundane. So now that he's been murdered, I could never do what you're doing, trying to find your husband's killer. If Carl's killer is found, I'll be grateful, but if not—" She splayed her hands in a hopeless gesture. "I have faith in the police, but if they can't apprehend the killer, then I'll learn to live with that. But you—you're very brave, Vikki. No wife I know has that kind of courage. You're something out of the ordinary. Maybe you're ahead of your time, but you certainly are braver than any suburban housewife."

"It's got nothing to do with courage," Vikki insisted. "I'm only doing what I feel is right."

Catherine didn't ask any more questions; they both seemed talked out. Vikki wanted to keep in touch with Catherine Frost; she liked the woman, and they were as kindred as two souls could be right now.

"Just be very careful, Vikki," she warned as she saw Vikki out.

"Oh, one more thing." Vikki handed Catherine an envelope containing a sympathy card. Enclosed was a check for the balance of the payment she owed Carlton, fifteen thousand dollars.

****

The next day, a plain brown box arrived, addressed to Vikki. An apology gift from Al, for springing Mona on her? Another of those chocolate oysters would be nice—even without the pearl.

She unwrapped the package, and inside was deli paper, like the kind meat gets wrapped in. Something from the bakery? She unfolded the paper and jumped back in horror, screaming.

Billy ran in, knocking over a chair. "What? What is it?"

She turned away, her insides churning.

The note accompanying Carlton Frost's nose read, in plain block letters, "Next time don't be so nosy."

Chapter Ten

Vikki had to sell the house.

She dreaded going back there and reliving her memories, but she'd delayed this task long enough. Her rational side knew packing up and leaving her Camelot for the last time was part of the healing process. Yet she'd put it off because the wounds were still too fresh; the house may as well have been leveled by a tornado. To her, everything lay in ruins.

She'd already decided to donate the furniture to charity. But first she had to empty all the drawers, in case anything turned up besides undies, hankies, and Motion Lotion.

So she went back to Camelot, alone, armed with a few dozen cartons and a box of Kleenex. Knowing more of Jack's tapes were probably stashed away somewhere, she went up to the master bedroom.

His night stand was closer to the door, so she opened that first. Inside was a travel alarm—now, why hadn't he taken that to Dallas?—a few e.e. cummings poetry books, and a small jar of ink. She knew what this was for—when she'd bought him the fountain pen, she'd had the stationers mix three shades of ink to make a vibrant violet blue, the color of his eyes—she'd always said she wanted to drown in them. When his eyes caught the light, they became translucent, like blue sapphires…

She opened the jar and spilled a few drops of the ink onto a tissue. It spread and seeped into the paper, bringing back another flood of memories—he'd penned many a love letter to her in that ink.

But she couldn't slip into any more reveries. She gave her cheek a slap, cracked her knuckles, and reached back farther, groping around. She grasped something plastic—reels! Three, four, five of them, numbered in Roman numerals. Although grateful she'd found them, her stomach fluttered. She tried to sort these mixed feelings. She was afraid to hear these, but didn't know why.

Now was not the time to quit searching. She opened the doors to his wardrobe and poked around for more tapes. She even rooted through his underwear drawer, finding nothing but silk briefs. She slammed the drawer shut on the memories of their passionate nights—and afternoons, out by the pool, on the porch swing…

Now on a whirlwind rampage, she emptied closets and drawers, dumping clothes into the cartons. In no time, she'd stuffed four cartons.

But something nagged at her as she glanced over at those reels every few minutes. She went back to her father's to listen to them.

****

Nobody was home, so she went into his studio and cued up the first tape. The first three were interviews with politicians and authors. Nothing noteworthy there.

But the fourth tape made her listen harder. And once she heard it, she wished she hadn't.

The whispery, flirty voice answering Jack's questions belonged to none other than the late Marilyn

Monroe.

It was meant to be an interview rehearsal, with Marilyn plugging her latest picture, studying with Strasbourg in New York, and her wish to be regarded as a serious actress, but the conversation drifted and centered around a common interest: the Kennedys.

It's a good thing you broke it off with the both of them, sweetheart, Jack said, his words stabbing at Vikki's heart. He spoke in the same soothing and intimate tone he'd used with her on the phone from his far-flung locations. *You were getting in too deep there. You're much safer with me. I'm only a television reporter. Besides, one of me measures up to two Kennedys any day.*

Her father's studio filled with the sound of laughter only two could share.

"I can't take any more of this." Vikki hit the Stop button and yanked the reel off the machine. The tape snapped in half. She pitched it in the wastebasket.

Jack had other women, but, like he'd always said, "You're free to do whatever you want, with whoever…"

She couldn't deal with that now. Now was no time to analyze feelings.

The next tape was marked XXIII. Ready for anything, eyes shut tight and hands cradling her head, she listened.

It was an interview with Long John Nebel, the radio talk show host. This time, Jack was the interviewee. Long John asked Jack his opinion on the Bay of Pigs crisis, the president's relations with Castro, and the Kennedys' vendetta with the mob.

"John F. Kennedy has a growing number of

enemies," Jack said. "But he knows this, because he's a smart man. He's said many times if someone wants to assassinate him, they will. He knew what he was getting into when his father got him this job. In the course of my work, I've found out specifically who some of these enemies are. I'm not going to mention any individuals' names, but I'm not afraid of them either. They might not even know who I am, and I don't care if they do or not. But mark my words, Jack Kennedy is being pushed into a corner. Of course he's not going to go on national television and say this. It's not good P.R. or good politics. Why worry the American people any more than they need to be, with missiles in Cuba aimed at us? But these bastards know who they are, and I know who they are." His voice rose. "And I'm not afraid to go on radio—and when the time is right, on television—and tell them I'm onto them."

Long John said, "I don't think I'm going to interview you on the air, Jack. I don't want them coming after me, either."

After another brief exchange, Jack thanked him and said, "Those bastards want to destroy our country and everything it stands for. And I'll be damned if I'm going to sit on the sidelines and watch it happen. Hear that, Marc Antony?"

"Who?" Long John asked.

"You didn't hear that, Nebel." Jack's words rushed out. "In fact, I'm taking this tape with me. When you want to interview me, and I guarantee the day will come when you will, I'll tell you all about it. Just remember, you'll have to get in line."

The tape ended. She shut the machine off. Marc Antony? She had to find out who that was. She remembered the other guy's name, Cassius. She was willing to bet her life those two were in cahoots.

****

The following night, hair in curlers, her house on the market, and her father out with Greta, she finally felt up to her regular pampering routine. He'd begged her to join them, but her need to be alone for just one evening outstripped her fear of being stalked, assaulted, whacked, or any of the other atrocious possibilities. Besides, her new Bauer sat next to her manicure items. She hoped her nails would be dry before she'd have to use it.

"Don't leave this house," Billy had warned on his way out. "I'll activate the alarm. The cops'll be coming around in a squad car every half hour or so, so don't get scared if one of them walks around the house, or tries the doors to make sure they're secure. And if you want to feel really safe, my thirty-eight is in the drawer of the nightstand, my side. You know my side, right? The side with the handcuffs on the headboard, that's my side."

"It's all right, Dad, just go! I'll be fine. Cripes, you're too much sometimes." She let out an exasperated breath.

"Don't start with me, brat." He flashed her a smile. "I worry about you. You'll always be my baby."

She had no argument with his "you'll always be my baby" routine. They embraced, and he tugged on a lock of her hair that had escaped a curler. "There's plenty to eat—and drink."

"Swell, Dad."

"We'll be back before midnight, and I'll call you when we're leaving." He backed out the door. "Lock this, now!"

"I'll be fine," she insisted for what seemed like the skatey-eighth time.

She relished this evening of solitude stretched before her. She planned to bake some fudge brownies, then have a long soak in Greta's oversized tub with the new Travis McGee novel and a stiff highball.

Two hours later, wrapped in her robe, she glued on false eyelashes as a dozen brownies cooled on the rack. The doorbell rang three times. She froze.

She crept down the entry hall and flattened herself against the wall, trying to peek through the curtains to see if a squad car was out there. No black-and-white, just a Cadillac parked in the driveway behind Greta's T-Bird.

The bell rang again, along with persistent knocking. She glanced at her Bauer. *Should I make a dash for it?*

"Vikki? You in there?"

She knew the voice; she'd heard it before. A fading Brooklyn accent, the tone patient, yet with a hint of concern. A voice that could reach Pavarotti's range in a *Rigoletto* aria.

"Vikki? Open up, *cara mia*."

Cara mia. Who'd called her that lately?

Him, that's who.

She disengaged the alarm, unlatched the four locks, and opened the door. There he stood, his hair more perfectly coifed than hers, a spreading smile gleaming in the porch light's glow. A long black coat exaggerated his height, a scarf circled his neck.

A striking ensemble, better than any window dressing of Bergdorf's.

"What are you doing here?" She stood rooted to the

floor, too surprised to be angry—or embarrassed he'd caught her with fake lashes on one eye.

"Your godfather sent me."

Her jaw dropped. "What for?"

"He wants protection for you and—I'm it." He took a bow. His hand spiraled through the air on his way back up.

She didn't know whether to laugh or slam the door in his face. All she could do was stand there, stunned. Her mouth hung open as she looked him up and down, drinking him in, watching his hands rubbing together, those manicured nails…

"Well, are you going to let me in, or do I have to protect you from out here?" His breath escaped in puffs of steam.

"I wouldn't let you protect me if this was Berlin and the Gestapo was after me." She leaned on the door to close it.

Of course his hand shot out and held it open. So it stayed open. "He hired me to do a job, and I plan to do it and do it right," he snarled.

"Then I'll call him right now and tell him to relieve you your duties, because I don't need a bodyguard, least of all the likes of you." She belted her robe more securely around her waist.

"Think it over, Vikki." He aimed his pointer finger at her. "You're already in danger. Even if your father is armed here, with all due respect, he's not the young wiseguy he was in the thirties. Sure, he'd throw himself in front of a flying bullet to save your life, but then what? You're not being properly protected. Face it. And please, it'd be nice if you'd let me in. Tough as I am, I could use some liquid refreshment."

"Then I'll bring it out to you." She made another move to shut the door, blocked again with the powerful arm that she remembered pulling her into a crushing embrace.

"Vikki, please. Let's be civil to one another." The snarl gave way to a Pepsodent grin.

"Civil?" She gave him her best smirk. "Oh, it was real civil, after letting me think you were the lonely bachelor starved for affection, when all the while you've got your betrothed holed up someplace, and she shows up in her hotrod."

"I didn't think it was necessary to mention her." He gave a casual wave. "Can I come in now, please?"

She ignored his pleading tone. "You conveniently left that out, knowing what my status was—widowed and lonely. You took advantage of me!"

"It's not what you think, Vikki. Mona and I don't love each other. Can I come in now? Some appendages are starting to get frostbitten." He jumped from one foot to the other.

"I don't care a—" It registered. "Wait. You don't love each other? What do you mean?"

"The marriage is arranged, like in the old country. For reasons that have nothing to do with love—oh, it's a long story. She's a nice enough girl, but we won't be sharing the sheets. Can I please come in now?" He looked over her shoulder into the house. "Looks nice and warm in there."

She had to hear this. Even if she had to back down and let him in.

****

Ten minutes later, he reclined in her father's Barca-Lounger with his shoes off, sipping a Scotch on the rocks, filling her in about his upcoming arranged nuptials.

"The families have always been close. Blood close. Our great-grandfathers were brothers. I don't even know what degree of cousins we are. But it's far enough that we can marry without the Pope's permission. Mona's parents both died when she was young, and my mother raised her; we've been like brother and sister since we're ten years old. I already told you Mama's fading fast. She wants to see us married before she dies. She'd also like to see a grandchild, but that just ain't gonna happen."

"So you're marrying a cousin you don't love just to please your dying mother?" Vikki didn't know whether to be impressed with his selfless devotion or write him off as hopelessly old-fashioned and weak-willed.

"It's mainly because of the exorcism." He sipped his drink.

She blanched. "What exorcism?"

"When Mona went back to Trapani to take care of her elderly aunt, Zia Rosina Maruccio, she got very sick herself. Mona figured somebody put the *malocchio* on her, you know, the evil eye." He extended his index finger and pinkie in the gesture of the old curse.

"I know it all too well, along with the other Southern Italian superstitions. My family indulged in their own brand of mumbo-jumbo." She nodded, exposing her amused smile.

"A priest came over and banished Satan, and then Mona recovered. She brought Zia Rosina over here and put her in a nursing home in Palm Beach, where she'll probably celebrate her hundred-and-fiftieth birthday. Mona's got this new lease on life and agrees with

Mama that we should get married or the evil eye will catch her again and she'll spend forever in purgatory. She thinks the sanctity of marriage will keep Satan's soldiers away so they'll go haunt some other doomed Campobello di Mazara *paisans*." He drained his drink and helped himself to another.

"And you have no say in all this?" she questioned him.

"I'm doing it for Mama. No other reason. I plan to lead my own separate life, marriage or not. When the time comes, we'll get an annulment, and that'll be the end of it. Rosie's paying for the wedding, because there's no money in either family to pay for it. He's throwing us the big old-world bash at the Fontainebleau. He wants Mama to die happy, too."

"So when's the blessed event?" She didn't want to ask, but not knowing was worse.

"Easter Sunday. The doctors assured us Mama will live that long, and if I know her, she'll hang on till we say the I do's. She's living for this wedding. It's what's keeping her alive."

"God help her." Vikki shook her head. "Why don't some people change with the times?" Her anger blossomed into respect, tinged with disappointment she couldn't fight. She couldn't yet hold her emotions in any semblance of order.

"Mama made every sacrifice for me." He came back from the bar and settled in the lounger again. "The least I can do is let her die happy. When my father died, she was both father and mother to me and my sisters. She worked all day and still had time to cook our meals and make our clothes. She even taught me how to shave."

Vikki had to stop for a minute and try to picture that. "But does she know you don't love Mona?"

"That's not the issue," he stated firmly. "I'm doing my duty as a good son."

"Does Mona know you plan to stay like brother and sister once you're pronounced man and wife?"

"Oh, I spelled it out, all right." He swirled the drink in his glass. "In Sicilian and English."

"She's cool with it?" Doubt crept into Vikki's tone.

"She has to be. I'm not giving her a choice." He took a sip, then a gulp. He smacked his lips. "Well, she does have a choice. Go through with this thing on my terms, or stay an old maid. But that'll never happen. She wants that band on her finger and that officiatin' from the priest and the march to the altar and back."

"It sounds as win-win as any Sicilian marriage." Vikki's flat tone echoed her feelings about the whole thing. "Meanwhile, back at the ranch, where do you plan to camp out while you're supposed to be guarding me?"

He sat forward. "Rosie was going to talk to your father about letting me board here, but I don't know if he did yet. He wants me to stay as close to you as possible. Physically, that is."

"Is that right?" She got up and refilled her drink. "For your information, I'm not even going to be here much longer; I just listed my house and I'm getting my own place."

"Then I'll have to camp out with you." His lips curled. He stroked his chin.

Her head snapped up and she caught his smug grin. "No dice, pal." She lit a cigarette, trying to keep her hands steady.

"I'm following orders." The grin vanished. "He wants us under the same roof. He wants you protected, Vikki. He's not kidding around, this isn't a game here. This is your life you're talking about, and this campaign of yours involves some very dangerous elements. You should be glad you have someone who cares about you enough to take care of you like this."

"I can take perfectly good care of myself. We're all armed and good shots around here." She gestured at her piece on the table. "My father can protect me—and himself."

"Oh, Rosie's sending a bodyguard for him, too." He crossed his legs.

"What for? Just because the detective I hired—" She stopped there. She didn't know how much Al actually knew about Frost's murder, and who his killer might've been. So she kept quiet.

But his nod told her. "That's just it. These guys you're after will stop at nothing, Vikki. If they have the slightest hunch you know too much, out you go." He jerked his thumb in the direction of the door and drained his drink.

"I'm not afraid." She didn't want to tell him she sensed Jack watching over her. "I know it's dangerous. Danger is part of life. We can step outside and get mowed down by a truck, too."

"Trust me. Just let Rosie do what he wants to do for you."

"Why what he wants?" She tried to keep her voice down. "I'm no little girl. I'm thirty years old."

"But he loves you like his own little girl. And you'll always be like a kid to him. I know, because—" He stopped. "I wish I had what you have. Just think about it—you have two fathers. I don't have one."

She sighed. Humoring elders was also part of life.

He stood and stretched. "It's late. We can talk more tomorrow."

She ran her eyes up and down his length and up again, and their gazes fused as they had that first time in the galley. He reached down to help her to her feet, and there it was again, that magnetic pull. But he didn't try to kiss her. He simply gave a reassuring nod and headed for the door. "I rented a car at the airport. I'll bring my bags in, and if I can talk to your father about staying here—"

"Wait." She followed, blurting out, "He's not home. I'm alone here."

"Oh, he's not home?" His eyes roamed the room, then up the stairs.

"No, but he should be back soon. Why don't you just sit back down and make yourself comfortable." She hoped she didn't sound too inviting. Their eyes stayed transfixed on each other. Neither made a move. She didn't dare, but if he came to her, she wouldn't push him away. She wanted him to take that step. How badly she wanted to breathe in his cologne and the wintry scent of that Mediterranean hair.

"Well, thank you, then." He returned to Billy's chair, but kept his shoes on.

She offered him another drink, which he refused.

"What do you want out of this, Vikki?" he asked. "Blood vengeance? Or something more righteous?"

She sat back down and tucked her feet under her. "I owe it to Jack to find out what happened, so he can rest. It's my faith that tells me his spirit isn't resting in peace until I do. I suppose part of my motive is selfish, too—I can't stand knowing somebody's walking around out there, breathing, having gotten away with murder. Call it what you want. But the main thing is—I need to be able to let him go, so I can move on, and this is the way for me to do it." She gave him a penetrating look. "Now I want to ask you why you want to jeopardize your life getting mixed up in this, guarding me from all this alleged danger. Are you that brave, or just greedy? How much is Rosie paying you for this gig anyway?"

"Nothing extra. I'm still getting my regular pay." He reclined and stretched his legs. "I'm not doing it for the money. It's out of appreciation—Rosie took me in and gave me a chance when I was at the lowest low of my life."

He didn't seem to want to explain that, so she asked him. "Well—what happened? If you don't mind my asking."

He spread his fingers and hesitated. "My father had a nice seafood restaurant in Trapani, Fratello's. When it became successful, he opened one in Palermo, right on the waterfront. But certain people of less-than-desirable character took them over and forced my family out— let's just say against our will—it was leave or else. We came to this country when I was ten. We already had relatives in Brooklyn since the turn of the century. But when my father died seven years later, I dropped out of school and worked two or three jobs to support my mother and lead a respectable life. I wanted to open another restaurant in his memory, but it isn't as easy here as back home." His tone somber, his words halted as he struggled to relive these memories. "So I worked in construction. My mother's health started to fail, so we moved to Florida for the warmer climate. Then I almost got killed in a motorcycle accident, and after two years of physical therapy and six back and knee surgeries, I lived hand to mouth, took any job I could find. I couldn't work construction no more, so in order to make my body useful again, I earned a black belt in Isshinryu Karate. That's when I met Rosie, at the Hialeah racetrack, when I worked there. I was at the window betting my last two bucks, and we got talking. He took me into his home that night, and I started my life over. He stood between me and starvation." He hesitated again, and she saw his eyes searching for words. "I'll be very honest. I didn't want to come up here to do this. Not because I can't do the job. I'm a decent shot, too. But it's—" He gave off a vague smile and took a breath before continuing. "You intimidate me—a little."

Now that surprised her more than the *malocchio* story. "Why?"

"You're educated, you're intelligent, you're independent...you want me to go on?" His eyes pinned her.

"No, you don't have to. But you certainly don't have to be intimidated." She cringed inwardly, flattered and uneasy at the same time. "I'm not superior to anybody."

"Well, maybe in time I'll feel more like an equal around here. But when Rosie told me I was coming up here, I thought—I don't want to fail at this. I'm brave, I'm bigger, I'm stronger, but she's smarter—all I can say is I want to do a good job." He gestured with his hands. This time she didn't interrupt. "Then in the last few days I started thinking of reasons I should come here—and I realized it's a need more than a duty—to protect you. If my father'd had somebody who cared enough about him to get him some protection, he'd be alive today." He looked right at her. "Face it, Vikki— with all due respect, you're not a hundred percent yet, emotionally. I know because, like I told you, I had some tragedies in my time, too."

"I'm glad Rosie helped you out. He's got a heart of gold." *So, why send him away? Let him prove himself. Besides, having him around might be amusing—at appropriate times.* "But I'm not ready for any kind of personal involvement."

"As long as you say so," he agreed quickly enough.

"With anybody."

"It's your call." He shrugged.

"Besides, you're getting married." She made it a point to remind him.

"I already told you what that's all about."

"No matter how you see it, I'm not going to be your *comare*," she drove home.

He blinked in surprise. "Did I ask you to?"

"Not tonight, but—you know what happened New Year's Eve."

"Did I ask you to then?" He sat back, apparently enjoying this exchange.

"No, but—you know what happened."

"Yeah, you made a lunge for me in the galley and never had your *strufoli*." A dreamy smile spread his lips. He gave them a tantalizing sweep of his tongue.

"Whoa, buddy." She held out a hand. "I made a lunge for *you*?"

"That's how I remember it." He closed his eyes. That dreamy smile widened.

"You've got a short memory, *malandrine*," she

informed him.

"What's the difference? We enjoyed ourselves and each other's company that night, and if you keep your word, it won't ever happen again. You're the one who brought this whole thing up. Not me. I came because I want the job. I see it as a—test." His lips curved upward. That smile would melt M&Ms in her hand.

She still wasn't sure of Rosie's intentions, but she wanted to kick herself anyway, for even bringing it up. "You're right, my emotions are all twisted up in knots. After what happened between us New Year's Eve— then this fiancée of yours comes out of the woodwork—let's just change the subject, or just listen to music and not even talk. Do you like Italian opera?"

"Like it?" He beamed. "It runs through my veins."

"Puccini?"

"The master of them all." He kissed his fingertips. *"Meraviglioso!"*

"What's your favorite?" She figured he didn't have a favorite, but needed to know anyway.

"Tosca, of course." He nodded, like the world should agree with him.

"A man after my own heart. Do you cry when she jumps off the parapet in the end?"

"Not any more." He smirked. "I did the first hundred times."

She headed for her father's record collection. "I'll play my favorite—featuring Renata Tebaldi, Carlo Bergonzi, and Giorgio Tozzi."

"Ah, yes, Renata," he singsonged. "Puts Maria Callas to disgrace."

She smiled as a spark flew between them. "We could talk all night just about opera alone."

"We'll learn more about each other in time," he promised as she placed the needle at the edge of the record. "No sense sitting here sharing life stories in one shot. That's no fun. It's better to get to know a person gradually, through actions rather than words. Like the acts of an opera. Slowly and suspensefully building to a climax."

"Well put. Damned poetic, I must admit." Then she admitted to herself that she wanted to know more about this engaged man who shared her passion for opera. Test, he'd said? This was going to be more of a test for her than for him. A test of temptation. *Oh, Rosie, what have you done?* She had a hunch her wise old godfather had sent this handsome Sicilian opera buff for a mission other than just to watch her ass—to keep it out of danger, that is.

She turned the phonograph volume up. "I like my opera loud."

He settled into her father's chair like it was made for him. "So—" He took a deep breath, and she could tell he was struggling to keep the conversation going. "Rosie told me you like guns."

"I had no choice." She gave him a winning smile, but he wasn't looking, so she kept it on till his eyes sought hers again. "I grew up with them. Between my father and Rosie, they had a whole arsenal. Rosie had a hunting lodge in Vermont before he started having back problems. So they always had hunting rifles and shotguns around, too. Then there's my dad with his collection of Smith & Wesson six-shots and other assorted revolvers from his heyday in the thirties."

"What was the first one you ever shot?"

"I was nine years old when my dad started teaching

me to shoot. It was at the lodge, with a twelve-gauge pump shotgun that nearly took my arm off. When I turned seventeen, he took me to Rodman's Neck Police Facility, New York's main pistol range, in the Bronx by the East River. He somehow got me in there. With my birthday present, a cute little twenty-two Beretta."

"What kind of shot were you?" he asked.

"At first?" She laughed. "Terrible. But I caught on. I like to paint, too. They're two entirely different arts, although they each require a steady hand. My father let me shoot his three-fifty-seven Magnum once at the range, and I didn't realize it would kick the way it did. It knocked me backwards a few feet. I wanted to be a showoff and hold it with one hand, but of course you have to use both. I was just like any other kid wanting to use an adult bowling ball or some other grownup thing."

Al clasped his hands behind his head. "I like antique firearms. With my first paycheck from Rosie I bought a forty-four Derringer, just like the one Booth used to kill Lincoln. It's a small piece—would fit into your hand—but it can put its half-inch ball through somebody's head. Only fires one shot, then needs to be reloaded. They don't make 'em like that anymore. I'm really proud of it, being it's the only antique I own. I can't afford any more right now. But I'd like to collect muskets someday, when I'm rich."

She nodded. "I just like the modern ones. More reliable. And you don't have to reload them as often." They shared an easy smile.

By then, they were on Side Two of *Tosca*—he treated her by singing some of Mario's part, and wow, what a voice! A few minutes later, Billy and Greta came home. Billy went right over and shook hands with Al like he knew about this all the time. After a cordial exchange, Greta showed him upstairs. He hauled his bags and his crate of long-playing records up into Thomas's old room.

"Dad—" She put the *Tosca* album away as he plopped into his Barca-Lounger.

"Don't worry. He wouldn't dare put the moves on you."

"How is it you always manage to read my mind?" Fists on hips, she cocked her head.

"I don't." He yawned. "That's Aunt Tessie's talent. I just know you too well."

"I can handle him, Dad," she assured him. "Even better than a Bauer."

"Don't I know it." He gave her that reassuring grin she loved on him. "I think he knows it, too."

"And when the time is right, I'll know it. If the time ever comes."

"It will. But it's not something you should put a deadline on, or worry about a respectable amount of time, or any of that horseshit I went through. You'll know when you're ready. Meanwhile, he knows he's got a job to do, and I think he'll do just fine at that. He's not as dumb as he looks." Billy gave her a wink and a click of his tongue.

"No, but I just hope he doesn't get into any real danger—I mean I hope nothing happens to him. He almost died in a motorcycle accident, you know." She wasn't sure how much of Al's past he knew.

"Then he's no stranger to risks." Billy glanced up the stairs.

She reached for Al's black coat draped over the

sofa back and toyed with one of the buttons. "I couldn't live with myself knowing another life was wasted because of me."

"I wish you'd stop thinking you're responsible for anybody's murder," Billy said. "These guys know what they're diving into."

"I just don't want anything to happen to Al." She grasped the coat's sleeve and stroked it.

He sat forward. "You're stuck on this guy, aren't you?"

Her fingertips glided over the cashmere sleeve. "No, I mean—he's good company. But he's getting married. He's not available."

Billy gave her his "who you shittin'?" look. "According to Rosie, who's pickin' up the tab, the marriage is arranged, and it'll be annulled soon enough."

That reassurance lightened her heart; it actually took a little leap. But she wouldn't dare let her heart get the upper hand. "This is a business relationship."

"Okay, but don't ever lie to yourself," Billy advised in his wise, sage tone.

"All right, Dad, I do feel something for him. Don't ask me what it is yet, though. You know what I'm still going through. He's personable. He's charming. We have some of the same interests. It doesn't hurt that he's this side of gorgeous. He likes me. I like him. That's all for now."

"Then forget bodyguard. Just think of him as your very own personal chauffeur/handyman/butler/go-fer/admirer. And maybe even friend. For now."

Chapter Eleven

Al became her chauffeur/handyman/butler/go-fer/admirer, friend—and more. Short of standing over her when she brushed her teeth, he never let her out of his sight. He went way beyond the job description: held her chair out for her, helped her on and off with her coat, and proved himself handy around the house, taking out garbage and changing motor oil and whipping up a mean veal scallopini on Cook's days off.

At least he let her sleep alone. He didn't make any passes, or ask her to dance to his Jimmy Roselli albums. She caught a glimpse of him one night going into his bathroom in nothing but a pair of boxers. Normally she'd have made him well aware he was under observation. But this was neither the time nor the place. He knew his status, though—too well, it seemed. Not only her thoughts of him but her dreams brought her to her knees clutching her rosary and begging not to be led into temptation.

He had a set of weights delivered to the basement and, with Billy's okay, mirrored an entire corner, floor-to-ceiling, to indulge in his favorite spectator sport: watching himself in motion. While he lifted, he blasted opera records, the music coming clearly through the air vent in her room. She didn't have to peek in on him; she just closed her eyes and pictured him supine on the bench, a sheen of sweat over his straining muscles as he bench-pressed barbells and sang *La Boheme* arias between grunts. Imagining it was more alluring than actually seeing it.

Despite her increasingly impure thoughts about him, their interactions stayed innocent; they played chess and cards and shot pool. She beat him at every challenge except one: matching her cannoli for cannoli, delivered from Valore's Bakery because he wouldn't leave her unattended.

His constant surveillance did put her on edge, but she would have been hard pressed to find one woman who'd trade him for a pit bull.

Never again did he mention his impending wedding, although letters from Mona piled up on the hall table. He stuck them into his pocket, in no hurry to read them.

One night when he was in the den watching *Gunsmoke*, she sneaked into his bathroom. "Just a peek. I won't touch anything," she whispered over and over as she tiptoed across the hall, not knowing why she whispered or tiptoed. Holding the shower curtain aside, she peered in and took stock of the items lined up on the edge of the tub: Prell shampoo, Tame creme rinse, and a box of Mr. Bubble.

Running her eyes over the items on the vanity— Stripe toothpaste, Vitalis, a bottle of Zestabs vitamins— she glimpsed a half-zipped toiletry bag. She tried to peer inside without touching it, but couldn't see much, so she carefully slid it open and peeked in. Along with the usual nail clippers, razor blades, and Q-Tips was a Miss Clairol hair color kit in "Midnight Raven."

"Does he or doesn't he?" she mimicked the famous tagline, and couldn't help smiling. So at least it wasn't boot polish.

Then she got out. He always visited either the bathroom or the refrigerator during commercials.

****

Al inhaled a lungful of a familiar perfume when he entered his bathroom that night. Aha! She'd been snooping. He rummaged around in his toilet bag, but everything seemed in place. Okay, so she found out he dyed his hair. Instead of feeling violated, he gave himself a smug grin in the mirror. She now knew something intimate about him. Her curiosity was a major step forward. They'd grown familiar with each other's habits and body language. Aside from her favorite operas and guns, he already knew how she liked to be held and kissed, and he'd knocked down a major barrier that day in the galley, but he had a long way to go.

Until Jack's murder was solved, he didn't stand a chance. That's why he made it his mission, too. He wanted her to get past her grief and rage and start living again. When she was ready to start her new life, he wanted to be part of it.

****

"That was a nice dress you wore to dinner last night. Did you design it yourself?" he asked the next afternoon as he joined her in a stroll across the Brooklyn Bridge.

"Now I know you're an endangered species—besides loving opera, you notice what I wear. Who told you I designed clothes?" Either her father or Rosie must've told him, or he'd done his own snooping. She wondered what else he knew about her that he couldn't find out from her yearbook.

"Greta."

"Greta?" She snickered. "Well! You figured you could get more background out of her than my father or Rosie?"

"No. It just came up in the conversation. We were talking about your father's musicals, and she told me you designed the costumes." He inched closer to her as cars whizzed by.

"Did she also tell you I have a master's degree in political science from Georgetown because I wanted to follow in my grandmother's footsteps in politics and eventually run for Congress?" she quizzed.

"No. None of that. Sounds more interesting than designing costumes." His pace slowed as he looked at her.

She slowed to match his pace and his gaze. "Not to me it isn't. I realized politics wasn't for me after my first job in the real world. I was a political consultant in D.C., and it didn't take me long to learn I'd just as soon leave it to the cutthroats. Politics is about who can screw who. The degree taught me to present a convincing argument and get people to believe every word I say. But it's not my idea of a career. It can come in handy sometimes, though."

"Is that where you learned your poker face?" His hand found its way to hers, and they clasped.

A warm thrill shot up her arm. "No, I learned that from playing poker."

"So are you planning to return to the world of costume design?"

She noticed how well their hands fit together. "I'd like to, as soon as I feel like I can create something that doesn't look like it came out of a nightmare."

"You ever design for other productions?" he asked.

"No, it's only a creative outlet for me, like my dabbling in watercolors. I was living my Camelot and wanted to start having babies, which just didn't happen, so instead of raising children I did the costume thing, played the piano, painted landscapes, and fulfilled my social obligations, like teas and card parties and benefits, in little hats and white kid gloves, all those 'noblesse oblige' things society matrons do." Hands clasped, their arms swung in perfect rhythm.

"I'd have thought a woman like you would find that life—how you say—a mismatch. I just can't see you as a society matron, or any kind of matron. You seem more suited to the career life than card parties and charity balls." He kept his gaze fixed to her, only glancing at the road for a blink or two.

"No, I enjoyed it while it lasted. You see, when Jackie came to the White House, I decided that's who I wanted to emulate. If I couldn't be her, I wanted to be just like her. We weren't far off Camelot, believe me. I was living a fairy tale that whole time. But like all fairy tales, it had to come to an end."

"You didn't feel like a misfit?" he continued his questioning.

"No. Not for a second." The memories hurt, but her desire to become closer to him outweighed the painful dredging up of her past. "I made myself fit in."

"Are you going to look for that again? The high society life?"

She pulled her wool cap lower over her ears as a gust of wind chilled her. But she wasted no time in reclasping his hand. "No. That was a part of my life that's over. I can never recreate that. I can never replace

Jack. I have the beautiful memories, and I'm happy for that. I need to seek out an entirely different walk of life now."

"Why do you feel you need to seek out an entirely different life now?"

She relished his curiosity, but now he sounded like a therapist. She examined his Roman profile. His hands cupped a cigarette as he lit it. "Okay, level with me once and for all. Did Rosie really send you up here to be my bodyguard? Or—some other reason? You can tell me. I'm no pigtailed ingénue who has to be protected from the truth. Come on—out with it."

He glanced down at her without turning his head. "Rosie sent me to protect you from 'the tangled web of the JFK plot' in his exact words." Smoke escaped his lips as he spoke, and the wind whipped it away. "He said to me, 'She can be just like her old man. When she sets a goal, nothing stops her.' He told me about your hiring of Detective What's-'is-name, who got whacked, and he thinks that'll lead to more trouble. He didn't send me up here to be your shrink or your car mechanic or show you how to shoot pool."

"I've been showing *you*," she corrected him.

"I mean he had one reason in mind, and that's it. You're drifting toward the deep end, little girl, and I'm your lifeguard."

They walked a few paces silently, and she looked down over the river.

"Now, you level with me," he challenged. "You think he sent me up here to be your gigolo, don't you?"

She faced him. He'd taken off the wraparound shades, so she swept her glasses off and their eyes met. "I know Rosie has only the best of intentions, but I can't help thinking he's got a hidden agenda here. I'm widowed, I'm trying to get my life back together, I'm vulnerable, and he sends a—he sends you."

He flexed his arms as they walked again. "But he would've sent me up here even if you were married, or taken, or however you say it. Rosie's treated me like family, but when it comes to business, it's business. Besides, I'd make a lousy gigolo."

"Now, that's a relief." She grinned. "I'm glad you admitted that, because if that was Rosie's intention, whether you'd make a good gigolo or not, you can turn around right now and hightail it back to Palm Beach."

"I told you why he hired me. And if he did ask me to come up here to—to be kept, I'd a walked right out of there and got me another job. I got no respect for guys who sponge off women. I see so many of 'em down there, too. Laying on the beach, prancin' around in mink coats even when it's stifling out, cruisin' in convertibles. I wonder if they respect themselves."

"They probably love every minute of it when they're doing it, and then hate themselves in the morning." She playfully leaned into him and bumped him.

"Could you ever see me like one of them guys?" he asked like he expected an answer.

She didn't want to admit she'd had him figured for "one of them guys" till very recently—like last week. "No, I see you as a hustler, but one who pays his own way. Although you like having a woman around—or maybe two. Or more."

"*Certo*. 'Atsa me." He nodded and flicked the butt off the bridge in a perfect arc. "Sometimes two or more's good, but one's easier to handle. Depends on the situation—and the woman."

She pushed a twinge of disappointment away. "How long did Rosie say you'd be on this assignment?" She didn't know what else to call it.

"However long it takes to nab Jack's killer. And when we do, you won't have anything to be afraid of anymore."

"I'm not afraid now." She spoke the truth.

"Didn't you learn anything from the stories your father told you that happen to be true?" he asked as he rubbed her fingers with his.

"I know murderers are cold, calculating, and heartless, and I know I'm probably better off with a bodyguard. All I said was that I'm not afraid. It's my faith." Then she decided to reveal her reason to him after all. "I know Jack's protecting me; he knows I'm doing this for him, and he won't let any harm come to me."

"Why couldn't he protect himself, then?" Al asked. "Or hire protection?"

"Jack never would've wanted a bodyguard, no matter how famous he became or how much danger he was in, and he put himself in a lot of danger. That's why I'm thankful for the short time I had him. I knew in the back of my mind one of his escapades might get him killed. He knew that, too. He had every intention of going out young, in a blaze of glory. He was destined to die a hero. He gave his life trying to expose the assassination plot of President Kennedy. Not even those Secret Service guys could say that. They all lived." Her eyes followed a tugboat gliding down the river.

"I admire him, Vikki. He lived for the moment. Not many guys have the brass to do that. And I admire you, too. You're not like any woman I've ever met. But I still gotta protect you." He squeezed her hand. She responded, their body heat mingling.

She stopped him just to take in the view from the bridge: the tall buildings glowing warmly in the cold morning sun, the Staten Island Ferry leaving a trail of semi-frozen river in her wake. "So if I jumped off this bridge, you'd jump in after me?"

"You betcha life."

"Rosie must be paying you a fortune." She shook her head, and they resumed walking. "I guess it's good to know my life is worth a few bucks."

"I told you, I'm not doing this for money, Vikki. Ask Rosie. He'll tell you I never do nothing just for the money."

She had him figured for a frustrated Mafia soldier, never rising as high in the organization as he'd have liked. He was only Rosie's button boy. So he took on these small-time jobs with enough elements of danger to make up for what he'd missed. Okay, so sponging off her was beneath him, but why did he display such chivalry all the time? An involvement was out, but hell, a wink or an accidental brushing of his hand wasn't too out of order.

But like her father said, any calls would be hers. Just because Al was Prince Charming didn't mean she had to be the Ice Princess.

Jack—and God—would understand a little flirting now and then. Just a little.

"Okay, you can buy me lunch and prove you're not a gigolo," she teased as they left the bridge and headed toward Greenwich Village.

"You're on." He clapped his hands. "I'll even

spring for a taxi. It's got nothing to do with proving I'm not a gigolo. I'm just freezin'. I guess I got spoiled, living in the sun."

"All that red-hot dago blood," she commented as he flagged down a dirty yellow cab.

"It's far from hot now, and it's shriveled parts of me I don't even know the English words for." They shared a smile.

"That's okay. You ever notice the most vulgar words sound like music in Italian?" She also noticed his Brooklyn accent shining brighter every day.

****

Loud singing woke her up the next morning at 8:00 on the dot. *Is Enrico Caruso across the hall?* It was the second best thing—Al singing in the shower. He had the radio in there with him and was singing Puccini's "Nessun Dorma" from *Turandot*.

The title meant "nobody sleeps," and it sure was appropriate. Sheesh, would he perform this matinee every day from now on?

Chapter Twelve

Her realtor suggested she sell the house furnished. "Buyers like it when sofas, tables, appliances, and draperies convey," she explained. "They think they're getting something for free, and it adds to the value of the house."

"Why didn't I think of that?" Vikki's estimation of realtors went up a notch. Why bring all those painful memories to a new dwelling? So she left the furniture in place, only taking her hi-fi and her antique jewelry armoire. Her mother's paintings would have to go back into storage.

She set aside the next day to empty the remaining closets, the basement, and the garage. But this time she had company. Al wouldn't even let her go to her own house alone. His adoring gaze roved as he followed her through the rooms.

"If you want to help me, you can remove the paintings from the walls. And carefully, please. My mother did those."

"She painted all these?" He held one painting at arm's length, tilting his head this way and that, taking it all in. He listened to opera the same way, only with his eyes closed.

"No, she didn't do that one." She plucked a book off the shelf, Chambers Biographical Dictionary, and flipped through the pages till she came to the one she wanted—her favorite artist.

"That was done by Henricus Van Meegeren, who died right after the war. Here's a brief bio about him." She held the open page out to him.

His eyes lit up with amusement as he read about the notorious Van Meegeren. "A forger? Sold paintings to the Germans?" He looked up from the book and back at the painting he'd been admiring. "Was this one of his famous forgeries?"

"No, this was never behind enemy lines. He signed it, and it's his. But I learned about him in one of my art classes and found this painting in a gallery in London. Like so many others, he died before he was really recognized. Like my mother. And those are hers." She pointed to the row of paintings going up the staircase. He climbed the steps, stopping to study each painting.

"This one at the top is different from the others," he commented.

"I did that one." It was a scene of a music room full of instruments, one of the last watercolors she'd painted.

"Oh—" His hands cut through the air. "I didn't mean your mother's weren't good—I meant—"

"It's okay, Al. Art is so subjective."

"Well, let me get to work taking them down." So he got to work and she entered Jack's walk-in closet. Where to begin? His scent lingered longer in here than in his study. As she scanned the rows of shoes and hanging suits covered with plastic garment bags, her eyes filled with tears, and by the time she'd filled two boxes for the Salvation Army, she grieved openly.

Al came over and stood in the doorway. "Are you all right, *cara mia?*"

"This is like giving part of him away to strangers, but keeping it all would be too painful. This is the worst chore I've had yet."

"I understand." He gave her a one-arm embrace.

"I know you do." He left her alone, and she took shoeboxes down from the top shelf, figuring they'd contain more Gucci loafers or boat shoes.

When she lifted the lid off the first one, she gasped. "Oh, no…"

The box was stuffed with reel-to-reel tapes.

She found Al removing pictures on the bottom step as she descended the stairs. How strangely bare the walls looked. "I found more tapes. We've got to listen to these now. Let's go." They headed back to her father's studio.

Hearing Jack's voice was becoming more bearable. That first time had been torture. But the tapes were reassuring, convincing her that he lived on, in some otherworldly, immortal way.

After two solid hours of listening to monologues about Civil Rights, Vietnam, and UFOs, the sixth tape caught her interest. Once again, Jack discussed President Kennedy with someone she didn't know— and since Jack gave him a code name, she was sure she'd never know.

"March first, sixty-three—I'm with GW-6, a Fed who's agreed to give me information about some behind-the-scenes activities. What can you tell me about these three assassins, GW?" Jack asked.

GW replied, "A, B, and C are rumored to do a lot of work for the Cuban Revolutionary Council, which was created by the CIA's Howard Hunt. Some people refer to this group as another Murder, Incorporated. It's been rumored the Council have been trying to hit Castro for a while now but haven't had any luck."

"A continuation of the original Murder, Inc., or is this another group altogether?" Jack asked.

"They're known to have formed right after Murder, Inc. folded. But that could just be a coincidence in the timing. This group has a high turnover, and some of them are agents who are sheep-dipped."

"Please explain sheep-dipped," Jack requested.

"That's an intelligence term referring to a formalized covert personnel system to conceal agents. An agent is given another name and the credentials and background to make him appear to be something he's not. Three personnel files are maintained: a regular life file, active duty file, and a phony file. A CIA or U.S. Army agent might be put through Marine Corps training without the Marines knowing that he's their agent, or an agent might be made to appear to be a defector to obtain the confidence of radical groups in the U.S."

"Are A, B, and C agents who've been sheep-dipped?" Jack asked.

"I'm not at liberty to divulge that. You'd have to go to another source to find that out."

"Thanks, I will," Jack replied, and the tape ended.

A shape formed in her mind. "Can A, B, and C be Antony, Brutus, and Cassius?" she asked Al.

He chewed on a pencil because he'd run out of cigarettes. "That could be their code names. Very logical deduction, Watson."

She couldn't help smiling. "It's Sherlock Holmes who was the smart one. Watson was his sidekick. Okay, Watson, then how do we find A, B, and C, the ones who are still living, I mean? We already know Cassius is dead."

"That's the problem." Al studied the chewed-up pencil. "We don't know if they're dead. It wouldn't surprise me one bit if they were. Considering…"

He didn't have to finish. She nodded, mentally exhausted all of a sudden. "Okay, I've got to think. I'll do some chores around the house, mindless stuff, to keep my brain on this."

"I'll help you."

She tossed him a grin. "I know you like to cook, but was housework in the job description?"

"I can do heavy stuff, like move the couch if you have to vacuum under it."

"But I'd still be the one doing the vacuuming," she supposed out loud.

"I like to watch you in motion." He gave her a cocky grin.

"Okay, you can really be a captive audience. I promised Greta I'd lay some mousetraps in the basement. Seems the mouse population has expensive taste and likes Westchester County."

He stood in the doorway and let her pass. "Well, nobody said this job was going to be glamorous all the time."

As she laid the mousetraps, each holding a bit of cheese, she thought of how simple minded and unassuming a mouse was, innocently sniffing around a piece of cheese, not even suspecting it could be a booby trap furnished to snap its head off.

Simple minds—sniffing around bait—booby trap…

"Hey!" She sprang to her feet.

"What?" Al sat at his bench, idly lifting one of his dumbbells, lost in thought.

"I have an idea to nab either this Brutus or Marc Antony." She placed the last trap next to the laundry room door.

"How? Put a contract out on them?"

"Get them to come to us! Just like I'm doing with these mousetraps. Rosie can spread the word to his cronies in Miami that he wants a hit done, he's willing to pay an astronomical undisclosed sum, and he wants nobody but Brutus or Marc Antony for the job. He won't say who the target is; we don't want to spill our cookies in the lobby. So we'll have to wait for either of the hit men to surface. The prospect of a big payoff should make them come slobbering. Rosie can just let it be known in his circles about this, so when one of the guys turns up, we can be sure it's him. Rosie can use his alias. What is it, Ponce de Leon?"

"Yeah." Brow furrowed, he looked pensive, but his eyes brightened as his interest was piqued. "The Fountain of Youth guy. Wishful thinking."

"Now—when one of them gets word about the job and inquires to Rosie about it, the hit man can call us here. We'll have another phone line installed here, so when he calls we'll know it's him. When he calls, we can set up a meeting with him." Vikki made fists and pumped them in excitement.

He nodded and placed the dumbbell back in its rack. "Sounds like a plan. These guys aren't much smarter than rodents. If we really hit the jackpot, we can get both of 'em, but chances are only one'll turn up," he said. "This won't happen overnight, though. It has to go through all the channels; word has to get around. You'll have to be patient."

That was like telling her to hold her breath. But all her life she'd gotten what she went after, one way or another.

"Jack, I promise this will work!" she vowed as Al swiped the cheese from the nearest trap—without setting it off—and popped it into his mouth.

"See, I'm smarter than the average mouse." He chewed and smacked his lips.

****

Ma Bell didn't waste any time installing that extra phone line. The new desk phone sat on the coffee table in the living room. Billy called it the "red" phone even though it was black. He had extensions installed in his studio, his bedroom, and his bathroom so they wouldn't miss any calls.

"I wish I could do something other than glancing over at it every few minutes, willing it to ring." Vikki wandered across the room to look at herself in the china cabinet mirror, unable to remember the last time she'd visited the beauty parlor. She could use a facial and a hair styling, but she just didn't feel like indulging herself yet.

"Get out and do something else, get it off your mind," Billy suggested as he dusted his piano keys. "It'd be great to see you go back to designing clothes. When Les and I start working on our next production, I want you to design the wardrobe again. We're gonna do something set in France. You like those frou-frou can-can costumes, don't you?"

"I'd love to, Dad. But right now all I can think of designing is a way to find Jack's killer." She paced back and forth.

"I have a feeling one of those guys'll be giving us a buzz on the blower there. That was a damn good idea you got, just from setting mousetraps."

"Well, the theory certainly works," she assured her dad. "We caught five mice already."

****

Benzo Battolini rolled off the whore he'd just laid three times, gave her a whack on the behind, and slid off the bed. "Gotta go, darlin'. I got an appointment with a yacht salesman."

"Take me on your yacht when you get it, Benny?" She fluffed the pillows and lit a cigarette, looking like she had no intention of scramming.

"If you get outta here and let me get dressed." He opened his closet, and as he pulled a shirt off a hanger, he glanced at his gun Scarlett. But he didn't want to think about the hit he'd done on the president, or the bonus they'd given him for doing it so well, or any other jobs for a while. He wanted to lay low and enjoy his money.

The phone rang, and he took it in the other room. The whore still lolled by his bed, all ears. He didn't feel like talking to anybody, but it might be something important, though he couldn't figure what. Everybody important to him was dead.

He swept the receiver off the cradle. "Yep?"

He listened for no more than five seconds, and only had to repeat what he'd said yesterday and the day before. "Look, I ain't interested, okay? This is the third time you called me, and don't call me again about this, hear?"

He slammed the phone down and yanked the cord out of the wall. Hell, he'd have it disconnected. Why was he paying for a phone anyway?

Now some sumbitch from New York was looking for him to do another hit, "a b-i-i-i-g hit for b-i-i-i-g bucks," his fixer had said. But not who or where or how much. The clients wanted to meet with him before they'd tell him anything.

But he wasn't interested. Why couldn't they get that through their thick heads?

That night, while he mulled over a list of names for his new fifty-four-foot yacht, his front door started to bang. "Hey, Ben, you home? Open up."

He knew who it was and felt like ignoring it, but he had to get these pains in the balls off his back.

He threw the door open. "Look, Pippi, I gotta keep a low profile. I don't want to do hits for a while."

"But Ben, this guy won't leave us alone." Pippi rushed in, out of breath. "He wants this job done, requested Marc Antony or Cassius, and isn't taking no for an answer. It must be somebody important."

"Who do they want hit this time? LBJ?" After President Kennedy, everything else would be anticlimactic. He knew it wasn't his usual bosses, who'd assured him Guy Banister was the last hit they'd need him for. "Who is it who wants me anyway? I'll call 'im myself and warn 'im off."

"Uh—" Pippi dug a piece of paper out of his wallet. "Here. Here's his number. A Ponce de Leon."

"I'm gonna call this Ponce de Leon and tell 'im to buzz off, 'cause he's just gonna keep askin' around, and I don't want my code name gettin' around too much these days. Maybe in a year when this thing's died down, but not now. See ya 'round."

He slammed the door and headed for the phone.

****

That night, as Vikki and Billy helped Greta paste S&H Green Stamps into books, the phone jangled.

Greta looked up. "I think that's your new telephone, Billy."

Vikki jumped. Her heart leapt. They looked at one another, and he made a mad dash for his studio to pick it up.

"I want to listen in on the extension." Vikki clutched the receiver in the living room.

"Okay, but don't breathe, and whatever you do, don't crack your damn knuckles!"

Greta held her crossed fingers up to Vikki.

"Hello," she heard her father's voice.

"You the fella wants a job done?"

She detected a southern drawl. Her heart pounded so hard she wondered if the caller could hear it.

"That's me. Who are you?"

"This is Marc Antony. I decided we don' want no part of it. Take this as a warnin', too, pardner. Back off. We're not doin' no more hits right now. Go about your business, but stay out of ours, or you're askin' fer trouble, and if y'all want trouble, I'll give it ya, hear?"

Before Billy could utter a response, the line went dead.

Her hand still frozen to the receiver, he came back into the living room.

"Well, that's that." He reached behind his ear for a cigarette. "We've been warned off. Let's consider ourselves warned—and sufficiently threatened."

She didn't want to let go of the phone. She wanted to prolong the moment of hope—when she thought she'd found one of them.

"Hang up the phone, Vikki. I'll have them come around to take it out."

She dropped the receiver into the cradle and let out a sigh. "So it's over." Then why did a tinge of relief lurk beneath her shattering disappointment?

But it was more than that. "Dad, none of my goals have ever escaped me so fast—in the space of a twenty-second phone conversation. I'm not a quitter."

He fixed his eyes on her. "Marc Antony doesn't want to take us up on our offer. We'll have to think of another way to get to the bottom of this. I get my best ideas when I'm at the piano. You want to listen to the new songs I'm working on?"

"No. I get my best ideas in silence." She kicked at the table leg. "Damn, and I thought that bait idea was so good."

"It was, and he called. He's just not interested in any jobs now." He headed for the doorway.

"But we had him right there on the phone!" She couldn't give up.

"We'll find another way," he answered over his shoulder. "There's more than one way to skin a cat. And catch a mouse. And believe me, these guys ain't got nothin' on mice."

Her blood heated her veins. A volcano waited to erupt inside her. "I'm going up to my room." She didn't want to revel in the joy of music or the sweetness of pastry, or chuckle along with a sitcom laugh track. She just wanted to figure out another way to make this work, and assure Jack she wasn't going to let him down.

She grabbed an anisette bottle on her way up the stairs.

Shutting out the world, she curled up on her bed in the darkness. "I'll keep trying, Jack," she whispered into her pillow. "I'll find a detective even sleazier than Carl Frost, I'll bribe the police force, I'll think of something." Brain-weary, exhausted, she didn't need to drink herself to sleep.

****

A hot breakfast beckoned, but she opted for her usual crullers and took her coffee black.

Greta went to meet with her publishers, and Billy was with his collaborator, so she and Al had the house to themselves. He insisted on making breakfast. She thought it was cute that he wanted to show off, so she sat and sipped her coffee.

"So the hit man refused your offer." Al heated up a skillet as Vikki flipped open the bakery box.

"Maybe he figured it was a trap, and it's a blessing in disguise and there's a better way." She resorted to rationalizing, and she only did that when she was desperate.

"I don't think he knew it was a trap." Al plucked a spatula from the drawer. "These guys don't win any prizes for matching wits. If they are the JFK assassins, they want to lay low, and I can understand why. If you'd just shot the president, would you go around taking more hits?"

"If I was greedy enough, I guess. We already know how greedy they are." After she poured herself another cup of coffee, she got a pad and pen to put her thoughts into writing. She drew a stick figure representing herself in the top left-hand corner, Jack's killer in the bottom right-hand corner, and a zigzagged path leading from her to him. She diagrammed in all the ways she'd already tried, and made a few random scribblings. While she was lost in thought, a phone started ringing. But it wasn't the kitchen phone.

It came from the living room.

"The red phone!" She leapt to her feet so fast, she knocked the chair over.

"You want me to get it?" He stood there holding the Aunt Jemima box.

"Okay, but hurry up! Take it in the studio!"

She dashed into the living room and picked up the extension the instant it stopped ringing.

"Yeah?" Al answered.

"You still want a job done?" The voice came through loud and clear.

"Who is this?"

"Brutus," came the raspy voice.

"Who's your source, Mister Brutus, sir?" Al asked.

"Ponce De Leon from Palm Beach."

Rosie's alias.

"Yeah, well—we got a call from Marc Antony saying the deal was off," Al informed him.

"Oh, that. Ya see, me and my associate had a disagreement. So I'm gonna go ahead and do it myself. I'm waitin' on a big payday and need a little somethin' to tide me over. Or it might be a big somethin'. Dependin' on who you want hit." The voice wasn't southern this time, but it sounded like it was coming from a really thick neck.

Al replied, "Well, I'm not going to discuss that over the phone."

"Our people can meet your people for a sit-down, talk about who it is, when you want it done, all the details. Tonight at ten sharp."

"Hold it," Al said. "This is too sensitive to involve any middlemen. The fewer people know about this the better. I'll have to ask you to meet direct."

The hesitation made Vikki think Brutus had hung up. But he finally spoke: "Then we meet direct tonight, then."

"Give me a few days, I need to"—Al cleared his throat—"transfer funds between financial institutions if we decide to proceed." He sounded like J.P. Morgan closing a railroad deal.

"Nothin' doin'. It's either tonight or it's off."

She held her breath waiting for Al's reply.

"All right, tonight then. Where?"

"The DeLenzo Funeral Home, exit seventeen. Visitin' hours'll be over, but ring the bell twice and I'll open the door," Brutus said.

"Yeah, I know where that is," Al replied. "My Aunt Maddiuch was laid out there. How will I know it's you openin' the door?" Al asked.

"Obvious. It's a goddamn funeral home. I'll be the only one there who's breathin'."

Click.

They hung up. Her knees trembled when she tried to stand.

He came back into the living room and sat next to her on the sofa as she cracked her knuckles one at a time.

"You think he's legit?" she asked.

"Yeah, he knew Rosie's top-secret mob alias. But he didn't give us much notice."

She tried to light a cigarette with a shaking hand. He whipped out a lighter and lit up for her. "How is he getting access to the funeral home? You think it's his family's business?"

"It's somebody's family's." He stood at the window, looking out. "One thing you gotta say about Italian funeral homes, they never have a slow season."

She took a long ragged drag. "I'm glad nobody's home right now. It's better they don't know."

"You don't want to call your old man and tell him about this?" He lit a cigarette of his own.

"No." She shook her head. "It'll be just the two of us."

"So, you give any thought to what you want to say to this guy now that we've practically got him cornered?" He sat on the couch and puffed away. She looked away from his intense gaze.

"I wrote down a list of questions."

"This isn't *What's My Line*, *cara*. He's not expecting an interrogation about Jack. He thinks we're just there to negotiate a hit." He flicked an ash into the ceramic ashtray.

She took another drag on her cigarette and blew it out toward the ceiling. "I'll start asking him questions. That's the only way to find anything out. I don't know how this is going to go; I don't know the guy. All I know is that he had some connection to Jack, and I want to find out what that is. Even if we have to take him prisoner and check out his alibi later. Rosie knows some people who were interrogators during the war. They can ask him the questions and get the answers I need to know."

Al asked, "Where's a suitable prison we can bring him to?"

"The best place would be my house—our house— the house I lived in with Jack. The wine cellar there.

But we're getting too far ahead of ourselves. All I know about this guy is that he's a criminal and he's greedy. I'll do the best I can knowing that. We're not following a script here." She put her cigarette down and sat on her hands to warm them.

"Then you're prepared to gun him down," Al said.

"No, I do not want to gun him down." She pounded her fist into her leg. "I want to know what happened to Jack! That's the mission I'm out to accomplish here."

"I just thought you should at least have Plan B." He sat back and crossed his legs.

Now she met his stare. "You're Plan B."

"Oh, so I gotta plug him." His lips spread into a half-smile, half-smirk.

"No, but you can rough him up if he's not cooperating. Then, eventually, we'll find out if he was directly involved with Jack's death or not."

Her heart started slamming again, and she enjoyed the rush it gave her. Like a sugar high but more exhilarating. She turned her wedding band around and around. "This has to work, Jack," she promised her departed love. "By tomorrow we'll be a step closer to the truth."

She looked up, but Al hadn't heard her. His singing floated in from the kitchen as he flipped pancakes.

****

This chain of events would've scared the typical law-abiding American spitless. In four hours, they were going to corner the guy who probably shot the president of the United States.

The entire day had her eating Sugar Pops out of the box, washed down with Cocoa Marsh or Yum Berry. The brief throwbacks to her days of innocence comforted her.

So did Al.

As she held a pool cue in a hand too shaky to make a decent shot, he assured her, "This will work out, *cara*. Assassins are driven by naked greed, and big bucks make them do things that would make a Times Square hooker blush."

****

Finally. Time to leave. Her heart seized every time she peeked at the clock.

As he drove, he clasped her hand for the twenty-minute ride. She sat next to him, snuggled up against his side, her feet tucked under her, trying to be brave. But still she trembled as the horror hit her—she'd never written a will.

Al doused his headlights and parked around the corner from the funeral home. She pulled on her gloves and a black ski mask as they walked through the biting cold.

With viewing hours over, the funeral home stood empty and dark. A small circle of light came from a streetlamp. A white Sedan de Ville sat in the adjacent lot. "Stay behind me," he ordered her as they approached it. By holding her glasses up to her eyes, she could make out a form sitting behind the wheel. She grabbed Al's arm and pointed with her gloved hand. "Hey. That guy in the car there. Maybe that's him."

Al quickened his pace and pulled her along. "Yeah, could be. Looks like there's nobody inside the place, unless he's stalking us in the dark."

She held her breath as they inched up to the parked sedan. "Hey. Yo. Hello? You Brutus?" he called out.

He shoved her behind him and shielded her with

181

his bulk.

"Hello in there," Al yelled, louder this time. If the guy couldn't hear that through his closed window, he had to be deaf.

"Hey, Brutus?" Now two paces away, they stood in silence. Al took one more step forward, peered in the window, turned, and looked down at her, his posture relaxed.

He let out a breath of steam in the frigid cold and jerked his thumb in the car's direction. "The guy's dead."

She gasped. "You sure? Don't you think we'd better find out?"

"You read my mind." Al tried the door. It was locked. They went around to the passenger's door. Locked. "Whoever whacked him locked him in, the son of a bitch."

"And a smart son of a bitch," she commented. "Gives him more getaway time before the cops can I.D. the poor sap. Okay, how good are you at breaking into Cadillacs?" She pulled off the ski mask and slipped her glasses on.

"I'll get the tire iron in the trunk." They cut through the lot to their parked car. "Now we know a shortcut," he commented as they headed back to the lot, the tire iron tucked under his arm. With a smooth backswing and follow-through, he smashed it against the driver's side window.

The glass shattered, tinkling like discordant piano notes. He reached in and felt for a pulse. "Dead as I'm alive. And still warm. Ain't been dead long. And—hey, get a load a this."

Vikki took a step forward, the glass crunching

underneath her boots. She peered in. Blood splattered the dashboard and the leather seats, black in the dark of night. A wad of money stuffed the dead man's mouth. "The final deposit," she said.

"Well, well, well. How 'bout that." Al smiled. "The bastard got too greedy, if that's possible."

Vikki leaned inside, groped around in the guy's pants pocket, and pulled out a wallet. A flurry of papers spilled to the ground. She picked them up, scanning them in the beam of Al's flashlight.

"What's he got in there?" Al asked.

"Just a few bucks, some toll receipts, nothing—" She gasped. "Wait! Here's a piece of paper with a phone number and today's date and 'DeLenzo's' written on it. This is the number of our 'red' phone."

"Then chances are he's Brutus." He nodded. "Or more accurate—the late Brutus."

"No shit, Sherlock." She stuffed the wallet and papers in her pocket.

"Hey, I thought I was Watson."

****

Al drove them back to her father's. She didn't want to talk; she didn't want to think. She turned on the radio and blasted WMCA. The Beatles singing "Please Please Me." Much as she loved the mop tops, she had to change the station; it was too upbeat for the moment. She fiddled with the dial till she found WQXR, the classical station. A Chopin nocturne floated through the speakers.

"Whoever whacked that guy knows what's going on." Al pulled to a stop at a light.

"Please, Al, let's talk about something else." Her chest tight with anger, she seethed in frustration.

After the Chopin piece ended, Al switched the radio off. "I'd like to hear you play the piano sometime."

"I'm not much of a performer." She shook her head. "I mostly like to play when I'm alone."

"How about we close the door to your father's studio some night, and you play and I sing?"

"I'd love that." Her frustration gave way to anticipation as she pictured herself and Al at the piano, voices blending in harmony. She always found making music with another person intimate and bonding.

"If I had my way, I'd have been an opera singer. Things just didn't work out that way." He gave an "oh, well" shrug.

"You have a great tenor voice. You probably would've made it," she told him in all sincerity. "I mean that. Your voice is so clear and strong, and you hit every note perfectly."

He glanced over at her and smiled. "That's very flattering. Thank you." He glowed.

"I'm not trying to flatter you. You do have a terrific voice." She let her gaze linger on his profile.

"Now you should let me have a chance to hear *you* sing solo."

"After my life gets back to normal," she promised him.

"You should try it now," he urged. "Sometimes music can be a great escape. When I was a kid, whenever I could afford it I'd buy a record. Didn't matter if it was Sinatra or Elvis or Caruso. I'd go to the cellar with the Victrola and sing down there for hours till somebody chased me out."

She just knew he'd take a hairbrush and pretend it

was a microphone and sing in front of the mirror, too. He didn't have to admit it. But somehow she knew.

When they arrived at the house, he got out first, helped her out, and shielded her all the way up to the door, gun cocked.

"The cops are gonna love that mess," Al said as they tossed coats and hats and gloves on the entry hall bench.

"It'll take a while to I.D. him, too." They went into the kitchen, and she spread the Brutus papers on the table.

Among the scraps she found a Louisiana driver's license belonging to a Victor Guarino, with a New Orleans address. "So he was Brutus." Her mind came to a quick conclusion, like the sum of two numbers. "Hey. I'll bet it was Marc Antony who nailed him." Paper rustled as Al opened packages of cold cuts.

"Coulda been. If he wanted to lay low, chances are he didn't want any of his cronies sticking their heads out of the dirt either." Al piled prosciutto onto a plate.

"And got to him right before we did," Vikki added. "Just think—we were that close to Marc Antony. Missed him by minutes."

"And not too many minutes. Brutus was as warm as me when I stuck my hand in there," Al said. "The blood was still wet, not too sticky yet—how you say— congealed?"

"It smelled like cordite a lot in there, too." Vikki stuffed a slice of prosciutto into her mouth.

"Yeah, it was a fresh hit, all right," Al agreed.

How they could talk about this while chowing on Italian deli amazed her and turned her stomach at the same time. She waved away the double-decker prosciutto-and-provolone sandwich Al offered her on one of Greta's Minton china plates. Good thing Greta wasn't home to see this.

Vikki lit a cigarette off the stove. "Rosie was right. They are starting to drop like flies," she muttered, standing in the kitchen doorway, dragging on her cigarette, shaking her head in bafflement.

"That's no surprise." Al spread horseradish on his sandwich. "If he was one of the president's assassins, he was supposed to lie low after the big Dallas hit. This is what he gets for being tempted by our money. I'll bet that final deposit stuffed into his trap was a Jewroll, too. I doubt there was even a fin in the whole wad."

"Let's talk about it later." The aroma of garlic sausage wafted over to her and beckoned. Her mouth watered. "The dead greaseball can wait. This can't." She stubbed out her cigarette and sat down to join the feast.

****

Billy knocked his cup over when she told him the next morning, but she pretended not to notice. "I'm not surprised the guy's dead, but I'm damn glad of it," was his only comment as they sat over their morning coffee, cigarettes, and pastry.

"My sentiments exactly, Dad."

"This is your classic high-powered conspiracy." Al sopped up the spilled coffee. "One guy's usually the ringleader, and the accomplices get knocked down one at a time, till nobody's left who can snitch."

It made her wonder if Jack really was one of the accomplices. With almost a physical reflex, she pushed the thought from her mind.

"Today's target practice day," she said to Al, as

much to change the subject as to stop from eating another cruller. They attended the firing range at Rodman's Neck Police Facility twice a week now.

"You taking the Bauer again?" Al asked her.

"That's the one I'm going to use from now on. We're getting to like each other. It's almost a fashion statement. I wish I could wear it on the outside of my purse, like a tote bag and an umbrella. It even matches a pair of my shoes."

After breakfast, they headed to the firing range.

She aimed at a silhouette's head from a distance of seven feet. The Bauer was light, and she had more control than she did with her old Smith & Wesson, but only having practiced with it a few times, she couldn't predict the outcome of this exercise. Her shot went through the head, a few inches left of center. She couldn't stop thinking about the Kennedy assassination as she aimed for the head once again, let out her breath, and fired. *What could have been going through those killers' minds? Did they think about how they would change history, slaughtering a beloved president, making his wife a widow and his children fatherless, or was it just another job? Oh, to get into the head of a person like that.*

She moved the silhouette back to fifteen feet and fired a few shots at the heart region. *Now, with Brutus gone, where to go next?* She listened to the exploding gunshots all around her. She'd have to come up with something soon.

The thought of failure was torture.

She moved the target back to twenty-five feet and fired another round. She gave the Bauer's barrel a kiss, something she did after every shot she'd ever taken.

"It's okay, baby, you're doing just fine," she said, as Al entered her partition.

She turned and watched him puzzle over her strange habit of kissing and talking to guns.

Chapter Thirteen

Vikki caught a glimpse of Al coming out of the bathroom. She ducked behind her door and peeked out. He sauntered down the hall, whistling the overture from *il Barbiere di Seviglia*, a towel hugging his credentials. She mentally slapped herself down after thinking, "What a tight ass!" and said three Hail Marys back in her room.

But Al knew where the line was and didn't dare step over it. He kept his emotional distance and remained all business. The few times she went out, even if it was to Walgreen's for tampons, he trailed her. She wasn't even embarrassed anymore, and he certainly wasn't. So she started sending him out for her tampons.

****

One snowy night, she got out her wedding album. After sitting with it in her lap for several minutes, she opened it and turned to her favorite picture—a close-up of the new bride and groom snuggling in the limo, toasting with champagne flutes. For the first time since he'd left her, she fixed her eyes on Jack. She studied his face for a long time, searching for something in those violet-blue eyes that she'd never found when he was alive—any hint of anguish or a hidden side of his personality.

"Oh, Jack, what was going on in your life?" she whispered into the expressive eyes, fixed not on the camera lens but beyond it, on whoever would see this photo decades from now. "I'll find out who did this to you, no matter what gets in my way. I won't let you down." She didn't cry. Her grief had morphed into a hardened fury and a solid resolve. But once again the question tormented her, and now she asked him directly: "What were you doing in Dallas the day John F. Kennedy got shot?"

****

Mounds of dirty snow covered the ground. Icy wind rattled the windows. She paced the floor like a caged lion. All the dead ends frustrated her even more.

She called Carlton Frost's partner. A buzzing tone told her the line was disconnected.

She called Catherine Frost, his widow. Maybe she could recommend some of his colleagues—it was worth a try.

"So how are you doing?" Catherine asked.

"Oh, I'm trying to get through each day. What about you?"

"I'm moving to Beverly Hills and starting a new life." The voice lifted, but still dragged with sustained grief.

"Well, good for you!" Vikki hoped her encouraging tone would help Catherine look forward to that new life.

"Carl's million-dollar life insurance helps."

"Wow." Vikki blinked. "He really did want to make sure you were well taken care of, didn't he?"

"I, er—hope you looked into that, Vikki. I don't know what kind of policy Jack had, but—" Catherine trailed off.

Jack's estate was substantial enough, but a mansion

in Beverly Hills wasn't her idea of a substitute for a slain husband.

"I'm okay that way." She spoke the truth. "But meanwhile, I'm at another dead end. I need another detective. Carl's office line is out of service, so I assume his partner has closed up shop. Did Carl have any other colleagues I can call?"

"His partner closed the office and left town soon after Carl died," Catherine said. "I don't know anybody else. I'm very sorry. Can you find someone else through NBS?"

"I'll ask Linc. But somehow I don't think he'll give me any more names, even if he knows any. It looks like I'm on my own with this."

"Why don't I take you to lunch, Vikki?" Catherine's tone wavered, as if she'd regret this invitation. "There are a few things you might want to know."

"About what?" Vikki braced herself.

"Let's just wait till we meet."

Uh-oh. Had Catherine stumbled upon something? "How about dinner tonight? I don't think I can wait a whole day." Vikki's hands began to shake.

A cab picked her up, with instructions to wait for her outside the restaurant and take her home, so she insisted that Al not tail her. "For God's sakes, it's dinner with a girlfriend. Besides," she reasoned, "Brutus and Cassius are dead, and Marc Antony is lying low. I'm out of the danger zone for now."

For once, she got her way. They met at O'Henry's in the Village. Catherine, dripping in mink and jewels, sat at the bar nursing a cocktail. She certainly hadn't wasted any time cashing in.

As they settled at a table, Catherine sipped her Tom Collins and said, "I didn't want you to think I'd come up with any leads. It's nothing like that. It's just something Carl told me when he was doing some work at NBS that I thought you might want to know about, and I'm terribly sorry I didn't tell you sooner. I struggled with the decision whether to tell you or not."

"Tell me what?" Vikki took a generous gulp of her Manhattan.

"Carl was on assignment at NBS about two years ago, I don't even remember what it was about, but he told me he'd gone to a few parties in Hollywood and Palm Springs. I think he wound up at Desi Arnaz's place. Anyway, he—" She took a deep breath. "He saw Jack there."

"At Desi Arnaz's place? So what?" She turned her palms up. "I'm thinking this whole thing had something to do with Cuba, and Castro, and connected to the plot that way. Maybe that's it?"

Catherine broke eye contact. "He was with a woman."

"Who?"

"Oh, please don't get too upset over this." Catherine played with the catch on her diamond wristwatch.

"Who was it, Catherine?" Vikki demanded.

She stared into Vikki's eyes. "Marilyn Monroe."

Vikki remembered the taped conversation and tried just as fast to forget it. "That's not a knockdown shock."

"It wasn't the only time," Catherine added. "Carl saw them together several times before that. The Arnaz party stood out because it lasted a few days."

"He was with her the whole time?" Vikki asked.

"According to Carl."

"Okay." She nodded and noticed she'd drained her drink. "So he really was having an affair with her. My husband and Marilyn Monroe. Another thing Jackie and I have in common."

Catherine lowered her gaze. "I'm sorry, Vikki, but I didn't want to tell you this the first time we met; it would've been too much for you. I'm just wondering now, because JFK's dead, she's dead, and you know the rumor—"

"Oh, yes, I know it, all right. She didn't die of any drug overdose. She was murdered because she knew too much and because of her affairs with the Kennedy brothers."

Catherine nodded. "I wasn't sure you knew. It's really not public knowledge."

Vikki looked for a waitress. "Jack knew all about it. One of the tapes he left behind was of him and Marilyn talking about JFK and Bobby. When Marilyn died—when was it, a year ago August?—it all had a shroud of suspicion hanging over it. Just like Jack's death. My Jack."

Catherine toyed with the bauble on her finger. "Maybe it all ties in, maybe it doesn't; I just thought you might want to know. I wasn't sure if you knew about Jack's…indiscretion, but since it was with who it was—"

"Oh, I'm glad you told me, Catherine. Every bit of information helps. Now I know who L.L. was in his notes," Vikki said.

"L.L.?"

"Jack had a code name for everybody he had

dealings with," Vikki divulged one of the dark secrets. "That's how I found out about Marc Antony, Brutus, and Cassius, and their connection to JFK."

A waitress hurried past, and Vikki flagged her down. "Another round, please."

Catherine nodded. "Carl did that, too. Never kept notebooks, though. But I always heard him speaking in code on the phone; everybody had a moniker."

"He called Marilyn L.L. because she played a character named Lorelei Lee in *Gentlemen Prefer Blondes*, Jack's favorite movie." Vikki swallowed. Her throat was awfully dry.

Catherine said, "I just wanted to tell you this to maybe provide some more clues—who knows? But if I caused you any more anguish, I'm sorry. I just wanted you to know. Carl, he—" Her eyes darted around the room, as if searching for words.

Vikki sensed another bomb about to drop.

"He saw Jack with other women on occasion, too—nobody famous, but now and again he'd glimpse Jack at some party or other with someone. He'd mention it to me in passing, 'Oh, yeah, and Jack Ward was there with some airhead,' nothing specific. I'm sorry, Vikki. I can't tell you how sorry I am. I just thought you should know."

"No, that's fine. I'm glad you told me." She stared into the depths of her empty glass, deep in thought. A wave of emotion came over her, nothing she could define, but that heavy burden of grief eased up on her. She now saw Jack as a different person. She had to talk about it right now; she couldn't keep it bottled up. "Catherine, all of a sudden I'm seeing Jack not as the saint, the hero I set him up to be in my mind. I'm seeing him as just a man, now. A man with needs, like the rest of them."

Catherine contemplated her diamond ring, nodding her understanding. "It happens, Vikki. Men are men—when they're away from home, they tend to—stray. Especially a man in Jack's position."

"Oh, yes." Vikki shut her eyes. "There I was, sitting there in my Camelot with everything a wife could want, and there's my husband sticking it to Marilyn Monroe—and whoever else."

"Don't blame yourself, Vikki."

"Oh, I'm not. Not by a long shot. He told me before we were married he wasn't a one-woman man and I had the freedom to see whomever I wanted. I just didn't want anyone else." Vikki shook her head. "Poor Marilyn."

Catherine screwed up her face, tugged at a dangling earring, and pulled it off. "Why poor Marilyn?"

"I feel sorry for her. Never found true love. Wanted to marry Bobby, was madly in love with him, had that torrid affair with JFK, and look what happened. What a tragic figure. I can't hate her, no matter what. I just can't. I can't hate Jack, either. I'm learning a lot about men. They're not all like my father."

Catherine smiled. "They never are. No man can ever live up to a father image. I adored my father; he was my hero."

"So is mine." Thoughts of her dad brought a smile to her lips. "But I felt that way about Jack, too. Till very recently."

Catherine said, "I admire your sensibility."

"It's more like resignation. But I'm seeing reality

instead of that little Camelot storybook I thought I was living in. He was all too human. Just like I am."

"We all are." Catherine patted Vikki's hand.

"And none of us is without sin. But we just have to live with it, don't we?" The waitress brought their round, and Vikki stirred her Manhattan. "I always felt like I had to have a hero. First it was my father, then Jack. Maybe I just don't need one anymore."

"I don't think you ever did need one." Catherine sipped her drink. "You're a hero yourself. I wish I had your brass."

They shared a laugh and toasted each other. "Here's to wives everywhere. May they see the light."

She didn't join Catherine in eating dinner. All she wanted to do was get four sheets to the wind. Catherine understood. After two more Manhattans, Vikki slid into the waiting cab.

"I'll write when I get settled out there, Vikki. I'm real proud of you, my friend," she vaguely remembered Catherine saying.

She didn't remember how she got into the house, though. When she woke up on the couch fully clothed at one a.m., her mouth felt like an entire army had marched through it, she was dying for a cigarette, and the TV was on. The Late Late Show. *Gentlemen Prefer Blondes*.

****

It took the better part of the day to recover. Once the fuzziness gave way to clear thinking, she took a long hot shower and looked for Al.

She found him lifting his weights. "Let's go out into the cold for a brisk walk." She pulled on her mittens.

"Sure." He flexed his muscles. "But bundle up good."

Five blocks past Valore's Bakery, sweat trickled down her back as her breath came out in puffs of steam. They turned and walked back to the house, stopping at the bakery on the way. She ate a cannoli on the way home, her reward.

"Something bothering you, Vikki?" he asked over and over.

"No." But she still tried to figure out how to explain all this to another private detective if she could find a good one.

Al challenged her to a game of billiards, and this time she didn't care if she beat him.

He sensed her frustration and halted their game when it looked like she wasn't going to win as usual.

"I know how you feel about all this, and you're in a hurry to find the truth, but we can only do so much, *cara mia*."

She didn't want to discuss what Catherine had told her—not yet. "That's what gets me." She chalked her cue. "I was always in control of the outcome of anything I tried or did. I decided to get a degree, and I got one. I decided not to go into politics, and I didn't. I decided to devote my life to Jack, and I made it work out. Do you know how I met Jack? It was no accident; I made it happen. I was determined."

"What'd you do, put a Sicilian love spell on him?" He gave her a cocky grin.

"Hardly. I won Jack purely by my own efforts. I stayed in D.C. after I graduated Georgetown, still thinking I wanted a career in politics. I got a job as a political consultant with a couple of ex-CIA agents.

197

Jack was a reporter for the *Washington Post*. I always enjoyed his articles—they had a clever undertone of cutting-edge humor. Sometimes he mentioned personal details: his close calls as a stunt pilot, his solo in a sailboat around Cape Horn, the political and show business parties he attended...I was hooked." She aimed her cue and hit balls at random. "I couldn't wait for him to reveal another personal item, like the next installment in a serial. Then he became a television reporter for NBS. I was in my glory, able to see him every night at six and eleven. When *So Far So Good* came out—that was his memoir—I took the day off from work to read it. I devoured it, tore out the pictures and taped them to my walls. On television, he was as commanding and powerful as any president, and that was it—I had to meet him." She rolled the balls around the table in all directions, watching them hit the bumpers and bounce back. "So I spent every spare moment in front of NBS Studios waiting for an 'accidental' encounter. Finally it happened. First it was eye contact and a little small talk, 'I'm your biggest fan,' that kind of stuff. I had to talk fast. I read up on the items he reported so I'd be able to hold a conversation with him, and one day just blurted out an invitation to my place for dinner. He was so surprised, he accepted. I had him over the next night, and he fell in love with my *aglio olio*. I was already in love with him. When that evening ended, I'd already planned out the rest of my life... I wasn't going to let him get away. I wanted him and I got him." She stopped and stared into space, remembering her revelation of the other night. "He wasn't a Race Parsec-type of fantasy superhero. He was a man—just another red-blooded man." She came back to earth when Al waved a hand in front of her eyes. "Huh? Oh, sorry. That was me, always in control. But now a force stronger than my will has taken over and is trying to tell me I'm wasting my time pursuing this."

"Oh, you're not wasting your time." He shook his head. The light above the pool table glinted off his Midnight Raven hair. "I know how much this means to you. When you go after something, something you believe in, it's never a waste of time. Even if it doesn't work out. Never trying and later wishing you did try—now, that's a waste of time. But going after it—never. Especially a go-getter like you."

She kept rolling the balls around the table. "I might be a go-getter, but I'm no longer in control, and that's what exasperates me. Not only that, it scares me. It's not the mob or the mysterious murders that scare me, it's not having control that's scary. It means the winds of fate, whatever forces that make things happen, are stronger than I am. Happenings are random. And, well, that's scary. And humbling."

"Yeah, there's a lot to be humble about. And scared of. The unknown. Just who's up above or down below calling the shots. Unless it really is random, which isn't much better. We don't have all the control. But neither do the mobsters with the three-fifty-seven mags or the tommy guns. They're just mortals crawling around, like the rest of us." He twirled his cue stick. "Whatever else is around us, God, or the stars, or whatever or whoever, calls the shots. I know. Cath'lic school put the fear of God into me, but there's the guy with the horns and the pitchfork, too."

"I've never been too worried about him," she said

with conviction. "Who kicked who out of where?"

"I know. I just haven't read the Bible in years. I should get back to it."

She noticed the silver chain around his neck and wondered what, if anything, was on it. She asked him now.

"Oh, just a cheap medal I found when I was down and out, and I never took it off since." He pulled the chain out from under his shirt, and a silver Mary medal dangled from it.

"You found it?" She went up to him and studied it, too aware of their closeness.

"Yeah, right before I met Rosie. I'm lookin' around the racetrack one night after work, for spare change, and I see this shiny thing on the ground. I thought it was a dime, and I thought, Oh, good, I can get a Slim Jim or somethin' to eat, so I picked it up, and there it was. Somebody must've dropped it. I took it as a sign that things would get better, and sure enough, my whole life turned around. It was better than any amount of money I could've found. So I never take it off. It's my good-luck charm. I'm scared to take it off." He chuckled.

She took a step back and returned to a respectable distance.

"I know what I told you about Mona's family sounds like Rod Serling dreamt it up, but I have a few superstitions myself," he admitted, taking his wallet from his back pocket.

She nodded. "It's a Southern Italian thing. You should hear some of the stuff my family used to get up to. Sheesh! Pat Cooper never has to make material up for his standup routine. All those stories are real."

"Well, I got this, too." He pulled a bill out of his wallet and unfolded it.

"The first buck you ever made?"

"Nope." He held it up to her.

Her eyes widened. "Cripes, that's a thousand. Why are you walking around with that much money, Al?"

"Emergencies. You never know."

She let out a low whistle. "It better be a big emergency."

"When Rosie hired me, he saved my life, and I said I'd never be broke again. So I keep this in here. I carry the G-note 'cause it's hard to break; not like a fin or a ten-spot. So it better be an emergency for me to spend it."

"Well, if it makes you feel better to carry it. Just don't get pickpocketed." Her thoughts drifted back to her own problems.

"I haven't yet. Hey—" He lifted her chin with his finger. "Everything will work out."

"What if this never works out, if I never find Jack's killer? How can I live with my failure?"

"It's no failure. You can say you gave it your best shot. That's never a failure. But even if you don't find out what happened to Jack, you have to let go—and get on with your life." It sounded like a demand. "Most of all, you gotta have faith the sonofabitch'll get what's coming to him anyway. Maybe some other thug'll blow him away. Don't have to be you. He'll get his. They always do."

This pep talk helped. "I know enough about 'the business.' It's a consolation, but I still want to do this myself. And I *am* trying to get on with my life."

"You're doing great so far. You whip my ass at

pool and chess and cards all the time. That should make you feel better." He gave her a dazzling smile.

"For a minute or two. But they're just games. They don't mean anything."

"I'm still trying to find something I got the upper hand at with you." He pinched her chin between his thumb and forefinger.

She wanted to tell him he already had—she was falling head over heels for him—and that was no game; they were twin souls at heart. But the timing couldn't be worse.

All she could do was keep him interested so he'd stick around after this was all over…and think twice about his arranged marriage.

Beating him at everything didn't hurt, either. He was the type who'd stick around till he could win a hand of poker.

****

Rosie came back to town, but not alone. He'd brought his own bodyguard, Angelo Tivoli, and one for Billy named Roberto Tento. To Vikki, Roberto looked like photos of Rosie from forty years ago, and Angelo's neck was wider than her waistline. By contrast, Al wasn't as hulky, but he had bulges in all the right places.

Billy chuckled at having a bodyguard. "I haven't had one in thirty years," he told Vikki, and recounted the incident when some creep was stalking her mother. "So I hired an army of bodyguards. The stalker turned out to be a cop gone bad, name of Sid Cunningham. Rosie's boys eventually caught Sid, brought him to me, and told me Sid's fate was entirely up to me."

"What did you do?" She fully expected another

description of excruciating torture and a one-way trip over the G.W. Bridge.

"He was already beaten to a pulp, spittin' out teeth on my Persian rug. I told them to let 'im go. I didn't want his death on my conscience."

She blinked in surprise. Maybe that was why he quit the mob; he had a conscience. But she had to wait to read his memoirs to find out. He still wouldn't let her read them now. "When I croak," was his way of refusing her with Italian class.

Rosie treated them all to dinner, and she noticed the boys ate enough lasagna to feed a football league but refused any alcohol. They even passed on the rum cake. She guessed they didn't want to start their first day on the job with hangovers.

After dinner, they all went back to the house and sang Billy's show tunes as he played the piano. Once again, Al's rich tenor voice made her wonder, as she did every night alone in bed, what other talents he had under his belt.

She'd never know unless she made that first move. Although she was hardly ready for that, a little teasing wouldn't hurt.

But, out of habit, she got out the rosary.
****

Billy helped his bodyguard Roberto move into the last spare room—along with his collection of Dean Martin records. Having these guys floating around at all hours frying sausage and singing arias kept her life bearable.

Rosie and Angelo were staying at the Plaza, but they might as well have moved in too. Rosie hung around the house, calling contacts, and contacts of contacts, on the red phone, still trying to find out who knew what about the JFK plot.

She knew this was Rosie's new hobby; he hadn't done any "business" in a while, and his feet were real itchy. She even overheard him asking Billy if he knew who ran the local numbers racket. "I don't do that shit no more," he'd declared with conviction in his voice.

Rosie held an informal conference the next night in Billy's studio, while the boys feasted on fried calamari and valpolicella at the kitchen table.

"So. I got a surprise for you," Rosie announced. "And this is why I'm here. We're finally goin' to Dallas to pay my old buddy Sparky a visit."

Vikki choked on the smoke she'd just inhaled. *Finally is right!* The prospect of meeting the infamous Jack Ruby excited and scared her. Of all the people she'd have to meet during this whole thing, he was probably the least dangerous.

"His trial's over, and I called in a few favors to get a certain party in Dallas to arrange a visit," Rosie continued. "Sparky should talk to us. What's he got to lose at this point?"

"That's great, Rosie. Thank you. I hope he can tell us something. Wouldn't it be heartening to know he really did kill Oswald out of sympathy for Mrs. Kennedy?" Vikki asked.

Rosie snorted. "Nah, it's all one big plot. We might never know the whole story, but Sparky'll tell me what we need to know. We go way back." He puffed on his cigar. "He knows I still got a few connections and can make his stay in jail a little more comfortable if he comes across for us."

"You mean like bring him a matzoh ball with a file

in it?" Billy joked, drumming his fingers on the tabletop.

****

On Sunday night Billy poked his head into her bedroom. "Hey, babe, I have something that'll cheer you up. In about ten minutes. Make some Jiffy Pop and come join us in the TV room."

One of their favorite old movies must be on—they both loved Cagney and Bogey—maybe *Casablanca*. But she was more in the mood for Cagney. Her father's Cagney impersonation cracked her up, especially when he did a routine from their favorite classic, *White Heat*. "How you doing, Parker…You want some air?…I'll give you some air." He always did it eating a chicken leg, like Cagney's character Cody Jarrett in the movie. Whenever they had chicken, she knew she was in for a treat.

It seemed a hundred years ago when they'd last laughed like that. She was ready for some yuks now.

Tossing the Sunday *Times* on the floor, she gladly went downstairs and got out a tin of Jiffy Pop. "Is *White Heat* on?" she asked as Billy pried the cap off a Stewart's root beer bottle and poured them each a mug.

"Nope. It's the *Ed Sullivan Show*."

"Oh, great! Is Topo Gigio on again?" That little Italian mouse puppet was Sullivan's best guest, and she suffered the plate spinners and poetry readings just to see Topo, who was always on last.

"Nope. Them four British kids you like who play that bug music. Their first American television appearance." He slurped his root beer and wiped foam from his lips.

"The Beatles?" She held the pan over the flame and

shook it. Kernels began popping inside. "I didn't even know they were coming over here."

"I could've got tickets to the show, but I didn't even know about it till tonight, when I saw it in the paper." He brought the soda mugs into the TV room.

"That's okay, Dad. I'm sure they'll be around for a while. We can go see them another time." She followed him with her Jiffy Pop, tearing into the aluminum foil.

Rosie had taken the boys out on the town, and she didn't ask but had an inkling it wasn't to the Ed Sullivan Theater to see The Beatles. "We'll be back wit' the crack a dawn," he'd said before sliding into his rented Fleetwood.

So she, Billy, and Greta settled down in front of the television, and she munched on her popcorn like a kid at the movies. "Hey, Dad and Greta, do you realize this is the first moment I'm actually enjoying something since Jack died?"

The Beatles sang "She Loves You" accompanied by an ear-piercing surge of screams from the audience.

"What's with this 'yeah yeah yeah' stuff?" Billy grimaced into his root beer.

"That's the new thing, Dad. I have the 45, and it's great." She tossed popcorn into her mouth.

"I don't know if I like this bug music." He covered his ears.

"It's called rock 'n' roll, Dad." She and Greta exchanged eye-rolls. "You like Elvis, don't you?"

"Hey, I think I'll get one of them wigs." He ruffled his own short hair.

"Those aren't wigs, Dad!"

"Why don't women go for you like that?" Greta asked Billy, pinching his thigh.

"They did, back when I was that age." He tapped his foot along with the Fab Four. "You were too busy running around with Screwy Louie and missed out on all the good music."

The mop tops finished the song and took perfectly synchronized bows.

"You think they'll ever get really big over here?" she asked her dad, who now looked mildly interested as they began "Please Please Me," barely audible over the screams.

"With you kids, maybe. But them and that Elvis dude sure can't compete with ol' Blue Eyes and our crooners."

"Well, I think they're cute," Greta insisted.

"You're a little old for them." Billy put his hand over Greta's eyes.

"You're the one gettin' old, pops," she shot back.

"Hey, *I'm* too old for them!" Vikki sat riveted to the TV, swaying with the music—what she could hear of it. "They're only in their early twenties." But it was nice to be a kid again, even for the span of a few 45s. Then Billy started dancing around the room singing, "Yeah, yeah, yeah! Ooooo!"

It was almost as good as his Cagney with the chicken leg. She munched her Jiffy Pop and welcomed the brief happiness.

****

A night of carousing didn't affect the boys' schedules or appetites. When she came down the next morning, they all sat at the kitchen table polishing off a gargantuan breakfast of peppers and eggs.

"*Buon giorno*," Al greeted her and pulled out the chair to his left.

"Ditto. I'll just have a cruller. Or two." She plucked one out of the Valore's box and poured a cup of coffee.

"I got us on a flight to Dallas," Rosie informed her as she glanced at the paper. Nothing interesting except an article on The Beatles, which she put aside for later.

"When?"

"Departing eight-ten tomorrow morning." He poured sugar into his coffee.

"I think my impatience is rubbing off on you." She dunked her cruller into her coffee.

"That's the reason I'm here, doll. This'll be fruitful—Sparky and me, we used to share all kinds a stuff back inna old days—dough, broads, everything."

"I hope he still feels that way, Rosie."

"In our business, loyalty never dies, Annie." He covered her hand with his.

"I know. I just don't relish the thought of being in Dallas." The thought killed her appetite. She put the cruller down.

"It'll be in and out." He poured more sugar into his coffee. "We won't go nowhere near Dealey Plaza."

"Whatever you do, don't book us into the Hilton," She made sure to remind him.

"Nah, we're stayin' at the other side of town. I knew you wouldn't wanna be nowhere near there, either."

"Thanks, Rosie." Considering the nature of his business, he certainly was thoughtful at the right times.

"Now, when we get down there, we're not Rosie and his goddaughter. We're Ruby's attorneys, and I come up with a few good names—I'm Morton Horwitz and you're Sheila Horwitz of Horwitz and Horwitz.

And Associates, of course." He slurped his coffee.

"You might look like a Mort but I don't know if I can pull off a Sheila." Her glasses slid down her nose, and she pushed them back into place. She knew where he'd gotten the Horwitz, though—he was a big Three Stooges fan, and Horwitz was the real last name of the brothers Shemp, Moe, and Curly Howard. "I guess 'Dewey, Cheatem, and Howe' would give us away."

"Ya can't take nothin' for granted, Annie." He did an eye-poke gesture. "Nyuk, nyuk, nyuk."

"Wiseguy." She gave him a pretend poke in the eyes.

So it was her, Rosie, and their bodyguards. With Billy in meetings with his collaborator about their next musical, he and Roberto stayed home.

They flew first class, Al in the seat next to her. They didn't talk much. Al did mention that he wished he'd stayed at the house to watch The Beatles last night because he wasn't big on carousing. "I took off by myself and went to the movies." That greatly relieved her, and she wasn't sure why.

"What did you see?" she asked.

"Nothin' special. *The Pink Panther*."

She turned away to hide her smile.

As they were about to land, a stab of nervousness tensed her muscles. She gripped the arms of her seat. What kind of guy was Jack Ruby? Mean and nasty? Condescending? He intimidated her already.

"I wonder what Ruby's like," she wondered out loud, slipping her glasses off, always self-conscious wearing them in front of Al.

"No matter what he's like, I know he'll like you." He looked straight into her eyes. She wondered if his

wink was just a reassurance or something deeper.
Then she realized: Finally! A wink!
It was a good start. Now it was her turn.

Chapter Fourteen

Vikki and Al lounged in the sitting room of her suite—not in Dallas, but in New Orleans, where Rosie insisted on going after their visit to Ruby in jail.

But they took the train. Her godfather avoided flying whenever possible.

"Rosie spent a good part of his wayward youth here, in case he never divulged his salad days to you," she told Al as they sipped mint juleps and snacked on Cajun Cakes. "But he really came here for the *muffulettas*."

"Nah, he never talks about anything before Ike's presidency. And what are *muffulettas*?" Al devoured a cake and licked his fingers. "I'm almost afraid to ask. It sounds like something obscene."

"They can be obscene, I suppose. It's a fancy name for a Roman sandwich. They're drippy, gooey, and big enough to choke a racehorse." She sipped her drink and rolled the sweetness around her tongue.

"I'll have one to cleanse my palate between bites of jambalaya," he joked with a half-grin. "So now tell me—how'd the visit with Ruby go?"

"The Dallas County Jail gave me the creeps more than Ruby did." She shuddered. "It was so stark and uninviting with those gray cinderblock walls. I'd put my Bauer to my head before having to spend a day in that place."

"Did you two pull it off as the Horwitz attorneys?" He sipped his drink.

"Oh, yeah. Rosie introduced us to the guard as Morton and Sheila Horwitz, said he'd called ahead of time. He sounded so serious. I've only heard him speak like that a few times—when he gave numbers to his bookie and when he ordered a custom Cadillac." She took another cake and bit into it. "Rosie flashed one of the business cards he got printed up the day before and told the guard we were Mr. Rubenstein's attorneys for his upcoming retrial. Jacob Rubenstein is Ruby's real name."

"So how did it feel to be Sheila Horwitz with the prospect of defending the most infamous guy alive today?" He refilled his drink from a pitcher and sat back to hear her juicy story.

"The first thing I did was get out a tissue and wipe off my lipstick. I didn't think it apropos for Attorney Sheila Horwitz to wear Really Red in prison."

"Then how come you ain't wearing it now?" His tongue darted out and wet his lips.

"I was." She batted her lashes. "You kissed it off."

He growled with a smile that melted her.

"So the warden signed us in, another uniformed sentry gave us passes, and a third guard ushered us down this dank, echoing corridor to a mess-hall type of room. It was lined with long tables and metal folding chairs. The warden announced that Ru—our client would be right out. So we sat there, with a guard stationed at the metal door." She ran her hands up and down her arms. Reliving it chilled her. "It wasn't cold in there, but I couldn't stop shivering. I think it was just the creepiness of the place. Oh, man, I wished you were there with me."

He released a heavy sigh. "Yeah, so did I, but Angelo insisted on staying in the car. He didn't wanna see the inside of another hoosegow. And I can't blame him."

She sipped her drink and put it down, focusing on a faraway point. "While we sat there, I remembered my grandmother telling me about visiting her father in the Tombs. He was falsely accused of murder."

"Yeah, I heard about it." Al nodded. "That was a horrible place. Never saw it myself, but heard it was a real dungeon. I'm sure that Dallas jail was a country club compared to that."

She rubbed her hands together to warm them. "Oh, yeah, I couldn't stop looking at the concrete block walls and the bars on the tiny windows. Even the stone-faced sentry posted at the metal outer door looked miserable. I felt pangs of sympathy—not just for the poor souls locked up there but even for the guys who work there and could leave every night."

"So how long till Ruby showed up?" he asked.

"Maybe about ten minutes." She recounted the event she'd never forget for the rest of her life. "These eerie echoing footsteps got louder, and then two figures in gray stopped across the table from us. I didn't know the short guy was Ruby till Rosie stood to shake hands with him. He looked so pale and nondescript. But Rosie made sure to say his name. 'Good afternoon, Mr. Rubenstein,' he said. But Ruby's guard kept a tight clamp around his other arm. I figured I'd better stand, ready for a formal lawyerly greeting. Then Rosie cut right in: 'Excuse me, Mr. Prison Guard, sir, I'm Morton Horwitz, of Horwitz and Horwitz and Associates, Mr.

Rubenstein's attorneys, and as we're representing him in his upcoming retrial, we need to maintain client confidentiality. So I request you please step out of the room for approximately thirty or so minutes.' The guard kind of scowled, but Ruby's eyes lit up. Then he turned to the guy and said, 'Yes, Ray, I need to consult with my attorney, Mr. Horwitz, and his assistant—' and he faltered, so I saved the moment for him and said, 'Associate. Attorney Sheila Horwitz.' But it still left a sour taste in my mouth."

He grinned. "So then what happened, Sheil—er, Attorney Horwitz?"

"Ruby introduced the guy, Captain Ray Abner, as his personal guard, like it was a heroic feat to be so infamous as to require a personal prison guard." She pressed her lips together, still unable to believe she'd actually met Jack Ruby.

"They prob'ly keep him around to make sure Ruby don't bash his brains out," Al commented.

She nodded. "I'll bet he's on a tight suicide watch. So Abner warned we had thirty minutes, and then he got out and clanged the door shut."

"So the three of you's were alone at last." Al sat forward, elbows on knees, fingers laced.

"Finally. Rosie held out his hand for a hearty shake and said, 'Put 'er there, Sparky!' and Ruby broke into a big grin." She smiled at the image in her mind. "He commented about the pounds Rosie put on in the last few decades, and Rosie told Ruby he looked pretty well-fed for a jailbird. When we all sat down, Ruby told Rosie he knew he'd end up in jail, and his voice dragged. That's when Rosie introduced me—the real me, his goddaughter Victoria—and I leaned across the

table and shook hands with the infamous Jack Ruby."
She held up the hand that had done the shaking as she
whistled in wonder. "I can't believe I actually touched
the guy. It's like touching a piece of history."

Al smiled in appreciation. "Yeah, I've never met
anybody famous—or infamous. That's something to tell
the grandkids."

"His eyes were pouchy and, boy, was his hand
clammy, and what a weak handshake. But I kept
thinking, *This is unreal—the man who closed the case
of the Kennedy assassination forever, in the most
astonishing sequence ever broadcast live, who changed
the course of history, and here I am shaking hands with
him.*"

"So what'd you say to him?" Al asked.

She shook her head. "Well—nothing. There I was,
and I couldn't think of a word to ask the man, though
I'd rehearsed dozens of questions on the way. I just sat
there tongue-tied, my insides churning. So Rosie led the
conversation. He asked Ruby, 'So, Sparky, they let you
have booze and broads up here?'"

"What's this 'Sparky'?" Al tilted his head.

"That's Ruby's nickname from Chicago. He was a
hothead. Well, still was, up until November twenty-
fourth, anyway. He told us the jail nosh was dreck. He
hoped to get special attention, have meals prepared the
way he wants them, but Abner said if he had to eat jail
food, Ruby had to eat it, too. But he told us he gets
Scotch brought—brung as he said—up to him. They
didn't let him have any broads, but he was workin' on
it, he said."

Al laughed. "That figures. I'm surprised they didn't
let him have his broads. At least some of his strippers.

He did have all kinds of connections in Dallas and was in tight with the cops."

"Well, maybe not anymore." She ate another cake and wiped her hands on a napkin. "Rosie promised Ruby some of his homemade wine, and Ruby wanted Manischewitz for Passover. Rosie said he'd get a broad to sneak in some along with some Dago Red. Ruby told us one of his gals from the Carousel Club showed up the day he got booked. She hid a Beretta in her scarf to give him, but they arrested her at the entrance. When Rosie asked if she got out on bail, Ruby started to cry." Vikki looked Al in the eye. "Ruby said 'She's dead. A week ago Friday.' I was in tears, too, I felt so bad for him, and that poor girl."

"What happened to her?" Al sat hunched forward, almost tumbling out of the chair.

"Ruby said he always turns to the obits first in the paper, and saw her name, Theresa Norton. He figured it was another Theresa Norton. Then he saw the relatives' names, her age—it was his Theresa Norton. Nineteen years old. Some gals from the Carousel visited him and told him she was shot. Ruby got really emotional over that," Vikki remembered. "He might be a hothead, but he's a really sensitive, emotional guy." She took a deep breath, Ruby's pained face clear in her mind. "Then Rosie asked about his other chickadees, and he said some got jobs at Madame De Luce's, a whorehouse in Turtle Creek. Ruby said he never allowed any hanky-panky in the Carousel. 'That was a fuckin' high-class place,' he said." Vikki laughed. "Then he looked at me and put his hand up to his mouth like a naughty boy and said, 'Oops, sorry, my dear.' How about that, a murderer with manners," she joked. "Then we got down to business. Rosie told him we needed to find out a few things. He told Ruby about Jack being the television reporter found drowned in his tub at the Dallas Hilton on—" Her voice faltered. "On that same day."

Al leaned over and grasped her hand. "You don't have to tell me any more if you don't want."

She gathered her resolve. "Of course I want to tell you. Ruby looked straight at me and told me he used to watch Jack all the time. He offered me his sympathy. And again he had tears in his eyes. Then his eyes lit right up, and—get this—he told me he saw pictures of me, too. He stared at me and aimed his trigger finger at me." She mimicked his gesture, pointing her forefinger at Al like a gun. "I kept thinking—that same finger fired the shot in that startling scene beamed around the world the instant it happened."

"When could he have seen pictures of you?" Al asked.

"Oh—" She averted her eyes. "That's the spread they did on Jack in *Look* magazine. After Jack won his first Emmy, they interviewed him at home and insisted I pose with him for a few photos. I didn't relish that exposure. It happened only because of Jack being famous. To me, it was an invasion of our privacy. But it was enough to stick in Ruby's memory for two years."

"You musta looked pretty tasty in those pictures." He gave her a wink. "I bet you gave Marilyn a run for her money."

"They weren't that kind of pictures, Al." She lowered her lashes and batted them. "But Ruby gave me his approval. Then I remembered he was the owner of a strip club." She focused on the far wall, recalling her reaction. "For some strange reason, I felt flattered. His

217

look wasn't lecherous. He was like any other male appreciating a female."

"I'm sure none of his Carousel gals were nowhere near as beautiful as you." His voice rumbled like a purring engine.

She blushed. The room grew hotter than an oven. "Thank you," she murmured. "Nobody ever told me I was beautiful before." She looked down and ran her gaze over the floor.

"Then you've been with the wrong guys." He pulled his chair closer. "So go on. When he finished ravishing you with his beady eyes, what happened?"

"I plowed right in and told him I needed to know what happened to Jack that day. I told him about Jack's notes I'd found, saying he was onto this Cassius, who Jack thought was planning to assassinate the president. I told Ruby about Jack's tapes mentioning this Cassius, and the tapes mentioning Brutus and Marc Antony, and that I'd found out they're agents who do political assassinations and mob hits. So I asked him if he could tell us anything about these people. I told him I'm convinced Jack was killed, and that I need to know who killed him." She fought back tears as she had that day in front of Ruby. "I didn't want to start blubbering then and there, dressed up like Sheila Horwitz. But believe me, Al, it was hard to hold myself together."

"I understand, *cara*." Al nodded. "So did he know those clowns, or what?"

"At first he didn't. I told him everything I remembered from Jack's tapes, and Cassius's real name being Rino Tieri, and that he was killed here."

"So it was a dead end?"

"Almost…Rosie asked him how he knew Oswald,

and Ruby said he was an acquaintance, but they didn't go slummin' together, as he said. Ruby knew Oswald's uncle, Dutz Murret, pretty well. Oswald used to come in the Embassy Club and hit on the broads." Vikki couldn't hide an ironic smile. "And Ruby said, 'Damned if Oswald didn't score most nights.' "

"Maybe it was the gun in his pocket," Al suggested.

"Ruby told us Dutz was one of Marcello's lieutenants in New Orleans, and Lee was a runner for his uncle. But that didn't help me. Oh, how I wished I could've brought Jack's notebooks and tapes. I had a hunch Ruby could've picked up on some clues there. I was just about to tell him that Detective Frost got murdered going after Cassius, and we found Brutus dead ourselves."

"I don't think you shoulda told him that." Al sat up, eyes wide.

"I didn't. Ruby broke in and told me what he couldn't tell Gerald Ford and Earl Warren when they visited him. He asked Rosie if he remembered a guy named Gio Bati, who ran the scrap iron and junk handlers union and fixed the races. Rosie remembered him—the guy wore a jacket made of dog hair. He moved to New Orleans after the war and hooked up with Marcello's outfit. He had a son, Benzo, and when the kid was about seventeen, he wanted to get into the rackets, but his old man told him if he did, he'd kill him. Then the old man got whacked, and the kid joined the Army Marksmanship Unit. He did some hits that Rosie heard about, on a South American tin pot dictator, some African bishop or other, various political hits. In a few years, he was a world-class marksman."

"So how does Benzo Junior figure in the whole thing?" Al lit a cigarette.

"The Bati family are originally from New Orleans. Marcello kicked them out, but they sneaked back in. Then Ruby said Oswald was involved with the CIA but had never told him how. He did tell Ruby that a group of three assassins is sometimes given contracts by the Cuban Revolutionary Council, an arm of the CIA. This trio of gunmen has a high turnover, but it's always three hit men doing high-powered hits. Whoever needed a hit like that, they'd hire out one, two, or all three. They call themselves the Triumvirate. Ruby didn't know who they are but said some of the higher-ups in New Orleans would know. Ruby was never high up enough to know code names. But Ben Bati's old man, Gio, used to be one of the three, and there's a chance Ben might've taken over the position when his old man died."

"The CIA?" Al took a long drag on his cigarette. "Hmmm… "

"Yeah." She took the cigarette he offered her. He lit it with his lighter. "Ruby thought maybe Benzo Bati was one of the Triumvirate. They've been around at least since the war. The FBI knew about them, and Hoover looked the other way. Ruby never knew anybody else named Bati. So he told us to try to look Ben up here."

"Well, what are we waiting for? Get the phone book." Al got up and started rummaging through the desk.

"Well, there's more." She flicked her ash. Al sat back down. "Ben's boss used to be Nappy Dibrizzi. Ruby and Rosie both remembered this guy. He didn't learn how to read till after he had four kids. Ruby said he did fifteen in the Hothouse, and now he's clean. He was one of Marcello's soldiers, then worked his way up, got his button, was a made man before he was twenty-five."

Al shook his head. "This makes my head spin. Rosie never talks about his past in the rackets." He chopped the air with his hand. "He never told me he knew Ruby or anything like that."

She sat back and took a puff. "Well, I've heard legends over the years but mostly from my father, not Rosie. But Rosie told Ruby that he and Nappy used to hang out together and run numbers when he first started out, but he hasn't seen him in decades. Ruby said Nappy came back here when Marcello got deported. But even when Marcello sneaked back into town, Nappy stayed here, and they never seemed to get in each other's way anymore." She took a sip of her drink. "You know, my thought at that moment was that there was Rosie and Jack Ruby, reminiscing like two old friends. And here we were in a jail, and here's the guy who murdered Oswald." She shook her head in wonder once again.

"So this Nappy guy sounds like a lead," Al said.

"Well, he did say if anybody knows where Bati would be or if the three guys with the Roman names are the Triumvirate, it should be Nappy. He owns a restaurant in the French Quarter, il Tantino, the only genuine Italian restaurant in town. Ruby gave the fried eggplant high marks."

"And he ain't even eye-talian," Al joshed.

Vikki crossed her legs and pulled her skirt over her knee. "So I knew this could be what we're looking for.

Ben Bati could be the Marc Antony of the Triumvirate."

"Then we're in the right place." Al gave her an encouraging smile. "And not just for the muffa-whatever sandwiches."

"Ruby said it was worth a shot. No pun intended." The gallows humor gave her a touch of the creeps. "But he doesn't know where Bati is now. He went to work directly for Marcello when Nappy went in the pen. Started as a runner, then graduated to one of his hired guns. But he might've taken over his father's job as one of those three top hit men after the father died. He could still be here, so we're going to scour this town to find him."

"Did Ruby say anything about the assassination plot, like if he knows how many assassins were in Dealey Plaza that day?" Al asked her.

"No, he wouldn't say, if he did know. He wouldn't admit to knowing who was behind it, or the assassin or assassins, however many there were. All he said was there's a right-wing organization in Dallas, a bunch of Nazis, and they're very powerful. If they have connections to Marcello or Castro or anybody else, he doesn't know—or won't say."

"Ruby should at least tell Earl Warren that this Triumvirate might've been behind it." Al stroked his chin.

She shook her head. "He drove the point home that the Warren Commission's agenda is about one thing: Oswald did it. Alone."

"But this could save Ruby's life," Al insisted. "Why wouldn't he write Warren a letter, like a written testimony, or a deposition?"

"I asked him that myself. Why not tell Warren what he knows? But he said they wouldn't listen even if he sang it to the tune of "Hava Nagila" while spinning a dreidel. He begged them to let him testify in Washington, but they won't let him, because he wouldn't be safe in Washington. Though he believes he's in a lot more danger in Dallas, and so is his family. At this moment, Lee Harvey Oswald isn't guilty of committing the crime of assassinating President Kennedy. Jack Ruby is. He's a scapegoat. If Warren wanted him to talk, he could get him to Washington. They won't even let him take a lie detector test."

"So what kind of justice is that?" Al's voice rose as he threw his hands in the air.

"None, if you ask me." She took one more drag and ground out her cigarette. "Seems the Warren Commission wants to make it look like Oswald killed JFK and Ruby killed Oswald. Case closed. Ruby swears he was used for a purpose, and there will be a tragic occurrence if they don't take his testimony and vindicate him." Her voice trailed off as a flood of sympathy for Ruby tore at her heart. "He told us point blank he's going to die in that prison. Four hundred million people saw him shoot Lee. Then he started to cry again, telling us how much he hates himself and them all for doing this. He felt so bad for Mrs. Kennedy and Mrs. Oswald. Then he really started to bawl. You saw Oswald's wife, the Soviet girl?"

Al nodded. "Yeah, Pretty little thing. Hardly speaks English, except maybe 'I don't know nothin'.' "

"Ruby said he sent her some money—'At least the Kennedys got dough,' he said, 'but she's dirt poor.' Oh, it was sad, seeing him, hearing him talk like that." She lowered her head. "Ruby crying, telling us he was just a nice Jewish boy from the Chicago ghetto, trying to make a living. He got his orders for the hit—he thought dying in the chair was better than at the hand of a vengeful enforcer for a screwed-up job. But now—"

"Well, if they won't even let him testify, that says a lot about what went on behind the scenes," Al said.

She nodded. "He said Lee was a good kid, he loved Kennedy, he was just a putz. Ruby didn't want to kill him, but he had to, he said. He kept saying how much he hated himself for it. He caved in to them, but he will never make peace with himself." Vikki inhaled and held back tears of her own. Ruby's sorrow, with his days numbered, tore her apart. "I actually reached over the table and took his hand." She reached as she did that day. "I said, 'Please, Jack, it's over. There's nothing you can do about it now,' and I called him Jack. I felt like I'd known him for years. He's that kind of guy."

"Sounds like Oswald wasn't the only putz in Dallas that day." Al leaned his elbow on the chair arm and rubbed his temples.

"He actually told me he felt sorry for me, for being another victim in this crime. Me, Jackie Kennedy, Marina Oswald, all their families, all the Americans who loved him, everybody all over the world. Just because a couple of rotten eggs had to knock Jack Kennedy off the throne. And then he surprised me. What he said showed me he's looking at the whole picture, something the plotters didn't: 'They're no better off with Lyndon Johnson.' "

"Unless he was in on it, too," Al said.

She held up a hand to halt that idea. "Oh, God forbid. It's bad enough as it is."

"So what does Ruby's lawyer say about his chances?" Al asked.

"He said his lawyer doesn't know how the retrial will come out." She blanched as another slice of that scene came back to her. "Ruby told us a kind of sick joke his lawyer made, when Ruby asked if he'd get the chair."

Al splayed his fingers. "Well? Let's hear it. I'll decide how sick it is."

"Ruby's lawyer told him, 'Jack, if you get it, don't sit down in it.' Ruby said it broke him up. He exploded into a fit of giggles right in front of us. It floored me. I sat there, kind of embarrassed. There he was, such a contrast to his heart-wrenching outburst of a minute before."

"Sounds like he's an emotional wreck." Al went to the minibar and took out a bottle, unscrewed the top, and took a swig. He sat back down.

"Ruby said that, besides the right-wingers, Marcello wanted JFK taken out, to get Bobby out of his hair. He wanted to set it up 'to make a nut take the blame,' as he put it."

"Hey, can you find somebody nuttier than that Commie ex-defector?" Al asked.

She nodded. "Ruby told us about some other kooks Oswald hung out with. This right-wing militant segregationist, David something…Ferrie, that's it. He lost all his hair and glues on his eyebrows. Ruby called them a cast of idiots."

"And now Ruby's one of 'em." Al frowned.

"But if they were such a cast of idiots, how did they pull off the crime of the century?" Vikki challenged him.

225

He couldn't answer that. "So what's the role of this David eyebrow-gluing guy in the cast?" he asked instead. "Did Ruby say?"

She shook her head. "He wasn't sure. He's a CIA operative and used to work for Marcello in New Orleans. Ruby met him and Lee around the same time. He lived in Dallas a while, then moved here to New Orleans. He was an Eastern Airlines pilot, of all things." She snickered. "Makes you think twice about flying, with him at the wheel."

"He still alive?" Al asked.

"Ruby said he was, but he predicted before long they'll all be six feet under. Ruby seems to think Marcello was the instigator behind the whole thing. He threatened to take JFK out all the time. But maybe somebody else beat him to it. Ruby wasn't high enough up to know any of that. But Earl Warren doesn't want any suspects other than Lee Harvey Oswald—and him."

"Did he tell you who gave him his orders to hit Oswald?"

She nodded. "One of Marcello's lieutenants, he didn't give a name. But he urged us to find this Benzo Bati. He's a good bet. He might be back here in town now, on Marcello's turf. He always did hits for Marcello, but that's no guarantee he drowned my husband. Ruby said Dallas was swarming with Marcello's gang that day. So it's a ray of hope."

Al sat up straight. "So we have something to go on, and we're already here." His tone encouraged her. "Ruby say anything else?"

"No, right then a man in a white coat came in with Captain Abner and tapped his watch." She paused. "Now this was the most bizarre part of the entire visit.

Ruby saw the guards and dashed to the far corner, covering his face with his hands, as if warding off a blow. He shouted, 'No, I don't want it! Keep away from me!' I sat there, stunned. As if the whole thing wasn't weird enough to begin with…"

"What was that about?" Al asked.

The white-coated guy said, 'It's time for your medicine, Mr. Ruby,' and he sounded like a babysitter enticing a kid to drink all his milk. Then Abner grabbed Ruby's arm and said, 'C'mon, Jack. We go through this every time,' or something like that."

"He must be on meds for depression or being a hothead or something," Al guessed.

"I don't know what meds he's on, or what they're doing to him." She shuddered at the memory of that disturbing scene. "Each guy held Ruby by an arm, then Ruby turned back to Rosie and me, shouting over his shoulder something like, 'See what they're doin' to me? They're tryin' a kill me! This is cancer they shoot into me! I tell you, they're killin' me!' I sat there, helpless, couldn't move a muscle, my heart in pieces for this poor victim. His pathetic shouts echoed through the room and died out as they dragged him away. I sat there and dropped my head in my hands. I was emotionally drained. I still am. It'll take decades to get over all this, if I ever do." Her voice cracked, weak and weary.

"It's okay, honey, you're strong, you'll survive this." He came over, knelt at her side and gave her a warm embrace.

She leaned into him, welcoming the comfort. "I kept hoping Ruby was putting on an act. Rosie said even when he knew Ruby in Chicago, he had a short fuse, always babbling about the end of the world and the oppression of the Jews and somebody always out to kill him. But, my God, he seemed so genuine."

"So now we have some homework to do." Al clasped her hands between his. "Then you can write Jack Ruby a thank-you note."

Chapter Fifteen

Al helped her out of their limo on rain-slicked Bourbon Street and entered the crowded il Tantino Ristorante at her heels. Rosie, already inside, cheek-kissed and pumped hands with a guy wearing an Italian flag tie tack.

The brick walls enclosed candlelit tables and scenes of Pompeii splashed on murals. A mandolin twanged in the distance.

"Vikki, meet Nappy Dibrizzi, a very dear friend of mine. We call him Nappy 'cause he was the first one of us to come over from Napoli." After the introductions, Nappy led them to a table and swept the Reserved sign away.

With a snap of Nappy's fingers, two waiters reported for duty. One held a chair out for Vikki and the other took their orders.

Three bottles of Sassicaia Tenuta San Guido appeared, corks popped, and Rosie led a toast: "To truth and health. *Salut.*"

They all drank to that, and the two *paisans* started gabbing about the old days. Rosie steered the subject to the JFK plot before the antipasto arrived.

"Ever since I know Marcello, he always hated the Kennedys." Nappy signaled a waiter, who dashed over and refilled the wine glasses. "It's no secret he talked about hittin' JFK to get Bobby out the way—word got around that after JFK got it, Marcello said, 'Bobby's just another lawyer now.' But it coulda been Marcello, coulda been anybody. Looks like they wanted to take their time, set it all up."

When Rosie said, "We just came from Sparky in jail," Vikki knew they were close to discussing the reason they were all there.

"Yeah, when I saw him gun down Oswald on TV, I knew Sparky was a dead man either way." Nappy gave a sad shake of his head. "If he refused to do that hit, he'd be sleepin' with the fishes. So now he's gonna die in the chair. Couldn't win."

Rosie nodded, stabbing his fork into a rolled-up slice of provolone. "My goddaughter here, her husband died in Dallas that same day, and she thinks there's a connection with his death to the JFK killing. The cops gave up, and she's trying to find out herself. Sparky told us to track down a Benzo Bati. He said you were once his boss. Do you know where he is, by any chance?"

Vikki's pulse raced. She held her breath. *Antipasto can wait.*

"Haven't seen him in years." Nappy shook his head. "After I got released, I don't want nothin' to do wit' the rackets, but can't get away from 'em, you know?" He dunked his bread in olive oil. "They're always in here, so I can't kick 'em out. But I don't do no other business with 'em. They come in here, they eat and pay their bill and leave. Lousy tippers, too."

"You ever hear of the Triumvirate?" Rosie speared a red pepper on the antipasto plate with a toothpick.

"Oh, yeah." Nappy nodded. "Gio Bati was in it before he died."

"You think the son was, too? Or still is?" Rosie asked him.

Nappy grabbed some prosciutto. "Would make sense, him takin' over for his old man."

"Yeah." Rosie bit into his bread. "Ruby told us about this Triumvirate, three guys that do hits for the government, or—whoever."

"Yeah, they do a lot of—whoever." Nappy sipped his wine. "That would make sense he'd be in it. Benzo was inna slammer, too, went back in, got out again. Second-degree murder, but he had the best defense lawyer in Louisiana, Maverick Brown, who plea-bargained it down to manslaughter. Last time I remember seein' Ben down here in the Quarter was four, five years ago. He was eatin' dinner with Lee Oswald's uncle, Dutz Murret, and another guy I didn't recognize."

"You knew Oswald and his uncle, too?" Vikki asked, astounded that all these guys were interconnected.

"Just from around. Just a noddin' hello kinda thing." He nodded. "We had mutual friends. Lee and his mother used to live here. Dutz was one of Marcello's runners."

"Any ideas where we can start to find Ben Bati?" Rosie asked as the waiters delivered the entrées.

"Dunno where he could be right now. But you can try his missus, Polly what's-'er-name." Nappy banged his fork against his plate as he thought. "They're separated, but she might still keep tabs on him."

"That's what she calls herself, ya know, her business name," Nappy said. "But what the hell's her last name? Some real WASP name. Oh, yeah. Smith.

She's, uh—a madam. Used to be, anyway. She retired. Her house is on Conti, but I don't remember the exact number, it's down toward the river, near Decatur. She might still live there, I'm not sure. Since I been married again, I don't get around as much, ya know." He sopped up gravy with his bread and shoved it into his mouth, chewing with gusto.

"That's an unusual name, even for a madam," Vikki commented as Al jotted it down. "Polly was the name of one of Jack the Ripper's victims," she said to no one in particular.

Nappy wound his linguine onto his fork. "That's the name she always went by, anyway. She used to sing, too. Sometimes at the Jazz Alley on Bourbon and Saint Pete. You might find 'er there. Man, what a voice. What a body. Over forty and still looks va-va-va-voom." A dreamy smile came across his face as he twirled his fork against a spoon. "Hey, let me know when you come across her; tell her to stop in. It's been a long time. Too long. It'd be nice just to see her. You know—just talk. No monkey business."

Al looked at Vikki and squeezed her hand. This public gesture didn't faze her as being too forward. She knew it was his way of saying they were onto something. It didn't carry the playfulness of a wink.

Her mind raced ahead of her: *Will I ever see him again after all this is settled?* She pushed the thought away and tried to enjoy her bistecca. This wasn't about her and Al; it was about Jack. Her whimsy had no place here and now.

She cut into her steak, knowing Jack would've gotten a kick out of this Italian feast in the middle of The Big Easy.

****

They split up to track down Polly. Rosie knew his way around the French Quarter, due to his misspent youth there, and Vikki had a map, so they each staked out separate territory. The hired limo stayed parked at their hotel.

Rosie warned, "You can go in the bars and ask if anybody knows her or where on Conti her house is, or walk down Conti and see if you spot what looks like a classy cathouse. But tell 'em you're a relative and just wanna look her up, or they'll get suspicious and think you're an undercover cop or somethin'. Don't sound like you're anxious to find her."

"Then I'd better belt down a good ol' Old Fashioned." She turned to Al. "Are you an Old Fashioned kinda guy?"

"When I'm with you—I gotta be."

They shared a smile over that quip as they headed for the Jazz Alley, where Nappy said Polly sometimes sang. It was closed, so they went across the street to Maison Bourbon, and Al cased the joint.

"Al, you don't have to do that. Who even knows we're here? We came by train, spur of the moment," she said as they sat at the bar.

"Nothing's spur of the moment. Don't tell me how to do my job and I won't tell you how to do yours, little girl," he warned.

So if it made him feel important, let him case every joint like Peter Gunn. She gratefully sucked down half her Old Fashioned without stopping and enjoyed the buzz that followed. Al's eyes darted around over the rim of his glass. But she heaved a contented sigh sitting at the mahogany bar with the brass rail, and shut out the world; she didn't feel a bit threatened. Who the hell knew them in New Orleans?

"Aldobrandi!"

They turned around, startled.

"Huh?" Al's wary expression softened from astonishment to pleasure with a grin as he hugged and cheek-pecked a woman whose face Vikki couldn't yet see. But what she could see were the dame's hands all over him.

"Rita! *Madonna mia!* What the hell you doin' here?" He introduced Vikki without waiting for an answer. "This is Rita Remo, an, uh, we, uh, we go way back. Rita, this is Victoria Ward."

Vikki chuckled at his struggle to find a way to say "old flame." As old flames went, she was slender, redheaded, and her false eyelashes reached into floozy territory.

"I came for Mardi Gras and decided to stick around for a few extra days. Were you here for Mardi Gras too?" She sounded like she was trying to cover up a Brooklyn accent with a southern drawl—but why? Vikki wondered.

Before he could cook up a story, Vikki jumped in, fueled by the buzz and some reckless urge she couldn't define. "We're on a pre-honeymoon. We're not married yet." She draped her arms around Al's neck, and he gaped at her like she'd just sprouted a third breast. "When we met it was love at first sight, and we haven't taken our hands off each other since. Have we, Porksword?"

"Uh—"

Rita raised her brows in grudging acceptance, but didn't notice anything unusual about her former beau squirming like he'd just sat on a tack.

"Congratulations." The drawl flattened. "When's the big day?"

She'd addressed it to Al, but Vikki jumped right in. "Tonight. We're eloping."

"Hey, you're a sly one, you rogue." Rita chucked Al on the chin. "Last time, you had that little lady in Florida on hold, the family arrangement." She turned to Vikki. "How'd you manage to drag him away from that, dearie?"

"Nobody's dragging me. I just want to make sure the shotgun don't go off here," he fired back.

A few seconds of silence as all eyes met, then Rita addressed Vikki, "So, there's a bun in the oven. Hope it looks like you, dearie, and not this *faccia brutta* here."

Rita pulled a business card out of her purse. "Al, give me a buzz, and we'll get together. You can tag along, too, dearie," she added without really looking at Vikki.

"I wouldn't otherwise dream of imposing on your fond memories, but we're leaving town tomorrow. We have to get out of here before his other intended finds out about us, and I don't mean Mona, the spurned arranged bride—this is somebody else altogether," Vikki kept playing along, not caring what kind of damage she was inflicting on the smoldering embers of Al's affair with this woman. She got a kick out of getting back at him for his surprise introduction to Mona, and watched his squirming with unconcealed glee, something else she hadn't felt in ages.

"Another one on the hook—well, you haven't changed your spots, Poet. I thought you'd grow up and straighten out, but it looks like you're the same old tomcat you always were. Keep a close eye on him, dearie, or better yet, keep him in chains," she stage-whispered to Vikki. "Good luck making an honest man out of him."

"I already have." With her smug reply, she ran her fingers through his hair, rubbing her leg against his. She had to stop when he looked like he was enjoying it. "Some of his body parts have my name tattooed on them."

"Well, then, don't let him wear it off. Congratulations. Great seeing you again, Poet. Keep in touch. Nice meeting you, dearie." She gave a finger wave and turned on a heel.

He stammered a goodbye as Vikki sucked down her drink and burst out laughing at the sheer astonishment on his face. "Poet?"

"Now, what the hell was that about?" he asked through gritted teeth before polishing off his own Old Fashioned.

"Didn't think I had it in me, did you?" She signaled the bartender. "Didn't know I could have a little fun. Thought I was all surly and serious. Well, one thing Jack taught me was to make room for some absurdity when things get too serious. You have to take a break and stop and just go nuts, even if it's only for a few minutes. Do something madcap, something you wouldn't dare do in the day-to-day grind. He did those things too often. I don't do them often enough. But at this point, I was just about due to exercise my flip side. Sorry I ruined what could've been a perfect evening for you with an old flame."

"Yeah, I would've liked to get together with her again; we were a hot item for a while." He squashed his cigarette on the floor like a bug.

"Uh-uh-uh." She wagged her finger. "Don't forget, you've got sweet little Mona at home waiting for you to come back and marry her."

"She can wait. *Madonne*," he droned as his eyes followed the sway of his old flame's buttocks exiting the bar. "Would've been nice to get some of that again. Re-e-e-eal nice."

"Your job is to protect me."

"I can do two things at once." His eyes stabbed her. "Or three."

She eyed him up and down—and up again. "With only one brain and just enough blood to service one body part at a time? I sincerely doubt it."

Then she left him to figure that out while she addressed the bartender. "Another round for me and my Old Fashioned guy here."

****

The next night, Vikki and Al stepped out into a driving rain. Al, brandishing typical Sicilian chivalry, refused to share her umbrella, but she got wet anyway.

They stopped in three bars without learning the whereabouts or address of Polly Smith. It seemed nobody wanted to admit they knew a madam or the address of a brothel. The Jazz Alley was open, so they hung out there a while, mainly to keep dry, but the music helped.

When the piano player went on break, she approached him. "Hello, I'm Vikki Ward. You play a mean 'Maple Leaf Rag.' "

"Hey, thanks, any requests?" He mopped his brow with a handkerchief.

"Just one…okay, two. 'Stardust.' And where I can

find Polly Smith. She sings in here sometimes. Please? It's extremely important to me," she added, for good measure.

He shook his head. "I haven't seen Polly in a long time. She retired a few years back. She did run a booming business, on Conti. The best whor—uh, bordello in town. I don't think she lives there anymore. She might just run it like an absentee owner, if she does still own it."

She glanced at Al and tried to keep the hope in her voice. "Where on Conti?"

"I don't remember the number, but it's a big brick house, toward the river, fifth or sixth one in. She stepped down in—" He glanced upward. "Oh, early sixty-one. But I think she might still have a hand in runnin' the place. When she announced her retirement, she threw a big bash there, had the cops over, the mayor, seemed all of N'awlins was at that party."

Cops and the mayor attending a retirement bash for a madam in her French Quarter bordello? Things sure hadn't changed much since the good old days.

They hooked up with Rosie again in Jackson Square at 7:00 as planned, and she gave him her no-luck story.

"I didn't find out anything definite." Rosie frowned. "But I looked up some more old contacts here. Let's go for dinner, and I'll tell ya about it."

They all settled in at Galatoire's and looked over the menus, entirely in French. She put hers down, too agitated to get excited over the Creole cuisine.

"Okay, who did you find, Rosie?"

"I did some askin' around and found out another old friend of mine who lives here has connections to the cops: my buddy Maximo Astore. We called him Floody. Floody's an ex-cop and was one of the worst. Now he does whatever the hell he wants. Him and his wife Mimi own a string of hotels, resorts, horses. They live the good life on an estate in Kenner. He come down to Florida to visit me a few times. Now maybe I can get him to return the favor. He might know where Benzo Bati or Polly are. He used to know everybody, and if we're in luck, he still does. I called him, but he wasn't home. I'll try again later."

"Any way we can get to Marcello himself?" she asked after they ordered. "Why not go right to the top, as long as we're here."

"Nah." Rosie shook his head. "It'd be a waste of time; he won't talk to me."

"But I heard he was a real nice guy," Al said.

"We never had nothin' to do with each other," Rosie told him. "He was just another punk kid in Chicago. He was always jealous of me 'cause of my connection to Capone. Marcello wasn't in with Capone the way he woulda liked to be."

"So now what?" she asked, too weary to savor her shrimp étouffée. "I still have to find Polly. She's supposed to live in a suburb somewhere."

"Somebody that well known shouldn't be hard to track down around here," he assured her, tackling his oysters Bienville. "Let's eat first."

Afterwards, as they went in and out of more bars, she thought she saw someone tailing them, but she banished that thought immediately. This was no time to get melodramatic.

****

It was past midnight when they got back to the

hotel, but she didn't feel like going to her room to watch TV, mourn over Jack, or lie in bed sleepless. So she bade the gentlemen goodnight. When she was sure they'd retired, she headed down to the hotel bar.

But not a minute later, Al pulled up the stool next to her, sporting a polo shirt and khaki slacks. He'd shaved, too. Wow, what a fast dresser! Another point in his favor.

That good point wiped out at least two and a half of his faults.

"Can't give you the slip for nothing, can I? Or are you an insomniac, too?" she asked as he offered her one of his Newports. She welcomed the cold sting of menthol in her lungs.

"Both. I'm not about to let you sit at bars alone, little girl." He ordered a Moretti's and tossed a fin on the bar. So he planned on staying a while.

"I'm finally at the point where I can stand to be alone." She blew smoke toward the ceiling. "I don't need constant company; I'm not one of those people who has to be surrounded by admirers twenty-four hours a day."

"Who said anything about admirers?" he shot back.

She slanted him a look that didn't serve its purpose when she broke into a grin. He looked damn good, and she was glad he was here. Sitting alone at bars wasn't her thing, but it beat lying alone in bed.

"I'm your bodyguard, remember?"

"You're off duty now." She glanced at her watch.

"I'm never off duty."

"Then how could you have gotten together with your old flame?" she quizzed.

"I'd've got Ange to cover for me. I know the

reason for that act—you just didn't want me to be with her, did you?" His smirk told her he'd figured her out.

"I was just having some fun. I don't care who you go carousing with. What you do on your own time is your business." She forced conviction into her voice. In reality, the ugly green head of jealousy had reared itself and squeezed her heart.

"Then why the one-act play? It was like something out of a bad soap opera." He snickered.

"It was a spur-of-the-moment impulse, and I thought it was pretty damn effective. I had fun. She was sure convinced. So, you want to be with her so bad, go be with her. Tell her it was all a joke. Go ahead." She waved him away like a fly.

He sat there looking at her, even after his beer came.

"Go ahead. Go." But of course she didn't want him to move an inch.

His chest expanded, his muscles straining under his shirt. "It seemed like a good idea at the time, you know, one of those things you do without thinking, but now, sitting with you alone here—" He heaved a sigh. "What is it that you do to me? I haven't been the same guy since I've been around you. I'm becoming"—he shifted uncomfortably—"principled."

"So, what's wrong with that? Are there any particular benefits to being a jerk?" She hoped he'd give her a believable answer.

His gaze deepened as she removed her glasses with a provocative batting of her lashes, wishing she'd worn the fake ones.

"It got me places." He drew his barstool closer.

"Maybe when you were young. But you're not so

young anymore, and being a gentleman will get you a lot more places than you ever got as a wayward youth." She punctuated that with a come-hither smile. But he was already as hither as he could be in public.

"Yeah? Like somewhere near your territory maybe?" He cocked a brow.

"Now, what fun would it be, knowing way in advance like that?" She cocked a brow right back at him.

"How far in advance?"

"I'd rather you sweat out the—" An electric current shot through her. She hadn't felt anything like it since she and Jack were at the flirting stage—"anticipation."

Oh, yes, Aldobrandi Gambaloto Emiliano Raimondino Po turned her on. *I can't help it, God.* She apologized silently as her gaze left Al and she bowed her head.

"Anticipation tortures me more each day," he spoke with reverence, as if reciting his favorite verse. "Now I know how thin that line between agony and ecstasy really is."

"Okay, I know enough Shakespeare to safely assume you didn't steal that from the Bard." She called on her playful tone. "But if it's original, I must applaud it. Is that why she called you Poet?"

"I didn't make any rhymes," he said.

"You don't have to. Not every poem rhymes."

"Did it sound like a poem?" He sipped his drink.

"A weak attempt at haiku, maybe." She chuckled.

"If I knew how, I'd set it to music, *cara mia*. It came right from the heart."

She believed him. And now she had a lot of thinking to do. "I'm going up to my room—I have a few things to sort out in my head. Thanks for coming down here to watch me." The moment called for it, so she gave his knee a quick caress as she told him goodnight.

"It's my job," he declared.

"I wonder how many guys would give crucial parts of their anatomy for your job right now," she teased.

"A bodyguard wouldn't be very protective without certain parts of his anatomy, *cara mia*." He held his glass up to her. She could feel his eyes following her out of the bar as she walked out. In an instant he strode beside her.

"You don't think I'm letting you go alone." He cupped her elbow. "I just wanted to finish my drink. I can't knock them back as fast as you."

She ignored that.

Before they got on the elevator, she noticed someone out of the corner of her eye, watching them. Was it the same one she'd thought was following them before? He did have a fedora on, like the other guy.

But lots of guys wore fedoras. Rosie wore a fedora. Jack Ruby wore a fedora when he shot Oswald. What did that say about guys who wore fedoras?

She refused to worry.

She bade Al goodnight at her door. He waited till she was locked in.

At two a.m. she still hadn't slept. She sat up in the easy chair, thinking of what had transpired in the bar, on New Year's Eve, and everything in between. She was falling for another man, and as professionally as he behaved, she knew it wasn't any easier for him.

Their relationship was highly improbable and extremely improper.

Knowing all that, she reached over and dialed his room anyway. "May I speak to Al, please?" she asked Angelo.

"He went out."

"Did he say where?" she asked.

"Nope. But I'm coverin' for 'im. You want somethin'?"

"No. I'm in my room and staying here." Her voice flat, she fought the shattering disappointment.

"I know. I'm keepin' an eye on your door. *Ciao*."

Where had he gone? Not that she was worried. Just disappointed. And—yes, jealous. She tried to chase that green-eyed monster away with a vigorous scrub under a hot shower and a few purse-size bourbon bottles from the minibar.

She poured a can of beer over her head, slathered on face cream, and slept in curlers that night—for the few hours she slept.

****

She would rather have not found out where he'd trotted off to last night. The next morning when they met at breakfast, something pink fell out of Al's coat pocket. She bent over to pick it up for him, and he nearly knocked her over to get to it first.

It was a pair of lacy panties. With an embarrassed laugh he stuffed it back into his pocket.

"Do you want to know where I was last night?" he asked when Rosie went to the tobacconist next door.

"It's obvious." She didn't want to look at him. "Let's hear no more about it."

"You kept telling me to go," he blathered, "if I wanted to go so bad, to go—"

"I said I don't want to hear it." It killed her to keep

her voice at a civilized level.

"Okay. You're the one who said it was none of your business." He turned away and lit a cigarette.

That could've been me in his arms last night, the jealous half of Vikki bristled.

But at least your honor's still intact, argued her righteous half.

He'll probably see that woman again here—and again in New York, the jealous Vikki carped.

Don't be like those women JFK "couldn't get rid of," lectured Righteous Vikki.

Neither half of her walked away from that one satisfied.

****

Rosie and his old pal Floody hugged and cheek-kissed and back-slapped and yabbered away for a few minutes. Then Rosie did the introductions.

"Vikki, this is my *paisan*, Floody Astore. Floody taught me almost everything I knew by the time I got to New York. He was wise beyond his years when we were kids."

Wise beyond his years? He'd been a crooked cop. Well, from what her father had told her, some of the smartest ones were the crooks.

Still, he looked at least as well-preserved as Rosie. And his teeth were his own.

They all sat inside his glassed-in porch overlooking the river, and a violinist played Vivaldi while they ate manicotti.

Then, and only then, after espresso and cannolis, they got down to business.

"So, can any of the cops around here help find this guy, or any leads, or at least find his ex-wife, this Polly dame?" Rosie asked.

Floody nodded as he crooked a finger in the air. His personal server dashed over, flicked the ash off his cigar for him, and gave it back.

"Prob'ly." He puffed away. "Me, I don't know where either of 'em went. Bati I haven't seen in years. His wife, she got a mansion out of town someplace."

"Nobody seems to know where, though," Vikki said.

"She should be easy enough to find. Try Lieutenant Louie Lavoie at police headquarters. I know Louie all his life. He might not be able to tell you where Bati is, but I know he'll know where Polly is. I'll call him and tell him to expect you. I wish I could help you myself, but I'm outta action for a while now, doing legit business. It's just easier when you get old."

"Yeah, sure, I know." Rosie ran a hand over the hair he'd dyed between Dallas and now. "I'm gettin' old myself."

Floody went to call Lieutenant Lavoie as a bevy of servants swarmed in to clean up and ask if they wanted anything else. Rosie dropped a ten-spot in the violinist's case and asked for an encore. He played "Santa Lucia."

They said their *ciao*s under Floody's portico as Rosie's chauffeur waited at the open door to their limo.

"Hey, I owe ya one," Rosie told Floody. Vikki's eyes narrowed in suspicion, remembering her father's warning on one of his muses about the good ol' days: "Never let these guys do you a favor, 'cause they always expect one in return."

"Fugget it," Floody said, and she hoped he meant it as Rosie extended an invitation to Palm Beach.

Maybe at their age that's all favors were anymore.

****

Apparently Lieutenant Lavoie didn't do that kind of business during business hours, so he offered to meet them at the Burgundy Inn later on.

Settled at their table, Vikki glanced over her shoulder every few minutes. Al caught on after the third glance.

"What's wrong?" he asked as they ordered drinks and waited for Lavoie to show up.

She didn't want to tell him about this, or alert Rosie. She was probably just seeing things. The streets were still crowded, even though Mardi Gras was over; it could've been anybody.

She replied a blunt, "Nothing."

"You think we're being followed, don't you?"

She rolled her eyes. "Are you a mind reader, too? You read wrong."

"If you do, you'd better tell me," he demanded. "This ain't the set of *Have Gun Will Travel*, you know."

She tried to turn the tables. "It isn't nineteenth-century Tombstone, Arizona, either."

"I'll look out for anyone suspicious," he insisted. Then, to her annoyance, he turned to Rosie and opened his big trap. "We might have a tail on us."

"You're goin' back to New York tomorrow," Rosie ordered.

"Absolutely not, Rosie." She stood her ground. "I have to do this. I never said we were being followed. It was something Al dreamed up." She shot Al a sneer.

Amidst this three-way bout, Lieutenant Lavoie showed up in plainclothes. They all shook hands, and he sat down.

His story was the same as everyone else's. "I haven't seen Bati in years. She's around, though. She went by 'Polly' when she ran the brothel. Now she's probably gone back to her real name. What was it? Oh, yeah. Hortense."

No wonder she went by Polly.

After the thinly disguised bribe of a dinner, Lavoie made a call and came back with Polly's address in Metairie.

"Good, that's not far from here." Rosie greased Lavoie's palm before they parted company. "For the police fund," he said, but she knew better—that money was strictly pocket-lining.

****

In Vikki's brief phone conversation with Polly, she introduced herself, told Polly who'd referred her, and summed up her situation in one sentence: "My husband was killed, and I have reason to believe your husband may have killed him."

"Well, since you're a friend of Louie's and Floody's—they've always been mah best customers—you can come ovah and we can chit-chat." The melodious drawl floated over the phone wire.

"Can I come over now? Please?" Vikki begged. "I can't bear to be stuck here, frustrated, jerked around, stalked—" It poured out of her. "Pleeeeease, Polly," she pleaded in her most pitiful tone. "This means so much to me."

"A'right, c'mon ovah, sugar."

Vikki nearly cried with relief. She couldn't spend another night so close yet so far.

Chapter Sixteen

"I want to go see Polly alone, and I mean alone," Vikki asserted as their driver headed for Metairie. "She'll be much more willing to talk if it's just another woman instead of two bruisers and an ex-mob boss."

"Maybe she got a point there." Rosie told both bodyguards. He turned to Vikki. "You should be safe enough in there. But we'll wait in the car. You're packin' your piece, too, right?"

She patted her purse. "Oh, yes, I'm packin', Rosie."

Now that was settled, she looked out the window at the passing scenery, wondering if Al would visit his girlfriend again. Before that ugly green monster reared its head, a happy thought lifted her spirits. *You're closer to your goal.* But once she reached that goal, Al would return to his life and she to hers.

What life?

That was her next goal.

****

The car halted at the end of Polly Smith's long tree-lined driveway. Vikki let out a whistle as she ogled the antebellum mansion. "Madaming sure provides her a comfortable living." But when Polly opened the door—pow! The contrast between the tasteful digs and madam's appearance rivaled the difference between seared foie gras and chicken gumbo. Her brassy teased hair nearly scraped the eleven-foot ceiling. Bangles and beads dangled from her earlobes, wrists, neck, fingers, and ankles. But everything she wore, from her lipstick to her feathered satin slippers, harmonized in complementary shades of red—that matched the wallpaper.

"Take a load off, dawlin'. You look beat," she offered in a velvety drawl and guided Vikki to a plush fainting couch. "Kick your shoes off, stretch yur laigs."

Why not? She slid the shoes off and dug her stockinged feet into the deep pile carpet. "Do I call you Polly, or Hortense—or something else?"

"I prefer Polly. I'm much more of a Polly, don't you reckon?"

Vikki was thinking more along the lines of a Pearl or a Ruby, but Polly was suitable enough.

Polly poured an aged brandy, and a maid put out shrimp cocktail. "When you called, I was skeery. I thought you were either a cop or somebody trying to catch me with mah bloomers down. I still have a hand in the business, even though I'm not there on the premises no more. But I reckoned even if you were the law, I'd want to see what this is about. Some excitement is due me. It's been slow as molasses in January here lately."

Maybe she retired too early.

"No, I'm no cop." Vikki wiggled her toes. "I'm just a widow trying to untangle a web."

Polly twisted a cigarette into a rhinestone-encrusted holder. "Well, here's mah story: Ben and I started a high-class brothel on Conti Street. It got to be known as The Convent and I was the Mother Superior. The gals were the sisters. He recruited sisters as well as customers, and before long it was busier'n a stump-tailed cow in fly time. The money rolled in." She gestured and her bangles tinkled. "Brought in some beauties, too. All had big knockers, some real, some not. Didn't hurt business none. He always was a titty man. Business boomed. I ran a tight ship, and before long he started howlin' about the paltry allowance I was givin' him, and how I was spending it all on the house and clothes for the sisters and booze for the customers." A smile played on her lips. "But he had perks: he used to spend the wee hours upstairs, takin' away the sisters from payin' customers, eatin' up the profits, pardon the bad pun. We had another of our usual fights about how I never give him enough money. I tol' him he always spent the night sampling the wares for free, and he split. He walked out on me with an *au 'voir* and never came back. I haven't seen him in gon' on…" She paused and counted on her fingers. "Better part of eight years."

She got up and headed for her antique cherry secretary. "This was mah callin' card." She handed Vikki a gold-embossed card with a phone number—no name or address.

Vikki nodded. "Very discreet. How long were you and your husband together?"

"Five years. I found mahself expectin' and wanted to legitimize the chile. Now he's at military school, gon' to West Point next year. At least my son's gon' the right way in life. I made sure of that. But Ben—" She sighed. "Ben Bati's short for Benzo Battolini, fer the record. But his middle name is t-r-o-u-b-l-e. Like a bad penny, it'll follow him around till he dies."

"I know the type." Vikki nibbled on a shrimp. "You have any idea what his connection might be to what I told you about on the phone?"

"Well," Polly began—the way she said it, "well" was two syllables—"after leavin' the Army, he joined the Carlos Marcello organization. Then he worked for Nofio Dibrizzi, a lieutenant of Marcello's they all call Nappy. Then he joined Dutz Murret, over on Lafayette Street in the Vieux Carré, where they ran a bookie joint together for a while. Lee Oswald was his nephew and used to work out of Felix's Oyster Bar and Restaurant as a runner for the Marcello gang, too. They're all thicker'n thieves. That's why I wasn't surprised when I found out they nabbed Lee for JFK's killin'. They're all connected, like a fence made o' bobbed wahr."

"I noticed that, too." Vikki nodded. "They all seem to know each other."

"Yeah, they're birds of a feather, a'right. It was no surprise when Ben got mixed up with Dutz and that Fair Play for Cuba thang Lee and his cronies worked for, handin' out leaflets on the corner, all that crazy stuff. Then they did a flip-flop and went against Cuba. Enough to make your haid spin." She twirled her forefinger around her ear.

"Yeah, that CIA splinter group, the Cuban Revolutionary Council. A Fed told my husband about it, in a taped interview," Vikki remembered. Once more, her memory flashed back to the job she'd had in D.C. "Why wouldn't these guys be tight? They all have a common goal."

"Yey-ah, I used to hear Ben and Dutz and their friends talking late at night when I'd come in, catch a few snatches of chit-chat." Polly nodded and her earrings clinked. "Seems Lee was a CIA recruit. After his Marines hitch, they sent him to the USSR, where he married that Russky gal and defected over there. Then they brought him back to the U.S.—lots of shady stuff going on with him and the CIA. And Ben, he always wanted to be a big hotshot, like in the movies. He went to marksman school in the Army and was a crack shot, so it didn't take him long to get mixed up with those gents." She held up both hands and shook her head. "I don't want to go off half-cocked—he never told me direct; I just know what I overheard."

"You ever overhear anything about him being in a group called the Triumvirate?" Vikki perched at the edge of her seat.

"Yey-ah, I knew he was in somethin' like that. I thought it was one of those crazy lodges like the Elks or somethin'." She tapped her fingers on her chin.

"Oh, no, it's hardly like the Elks," Vikki corrected her.

"Well, I never paid much attention to his comin's and goin's anyway." Polly examined her lollipop-red nails. "I was too busy with the business and raisin' the boy. Ben did his thang, and I did mine."

Vikki couldn't help being astounded at how little some wives knew about their husbands. Then she stopped herself cold. Who was she to talk? "The Triumvirate are a trio of top-rated assassins. And it looks like your husband's the cream of the crop."

Polly didn't bat a false eyelash. "Figgers."

"Do you know where he is now?"

Polly stretched her shapely legs and propped her feet on her cocktail table. "Well, I ain't seen him since Junior's tenth birthday, and he's gon' on eighteen now. He don't keep in touch with the boy like a normal daddy, either. Oh, no, he just tosses a few greenbacks this way on the kid's birthday, if he remembers, and at Christmas, if he's feeling generous. Postmarked all over the U.S. and sometimes even Yurp—one came from It'ly, an international money order. So he gets around. Hard to pin down."

"Didn't you ever try to sue him for child support?" Vikki probed.

"Once, but I don't need his scummy money now. I support me and mah boy comf'tably. He ought to've come see the boy once in a while, watch him grow up. I don't chase him around, though. Any man who walks out on his wife ain't worth mah time. He's always on the lam. I do hear about him now and then, through this one or that one."

"How come you never divorced him?"

Polly shrugged. "I'd rather stay married, 'cause I don't want to wind up stewed in Sin City, married to some dude whose name I don't remember the next day. So it's like an insurance policy for me."

"When did you hear about him last?" *Oh, how I wish I had a tape recorder!* Vikki thought.

"During Mardi Gras, I overheard some good ol' boys gabbin' at a shindig in Fat City, and by what they said, Ben could've been in Dallas that very day."

"It looks like he was," Vikki confirmed. "So where might he be now?"

Polly took a long drag of her cigarette. "Oh, Lordy, he could be anywhere. He likes to stay on the run, has the itchiest damn feet I ever know'd. He could've gotten hisself killed since the JFK shooting, for all I know. I'm always waiting for that phone call from the morgue or whoever calls you to tell you your husband's dead—yikes!" Her hand flew to her beaded neck, and she hiccupped. "Oh, I do apologize, dawlin'. *Faux pas.*"

Vikki nodded. "It's okay. I'm learning to handle it."

"I'll sure let you know when I hear from him next or if I hear anything about where he is."

A welcome wave of hope washed over Vikki. "Polly, how can I thank you?"

"By comin' on back after you find out what happened, and we'll go out and pull a plank off the wall. You come on back down here and be mah guest. We'll really whoop it up. We'll each have something to celebrate, if Ben did have something to do with it. I'd love to see him git what's comin' to him once and for all." Polly stood, and Vikki followed her lead.

"It's a deal." She trailed Polly to the door.

When they hugged, Vikki caught a whiff of Tabu perfume.

Out on the street, she looked both ways. Nope, nobody lurking around. Al jumped out of the limo and helped her in.

"Well?" they all asked at once.

"Ben's on the lam, and all arrows point to us having our man." She rambled on about his CIA involvements, her mind working a mile a minute. "Rosie, Remember those ex-CIA agents I worked for at that security consulting firm in Washington D.C.?"

"Yeah?"

"They gave me an open invitation to come back whenever I wanted." Actually, it was one guy in particular, Ray Strauss, who'd had a wicked case of the hots for her. The only single guy in the firm, he courted and wined and dined her with dogged persistence. But he just didn't ring her bell. Then Jack came along...

She didn't want to reveal all this. But her mind wandered back to Ray. He'd taken her to the nation's capital's best nightspots, restaurants, and cultural events. They'd spent hours engaged in long, deep discussions. He was a genuine human being; she just couldn't return his ardent feelings. He promised he'd be there for her if she ever wanted to come back, and he said he'd reserved a special place in his heart for her. Sweet without being saccharine. Personable. Genuine. But the sparks only flew one way.

They still exchanged Christmas cards, and he always enclosed a little note wishing her well, never failing to mention that he was still a bachelor.

So she hoped a decade hadn't changed his feelings.

It was a long shot, but stranger things did happen.

****

"Now I'm gonna take you for the best New Orleans meal you've ever had." On their final evening in New Orleans, Rosie led them down Decatur Street toward the river. A steady wind gave her a chill, and Al kept her warm as well as covered.

"Oh, not more Creole, Rosie. I'll settle for a Howard Johnson," Vikki moaned.

"Nope. Even better. Remember those muffulettas I told you about?"

"Oh, yeah, we never did get around to having those." Thoughts of a drippy sandwich spurred her hunger

"It's here." They entered a small deli under a sign, Progress Grocery, and Rosie ordered four muffulettas.

They sat at one of the small tables and chowed down on the jawbreaker sandwiches heaped with layers of provolone, mortadella, Genoa salami, and capicola ham. The spread on top, a mix of chopped olives, garlic, celery, and onions in oil, soaked into the huge round Italian roll, as big as the plates they were served on.

"Now this is livin'." Rosie happily chomped. "We gotta get one of these places in Palm Beach."

"That could get dangerous," Al commented.

They walked off their muffulettas, stopping in bars and listening to jazz till three a.m. just like regular tourists.

Until the shots went off.

She'd heard shots enough times to know they were no firecrackers. At the second shot, Al cried out in pain.

He drew his gun and sprinted down the street after a shadowy figure. Angelo shoved her into the doorway of a closed store. "Get down!" He slid his gun from its holster and covered her body with his.

Rosie crouched, his gun drawn.

Two shots rang out in the distance.

Al came back, clasping his left arm. "I got him in the leg. But he jumped in a car and took off. Runs like a racehorse, even with a limp."

"Are you all right?" Her heart stuck in her throat. "You're going to bleed to death!" She rushed up to him and examined his arm. "It's not hemorrhaging, but I'm worried sick anyway." She looked into his eyes.

He gave her a smile that looked forced. "It's not serious, just grazed me. I'll live."

"We have to get you to a doctor!" she shrieked.

"Yeah, I'll find you one." Rosie took Al by his good arm. "We'll go to the Lorraine Hotel; it's a block away." Al still insisted on walking directly behind her.

"I'm okay, it's not bleedin' too much. I'll wrap a belt around it. I don't need a doctor." Al walked with his arm up.

"The hell you don't!" Rosie barked.

"I've been shot before." Al jammed his gun back into the holster.

"Then you're running outta chances." Rosie picked up the pace.

"I'm not sittin' in no emergency room all night." Al spat on the ground.

They reached the hotel entrance. Vikki opened the door for them. "I ain't takin' you to the emergency room," Rosie said. "I'll find you a doctor who'll keep his trap shut about the whole thing. In other words, a doctor who's got a price. But just walk through the lobby to the phones like nothin' happened."

A stab of fear took her breath away; getting shot at stretched even her limits. The thought of him dying made her shudder till her teeth rattled.

They entered the lobby and followed Rosie to the pay phones.

"Whoever you thought was tailing us since we've been here finally had the brass to take a shot," Al said to her.

"I never said anybody was tailing us!" she hissed under her breath.

"Well, they are now." His eyes darted around as he held his arm.

Rosie called his buddy Floody and got the name of a trusted sawbones. "We're goin' to see a Dr. Plante at the edge of the French Quarter here. He'll fix your arm, we pay him his fee, and then that's the end of that. Damn. For this money he don't even do a house call.

I'll be a crab's ass."

Looking as casual as possible, they made their way back through the lobby and into a taxi.

"Uh—I didn't say nothin' back there, but I should tell you now, Al." Rosie nudged him. "Plante's not a people doctor."

"What does he do?" Al asked. "Fix sick plants?"

"Nah. He's a vet."

"A vet? Like a guy who works on cats and dogs and birds? Why the hell'd you get me a vet?" he thundered.

"He's the only doctor Floody could get," Rosie said. "His usual doctor is over at Marcello's place tending one of his boys. So he's the only one could do it."

"Yeah, but—a dog doctor?" Al gestured at his head. "Do you see floppy ears and a tail here?"

"Hey, a wound's a wound. What's the difference it's a human or a bird or a gol'fish? Just sit there an' cool your jets. Your heart beats faster, it'll make it bleed more." Rosie squeezed Al's good arm.

Al mumbled in Sicilian, and Vikki grasped his hand. "It'll be okay," she soothed. "I'm sure a vet's just as good if it's a superficial wound like you say it is."

"Dammit, I should've never got into this mess," he groaned, blowing air between his teeth.

She hoped he didn't mean that.

"Ah, shaddup, willya?" Rosie gave Al a light smack on the side of the head, and it worked. Al didn't make a sound till they got to Dr. Plante's estate.

"Well, well, a two-legged patient," the doctor remarked as he led Al into his examining room. "Don't get too many of those."

He closed the door. Vikki paced the waiting room like an expectant father.

Ten minutes later, Al came back out with his arm bandaged and holding a bottle of pills. "He'll live," Dr. Plante assured them as Rosie peeled off several bills and stuck them into the doc's shirt pocket.

"Not them things you give horses, are they?" Al studied the pill bottle's label. "I used to work with horses, and horse tranquilizers will put me out of my misery permanently."

"No, no." The doc chuckled. "They're people pills. You should have that looked at when you get back home, too. But it should be all right."

"Thanks so much, Doctor." Vikki pumped his hand, but Al kept mumbling as they piled back into the waiting taxi.

Plante followed them out and reached into his pocket. "Oh, here. For Mr. Al. This'll make you feel better, too." Al promptly unwrapped the proffered lollipop and shoved it into his mouth.

Only when they got back to their hotel did Al take a look at the wrapper. "God dammit, look what that *ciuccio* gave me!"

She took a look and couldn't help cracking up.

It was a doggy lollipop.

⚜⚜⚜

"The last thing I want to do is sleep," she admitted to him at the door to her suite. "Why don't you come in for a while?"

"Yeah, I'm a million miles from sleep myself."

No innuendo, no suggestive winks. She simply needed company.

She got wine and glasses from the minibar and they

settled on the couch—at opposite ends. "You think he'll come back tomorrow and try again?"

He slid closer, took her drink, and held her freezing hands. "No, I got him in the leg. I think I nailed him with my second shot, too. He's lucky if he'll be walking six weeks from now."

"Who? Who could he have been?" Her eyes searched the unknown, her hands warming inside his.

"A lousy shot. No expert hit man, that's for sure. Somebody who doesn't want us to find Bati, obviously. One of his goons, maybe. Could be any of 'em. The JFK plot is a complicated one. Could be one of hundreds of people."

"How did he find out we're looking for Bati?" she further probed the unknown.

"People have big mouths, and we've been asking a lot of questions." He rubbed her fingers. "That *chiacchierone* detective, maybe, who got himself whacked here. Somebody who knew that dead Brutus guy maybe. Could be anybody."

"I've never been shot at before." The thought made her shudder.

"Well, if you're gonna play Super Sleuth and chase after people who kill presidents, get used to it." He gave her a half-smile, half-smirk.

Despite his stern tone, his gaze into her eyes halted her shivering. He patted his wounded arm. "Now you know what bodyguards are for."

Chapter Seventeen

"It's been great talking to you again, Ray. I'm sorry I wasn't better at keeping in touch. But, God, I hope you can help me." Vikki hadn't gone into details with her ex-employer, even though she was on her father's "red" phone and Ray was on his "secret" phone he used under an assumed name. His phone was actually red. When she'd worked for him, no one was allowed to answer it but him.

"You want to come down here to talk about it?" His breathless tone suggested his intentions. "It's been a long time."

"I'd rather you come up here." She didn't want to see Washington D.C. again, where she'd first met Jack. It was more of a reminder of him than New York was. "I'll pay all your expenses." She knew he wouldn't accept that offer; he wasn't of Carlton Frost's ilk.

"No, I won't hear of it, Vikki. But I'll come up this weekend, how's that?"

"Perfect." She let out a relieved breath. "Let me know what flight you're on, and I'll come meet you."

She headed into the kitchen and opened the fridge to browse.

Al got up from the couch and tossed the Word Jumble aside. He followed her into the kitchen and helped himself to some cold cuts as she cut herself a slice of banana cream pie.

"I'm coming with you when you meet this CIA guy." He slapped mustard on his bologna and capicola sandwich.

"It's not necessary. I've known him over ten years, and he's a gentleman. Besides, he's no longer in the CIA." Standing at the counter, she decided her slice of pie was too small. She grabbed a fork and ate straight from the pan.

"Still, you'd better make sure he's not wired." He took a swig of 7-Up from the bottle.

"Why would he be wired?"

Al's eyes pinned her, and once again she wished she'd taken off her glasses. "Are you joshin' me? You plan to discuss who killed John F. Kennedy with a CIA agent, a plot your husband got killed in, and not expect him to be wired? You're more naïve than I thought, little girl."

"First of all, I'm not naïve. Second of all, he's no longer a CIA agent. And third, stop calling me that!" She halted her fork halfway to her mouth. "What happened to *cara mia*?"

"When you act like a *cara mia*, I'll call you one. Still, I'm going. It's my job. Besides, I don't trust the guy." He cut his sandwich diagonally.

"You don't even know him." Then the penny dropped. "Oh, I get it." She placed a fist on her hip. "This is your sweet revenge because I didn't want you to go rendezvous with Rita. But you went anyway. Now you're going to spy on me while I meet Ray. Well, forget it. Go see *McHale's Navy*. It's been held over at the Pix."

"Nothing doing. My job is to protect you." He bit into a pickle.

She thought a minute. Maybe having him there wouldn't be such a bad idea, just in case Ray tried to rekindle his one-way flame. "Okay, you can come. But remember, this means everything to me, and I don't want you ruining it for me with your Sicilian macho routine."

"Me? Macho?" He took a sip of soda and belched. "Do I come across that way?"

Putting the pie away, she shook her head and left him to his snack and his bodily functions.

****

The years hadn't put much wear and tear on Ray Strauss. He'd managed to keep his hair, his physique, and his taste in tailored clothes. All in all, he still looked like he could turn a few heads. It got her wondering what might have happened if she'd never met Jack.

"Vikki! So good to see you!" They shared a warm hug. Al politely hung back.

"This is Mr. Po, my bodyguard."

Al shook Ray's hand, greeting him with a formal "Pleased to meet you, sir" instead of the customary "Ha'ya doin'?"

"What's with the escort?" Ray asked as they made their way through the terminal.

"Various reasons. He's a driver, too."

Al didn't skip a beat. "You know how women drive in New York, chum? They all should have men cartin' 'em around." So much for the polite routine. She knew the "sir" had been a one-shot deal, too.

Walking through the parking garage, Ray asked, "So can you tell me what this is about, or would you rather wait till we can speak in private?"

Al opened the trunk of his rented Cadillac and tossed Ray's bag inside.

"Well, you see, Al's coming with us." She turned and approached the back door. "He has to protect me at all times. That's what he was hired for."

Al opened the back door and helped her in.

"Protect you from me?" Ray's eyes went hound-dog round as he slid into the seat next to her. "We're old friends."

"Don't take it personally." Al jingled his keys.

Ray placed his hand possessively on her arm. "Are you in any danger, Vikki?"

"Not right this minute," she assured him as Al got behind the wheel.

"She's in a lot of danger, pal," he warned over his shoulder, "and now, whether you like it or not, so are you."

"Just get us home in one piece, Al," she instructed him.

But of course he kicked in another two cents. "It involves the death of her husband and President Kennedy, who both might've been killed by the same outfit, and she's already been shot at in New Orleans. He missed, lucky for her, and got me. See?" He held up his bandaged arm. "Now she's back on the trail again in New York."

"Thank you for that summary, Al." She turned to Ray. "Yes, I'm trying to find Jack's killer, but I really don't think a twenty-four-hour-a-day bodyguard is necessary. It's my paranoid godfather."

"I can't blame him, Vikki. I just wish you'd stay out of the crossfire." Ray tossed his head in Al's direction. "An armed jock can't guarantee you safety."

"Ever think of hiring one for yourself?" Al shot back.

"Don't take it personally, Mr. Andretti," Ray retorted.

"Al, your job is to negotiate the Long Island Expressway, not debate my guests. And slow down." She turned to Ray. "I'm doing this for Jack, and I'll stop at nothing."

"Okay, I'll help you all I can, so start at the beginning." Ray turned to face her.

They drove to Liam O'Brimley's Steak House on the Upper West Side. She gave the hostess her name. "I have a reservation for three adults."

They worked on their filet mignon while Vikki filled Ray in. "So can you help me track the killer down?"

"I've never heard of this Ben Bati, but I'll see what I can do," Ray offered. "I personally didn't hear about any JFK conspiracy, but then I didn't go digging into that, either. If anybody in The Company does know anything about it, then nobody I know has divulged anything. All I heard was that the Dallas police and the government pinned it on Oswald alone."

"That's the official version for the history books." She stabbed at an asparagus spear with her fork. "But according to those in the know, Oswald didn't work alone that day, and he'd been in the CIA. And with every lead I pursue, I come to a dead end. Then another lead falls into my lap. I just hope I'm barking up the right tree this time. After this, I run out of trees."

"Well, I don't even have a tree anymore, since I'm no longer with The Company." Ray shook salt onto his potato. "But I'll see what digging I can do. Like I said before you left Washington, the offer will never expire."

She managed a weak smile as Al's gaze burned into her.

Ray's eyes brightened. "Hey, any chance we can go out to dinner while I'm here—just the two of us? I'd like to try a restaurant that just opened, Le Périgord, on Fifty-Second Street."

"Of course." She didn't look Al's way. "He's a bodyguard, not a chaperone."

"It's my job, *cara mia.*" He cut into his steak.

"Fine. You can do your job just as well by waiting in the car when Ray and I go out." She ate her asparagus as Al busied himself smacking the bottom of an A-1 bottle. "Tomorrow night you can sit in the car with the windows closed and bellow all the Puccini you want."

****

The doorbell rang at six on the dot the next night. "Al, I feel bad with you waiting out in the car while Ray and I go to dinner tonight." She headed for the door. "I'm not deliberately excluding you."

He swatted the air with his hand. "I'll survive. I'm not big on French cuisine anyway."

"Hey." She got an idea. "Take my portable tape recorder from the cabinet. Bring some of your opera tapes."

"Ah, yes, I can practice my singing—with the windows closed, of course."

****

The maitre d' seated her and Ray at a cozy table in Le Périgord. After they ordered cocktails, Ray leaned forward. "So, talk. Anything you want to get off your chest, tell me about it. I'm still the world's best listener."

"I know." She still couldn't figure out why she'd turned him down years ago. She did remember her Aunt Tessie giving her a Tarot reading predicting she'd soon be involved in a whirlwind affair. Aunt Tessie's accuracy rate had people lining up to get readings.

After the Tarot reading, Vikki had stayed on high alert, but when Jack came along, she didn't attribute it to Aunt Tessie—this wasn't going to be some whirlwind affair. This was head-over-heels love that led to forever.

"Well, I'm thinking straight again, and functioning, but I have my moments." She picked up her leather-bound menu.

He eyed her up and down, his gaze lingering on her eyes, no lower. "You look like you're doing beautifully."

"My dad and stepmother, my godfather—they've all helped me through it. I don't know where I'd be without them. Al has been—oh, never mind." She flipped her hand. "I didn't invite you up here to talk about him."

"I can tell there's something between the two of you." He watched her over the top of his menu.

"Like what?" Their drinks came. She ordered *sole anglaise* and he asked for *canard rôti*. Al liked roast duck, too. She almost got up and went out to ask Al to join them, but she knew he wouldn't want to intrude. He'd looked enough like a third wheel last night.

"A tension. It's almost visible." His unblinking stare intensified. "I don't have to be psychic to see it."

Odd he'd mention anything about being psychic.

"Al grates on my nerves sometimes, but having somebody on your back day and night can do that to a person." Vikki sipped her martini.

"Yeah, especially somebody who looks like he could give Marlon Brando a run for his money if he could act." Ray sneered into his gin and tonic.

The thought of Al in a tight Brando T-shirt warmed her inside. "He has a soft side under that armor, but he's an expert at not letting it show." She slid the olive off the toothpick with her lips.

"You'll get to see that soft side a lot more when he's no longer working for you and takes off the armor." He paused. "If he's still around." Ray and his subtle inquiries.

"He'll have no need to hang around after this is solved. He's getting married in a few months, and if I'm still entangled in the web, as my godfather says, he'll dispatch somebody else to my side—and back." She forced herself to believe it didn't matter whether Al was with her.

Ray's eyes lit up. "Then it's just as well it's a professional relationship."

"I must say, Al does a great job of putting his life on the line for me, and he respects Jack's memory. Propositioning a recent widow would be out of line, for anybody." That should quash any ideas Ray had lurking on his back burner, as she noticed him reaching for her hand.

"You're right." He pulled back. "And I apologize."

"For what?"

"I'm a straightforward guy, Vikki, so I'll tell you I was hoping we could be more than friends at some point—sooner rather than later. But you're right; I'm ashamed of myself for even thinking it so soon." He looked down into his glass.

"You can think whatever you want, at this point or any other point. I have no control over your thoughts." They exchanged familiar smiles. "But it'll be a long time before I commit to anyone again. If ever."

As they dined, they reminisced, and he filled her in on some Beltway gossip, but the topic wound its way back to the serious stuff.

"I'd strongly advise you to stay out of this search and leave it to the pros, Vikki," he warned again. "I should know. I've been embroiled in plots I can't talk about, nowhere as dangerous as this one."

She swallowed and put the fork down. "Let me tell you something, Ray. I'm not afraid. Not of some thug shooting at me, not of JFK's assassin stalking me, none of it. It's as if Jack passed his fearless quality on to me when he departed. Jack was never afraid of anything in his life." Her voice wavered as she fought a stab of grief. "Now I feel the same way. A lot of people called him plain foolish for doing some of the things he did. But there's a thin line between foolishness and courage, and if I cross that line, so be it. If something happens to me while I'm doing this, it'll be all the sooner I'm reunited with Jack, and I'll have died a hero's death, just like he did. So, melodramatic as it sounds, it's how I feel, and either way, I win."

His silent nod told her he had no argument there.

They ate quietly for a few moments. "Do you have any leads other than this Bati guy?" he asked.

She shook her head. "It was one dead end after another. Now he seems to be the last one left. But who knows, he might be a dud, too. Then I'm back to square one. At least I have an ally in his estranged wife. She'd like to see him strung up, too, but for different reasons."

"I'll do my best to help you, Vikki. At least I hope we can keep in touch on a regular basis."

"Don't see why not." She sipped her water. "If you don't mind being shadowed—by my bodyguard, I mean."

"Vikki, you know I'd never want to see you hurt. And I don't mind admitting that I'm worried about you, getting caught up in this—do you know the magnitude of this? It's the highest-level murder plot in U.S. history, if it was a plot."

"Ray, have you forgotten my heritage? I know all about high-level plots. Another good thing about being the daughter of an ex-gangster. Bodyguard or not, I'm fully loaded these days." She patted her purse next to her.

"God almighty, Vikki, you're carrying concealed now?" His expression of grave concern changed to that of intense veneration as his eyes widened and his brows shot up. "Hell, *I'm* not even armed tonight." He chuckled. "Well, I'm glad I'm with somebody who can protect me. And I'm not talking about Caruso out in the car, either."

Relief eased her tension. She relaxed as her taste buds delighted in the mustard sauce. The numbness wore off more each day as her senses started to live again.

****

When they got back from dropping Ray off at the airport the next day, she got a surprise phone call from Polly. "I'm coming to New York to visit my aunt in the Bronx. I'd love to call on you."

"Hey, great!" Vikki squealed. "Come stay here at my father's. You can bunk with me, and I can really use some female company," Vikki offered. "I haven't had any close girlfriends since before I met Jack. I need someone to sit up late with, munch Cheez Doodles, do our nails, flip through fashion magazines, and talk—girl talk."

"Hey, sounds like fun."

"The fun'll be all mine, Pol. I feel like we really bonded that day over shrimp cocktail and a common goal."

Polly arrived, gushing all over Billy and the best-selling author Greta Schliessmayer. She offered to buy a stack of Billy's albums and Greta's books on the spot, which they autographed and gave her. She held onto them like gold. "I know we've got another true crime story here, tracking down Ben," Polly said.

Vikki sat up straight as an idea hit her. "I have a friend who's an ex-CIA agent, Ray Strauss. He used to be with the Office of Central Reference, under the Deputy Director for Intelligence. Would you mind if I invited him over so he could get some information from you about Ben? He knows just what questions to ask. It may lead to something."

Polly frowned. "I don't want to get interrogated. I had more'n enough of that in mah career."

"I assure you it wouldn't be an interrogation." Vikki leaned forward. "Having him meet you might just be the thing that clicks, and maybe it will help track Ben down. You never know. He's a really nice guy, too. And single," she added, hoping that would spark Polly's interest enough she'd at least meet him.

"A good looker?"

"Well—yeah, I guess." How keen would Ray be on an ex-madam propositioning him? Well, he could handle himself. She just wanted him to ask Polly the right questions. After all, he was the trained snoop.

"Okay, if it'll help you. I'm a reliable witness," Polly agreed. Vikki sprang to her feet and dashed for the "red" phone.

****

Ray came back on Saturday, and they repeated the greeting at the airport. This time, Al kept the remarks to a professional minimum and just drove, but Vikki caught him eyeing Polly, whose *mah boy*-ing him through their initial exchange brought him down a visible peg. Vikki watched him squirm.

Once Vikki got Ray and Polly settled in front of the fireplace with a couple of brandies, Polly had no problem opening up. She told him about her failed marriage, Ben's mob and CIA connections, and the dialogue she'd overheard between the ol' boys at the Mardi Gras party.

Ray took notes. "Did Ben ever discuss JFK, or the possibility of his getting assassinated?"

"No, that would've been taa-boo, to discuss anything like that with the wife." Polly swirled the brandy in her glass. "He'd never admit he was in Dallas or had anything to do with it. Ben didn't care about JFK or Bobby either way, but Marcello—now he had a real vendetta goin' with the Kennedys." She sipped her brandy. "But Ben just did his job and went about his business. I reckon he saw himself like the Kennedys— racing yachts, having gorgeous gals crawling all over 'im. The only thing he couldn't fake was the education. He came from a poor immigrant family, settled in

273

N'awlins, and joined the Army. That's where he got what smarts he has."

"Did you hear any of those old boys mention Jack Ward's name?" Ray asked.

"Never." She shook her head.

After Ray probed about Bati's possible whereabouts, Vikki asked, "Could he have gotten deported?"

"It's possible." Polly pushed a hairpin back into place. "He's done amazing things. After all, Marcello was deported once, on Bobby Kennedy's orders, and slithered back into the country. Made Bobby holler like a stuck pig. I don't know if Ben would be that clever, though."

Ray clicked his pen closed and shut his notebook. "Well, thanks, Polly. You are very helpful. I'll have more questions the further I look into this." He stood. "Now, which of you ladies would like to be taken to lunch, or may I have the pleasure of escorting both?"

Vikki smiled and glanced over at Al. "Would you like to join us?" she offered. "You don't have to wait out in the car this time."

He brandished a grin. "Hey, our double date!"

A secret thrill rushed through her as she bit her lip to stop a delighted grin.

And what a double date it was. Polly and Ray got along like long-lost soulmates. In about two sentences, they discovered their mutual interests, namely football and drag racing. While they sat in animated discussion, that left Vikki with the other odd one out—Al.

"So—what's new?" Vikki asked Al over raspberry torte as Polly and Ray debated the merits of the New York Giants' defensive line.

Al solved that problem by moving his chair close enough to touch her thigh. A hot tingle fluttered through her. She didn't pull away. "Now we can talk. Unless you want to referee there." He gestured toward the debating duo.

"They're enjoying themselves." She looked across the table. "Let's just flake off and leave them alone."

"You mean move to another table?" He glanced around at the crowded restaurant.

"No, just leave them be. I think Ray will make some progress, do some digging on Bati, with the information she gave him."

"I'd love to personally find the bastard who did this," Al said with sincere conviction.

That softened her heart. He wanted to be her hero. "Well, if you do, hand him over to me, please."

"We'll work him over together, like a duet. The way we planned to do with Brutus." Their eyes met. He winked. He then glanced down at her half-eaten torte.

"Go ahead, finish it." She pushed the plate toward him. Wow, I do care for this guy, she thought. Never had she given up dessert to anyone.

"Thanks." He dug in.

"It's amazing how many people were involved in this, with all their aliases and wanderings." She watched him attack the torte with verve.

"They certainly are the scum of the earth. Anybody willing to take money to murder the president isn't gonna be your average shmo that you can find in the Westchester County phone book." He patted his mouth with his napkin.

"I'm so desperate, if Ray can't come up with anything, I'm going to ask my Aunt Tessie for a psychic reading." She took her water glass and sipped, glad the ice had melted.

"I thought that was all mumbo-jumbo to you." He ate one more forkful, leaving the plate clean.

"She has been right a few times, although I don't want to resort to the supernatural. It's against all my principles. But I am desperate. I'm beyond desperate. I'm beginning to think it's hopeless." She sighed and shook her head.

"It's never hopeless." He clasped her hand, and she welcomed his touch. "Just slow down. You'll get old before your time. And believe me, we get old fast enough."

Just then, Ray turned to them. "I'm so sorry, we didn't mean to ignore you—we just got into this discussion, and—"

"It's fine, Ray." She waved the apology away. "Al and I didn't want to intrude."

"Oh—not at all." Ray's tone bared his embarrassment. "I almost feel like I'm intruding on you two."

The way he said "you two" had such a ring of intimacy to it. "How can you possibly be intruding? Al and I are friends." She realized she'd blurted that out. "I mean—"

"As opposed to enemies," Al amended.

Vikki half expected him to go into a routine like she did when Rita showed up, but thank God he didn't. He only took Polly's arm on the way out and, making a big show of it, asked the ex-madam out the following night. "This time you can be the one tagging along," he breezily informed Vikki.

"Touché," she muttered.

But she knew Al deserved a night off.

So Roberto covered for him the next evening. She had the option of staying home and watching her father rehearse his new songs, with Roberto singing harmony, or tagging along with Rosie and Angelo to the fights at Madison Square Garden.

She didn't especially want to do either. Watching guys beat the crap out of each other was too much like reality, and show tunes were too much the opposite. So she made some plans of her own.

Slipping out of the house unnoticed for a few hours would be like biting into the forbidden fruit— dangerous and delightfully perverse. Her private time in the bathroom just didn't compare.

Wrapped in her robe, she sauntered past her father's studio and halted at the door. "I'm going to have a nice long soak." Billy and Roberto gave her their nods from the piano. Nobody would miss her; they knew she took long baths. She'd be back home packing on a mud mask before Al and Polly returned from their "date."

Upstairs, she called a cab and instructed it to wait on the corner. She got dressed, slid the Bauer into her shoulder holster, and stuck a cigarette case and lipstick into her coat pocket. Slipping out the basement door, she breathed in the fresh air of freedom.

Ah, to sit alone in a smoky bar…what heaven.

The cab dropped her off at Bleecker and Broadway. She headed for The Bitter End, where she had seen Bob Dylan perform for the first time. For that, she felt obligated to keep patronizing the place.

The sidewalks weren't crowded. An icy wind howled, rattling the garbage cans and swirling the litter.

She tied her scarf more tightly around her neck and nestled her chin into her fox collar.

When she opened the door to the bar, a warm rush of air blanketed her like a down comforter.

She pulled off her gloves and scanned the smoky room for a seat, but the place was packed. On the raised platform that served as a stage, an acoustic guitar leaned against an empty stool. Whoever it was must be good to generate this kind of crowd.

With patrons four deep at the bar, it took a while to get served. Her drink sloshing over the sides of her glass, she nudged her way toward the empty stage. As she inched along, somebody bumped into her so hard the glass slipped from her hand and crashed to the floor. "What the—"

He babbled one apology after another, not letting her get an insult in edgewise. "Let me buy you another one, what were you drinking?"

"Never mind, I'll—"

"No! I insist!" He flashed her a smile. Crowns. "Please, tell me what you were drinking, and I'll buy you three more. I'm so clumsy. Please. Now, what were you drinking?"

"Seven and seven." She hadn't let a man buy her a drink at a bar since before she met Jack. But she felt a twinge of sympathy for the klutz; he probably got more than his share of rejections in bars.

She had a hankering for a buzz and gave him a grateful smile when he handed her a full glass. "You didn't have to, but thanks." She sipped and picked up where she left off.

Even without music playing, the room was too loud for normal conversation. Leaning into her ear, he introduced himself. "I'm Aladio. I drive a truck and just got back from the Gulf Coast."

"I'm Victoria." She always used her full name when she wanted to keep her distance.

The air grew warmer and smokier. She took a lengthy gulp of her drink as a trickle of sweat ran down her back.

"Is it hot in here, or is it me?" was the last thing she remembered saying as a wave of dizziness came over her. She lost her balance, swayed, and grabbed onto a wooden beam to steady herself as the room spun.

"Heads up!" she heard Aladio's voice as he caught her and half-dragged her through the crowd to the door. "Make way! She had one too many," he warned the few patrons who gave her a passing glance. His voice seemed far away, yet he was right next to her.

"What's the matter with me?" she asked over and over, but couldn't find her voice. The crush of bodies choked her as he maneuvered her out the door and onto the sidewalk. Several gulps of cold air did nothing to clear her head. Her lids got heavier; she struggled to keep her eyes open. A bulky figure appeared on her other side and clutched her elbow.

They half-dragged, half-carried her down a few dark side streets and turned up a narrow alley, then ushered her into an abandoned brick building. Forcing her eyes to stay open, she noticed the door had a square peephole cut into it. *That looks so familiar.*

Clasping her arms with an iron grip, they steered her down a flight of rickety wooden steps. With no energy to shout or put up a struggle, she teetered on the edge of awareness as if drugged.

They pushed her down to the hard floor. Her head

rolled to one side. Her eyes closed. When she opened them again, an intense beam of light blinded her. She shielded her eyes with her arm.

She tried to remember how she got here. Some guy had rammed into her, made her drop her drink, insisted on buying her another one…

Good God, he'd slipped her a mickey!

Chapter Eighteen

Al enjoyed Polly's company but needed to get back on the job. He glanced at his watch for the third time in twenty minutes. "I can't stay out much longer. Duty calls, you know."

"You enjoy takin' care of her, don't you?" Polly asked. "Sure is an assignment no red-blooded bodyguard would pass up."

"Oh, yeah. I'm cut out for this kind of thing." He closed his eyes, savoring Vikki's image in living color. "Goes to extremes, you know? One minute we're sitting in a bar like we're doing now, having a nice talk, next minute I'm chasing after some lug who's shooting at her."

"Nobody said it'd be like slidin' off a greasy log backward. Like mah former line of work, it can get messy sometimes." She tittered, patting her hair down.

"I'll admit, I wouldn't want to trade places with you." He finished off his wine. "That line of business is strictly women's work."

They shared a laugh.

"She's a brave gal, doin' this." Polly lit a cigarette. "Musta really loved that husband a hers."

"Oh, yeah, she did." A familiar twinge of jealousy crept into his heart, and once again he pushed it away. What a waste of time, being jealous of a dead man. "And she's not going to open up to me till her quest is fulfilled. She's not willing to give up her obsession to commit to me. That's why I wish I could carry it out for her, or at least help her do it."

"Al, you can't blame her for being obsessed with this." She took a drag and blew out a stream of smoke. "Wouldn't you do the same thing, if someone you loved got killed an' you wanted to find out who did it? What if the victim was Vikki?"

"Of course I would." He splayed his fingers. "I wouldn't think twice about it."

"And I know she'd do the same for you, too."

He shook his head. "I don't think so. Jack was the love of her life."

"Our lives don't always have just one love, mah boy." Polly flicked her ash.

"I can't expect her to give up searching for Jack's killer, as much as I hate to see her putting herself in danger all the time. But it kills me to watch her risk her life to find this bastard. It just kills me." He glanced at their wine bottle. Empty.

"But it'd kill you more to ask her to stop, for your own selfish reasons. So let her do it." Polly blew out a stream of smoke.

His eyes landed on the lipstick stain on her cigarette filter. It reminded him so much of Vikki... "But she's not going to be open to committing to me till she finds Jack's killer," he said. "If it takes the rest of her life."

"You don't know that." Polly propped her elbows on the table. "Why don't you try?"

"Because she'll tell me to flake off." He fished a cigarette from his pack and lit it on the end of hers. "She's already said she doesn't want an emotional involvement, doesn't want to be my *comare*, all that."

"Then try again and again. Look. This is something you have to persevere on. And you know what the first step is, don't you? She's not goin' to commit to you as long as you're engaged. So, about this little bride of yours back home." She leaned forward. "You're bound to break somebody's heart sooner or later. I hope you realize that."

"Nah." He waved both hands. "Mona's not in love with me, and I'm not in love with her. We're both going into this with our eyes open."

She shook her head and her earrings jangled. "Do go on."

"Huh?" He looked over at her.

Her eyes penetrated him. "Why don't I believe you?"

"I told you, she's an old-fashioned Italian girl. Let me tell you something about old-fashioned Italian girls." Al motioned up and down with his hand. "They don't marry for love, arranged or not. They marry for security. Then once the *bambini* start coming, they're so busy ruling the roost, their husbands slip out and stray, and it's more than okay with them. It's a relief."

"How about the ones who *are* in love with their husbands?" she challenged.

"Mona's not in love with me, I said. She's like my sister." He took a long drag.

"How often do you hear from her since you're on this job?"

He shrugged. "Often enough. She likes to write letters."

"She misses you." As she gave him a smile, her teeth gleamed in the glow of the candle between them.

"Nah, it's just chatty stuff, like she got a new chicken cacciatore recipe, the weather, junk like that."

"Does she write about the upcomin' wedding?" Polly shrugged into her beaded sweater.

He rolled his eyes. "Does she! Described the gown down to the last thread, the cake, the flowers, everything. But all brides are like that. They get all worked up about the whole deal."

"She sign them 'Love, Mona'?" Polly examined her red nails.

He thought for a moment and shook his head. "I never noticed."

"She tell you she misses you?"

"You can miss somebody without being madly in love with them," he stated.

She shot him a disapproving glare. "You're givin' this gal the brown end a the stick, you know that?"

"Why?"

"Do I have to hit you ovah the head with a bag a hammers?" She rolled her eyes and raised her painted-on brows. "The lady is countin' the days till this weddin', and you're happy as a dead pig in the sunshine."

"It's an arrangement." He cut the air with his hands. "When Mama dies, we're getting an annulment. She knows that."

"You mean *you* laid down the terms, and *she* went along with it." Polly twisted a new cigarette into her holder.

"No, it's mutual. We agreed we'd split up once my mother was gone."

Polly hawmphed. "She's a clever gal. Very crafty. You don't understand the inner workin's of the feminine mind at all, mah boy. Once you're hitched, just wait and see how hard it'll be to get out of it. Annulments ain't easy to get, you know. It's not the same as a divorce. The easiest grounds for annulment is non-consummation. You plan to hit separate sacks?"

"I told you, it's not that kind of a marriage. I'm— we're doing this to make the rest of Mama's days happy." Al cracked his knuckles, wondering where he'd picked up the habit.

"Oh, Mama's not the only one who'll be happy. Just wait till the weddin' night, when she comes out in that itty-bitty negligee and starts vampin' you. You'll see your willpower shrink in two shakes of a rooster's comb."

"I won't let her vamp me." He took a drag.

Polly laughed out a puff of smoke. "Don't kid a kidder, mah boy."

"How do you know all this?" He folded his arms on the table. "That's just not the way I planned it."

"Some things you just can't plan. You're a danged fool if you think this is goin' to go to plan—yours, anyway. Let me offer you some sage advice, before it's too late." She wagged a finger. "Don't marry this gal."

"What?" His voice broke. "And break Mama's heart?"

"With all due respect, Mama doesn't have long to go. This gal has to live the rest of her life, and so do you. Don't do this to her. Break it off now, like a man, before it's too late. And you'll have a clear conscience."

"I do have a clear conscience," he insisted.

"How can you say that when you did what you did that night in N'awlins, fannin' that old flame a yours?"

She lowered her fake lashes and fanned her face with her fingers.

"Rita? Oh, I—" He lowered his head. "I'd better confess now, before I make myself look even worse. I didn't get together with any old flame."

"Then where'd you get those lacy unmentionables Vikki told me fell out your pocket?" She raised a brow.

"A raunchy sex shop on Bourbon Street," he told her. "I'm not interested in Rita anymore. I got my sights higher than that now."

"So you just did all that to make Vikki jealous?" Her lips split into a smile.

"Not so much that but to get back at her for that campy act she put on to make Rita think we were engaged. *Madonne*, that threw me for a loop." He waved his hands.

"Then it worked. It was good enough to get rid of Rita, too." She gave him an assuring wink.

"Rita believed it, not because she's dumb but because she knows me. Well," he tossed his head. "The old me, anyway."

"You and Vikki are just piddlin' around. All this game-playin', one-uppin' each other."

"I can't just sit there and take it. I have to fork it out, too," he said.

"Aside from that courtin' ritual, you have to tell that bride-to-be of yours that it's ovah. Otherwise you'll ruin both your lives. She won't give you an annulment or a divorce. She's just tellin' you what you want to hear. Once she's got that piece a paper signed, she's got you by the *cajones*," Polly stated, as if reading his fortune from a spread of cards.

"How do you know so much about old-fashioned

Italian girls?" he asked.

"Because I used to be one myself."

His jaw dropped. "You're Italian?" He studied her features—the wide-set blue eyes, the long thin nose, the rosy cheeks. But that could be rouge. He knew ladies loved to slather that on.

"Shuur am. Ortensia Bernadette Russo Sidonia. Fell off the boat from Sassano to N'awlins before I could talk. So I learned to speak Italian with a Cajun accent."

"Where's Sassano?" he asked her.

"About forty miles southeast a Napoli. A small village, never even seen it on a map."

"Your mother's maiden name is Russo?" That gave him a warm old-country feeling. "That was my nonna's maiden name."

"*Paisano*! All Russos are related. That's why we're all *pazzo*." She circled her forefinger around her ear. "All that interbreedin'."

"Oh, that's what it is." He gave an exaggerated nod. "I thought it was all that grape-stomping in the hot sun."

"So you gon' do the right thang?" Her hand grabbed his, and her eyes pinned him. Being in a half-nelson couldn't have been more restricting. "Remember, you'll never have Vikki unless you're free. And trust me when I say once you're hitched, you're gon' stay hitched."

He shifted his gaze downwards, to the bottom of his wine glass. "I know Mona wants the old-fashioned wedding with all the trimmings." But was she in love with him, or with her wedding day? "I thought I was doing what's right by her and by Mama, and let things take care of themselves later."

"It don't work that way, Al." She gripped his hand. "Think long-term, your future, beyond your wedding day. If you want Vikki, end this farce and pursue her."

His heart raced at the sound of her name. "It looks like she's getting tight with that ex-spy again."

"She ain't innerested in him." She sat back and scowled. "He told me he knows you two got a thing goin', and he's keeping his distance."

"When did you talk about that?" he asked.

"Between arguments about the New York Giants' defensive line and LBJ's increasin' our involvement in Vietnam. You just didn't hear us; you were too busy having your own cozy little powwow."

Al shut up to think. Polly shut up and let him think.

He drained his water and chomped on the last ice cube. "You're right. I shoulda got a second opinion. Besides my mother, I mean. A second opinion from somebody who's not so involved in it they can't think straight. That's my problem, I only look at things one way—mine."

"You'll grow up, and your eyes'll open." She gave him an assuring nod. "You've already matured about fifteen years since you sat down at this table."

"Hey, thanks. But there's a difference between maturing and aging. I hope I still look like I'm nineteen when I get up from this table." He smoothed down his Midnight Raven hair.

"Just don't act like it." She gave him a cocky grin.

Another glance at his watch told him his "lunch break" was over. "I really need to get back."

He helped her into her coat and left a generous tip.

"Telling Mona I don't want to marry her will be

harder than being tailed by a hit man," he muttered as they left the restaurant.

"Just make sure you're protected," Polly warned, gesturing at his lower anatomy. "With your cup."

****

Vikki inhaled deep breaths to stay calm. As stealthy as a panther, her fingers crawled to her holster. To her horror, it was empty. "What—what am I doing here?" she asked Aladio, who sat in a chair a few feet from her.

"We already took the gun, lady," the guy holding the flashlight said. She blinked in disbelief. Her eyes adjusted to the dimness. She couldn't stop staring at him. The wavering light contorted his grotesque, almost comical features, mocking the terror of her situation. A frizzy rug crowned his head, his crooked eyebrows crept up his forehead like two hairy caterpillars...

Glued-on eyebrows! Her mind flashed back to the Dallas jail and Ruby telling her about that CIA kook who ran around with Oswald—oh, what was his name?

She looked around as she struggled to sit upright. The place had been a saloon—a long time ago. Empty shelves loomed up behind the long curving bar. A few beat up tables and chairs stood scattered around. She remembered the covered-over peephole in the door.

That was from the Prohibition era, when this saloon became a speakeasy.

"Let's get this over with, Dave. I'm hungry." Aladio got to his feet. "I could go for a steak dinner with onion rings."

Dave—she silently repeated the name as if learning a new language. Dave...

The guy with the glued-on eyebrows was David

289

Ferrie!

"We have to be careful," Ferrie retorted. "I still haven't decided what to do with her body after we're finished with her."

"Leave it here." He swatted at her as if she were a fly.

"How 'bout when it starts to rot? No, too easy to trace it back to us." Ferrie paced.

"You got that gasoline can?"

"Yeah, but it'd be easier to stuff it into a bag and dump it off a pier." Ferrie righted his wig and smoothed down his brows with his thumbs.

"It'll float."

"Get a coupla bricks," Ferrie ordered.

She realized with horror that they were talking about how to dispose of her corpse. Her heart slammed as she faced her impending death. So this was it, her final moments.

"Now." Ferrie turned to her. "Tell us why you got your CIA friend nosing around us. Who else is in your little circle, and what exactly do you know about our whole thing?" His voice squeaked, and he rushed his words as if out of breath. "Cooperate, and we'll go easy on you."

She shook her head, her mind still not fully aware of what he was asking her. "What CIA friend?"

Ferrie lunged at her, and before she could raise a hand in defense, backhanded her across the face. "Don't play dumb with me. You know I'm talkin' about Strauss. You got him involved for a reason. Now what is it?"

"R—Ray?" What did he have to do with Ray? Her brain ached as she struggled to make the connection.

Yes, they were both in the CIA. No, she couldn't implicate Ray. After a few more seconds of her silence, he grabbed a hunk of her hair, nearly tearing it from her scalp. "You talk or you're gonna wind up just like the rest of 'em."

Her slamming heart took a sickening leap to her throat. Had Ray told them of her involvement in this whole thing? Or had they just stalked her all along? Was Ferrie the one who'd shot at her in New Orleans? Good God, was he Jack's killer?

She was in no position to ask questions. She had to think quickly. Bluff them out, like in the Br'er Rabbit story she'd never forgotten from childhood. "I don't care what you do with me, but right now—I can't think—my mind's in a fog from whatever you put in my drink. Please, take me home, and when I'm better I'll tell you anything you want to know. Just don't leave me here. I hear rats! I'm afraid of the dark!" She scurried into the corner, drew her knees up to her chin, and covered her head with her hands.

"Maybe we'll do that after all." Ferrie sneered. "Leave you here to rot."

"Please! Kill me, but don't leave me here! I hate rats, and I hear them all around here! Whatever you do, don't leave me here alone!"

"You'll tell us what we want to know first," he rasped. "And if you don't want to tell us, you'll think again."

"Okay, I'll tell you whatever you want, when I can think straight. You drugged me so much, I feel like I'm about to drop." She gulped the fetid air. "But, please— don't leave me here alone!"

"Afraid of rats, are you? Then we *will* leave you

here, till your head gets straight, and once you're gnawed to the bone by rats, maybe then you'll tell us what we want to know." They turned and stomped out, slamming the door behind them.

It worked! Crouched in pitch blackness, she heard their receding footsteps. Relief mingled with the dread of being trapped here, but her bluff had worked. "Born and bred in the briar patch." She recited the line Br'er Rabbit hollered out to the fox. "Born and bred in a speakeasy. Well, almost." Now maybe she could use what she knew about speakeasies to get out.

She stood and grabbed the wall for support, testing her balance. Her head still fuzzy, she paced around the room, flexing and blowing on her fingers in the bone-chilling cold. They'd taken her cigarette case along with her gun, so she couldn't even light a match. Bumping into tables and chairs in the dark, she groped her way behind the bar. Sweeping over layers of dirt and grime, her fingertips crawled along shelves that once had held rows of bootleg bottles of booze. The cloying, dank smell of neglect and decay churned her stomach.

Her fingers brushed against something dry and brittle. A dead rat. Recoiling, she jumped back. How many more rodents lay here, decomposing—and how many live ones were scurrying around? She tried to stop shuddering and moved forward again, digging into her memory for her father's speakeasy stories. During Prohibition, he'd installed a false panel behind his bar. It led to the sewer, where they'd dump the bottles when the Feds showed up.

Fingering the shelf like a blind woman reading Braille, she felt a narrow gap in the wall. Good God, a false panel? She pushed at it, banged on it, kicked at it. It held fast, sealed tight. She drew back and threw her weight on it. It started to give. *Please open!* she begged.

One more shove, and the mechanism gave so suddenly, she tumbled into a tight, claustrophobic pit. Her elbows and head slammed against hard slimy bricks. She landed with a splat, sprawled at the foot of the shaft, face down in pungent filth.

With only her hands to guide her, she got up and treaded the slippery surface as a thick liquid seeped into her shoes. She continued down the steepening slope, wading deeper into the sewer's bowels. Fingers splayed out before her, she groped along the encrusted stone of the narrow passage. The odor of methane gas and putrid waste grew stronger with each step.

She breathed through her mouth, tasted the filth. She tried to imagine a field of flowers, Al's cologne, anything that smelled good.

Reaching up, she touched the low arched ceiling. After a few more paces, the tunnel ended. Turn right or left? Did it matter? Would one way promise escape while the other way brought certain death? She followed her instincts and took the passage to the right.

The slimy floor sloped farther downward. Standing ankle-deep in the thickening sludge, she pressed her scarf to her nose to ward off the stench, but it far overpowered her perfume. She tried to breathe without retching.

With each step, her feet squelched and sank into the murky depths. She struggled to move. Although on a downgrade, it was more like climbing—she had to pull each foot out of the muck before plopping it down again.

Fumbling her way along, she took a deep breath of the putrid air. "Hello! Somebody help me!" Only her echo answered. Why couldn't an emergency sewer worker be down here? Something cold plopped onto her head in the spot where Ferrie had grabbed her hair. She stopped slogging through the scum and touched her stinging scalp. A few more drops landed on her hand and slithered down her cheek. She shivered and wiped the cold water off with her scarf. It reeked with the fetid odor. She yanked it from around her neck and flung it away.

The water rushed faster around her ankles as the ground slanted more sharply. She slid with each step, losing her balance a couple of times. Her shoes were now entirely soaked through, her feet numb with cold. Her slacks clung to her legs, and her shoes were nearly pulled off her feet with every step through the sludge. Oh, if only she'd worn boots!

A small slimy object nudged her, and she tried to kick at it. Thankful she couldn't see what it was, she knew it was another bloated dead rat.

As the filth clung to her, she plodded along the slippery surface, struggling to keep her balance. It had to end somewhere, but she feared her fate when she did escape. Would they come and find her again? Break into the house and drag her from her bed? Stalk all of them and shoot whoever opened the door first? She shuddered, but not because she was drenched and chilled to the bone.

As she forged on over the slimy ground, she thought of happy times, holidays with her family, her blossoming relationship with Al. But she forced herself back to reality as trudging became even harder. Her left shoe got sucked from her foot, so she let the other shoe slide off, too. The sludge now squelched between her toes.

Coughing and sputtering, she blindly floundered through the endless passage, her hands raw from the caked lime, algae, and filth covering the brickwork enclosing her.

Rushing water sounded closer all the time, like countless toilets flushing all at once, emptying here at the receiving end of modern plumbing. No one would hear her screams for help over the noise.

Now up to her knees, viscous as poured concrete, the sludge became impossible to slog through. Her flesh crawled as the cold slime seeped through her drenched slacks. She gagged. With every few steps, the bottom angled down more sharply. She slipped and slid, nearly falling over. The water lapped around her thighs. Within minutes it would be waist-deep. What to do then? Turn back? Keep going, hoping for an escape? Or would that mean drowning in a flood of waste and filth?

She forged on. She couldn't turn back, knowing what awaited her when—and if—they came to get her.

Images flashed in her mind—bullet-riddled or strangled corpses, all connected with the JFK plot—just like her Jack.

Now she might be one of them.

With each tortured step, she took short gasps, inhaling the foul air. Her lungs ached. The fumes nauseated her. The rushing water came waist-high. She tasted the smell of it. It coated her tongue. As the current shoved her against the wall, her hopes of escape vanished.

She yelped in pain as her head banged against a

sharp object. A pipe? She reached out, closing her fingers around the encrusted rungs of a ladder.

She stood on tiptoe, choking and gulping. Her hand clamped around that bottom rung, grasping it for dear life, her only escape to the street.

She tried jumping, but sludge soaked her, weighing her down. Her stockinged feet couldn't grab the slimy wall.

An idea came to her—from where, she didn't know, but tears of appreciation stung her eyes. If she wasn't strong enough to haul her body up to that rung, her suede slacks were.

She unbuttoned, unzipped, and wriggled out of them. She slipped one pants leg over the bottom rung and knotted the legs together in a crude stirrup. Grasping it with raw hands, she pulled herself up, inch by inch. With one foot through the makeshift stirrup, she hauled her weight upwards until her fingers and toes curled around the ladder's rungs.

Clenching the rusty ladder, she wondered for a split second whether to get her slacks. Forget it; the ladder was as slippery and filth-encrusted as the passage walls; she couldn't risk it. She'd come this far. She'd wear her coat once she got out.

As she crept, rung by rung, not daring to go faster for fear of slipping, one of the ladder's bolts worked loose from the wall. The ladder quivered under her weight. "No—please—don't come loose now," she begged.

Above her head, she heard a whoosh followed by a metallic clang, like the sound when she drove over a manhole.

Sweet Jesus, a manhole! With another metallic

clang, a flash of light skimmed over her. She began banging her fist on the underside of the manhole cover. "Help! Get me out of here!"

She couldn't budge it. It weighed a ton. Through the tiny square hole in its center, beams of light flashed as cars approached and sped past. Exhaust fumes choked her. "Please!" She banged and screamed her throat raw. A hunk of metal stood between death and salvation.

Voices murmured above her, and with her last hope, she balled her fist and pounded on the unforgiving steel. "Please get me out of here!"

The cover started to move as someone worked it loose, and with a slow scraping sound it slid aside. She blinked. Dark figures hovered around the opening.

A hand reached down. She thrust out her scratched, frozen fingers. That hand grasped hers in the warmest, most comforting human contact she'd ever known. Strong arms pulled her through. She experienced a rebirth. No glued-on eyebrows; he was just a guy in a shabby coat and a tam, smelling of turpentine. She scrambled out onto the asphalt and rolled onto her side, gulping for air. Bodies bent over her, horns blared, rotting garbage reeked. Once again she breathed the fresh air of freedom.

Shivering, she whispered, "Thank you," and her eyes slid shut. She didn't even care where they took her—she'd escaped the catacombs alive. Nothing else mattered.

She heard "hospital" and "hypothermia" among the buzz of the small crowd clustered around her. Whoever had pulled her out carried her like a bouquet of flowers.

A yellow cab pulled up alongside them, the back

door opened, and the gent in the shabby coat helped her inside. "The emergency room at St. Vincent's," he told the driver as he slid in next to her. "You're pretty banged up." He pulled her coat around her with those big comforting hands. But it didn't stop her shivering.

"You don't have to come with me," she protested weakly, surprised he'd cared enough to make sure she got there.

"It's all right." The gentle voice soothed her. "I just want to make sure you get to see a doctor."

"Can you have the cab take me to Larchmont? I'll pay for it."

"No, you should go to the hospital first," he insisted.

The cab pulled away with a screech, and she fell over against him. "Sorry." She leaned the other way.

"It's okay. What happened to you, anyway?"

"I just—I was walking along, and fell into the manhole." The last thing she wanted to do was explain any of this.

"Jesus, somebody ought to call the city about that. You could've gotten killed."

If only he knew the half of it. "I know," she whispered as the cab swayed, jerked to a stop for a light, and took off again.

His hand, wrapped around hers, was splattered with paint. "Are you an artist down here?" she asked, to keep her mind off the horror of her ordeal. There would be enough rehashing that later.

"Yes, I am. I'm Franck LeJardin, Junior, and my work is on display in a gallery on Vestry Street. I'm a sculptor, too. I'm the first one in my family to be able to make a living from it."

"Good for you." She gulped some more precious air. "My name's Vikki. How about, when I'm cleaned up, I'll stop by your gallery."

"Oh, I'd love that. I have a card here somewhere I'll give you." He patted his pockets.

The driver veered off to the right and screeched to a halt before St. Vincent's emergency entrance. As Franck helped her out, she thanked God for her steady footing. Her shivering subsided. "I think I'm okay now. I'll just call home and—"

"No, I want you to sign in and see a doctor." He walked her through the glass doors.

She sank into the only free chair in the crowded waiting room, not knowing where to begin explaining if a doctor—or worse, a cop—started asking questions.

An attendant gave her a form attached to a clipboard. She filled it out using a fake name. "You'll be seen to in under an hour."

That was plenty of time to get the hell out.

She approached Franck waiting at the entrance. "Thank you for taking me here. I don't have any money on me right now, but—"

"No bother." He held up a paint-stained hand. "I was glad to help."

"I don't want to hold you up any further; I'm signed in. I'll be okay."

"You sure?" he asked.

"Yes, really." She nodded.

He handed her a card. "I hope you can come by the gallery."

"I will. I promise." She glanced at the card. "My mother was an artist right here in the Village."

"Was she?" His eyes lit up. "What was her name?"

"Prudence Mul—McGlory. Or maybe she went by Muller. I'm not sure."

"I know that name." He scratched his head. "Where have I heard it before?"

"She didn't do too well in the business. She died very young, too."

"Oh, I'm so sorry." He placed a hand on her shoulder. "I'll have to remember where I've heard that name. Well, Vikki, I hope you'll be okay."

"I will, and thanks again." She tried not to sound too anxious, but all she wanted was to get out of here.

As he departed, she found a pay phone and called her father.

She'd been here before, once when she'd stepped on a nail and another time when she and her cousin Johnny were in the Village drinking. He got into a fight and got his nose broken. In the midst of the fight, he'd gotten robbed, and her mad money wasn't enough for a cab. So they'd walked. Well, now she knew the real scenic way to get here.

She waited for her father without being noticed, even though she was a sorry sight, stinking and filthy. She hoped someone wouldn't take her for a derelict and toss her out. It must've been the leather coat with the fox collar that did it. Even though it was now matted and reeked of sewage, it wasn't the usual attire of bums. She kept her eyes riveted to the curb where the ambulances pulled up.

Her father's car pulled up and screeched to a halt. He rushed up to her with Roberto on his heels. She went limp in his arms.

"Jesus, Vikki, you almost gave me a heart attack!"

She cried tears of relief for both of them. "I'm so

sorry, Dad. I just had to get out of the house. I've been living like a prisoner."

"Did you get a good look at the bastards who abducted you?" He held her at arm's length and looked her over.

"I sure did. One of them was David Ferrie, the CIA guy Ruby told us about. I'll bet my life on it. There can't be two of him in the world."

"Holy Christ, now they're onto you." His eyes darkened. "I think it's about time we call the cops with this."

"No!" She stomped her stockinged foot. "I don't want to take this to them. It'll be too much of a mess."

"We'll talk about that later. Meanwhile, if you ever try to leave the house again, you won't even be able to go to the bathroom alone, you hear it?" His teeth clenched.

She'd better hear it. When he held her by the shoulders and stared her down like that, he meant business.

"Yes, all right. I'll behave myself. I won't set foot outside the door, not even to get the paper, the milk, the mail, nothing."

He insisted she get treated, so they waited. A nurse walked her to a cubicle, pulled the curtains around it, and a doctor finally came to look at her.

How to explain this?

"I fell through a manhole."

That seemed good enough for him, rather tame for Greenwich Village after midnight. After cleaning her up and getting antibiotics and a tetanus shot into her, they released her.

Her father and Roberto walked her to the car.

Catching the glint of Roberto's gun in the white hospital lights, she remembered. *Oh, no, the Bauer's gone.*

As they helped her into the car, she glanced around for stalkers and fake eyebrows. "Thank you, God, for sparing me," she whispered, head bowed.

On the way home, her father tried to perk up her spirits. "You don't have to be a prisoner; you can go out, but with Al, not alone. Go to a museum, go shopping. New York is at your feet. The whole damn world is at your feet."

"I guess then Al will really be earning his money, following me around museums and the ladies' lingerie department at Saks." She rested her head on the seat back, watching the city lights whiz by.

"So you might open his eyes up to a couple things he's never seen before," her father urged. "Take him out on the town. You both love opera—go to the Met. Go dancing. I'll bet he does a mean cha-cha."

"He held his own on the dance floor on New Year's Eve," she mused.

"So there you are. You can do something different every day—and every night."

"Of course these things you're talking about sound just like dates, Dad." She looked over at him in the red glow of a traffic light.

"Yeah, and he's getting paid for it." He grinned at her. "The guy has the best of both worlds. Paid to escort my princess all over New York. And who says you gotta stop at New York? Why don't you get out of town for a few days, have him escort you to the islands, or to Aspen, or wherever. It'll take your mind off all this— all you've been through—with a change of scenery."

"And he insisted he wasn't a gigolo," she teased.

He drew his brows together. "Gigolos don't throw themselves in front of speeding bullets."

"You got me there," she admitted.

"I know the gigolo type. And it ain't him."

"I don't want to give up, Dad. Even for a few days. If I'm out of town, nothing gets done. I don't want to run away. I want to stay right here till this is solved."

The foul odor emanating from her body and clothes disgusted her. She couldn't wait to scrub her skin raw. God, she stank.

"Okay, suit yourself." He waved his free hand. "But I just want you to live a little."

"I'm going to start to live—again. I have to." She gave a resolute nod.

"Then ask your bodyguard, or whatever you want to call him these days, to get his tux pressed, slick his polished hair back, and take a nice bath with Mr. Bubble, 'cause you're goin' out on the town."

"How did you know he uses Mr. Bubble?" She sat up.

Billy looked away. "I ran out of my own and had to borrow some of his."

"Well, at least you don't dye your hair." She went back to the passing city scenes—canopied apartment buildings, double-parked cars, throngs of pedestrians, blinking WALK signs.

"And he does? How do you know?" he asked.

"I, uh—happened to pass by his bathroom and glimpsed a box of hair dye," she confessed, but not the whole truth. "In Midnight Raven, no less."

"Glimpsed, huh?" He shot her his "who you shittin'?" glare she could never argue with—not since she was three years old.

"Well, I was browsing a little," she added to her confession.

His glare didn't waver.

"All right, so I was snooping." Now she came out with it. "He knows enough about me—he buys my tampons, for God's sake."

Billy chuckled. "A word of fatherly advice here, babe. Any guy who's cool with buying a woman's feminine products is a rare catch. You'd better hang on to that bastard."

"He's getting married, Dad," she reminded him.

"Hang on to him anyway. I have a feeling it won't last."

Once more, she fantasized about romance with Al. But she cut it short, as she did every time. She wasn't ready. "The guy's getting married. Arranged or not, I'm not going to be anybody's *comare*."

She found herself hoping the marriage wouldn't last, or wouldn't happen at all. But that would take a miracle, so she hoped for a quick change of heart on Mona's part.

Or better yet, his.

****

Back home, safe and warm, she headed for the tub and poured in half a box of Calgon. She soaked in that hot water, bordering on scalding, for over an hour, refilling the tub as the water cooled. She rubbed herself raw with her bath mitt and plunged her scratched hands in the Pond's jar.

She didn't even remember crawling into bed, but the next sound she heard was a soft knock on her door. She looked at the glowing face of her alarm clock. 2:30.

"Come in." She rubbed her eyes, still half asleep.

Al rushed in, knelt at the bedside, and they clung together like two victims about to drown.

"Vikki, don't ever do that again, don't ever leave the house alone."

"I won't. I promise," she whispered, now fully awake. "I don't want to talk about kidnappers and their CIA connections. All I want to do is put the nightmare behind me and move on."

"I understand. You never have to mention it again if you don't want to. It's entirely up to you." He relaxed their embrace and she sat up, pulling the neckline of her nightgown to her chin. Not that he could see her décolletage in the dark. That was just her old school modesty.

"You know what my dad suggested? Us going out on the town, to shows and stores and just living. Something I really need right now." She clasped his hands and inhaled. He smelled so nice and clean.

"That sounds great, *cara mia*, but your dad wants to make sure you're really safe this time. So it won't be just us." He slid her vanity stool over to her bedside and perched on it.

"Oh, no. Don't tell me—more bodyguards." She leaned over and raised the window shade. Moonlight drifted in and illuminated him.

"Well—yeah. But more like security guards. There's one stationed at the house already. He's got front yard detail."

"What else?" Caution steadied her tone.

"You shouldn't mind this, since you design costumes." His teeth glowed as he smiled.

She blinked in surprise. "He wants me to wear a

costume?"

"Well, nothing drastic. Just a wig and glasses."

She chuckled. "Ah, what the hell. That might be fun."

****

The living room wall had a hole in it the next morning. "Holy Jesus, what happened?" she asked Al as he came in with the paper.

"Oh, Rosie did that. When he found out what happened to you, he got kind of, uh…upset." He unfolded the paper and slid the sports section out.

"What did he put through it? His head?" She examined the gaping hole and wondered how many victims had suffered the same fate.

"Nah, just his fist. Then he mumbled something in Sicilian." He opened the sports section and spread it on the kitchen table.

"Oh, no, don't tell me it was a familiar vow." She knew them all.

"Okay, I won't tell you. Just don't be surprised if you see David Ferrie's name in the obituaries one of these days. And the other guy. The same day." He rested his elbows on the table.

"It's not like I'm going to look for it." She filled the coffeepot with grounds.

"He says he's gonna frame the obit and cover the hole in the wall with it." He got up and fetched two cups.

"Oh, Greta will love that. It'll look just dandy next to her Chagall there." She got the milk from the fridge.

"You think Ferrie might be Marc Antony?" He took the lid off the sugar bowl, looked inside, and replaced it.

306

"No, not the way Ruby described him. Ferrie's a low-level CIA operative, not an assassin. But he knew Ray somehow. I'll have to call Ray and tell him what happened. He might be in danger." She poured milk into the creamer.

"Ray can take care of himself." His tone carried a sharp edge, resentment lurking just beneath the surface.

"I know he can, but I still have to tell him what happened and warn him." She inhaled the rich aroma of percolating coffee. "Why does coffee have to take so long?"

"If you ever bring instant coffee into this house, I'm moving out." He went back to his sports page.

So she phoned Ray, but he was out of the office. By that afternoon he still hadn't called back, but he was busy. She went upstairs to take another hot bath.

****

Al never asked for advice in his life. Everything he did was from the seat of his pants, or on orders from some boss or from God.

But there's a first time for everything, and now he needed the advice of someone wiser—and with "the inner workings of a feminine mind."

So after making sure Vikki was upstairs teasing her hair or whatever she did to it that made him want to drown in it, he looked up Polly's number in his little book. She answered on the first ring.

"Hi, Polly, it's Al. Vikki's bodyguard."

"Hiya! I haven't stopped thinkin' about you for a minute since I got back. Well—have you changed the course a history yet?"

"You mean have we found the killer? Nah." He stretched the phone cord and reached the sofa.

"I meant did you break it off with your fiancée?"

"Oh—yeah, that'll change the course of history, too. No, I haven't yet; that's what I'm calling you about." He sat back and put his feet up on a throw pillow.

"Well, only one person can do that, mah boy, and that's you. Sorry I can't do the dirty deed for you."

"No, I decided that's what I'm going to do—have to do. But what I need to know is—how. I've never ended a relationship." He fingered the phone cord. "I don't want to hurt Mona. I want her to get on with her life. I know she'll meet a great guy. We're really not meant for each other. We'd fight all the time. We have nothing in common. The biggest thing is, I don't love her that way—like a husband should."

"So what do you need to know from me?" she asked.

"How to say it."

"You just said it, honey. Tell her exactly what you told me, and your problem's in the past. But—you got to do this in person. Verbatim. Just what you told me."

"I already forgot what I said." He laughed.

"Then write it down. She'll meet someone who'll give her the love she deserves, you got nothin' in common, you'd fight all the time, and you can't stay away from other women, one in particular—"

"Hey, I never said that!" He gripped the receiver.

She let out a guffaw. "Just kiddin'. But we do know it's the truth."

"She don't have to know that, does she?" he asked her.

"Course not," Polly said. "Think of it as something you're doin' for her, not for you. That's what diplomacy is all about."

"Okay, you're right. So—" He got up, found a pencil on the desk, and tore up a cigarette pack to write on. "You're a great girl, you'll make somebody very happy someday," he muttered as he scribbled. "What else?"

"You don't love her the way—"

"Yeah, the way a husband should," he finished for her.

"Skeer up a few of your faults, too. That'll make it easier for her to take. Then she won't think she's losin' so much. Tell her you don't empty ashtrays till they're piled to the ceilin', you leave your dirty shorts in a heap on the floor, you smoke while you're cookin' and sometimes drop ashes in the pasta fazool, your quick temper, your swaggering arrogance—"

"Hey, wait a minute!" he broke in. "Where'd you get all that?"

"Well, in'it true?"

She had him there. But how…

Ah-ha! How else? "Vikki told you all those things about me?"

"And that's just the beginnin'. I won't even tell you what she said about your bathroom habits."

"Bathroom habits?" He looked up, half expecting to see Vikki crouched on the stairs, listening in.

"Oh, just that she hears you singin' opera in the shower. Not that she complains. She loves it. But let's take first things first. Finish your business with Mona. Then, if you need any advice how to handle Vikki, we'll take that up later."

"Yeah, I told you, I can't rush it. She keeps saying she's not ready, and she's right. She's still so hung up on her husband, she won't take her wedding band off, she talks about him all the time, and you know how obsessed she is about finding this guy who did him in." He tapped the pencil on the receiver.

"Well, take care of the business at hand first. Then if you're still alive, you can call me." She followed that with a throaty chuckle, but he couldn't appreciate her humor just now. She didn't know Mona and her collection of Tuscan butcher knives.

"Okay, I know what I have to say. Listen, thanks a lot for that help, Polly. If there's anything I can do for you, just let me know." He walked over to the phone base.

"Oh, I will. But let me know how it goes."

"Will do." He hung up and stared at his scribbled cheat sheet. The length of the flight was more than enough time to memorize that. He started practicing in front of the mirror, like he'd done since he was a kid singing opera arias and Sinatra ballads with a hairbrush microphone.

If only he could sing this to the tune of "LaDonna E' Mobile," take a bow, and leave, it'd be a hell of a lot easier.

****

Vikki entered the kitchen the next morning and headed for the pastry box.

"Al asked me for a leave of absence," Rosie told her as she flipped the lid open.

"How long? What for?" She suddenly lost all her desire for crullers.

"Has to take care of some personal business, he said." Rosie went back to the racing form.

"What kind of personal business? Is he"—she let

the lid fall shut—"getting married now?"

"Didn't say, but it can't be that. I'm pickin' up the tab for that bash at the Fontainebleau, and it's not supposed to be till Easter. Unless he's gonna elope."

If only she could see the humor in that. She didn't want any coffee, either. Would Al—and especially Mona—go against old world custom and elope?

She conjured up a thousand reasons why they wouldn't. Italian girls like Mona lived for that walk down the aisle, the white gown, the flowers, the receiving line with the satin money bag, the first dance as Mr. and Mrs. She knew that well enough, having been one of them.

Elope with Jack? Well, maybe she would have. But of course she would have come back and had the church wedding, too.

But this was Al, and he wasn't the impulsive type. Certainly not adventurous enough to elope. But when Rosie made another offhand comment from behind his racing form about Al going back home to Palm Beach, she bent over as if sucker-punched.

"Back to Palm Beach? What for?"

"I dunno." He lowered the paper. "Ask him."

"No. No, it's none of my business." She waved the idea away. "I can't ask him. But how long is he going for?" She had to ask.

"Coupla days."

"It can't be an elopement, then. Unless he's bringing her back with him…" Her voice trailed off as she looked up. Al stood in the doorway, blinking at the bright light streaming through the kitchen window. He pulled his shades over his eyes. "I hardly got any sleep last night. My eyes ain't a pretty sight." He took three eggs from the fridge and balanced them in one hand on his way to the stove.

"Why did you hardly get any sleep?" She had to know. Would he tell her?

"Just have a few things on my mind." He cracked the eggs into a frying pan.

"Al—" She glanced over at Rosie making notations on his racing form and trying to reach for the phone at the same time. "You can talk to me, any time you have a personal problem. I'm a great listener. I'll be happy to help you with whatever's bothering you."

"That's okay. I think I got it fixed. I'll sleep well tonight, that's for sure." He turned the burner on under the pan.

"Rosie told me you're taking a few days off. When are you leaving?" She leaned on the counter, trying to look and sound nonchalant. But she was no actress.

"This afternoon. Just don't let the other boys get fresh," he kidded, and she could tell he winked underneath his shades.

She watched Al flip the eggs with a flourish, like he did everything else.

"I hope it turns out all right," she offered.

"Me too." He turned to face her, and she could sense his tiredness in the way he struggled to grin. What the hell was this problem he had to work out? She burned with curiosity but didn't dare ask him.

He ate his eggs without volunteering any information, and she watched the clock till he had to leave.

"I'll see you in a few days, *cara mia*. Keep the home fires burning for me."

"Sure." He gave her a cheek peck, turned, and

galloped down the driveway, leaving her longing for more.

****

Polly called her later that day and said she couldn't reach Ray. "I've been tryin' to get him on the phone for a week now. I found a picture of Ben, a spare passport photo, to show him. Have you heard from him?"

"Gee, no, now that you mention it." Vikki sat at the desk. "He still hasn't returned my calls. I didn't think anything of it, but now it does seem odd. I had my own kind of—incident the other night." She decided at that moment to tell Polly about it.

"What happened?"

"I was kidnapped. A couple of CIA guys who wanted to know what I know about the JFK plot and about Ray." That was all she wanted to say about it.

She gasped. "Oh, Lordy! Are you all right? How did you get out?"

"I bluffed my way out. Through the sewer." The stench rushed back to her, and she took a deep breath through her mouth.

"Did you get hurt?"

"Not seriously, but if my father hadn't owned a speakeasy thirty years ago, I'd have probably died in there. I found one of the false panels he'd told me about." Talking about her escape wasn't so painful.

"Someone up thar was lookin' after you, kid!"

"Oh, I know." She nodded, glancing heavenward. "But it doesn't get me any closer to finding out what I need to know."

"I wish I could help you find that snake."

Vikki reached for her phone directory. "I'm going to call Ray again." She slid the tab down to the letter S and pushed the bar down. The lid popped up, displaying the "S" page.

"Yeah, thanks. I just thought it odd, 'cause he didn't say he was fixin' to go away or anythang," Polly said.

Vikki hung up with Polly, called Ray's office, and talked to one of his partners.

Stunned and sickened, she dropped the receiver and staggered to the couch, holding her stomach.

Billy found her curled up there—how much later, she didn't know.

"You okay?"

"Ray Strauss got murdered." In a perverse way, it seemed easier to say it each time.

"When? How do you know?" He sat next to her.

"I called his office. He was found dead in his apartment, shot through the head. They ruled it a suicide. I'm wondering who's next, Dad." She wasn't afraid; she wasn't panicked. She sat still, now strangely and frighteningly calm. It seemed all the adrenaline had drained out of her and she had nothing left but acceptance, a stark resignation. "It'll be one of us."

"Look, we can call this whole thing off." He hugged her and brought her head to his shoulder. "You want that, just tell me, and Rosie'll get rid of Al and these other guys, and that'll be the end of it."

"No, Dad. Losing Al is more unbearable than someone stalking me, shooting at me, or kidnapping me. What kind of life could I have without him?" Only now, with the question out in the open, did she realize how much she needed him in her life. "No, I don't want to quit. And I don't want to lose Al."

"Are you in love with this guy, babe?" He tilted her

chin with his finger.

She nodded. "Yes. Now I can say it. I'm positive. I'm in love with him."

Talking about it took the edge off her shock, her sense of unreality, knowing she was the cause of all these murders. "God help me, but I'm in love with him."

"I don't think he'll be married for long, if at all," Billy assured her. "I think he went down there to break it off with her."

"You do?" She sat up. Her heart leapt, but with joy this time.

"It's just a hunch, but my hunches are usually right. He's pretty stuck on you, too." He gave her his winning smile.

"I'm not so sure. He hasn't—well, you know." Her hands fluttered. "Shown it."

"He's not supposed to show it. He's a professional. When this is over with, he'll be more—attentive, if you catch my drift." He wiggled his brows like Groucho.

"Then again, he might split as soon as he finishes this job. I have to admit my fear of that, too." It sounded more ominous now that she'd admitted it out loud.

"I don't think so, somehow." He shook his head.

"How do you know all this?"

"I'm a fella." He spread those long fingers. "We all think alike. I also see the way he checks you out, with obvious approval, when you're not looking."

"If it's so obvious, how come I never see it? I can't ever remember being in the same room with him and taking my eyes off him."

"Maybe I'm just more observant than you are." He

chucked her on the chin.

"Oh, I hope you're right, Dad. I'm also worried he's going to get it next, like he almost did in New Orleans. It's one thing to put myself in danger, but everybody else—" She shuddered.

"If some high-powered hit man wanted to get you, or Al, or any of us, he would've already. These guys don't wait till the weather's nice or till Saturn is in conjunction with Pluto. Ray was in the CIA, wasn't he?" He pulled off his shoes and slid into his slippers directly in front of his lounge chair.

"He used to be," she said. "Before I worked for him. But now I'm wondering. Ferrie asked me about him when they had me in that old speak. But Ray didn't know anything about the JFK plot."

"So he said." Billy picked up his shoes and deposited them in the hall closet—just the way Greta had trained him.

"You think he was keeping something from me?" she called to him across the room. "Something about knowing David Ferrie or something to do with the CIA's involvement in the assassination?" rushed out in one breath.

"All these guys are secretive, lead double lives, the whole bit. He was snooping where he shouldn't." He came back and sat next to her. "Didn't you say he had a private phone line he used with a fake name?"

She nodded. "Just like your red phone."

"He had that for a reason."

"I don't want to know." She turned away.

Just then the front doorknob jiggled and the door swung open. Al trudged in, stamped his boots on the mat, and dropped his valise on the floor. Her heart tumbled. Billy got out of the way.

"Hi." She kept her tone casual, like she hadn't been counting the hours till his return.

He held out his arms. "*Cara mia.*" He wrapped her in a welcoming hug. "It's all over between me and Mona, Vikki. I'm a free man now."

She refrained from jumping up and down. It wasn't easy, but no way would she be like those women JFK "couldn't get rid of." She just stood there and said, "Really? And no black eye?"

"Ah, that's not where she hit me."

She didn't hide her smile as she helped him off with his coat. "What'll it be, Chivas Regal, anisette, a goblet of chilled *vino rosso*?"

"You know what I've been dyin' for the whole time I was away, but didn't want to ask for it?"

"What?" She hung his coat up.

"A great big glass of milk with that gooey chocolate syrup of yours."

"Coming right up!" She skipped into the kitchen, then stopped herself, remembering Ray's tragic death. She didn't want to hit Al with a casual "by the way, Ray Strauss is dead," so she fixed his chocolate milk, opened the pastry box, and saved the news for afterwards, when they'd all be in attendance.

She joined him in a glass of milk but sat in silence, lost in her thoughts. Of course someone in the CIA or behind the assassination plot had killed Ray. Just like all the others—including Jack.

Pushing all that aside, she focused on the here and now. Thank God Al was back where he belonged.

"It's so good to have you home." She stood, went over to him and gave him a heartfelt hug.

He grasped her hands.

"Home?" He looked up at her, a smile playing on his lips.

"Oh…" She covered her mouth with her hand. "Did I say that?"

Chapter Nineteen

"Ha-a-a-y, who's this gorgeous bombshell? What's Jacqueline Bouvier Kennedy doing here?" Al growled as Vikki glided down the stairs. Passing the hall mirror, she did a double-take.

"Yikes, I do look like her, don't I?" Her red kerchief, black wig, and dark glasses concealed her features so well it scared her.

"You should get great service at the Russian Tea Room. You just need to get the girly whispery voice down pat." He approached her and fingered the wig.

"Forget the girly whispery voice." She sat on the sofa and pulled off the disguise. "I don't know why all this is necessary. It's enough Dad hired those soldiers posted outside and I'm under virtual house arrest. The only way I'm allowed out of the house is in a car through the garage. Why do I have to go out in a Halloween costume?"

"For your safety, *cara mia*." He stood back and gazed at her.

"Then why don't you wear a disguise?"

He looked himself up and down and flexed his muscles. She tried to turn her head the other way. But it had a mind of its own. "Like what?" he asked.

"I don't know—how about you and Roberto sharing a horse costume? He can be the back end, of course."

He screwed up his face. "Much as I love horses, that wouldn't suit my personality."

"Then *you* be the back end."

He came closer. "Put the wig and glasses back on, Vikki."

She grew warm, and her pulse went into overdrive as she inhaled his clean scent. He'd just showered, and not with Mr. Bubble. "What for?"

"Put it back on, look in the mirror real close, and tell me if you feel like someone else."

She geared up again and turned to the mirror inside the china cabinet. "Yes, I suppose I do feel different. It makes me want to do things I wouldn't normally do." She twirled to face him, knowing he had the same idea.

"Tell me what kind of things, Vikki." His voice rumbled like a lion's purr.

She didn't need to answer that. They fell into each other's arms. His mouth claimed hers. She pressed herself up against his surging hardness.

"Will you come to the Plaza with me?" he breathed.

She didn't think she could wait that long. But she also didn't want to reach the point of no return right here in her father's dining room. Or anywhere in his house. Or at all.

"That's not a good Idea right now, Al."

"Then when will it be a good idea?" He ran his hands over her wig and it came off. "Oh, *managgia*," he groaned.

"Sorry, now I'm me again. Kind of kills the moment, doesn't it?"

"Vikki, you truly believe I just wanted to make love to you in a disguise?" He regarded her with mock hurt in his eyes and a playful smile on his lips.

"It helped, didn't it?"

"It doesn't matter what you're wearing. It's you I love." He cupped her chin to look into her eyes.

Did she hear right? She licked her suddenly dry lips and pulled away to get some air. "You—love me?"

"What do you think?" His heavy breathing convinced her. "I have no interest in even looking at another woman. I ended my engagement. Would I have done that if I didn't love you?"

"So—now what?" She swallowed, her throat parched.

"So now I wait for you. As long as it takes."

She took a breath and let out a sigh. "Al, I'm just not ready yet."

"You'll always cherish Jack's memory. But he's gone. And we're here. And you know he would've wanted you to love again."

"But not this soon." She took the wig from him and shook it out to occupy her hands.

"We don't have to elope. But it's not wrong to love each other." His tone became pleading. "If you want to keep it quiet, nobody has to know."

"It's not exactly easy to hide it, Al. My father knows—well, he knows there's something between us." She fumbled with the wig.

"I know. So does Rosie. And Greta. And the boys. And Polly." He counted on his fingers.

"Polly? How could she tell?"

"She was a madam, *cara mia*. You don't think she can tell love from lust?" He smiled.

Vikki faced the mirror, put the wig back on, and straightened it. He embraced her from behind, and they studied their reflections.

"I know it's a mirror, but I'm looking at someone else," she commented as he ran a hot trail of kisses down her neck. She shivered in delight.

"Then you can be someone else." His hands slid farther down and encircled her waist.

She turned around and sought his lips. When the kiss ended, she answered, "It's like living out a fantasy. It's scary, and deliciously forbidden at the same time. But why do I need a disguise to feel like this?"

"You don't." He pulled the wig off and tossed it on the floor, along with the glasses. "When the lights are out, you can be whoever you want. And I'll be whoever you want."

"You mean dress up as Don Giovanni or something?" She shook her head. "No. I want you to be you."

"Then let me take you to the Plaza." His hands caressed her curves, setting her on fire. His lips were a breath away.

"Not now. I still have some emotions to sort through first."

He took a ragged breath and released her. She went cold all of a sudden.

"You sure know how to keep Pizza Roma in business," he said.

"Why?"

"'Cause every time this happens, I need to chow my frustrations away." He headed for the phone.

"Oh. Okay. Order me one, too."

****

That night, she had a good stare at herself in the disguise. An idea started forming in her mind, and she got on the phone to Polly before any of it slipped away. This was too profound an idea even to write down first.

"Hi, darlin'. How's it goin'?"

"Fine, Polly. I thought of a way to get Ben to show up." A stab of fear shot through her as she voiced those words.

"Oh, yeah? What is it?"

"Well—" She rolled a sip of anisette around her tongue. "My father and Rosie are making me wear disguises now, and although I think the idea's a little over the top, now I know what it feels like to be someone else."

"Oh, yeah, baby, I know what that's like. That's what my business is all about."

"It's like acting in a play, isn't it?" Vikki asked her.

"Shuur is, but it don't always end when the curtain falls."

"Well, in the course of my studies, I learned how politicians deal with people—on their own level," Vikki said. "Don't talk down to them, but as one of them. That's how you get votes. They have to identify with you and look to you as a leader at the same time. Like the fictional characters in a story. The Kennedys' Camelot was a prime example. The First Family was the ideal family—people looked up to them and wanted a fairy tale to follow every day. It's a paradox, being above them and one of them at the same time, but you have to deal with people that way to get them to do what you want. It works like a charm—just watch any politician in action."

"Right you are, sugar."

"So I thought, why not work it to my advantage?

323

Then I started thinking of the kind of person Ben is, and thought of a way to get him to show up." She stopped to take another sip.

"Go on."

"Tell him we're going to open another brothel. A real high-class one, on Manhattan's Upper East Side. I'll be the madam, and you and Al can be investors. But I also want Ben's help—he did so well bringing in girls, we can use his recruiting expertise again, sign him on as a partner, and give him a cut of the profits. When his interest is piqued, I can pump him for information on what happened to Jack."

"Hmm." Polly's voice hummed over the wire. "It might work. I'll start spreadin' word around that the proposition's open, and hope he surfaces."

"It should work. It's dealing with him on his own level, something he's interested in. The prospect of making pots of money—the honest way. Well, not quite so honest, but it's downright respectable compared to the way he's been making a living. I just hope when it comes to a battle of wits, I'll win." Vikki forced determination into her voice.

Polly guffawed. "Honey, if it's a battle between the two a you's wits, it'll be like Eleanor Roosevelt versus Freddie Flintstone. Don't worry about outsmartin' him. Without his sniper rifle, he's just another *capo di cazzo.*"

Vikki had never heard Italian spoken with a Louisiana accent before.

****

"Rosie left these for you," Billy said the next morning when she sat at the breakfast table. He placed two neatly clipped newspaper articles in front of her.

The first one said that David Ferrie, a CIA contract agent who knew both Ruby and Oswald, and also worked for Carlos Marcello, had "suffered a brain hemorrhage" and was found dead in his New Orleans apartment.

The second article said that CIA agent Aladio del Valle, a close friend and colleague of David Ferrie, was killed in Miami the same day that Ferrie died in New Orleans. He'd been shot in the heart and his skull split open with a machete.

"Jesus, Mary, and Saint Joseph." She shook her head in disbelief as she read it again and again. "Did Rosie—" She finished the question with hand gestures.

"Don't ask, babe," Billy replied. "It's not polite."

****

With the card Franck LeJardin had given her the night he'd pulled her from the sewer, she and Al went to his Vestry Street gallery. She bought two paintings of tropical beaches, and Al bought a small sculpture of a ming tree. Franck wasn't there, so she left him a note thanking him once again and promising to come back soon.

She hung one painting over the hole Rosie had punched in the wall, and it held its own next to the Chagall.

Billy looked at the signature. "Oh, yeah, your mother shared her Tenth Street studio with an artist named LeJardin." He nodded, showing no particular interest. She knew her father had no passion for art; he'd never said much about her mother's paintings. But they were all she had of the mother she'd never known, so she'd hung them throughout her own Camelot. "This guy must be his son."

She ran a finger over the raised brushstrokes. "His work is nothing to drool over, but after all, the guy saved my life. If Greta doesn't like it hanging here, she can find something else to cover Rosie's hole. Franck said he's the only one of his family ever to make a living from painting."

"That's not hard to believe. I don't know what happened to his old man, but if this guy makes enough to eat selling this stuff, God bless him," Billy said.

"I plan to buy a lot more from him, Dad. He pulled me from a sewer and didn't ask questions."

"That was very noble of him, but you don't have to be his lifelong benefactress. Just buy him a small loft with a good bomb shelter in the basement." He looked at her with a twinkle in his eye.

"I feel like I owe him," she admitted, trying to acquaint herself with her new painting.

"Maybe he should join the rescue squad. He'd make a much better living." Billy gave the painting another once-over and turned away. "Hey, did I ever tell you about the time your mother sculpted a statue of me naked? And unveiled it in front of the whole family?"

"No, Dad, and I don't think I want to." She rolled her eyes. Another of his legends. "How 'bout you spare me this time?"

His eyes focused on some long-ago memory, and a dreamy smile played on his lips. "I gotta admit, it was the best damn art she ever created. A few more of those, and she might've made some bucks."

"Where is it now?" Vikki asked.

"I gave it to Les Fontaine." He lowered his eyes, as if he'd regretted it.

"You gave Les Fontaine *that* statue? The one of the guy with the—" She started to gesture but stopped short. That sculpture had stood on the mantel of her father's lyricist for years. About a foot tall, in flesh-colored clay, it had delicate facial features and the body of a Greek god. Its most prominent detail: an especially well-endowed, fully aroused male member.

She grimaced. "Oh, God, Dad! That's a statue of you?"

"In the flesh," he boasted, buffing his nails on his shirt. "I mean, in the clay. You never noticed it says 'Billy' in big letters on the base?"

She shook her head. "No, I never dared venture that close."

"Well, it was me, thirty years ago. But I can still hold up pretty well, if I don't mind saying so."

She didn't want to acknowledge his double entendre. But she was getting an idea. Maybe Franck could sculpt her nude for Al…

What a way to reward a local artist for saving her life!

****

Linc Benjamin came over the next night with a bottle of champagne. She took his coat, ushered him into the living room, and Billy popped the cork at the bar.

"By the way, Linc, what are we celebrating?" Vikki asked.

"My emancipation. I resigned from the network."

"What?" She couldn't have been more surprised if he'd told her Paul quit The Beatles and he replaced him. "Why?"

"Because it's been unbearable for some time now."

He sat on the sofa.

Billy poured them each a flute. "You kids want some privacy, or you wanna sit out here, or what?"

"No, it's okay, Mr. McGlory." He took the drink Billy held out to him.

They toasted his newfound freedom.

"I'm not the only one resigning," Linc said. "Several of the staff already quit. It's Whitefield. He's become insufferable."

"Herbert Whitefield?" Her eyes widened in surprise. "The V.P.? How?"

"He's always been obnoxious, pushy, greedy, and a coward, but his ego's got the best of him now. Since he got promoted to Executive Producer, he thinks he's running the Roman Empire, the British Empire, and the Third Reich, all combined." Linc took a sip of the bubbly. "I couldn't take it anymore. Not only that, he's been hitting the bottle even heavier than usual. Some days he shows up for work with half a bag on. He was a reformed alcoholic, but I guess he fell off the wagon again."

"Did you find another position?" Vikki asked him.

"No, not yet. I'm going to do what Jack always threatened to do. Sail around the world for a year, climb mountains, go diving in the Great Barrier Reef. I've always wanted to write a novel about Richard the Third. And not the monster Shakespeare made him out to be."

"I guess this is the winter of your discontent." Billy refilled their flutes, emptying the bottle.

"It's been the *year* of my discontent. I've had it up to here with Whitefield"—Linc gestured with his hand—"and mark my words, NBS will suffer for it, too. He wants to bring in all this absurd programming, these fist-in-the-mouth talk shows, create a variety show to compete with Ed Sullivan…now who could possibly compete with Ed Sullivan?"

"Maybe give Topo Gigio his own show?" she ventured.

"I'd rather have Topo Gigio run the network," Linc said.

Billy clapped Linc on the back. "Well, I admire ya, son. You gotta go with your gut sometimes. Take your year off and enjoy it."

"When's your last day?" she asked.

"End of the month. I haven't made any plans yet, so we'll get together again before I go anywhere." He took another sip. "So how about you, Vik? Any progress?"

"We're working on a way for my friend Polly to smoke out her elusive husband, Ben Bati." But she didn't want to say how.

His eyes widened. "Oh, he's the main suspect, isn't he?"

"He's the only one left."

"How are you going to get any information out of him if you find him?" he directed the question to Billy.

"Oh, ve haf our vays." He held his cigarette with his palm up.

"Okay, I don't need to hear the gory details." Linc waved his glass. "Are you—going to tell the press when it—when anything happens, if you catch him and find out he was Jack's killer?"

"God, no!" She shuddered. "I've been through enough. All I'd need now is the press hounding me. It was bad enough when Jack was alive. I always avoided the cameras, the lights, all that."

"You're a chip off the old block in enough ways." Billy gave her a shoulder hug. "I'm glad my kids aren't in showbiz. There's no business like show business, but it can get the best of you if you ain't got your head on straight."

"Don't I know it," Linc agreed. "It'll be good to get away for a while and be a nobody. And let Whitefield dig his own grave. He's making a big mistake. Alienating the staff, leading the network on the road to ruin. He's got visions of Emmys, but he'll be lucky if he doesn't get turfed out on his ass after the next season starts."

"Maybe he'll see the error of his ways when ratings start to plummet and his name doesn't come up on the list of Emmy nominees," Vikki offered.

"That pompous ass? He'll go to his grave thinking he's God's gift to broadcast journalism." Linc let out a sardonic laugh. "Hey, that reminds me. Did Jack ever tell you about the time he set it up to make it look like Whitefield got nominated for an Emmy?"

"No, was that another of his practical jokes?" Vikki couldn't wait to hear this.

"Oh, was it ever." Linc shook his head, chuckling. "He burst into Whitefield's office with this bogus telegram from Hollywood, telling him 'Herb! You've been nominated!' Whitefield's head could barely fit through the door. He goes to the travel office and gets a plane ticket to L.A., a new tux, the works, and he's about to get into a stretch limo to LaGuardia, when Jack comes out and tells him it's all a gag, and *he* was the nominee instead. So Jack shoves him aside, gets into the limo, and it takes off!"

She smiled. "That was classic Jack."

Billy said, "Whew, he must've had it in for this bastard."

"It was a friendly rivalry. But Jack never passed up a chance to dish it out. Whitefield went apeshit. Kept saying 'I'll show him. I'll win an Emmy and bash him over the head with it!' Of course it never happened. Jack won that year. Really stuck it to him."

She smiled. "You know, I've finally reached the point where I can remember things Jack did and not break down. The cross gets easier to bear every day."

"Hey, as long as we're standing around polishing off the champagne, how 'bout a pie to go with it?" Billy offered.

"Sounds great, Dad. I'll have the Large Super Supreme Special."

"You must be hungry." Billy rubbed his tummy.

"Starved."

"Want some wine to go with it?" He went for the phone.

"Sure. You got any chilled in here?" She opened the refrigerator door.

"I don't think there's any left. I'll go down the cellar and get a few bottles."

A surge went through her. The wine cellar. Right next to where Al was pumping his weights. "I'll go!" She dashed out of there and down the stairs like they were on fire.

He was doing bench presses. She headed for the wine cellar, rubbernecking as she walked by him.

"Just passin' through." She tried to keep the excited pitch out of her voice but couldn't help it. His heavy inhaling and exhaling did things to her, even at a distance of six feet. Her eyes strayed over to him. The straining muscles and bare chest didn't help her blood pressure any, either. *Man, that's some slab of beefcake.* "Dad's ordering pizza. Care to join us?"

He put the barbell down, stood, and stretched.

"You really have to do that in front of me?" she teased, eyeing him up and down. It was then she noticed he was wearing shiny black dress shoes.

"You're right," he said. "It's not fair. Strip down to your drawers and stretch, and we'll be even." Now he did some eyeing up and down of his own.

She broke into a smile and shook her head. "Fair? You don't play fair. Why don't you wear a sweatsuit? You're not even decent."

"I'm not?" He turned and primped in his floor-length mirror. "I think I look decent enough. Tell me what you object to, and I'll remove it immediately. Or you can do the honors."

"Well, you can start with the spit-shined shoes. What's the idea of that? In case you have to run out to a funeral?" Without thinking, she inched closer. He stepped around the bench and they stood within fondling distance.

"To answer that question, my loafers are at the cobbler's getting new heels, and to the first question, I wear nothing but boxers 'cause I don't expect to be seen down here. It would be nice to sweat and grunt in private," he replied a bit defensively, but maintaining his amused air.

"Any space that's on the way to the wine cellar in this house can never be considered private," she challenged. "There's more traffic here than in the corner deli."

"You want me to put a curtain up?" he offered with

a twinkle in his eye.

"No! Well…no, that's not necessary. Just—Greta might come down here and see you like that."

He burst out laughing. "Greta? Like she'd object."

She placed her fists on her hips. "What kind of place would this be if we all paraded around in our underwear?" she further goaded him.

"Nobody would think anything of it. Just like at a nudist colony. You only look out of place when you're clothed." He gestured up and down at her.

She didn't want to go into that. She'd been to a nudist beach on St. Maarten and fled without removing a stitch. But she wouldn't admit that to him.

"Okay, Al, your body is obscenely gorgeous. You don't give a damn about privacy; you'd strut your stuff in the buff if you could. But I honestly only did come down here to fetch a few wine bottles."

"Then don't let me keep you any further." He gave a mock bow and cleared the way.

"Thank you." She passed by. He had her so distracted, if she hadn't been in a wine cellar, she'd have completely forgotten what she'd come here for. She gathered up four bottles of Valpolicella, and he took them from her on her way out.

"Allow me." He now wore sweat pants and a guinea T-shirt, three sizes too small, of course. "Maybe someday I could be a contender." He recited a variation of the famous Brando line, gently pushing a strand of hair off her cheek.

She had to pry her eyes away. She took her glasses off so he'd be no more than a blur. "Don't start now, Al. Not with pizza coming in twenty minutes."

As she headed for the staircase, she noticed the

thermometer on the wall—it was only 62 degrees down here. So why was she sweating?

****

Waiting for pizza delivery wasn't as exciting as an iron-pumping Al dressed like Brando, but it was safer. So she headed back upstairs. Billy spread his favorite red-and-white-checkered cloth over the dining room table, stuck a candle into an old Chianti bottle, and put Al Martino's "Chitarra Romana" on the hi-fi.

"Ah, *bellissimo*, we're at Umberto's!" He uncorked the wine with a pop. Greta didn't look Al's way once—she sat next to Billy, clinked glasses with him, and undoubtedly played footsie with him under the table. Vikki hid a smug grin. So much for Al's claim that Greta had a roving eye for him.

Devouring the pie and wine, they gabbed about Greta's latest book and Billy's next musical. But the conversation drifted to finding Jack's killer. Vikki didn't dredge up the subject—Al did.

"So, what's Bati's connection to Marc Antony?" Linc asked, going into his pigeon-neck routine again. "Or do you think it's the same guy?"

"It very well may be the same guy." Vikki sipped her wine. "And now that I know Bati's wife, I'm hoping she can roust him out and make the connection."

"I'd go for the scatter technique, myself." Billy bit into his pizza.

Linc looked up. "What's that?"

"That's dismemberment of the body into burlap bags and spreading them along the Jersey Turnpike." He chewed and chomped, like this sort of chatter happened every night at the dinner table. "Or if it's summer, we can put him in the Sicilian oven."

"The Sicilian oven?" Linc held his pizza slice in midair.

Billy nodded. "That's stuffing a dead body into the trunk of a car when it's really hot out—"

"Dad, we're trying to eat here." Her appetite vanishing, Vikki put down her pizza and took a gulp of wine.

"It's okay, Vikki. I feel the same way," Linc said. "I'd like to catch the bastard and tear him limb from limb personally." His fist tightened around the stem of his glass.

She looked at him good and hard, although her glasses were off. "I thought you were such a peacenik."

"You know how I felt about Jack. If you find his killer, I want him to get what's coming to him!" Linc's voice broke with emotion.

Maybe it was the wine talking, or maybe Linc really did feel this way.

"I want to find him first. But I got a map of the Jersey Turnpike anyway," she added with a smirk.

"I'm just sorry Frost got taken out before he could find out anything, much as I disliked him," Linc said. "I want this bastard caught as much as you."

"After Jack got killed, I realized I couldn't rely on the law." Vikki picked up her slice of pizza, hoping her appetite would revisit. "We ran into one dead end after another, but I can't give up. Jack never would've given up if this were reversed."

"But have you thought about what you're going to do if—I mean, *when* you're sure you've got the killer?" Linc persisted as Billy leaned over and refilled his glass.

"After we've interrogated him and he's all but

confessed, we'll turn him in," she answered with a firm nod. "Then maybe they'll be convinced enough to reopen the case, if there's a live suspect in front of them."

"If you want to uphold tradition, it's easier just to pop him one," Al chimed in. "He don't deserve the justice system."

"Shooting's pretty messy, so make sure you don't do it on my rug," Greta warned. "Billy, remember you told me that cop bled all over your Persian rug after they beat the crap out of him, and you could never get the stains out?"

Billy jabbed his fork into his salad. "Yeah, and they hadn't even plugged him. Just roughed him up a little. But he was a mess, crappin' in his pants and all. Stunk worse than a body in a Sicilian oven."

This evoked a grimace from Linc. "Jeez, the things you folks talk about over dinner. And I thought journalists had cast-iron stomachs!"

A scattered laugh reverberated around the table as Billy uncorked another wine bottle. "Yeah, I guess we have a unique way of keeping a conversation rolling along." He held his glass up for a toast. "*Salut.* And when we do find him, Linc, you'll be the first to know. But if you're at another network by then, just keep it off the six o'clock news."

****

As they lingered over coffee and cake, Vikki relaxed, knowing Jack's killer was within reach. They were in the home stretch. She didn't know how she knew; it was just a gut feeling.

After Linc left, Billy and Greta went for a soak in their oversized tub, leaving Vikki alone with Al.

"So—what say we go to a movie? Or just stay home and play a few hands of gin rummy, or—" He helped her out of her chair, wrapped one arm around her back, and clasped her hand as if slow dancing. "Or come up with a better idea." He kissed her hand, his voice husky with lust.

She indulged in his closeness as they swayed to the imaginary strains of an Italian love song. "Hmm, if we were all alone in the house, I'd put a Sergio Franchi record on. It's been ages since I went dancing." She pulled away, once again fighting her desire. She grabbed her napkin off the table and wiped her forehead. "We can't let anything happen with my father home! Besides, I don't feel like going out, hiding behind that disguise, bundling up in the cold—let's just stay here and—behave ourselves." She didn't dare admit, even to herself, what she wanted to do, right there on the rug in front of the roaring fire, with Sergio Franchi singing "Core 'ngrato" in the background.

He poured them each an anisette and settled on the sofa. It was up to her how close or far from him she wanted to sit; the invitation was clearly open.

She left a hand's length between them. A small hand.

"How are you feeling these days, Vikki?" He crossed his leg over his knee and grabbed his ankle with his free hand. "Deep down?"

She thought for a moment. "Better than I have. I'll never get over Jack's death, but I feel alive again more often. Although time's passing, and I have my family around me, and—and you, I've been finding that recovery within myself. I've been praying and—it's easier when I don't drink."

"Almost everything is easier when you don't drink. But I'm glad I've been helping, too."

"Yes, you really are. I didn't want you here at first, when you showed up on the doorstep. But now I don't want to imagine what it would be like here without you." She let her heart speak, knowing it wouldn't scare him away. They were way past that now.

His arm slid around her and brought her close. Was that his heart thumping or hers? "Good to know I'm doing my job."

"It's more than a job now, Al. We both know that." She rested her hand on his chest. Yup, that sure was his heart thumping. Faster than hers even.

"Let me know when you feel fully alive." He kissed the top of her head.

"Then what?"

"Then I'll propose marriage to you, and if my prayers are answered, you'll say yes." He tilted her head back with his thumb and lowered his lips to hers. She savored his lingering kiss.

Then it hit her like an oncoming train. "W—wait a minute." She sat up. "You'd—propose to me? You'd want to marry me?"

"Not *would* want to marry you, I *do* want to marry you. I plan to ask, but when you're ready. If you say no, I'll ask you again. Till you do say yes. I hope you'll give in when the begging gets to you."

She fell back against the sofa cushion, dizzy. "But—you just broke off with your fiancée, and you talk like you want to be free—"

"Why do you think I broke off with her?" He played with her hair. "I never loved her. I love you."

"But—"

"Why all these buts?" His eyes pinned hers. "There's no 'but' here. I'm going to wait till I feel the time is right, and then I'm going to pop the question. But now it won't be such a pop anymore. I didn't want to spoil the surprise. But you did ask, and I always answer up front, *cara mia*."

"You don't want a traditional Italian marriage, do you?" she blurted, then wished she had held her tongue, sorry she'd opened her big mouth. "You did say you spelled it out to Mona that you wanted an arrangement."

"That was different. I didn't love her…for the gazillionth time." He twirled a lock of her hair around his finger. "Why? Do you have something against the traditional Italian marriage?"

"I've never had one. I had the traditional Italian wedding, but the marriage was far from traditional." Now she was comfortable talking about it, since he'd brought it up.

"Oh—because Jack wasn't Italian?"

"It wasn't just that." She tucked her feet under her. "He was Jack. He had his flaws, but I was so much in love with him, I took the bad with the good. That should be in the vows, besides 'in sickness and in health, for richer or for poorer.' It should include 'for faithfulness or unfaithfulness' to cover all the bases."

"He was unfaithful to you?" He whistled. "*Mama mia*, and you talk about him like he was a saint."

"I used to. But he was very human. I knew he had other women, but I found out to what extent after he died." She spared him the details about "L.L." for now.

"You're either very forgiving or way ahead of your time." He gathered her hair in bunches and let it fall through his fingers.

She shook her head and closed her eyes. "He told me before we got married that he had a tendency to stray. It was part of being in show business, but more accurately it was part of being Jack. So my option was to take it or leave it. But I was so happy in my Camelot, with comfort, security, a beautiful home, all the charge plates I could want, so a few flings with some starlet—" She reached over to the table and grabbed a cigarette from the silver holder. "I could've done whatever I wanted with whomever. Although I didn't. I was happy with my life the way it was. I didn't need anything or anyone else. But obviously he did." She offered him a smoke. He lit them both with his lighter.

"I'm sorry, *cara mia*. But not too many wives put up with the *comare* these days. I wonder when that tradition flew out the window, the *comare* and the understanding wife. After the war, maybe?"

"Could be. When we realized we could live without men." She took a long drag.

"Yeah, give a dame the vote and she wants to run the world," he said over a laugh.

She stabbed him with a glare that made him flinch.

"Hey, it was a joke, okay?" He held his palms up in surrender. "Go run the world if you want. Just leave enough time to make my supper and iron my shirts."

She shook her head, giving him a sweet smile. "We'll have a maid and a cook, darling."

"How about a bodyguard?" he asked.

"I don't think I'll need one any more." She stubbed her cigarette out.

"Hey, here we are talking about this like it's really going to happen."

She looked into his eyes, glad she was nearsighted. She saw every tantalizing feature so clearly—the parenthesis around his mouth, the crinkles around his eyes, flecks of gold in the irises, and every black lash. "You're really going to wait for me, Al? Until all this is over, and I'm functioning like a real person again?"

"To the ends of the earth." He ground out his cig, leaned toward her, and their lips met.

She indulged in his warm, soft, and deliciously slow kiss. Their bodies prolonged their embrace, and he lowered her to the cushions. Their kiss came to an end. She nibbled at his neck, pressed her body to his, desire coursing through her. Oh, how she wanted him…

****

Billy came down the stairs for a nightcap and glanced into the living room. He noticed the glow in the fireplace, Vikki's eyeglasses and the anisette bottle on the table. The couch faced the other way, but nobody was sitting on it. "Where'd they go?" Then he realized they hadn't gone anywhere—and they were on the couch, but not sitting. Before he got out of their way, he placed a long-playing record on the phonograph.

Jackie Gleason's *For Lovers Only*.

****

Vikki was upstairs cleaning her guns, and Greta and Billy were working in their separate studios when Al answered the door two days later.

"Hey! Polly!" He stepped aside to let her enter, picked her up and twirled her around.

"Howdy, mah boy—uh, man. Congratulations! You're free! I'm very proud of you!"

He took her coat and brought her valise inside. "Yeah, it wasn't easy, but Mona took it better than I

341

thought she would. I was prepared for a serious bout and coming back in bandages. I'd never admit this to anybody else, but I was…" He made circles in the air with his hands. "How you say, paralyzed. I've never felt that way before." He paused. "Well, I did, once, when my father was killed right in front of me. And I was a little kid then."

"I understand, babe. There's a little kid in all of us." She patted his cheek. "And there's a whole lotta kid in some of us."

He led her to the sofa and called up the stairs to Vikki, "*Cara mia*, you have a visitor."

Vikki approached the landing, peeking over the banister. Then she caught a glimpse of piled-up red hair and came flying down. "Polly! What are you doing here? My God! It's so good to see you!" They hugged and cheek-kissed.

As Vikki headed for the bar to fix her a drink, Polly clutched Vikki's elbow. "Have I got news for you."

Vikki spun around. "What?" She held her breath.

"Ben's comin' to town. He got wind of our proposed bordello purchase, called me, and I told him to meet us in New York on Friday to discuss the arrangements. You'll be able to meet him, talk to him, blow his brains out, whatever in holy haail you want."

"Oh, God! Polly!" Emotion burst out of her: grief, excitement, trepidation, all in a jumble. Polly held her close and they rocked back and forth in glee.

When Vikki calmed down, she looked at Al. He opened his arms and she stepped into his embrace. "Another step closer to the truth. The last, I hope."

She led Polly to the sofa. "When's he coming?

How can we set this up?"

"He's probably in the city by now." Polly kicked off her shoes. "He always liked to stay at the Pierre."

"The Pierre, hmm?" Vikki thought fast. She glanced over at Al, standing with his arms folded, head cocked, listening intently. "Al, you mind if Polly and I have some girl talk?"

Without a word he gave a salute and vanished.

"Now, this is what we'll do." Vikki clasped her hands, index fingers pointing up. "I'll be the madam of the new establishment. I'll tell Ben we want him as a partner and go over some details about a business plan. Meanwhile, I have a way to work Jack into the conversation. If I just walk in there and start asking questions about his involvement with Jack's death, he'll get suspicious." She watched Polly nod. "You told me a lot about him. I know how to get a man of his ilk to do what I want. I don't have to spell it out, do I, Pol?"

Polly's smile told her. "I'm a lousy speller, but I catch your drift."

"Okay, then—" Vikki shut her eyes and focused on her plan. "I'll have a good chance of finding out what I want to know. Also, I—" She halted. "I wasn't going to say this, but we're already good friends, and confiding in you will make my soul a lot lighter."

"Spill it, honey." Polly sipped her drink.

"I went to Catholic schools," Vikki said. "Between my parents and the nuns, I was raised the good Catholic girl. That comes with a lot of contradictions when you're at odds with raging hormones and what's right and wrong, what's a sin and what will keep your soul out of hell. Dressing like a high-class madam, taking on this role—" She took a deep breath and released it, trying to ease her mounting excitement. "I'm acting out a fantasy of sorts, and carrying out my mission at the same time. I've never done anything this outrageous before. It's a once-in-a-lifetime occurrence. And I think I'll be a lot more effective in carrying out my mission because I'm doing this only once. I'll never do it again—either I make it or break it in this one chance," she declared with a determined nod. "I'll go to confession later," she half joked.

"You don't need to go to confession, honey." Polly took Vikki's hand. "No one's gonna send you down there with what's 'iz name. God won't condemn ya soul to torture. You want to do this, you do it. Trust your instincts. This is your instincts talkin', and you gotta go with it. Dressin' up as a madam or call girl is far from a sin. It's the doin' it for real that might hold you up at the gates for a while."

Vikki returned her friend's smile. "Okay. So I'm going to do this. Everything is guiding me in this direction. It must work. And it will work! You have to deal with people on their own level. Well, this sure seems like Ben's level."

"I never even thought of him havin' a level." Polly took another nip.

"I'll cajole the truth out of him." Vikki glanced in the direction of her father's studio. "I don't want my family to know about this, either."

"You don't want your family to know we found him, finally?" Polly's eyes widened. Her spidery lashes spread apart.

Vikki shook her head. "They've been breathing down my neck since this whole thing started. This is entirely my doing. I want no interference." She cut the air with her hand. "I want to do it my way. This is my mission, and I'm going to carry it out. Now that we're this close to Ben"—she held her thumb and forefinger an inch apart—"I'm not handing the reins over to anybody. I can handle him."

Polly gave Vikki an assuring nod. Her earrings jangled. "If that's what you want to do, I'm with you all the way, honey. But you'd better take the bodyguards with you. Or at least Al."

"I don't want anyone interfering, for once." But how could she do this behind their backs now? She was practically a prisoner here. "I'll be up front with Al and tell him my entire plan. But if he gives me a hard time, I just may have to use some diplomacy on him." She knew just what kind of "diplomacy" worked on him.

"Be very careful with Ben, Vikki," Polly warned, shaking a finger at her. "He's got no conscience. He's as cold-blooded as a lizard. I don't want to see anything happen to you."

"I know what I'm doing, Polly. Trust me." Vikki squared her shoulders and sat up straight. "How can he pass up a chance to spend some time with a gorgeous redheaded madam in his room at the Pierre?"

"He won't. Especially if there's profit potential."

Chapter Twenty

After Polly left, Vikki went up to her room to plan this meeting with Bati. "Oh, if only I'd taken acting lessons," she enunciated in her best Kate Hepburn imitation. Playing Sheila Horwitz had been a piece of cake compared to this—the role of a lawyer wasn't quite the stretch a call girl would be.

She grabbed her bedside note pad and pen to draft a list of questions and his possible answers. She recited them out loud, opened her jewel box and took out her most valuable pieces, hidden under the plastic pop beads and other costume jewelry.

Of course she had to tell Al about all this. *What's he doing right now?* she wondered. She'd sent him to his room when Polly was visiting, and he hadn't come out.

With a reckless urge, she tried on her new curly red wig. When she looked in the mirror, that same forbidden shiver of delight came over her as with the Jackie getup. She was no longer Vikki Ward but a product of her imagination, ready to think, do, and say whatever her whimsy's urges desired—kind of an alter-ego.

That alter-ego knew what she wanted to do right now.

Before she changed her mind, she slid on her Frederick's of Hollywood push-up bra, slinked into a black sheath, slipped into stiletto heels, and glided down the hallway to Al's room. Her rap on his door echoed her heartbeat.

She counted, "One, two, three—"

The door opened. "Yeah, what—h-a-a-a-y." They eyed each other from head to toe in less than a second. "You look, uh…bedroomy."

"Sorry to wake you." But her smile told him *I'm not a bit sorry.*

"Are you kiddin'?" He clasped her hand and led her in. "This is even better than Jackie. Who are you supposed to be now? Rita Hayworth?"

"No, nobody. It's just another disguise, to throw them off."

"Well, you're throwin' me off pretty good." He sat on the rumpled bed. "Sorry the bed's not made. It was either make the bed or answer the door. The door won."

"Good choice." She glanced around. Not a dirty sock or pair of shorts in sight. The bed was actually made—the bedspread with nary a wrinkle. Bottles of cologne, aftershave, and a deodorant can stood lined up on his dresser like soldiers. A portrait of the Madonna cradling Baby Jesus hung on the facing wall. *Did one of the bodyguards double as a chambermaid?* she wondered.

"Sit down, then." He patted the space next to him.

She sat next to him, with breathing room to spare. His weight on the mattress tilted her toward him.

"Is that why you came in here like this? To ask me if this disguise could fool those clowns? Or is there a more underhanded reason?" His eyes took her all in at once.

"A few reasons, Al." She moved closer. The

tension heightened. "All underhanded."

"I'd like to put my hand under a few things."

"You'll have to restrain yourself for now," she warned, but moved closer by instinct.

"The only way to restrain me is to tie me up, *cara mia*." His voice caressed her ears like a velvet pillow.

Ah, the hell with being ladylike! I'm not Vikki right now. Vikki is in her bedroom praying over the rosary not to be led into temptation. She slid over and bumped up against his thigh. "Hmm, I need to get a disguise." His arms went around her.

Her mouth claimed his, and their kiss didn't end for many dizzying moments. She saw starbursts behind her closed lids as his hands slid over her curves and down the swell of her buttocks.

"We have to stop before it goes too far," she panted. "I need to"—she caught her breath—"talk to you about something."

He let out a ragged sigh and laid her on her side.

The wig askew, she plucked it off. "Ben Bati's at the Pierre. I'm going to go over there and talk to him. But I don't want my father or Rosie to know about it. I want to talk to him first—just like we'd planned to do with Brutus." She caught her breath.

"I don't think you should." His eyes narrowed.

"With all due respect, Al, what you think is irrelevant. I need to know what happened to Jack, and questioning Bati is the only way to find out."

"Don't expect the truth from a snake like him that easily." He placed the wig on his nightstand next to a pile of Mad Magazines.

"Oh, no? He's a man, isn't he?" Her seductive glance made him bolt upright. His eyes pierced her.

"No! You're not going nowhere near him!"

"Oh, yes, I am," she retorted in a strong but calm timbre.

He threw his hands in the air. "What if your plot doesn't work, or backfires? This isn't the parking lot of a funeral home, with me to protect you. You're going to his hotel room alone? He could rape you or kill you, for Christ's sakes. You're dealing with a fuc—a stone-cold killer!"

"I'll be armed." She stated the obvious. "He's not dealing with a pom-pom girl here."

"And you think he won't be armed?" He gave her the bitterest sneer she'd ever seen on him. "I'm not letting you out of my sight. Not only is it my job to protect you, and Rosie would stuff me into a Sicilian oven if anything happened to you, but I'm not letting you meet him alone. I'm going with you, and that's that!" For the first time, he shouted at her.

She looked away and thought a moment. No bodyguard in his right mind would let a woman do this alone. And since he was much more than a bodyguard… "Okay, we'll do it this way." Her eyes reconnected with his glare. "You buy the most expensive suit on Fifth Avenue, which I'll pay for, we'll meet him together, and you'll be an investor. I have a way to get the conversation to segue from running a high-class bordello to his involvement with Jack. If he gives us a hard time, whip out your gun and hold him at gunpoint. The same way we were going to deal with Brutus."

He *tsk*ed with an eye roll. "Yeah, and if we're lucky, he'll be dead before we get there, like Brutus."

"Hey, you never know. The way things have been

going…" She gathered herself together and swept the mass of red curls off the nightstand. "Dinner's at the usual time tonight. We're having Deacon Bob over. You, uh, might want to get presentable first. I mean—presentable for dinner with a man of the cloth. And let me borrow the new Mad Magazine when you're finished. I can use a few laughs, too."

As she slipped out the door, she heard him mutter, "Well, I hope she won't dress like that when the deac is here."

Chapter Twenty-One

She waited for Polly in the Pierre's lobby, Al at her side, her faithful .22 in her purse. She had dressed for the part—stylish dark auburn wig, brick-red lipstick, Russian sable over a beige suit, emerald-green silk blouse, and Enzo Arnolfo shoes. Her earlobes, neck, wrists, and fingers dripped with Tiffany jewels. She'd figured the diamond tiara would be a bit much. Instead, she wore her matching sable hat, hoping when she took it off the wig wouldn't come off with it.

Al strutted back and forth in his new Armani suit, sporting a new cut by her hairdresser. He looked like a million bucks.

"You're the epitome of the Fifth Avenue gentleman, Al." She refrained from jumping all over him by polishing her ruby ring on her sleeve. "If you were a male escort, the women would be scratching each other's eyes out to get to you."

"Oh, yeah?" He buffed his nails on his lapel. "Maybe I'm in the wrong business after all."

She glanced at her diamond-encrusted watch. "I hope Polly won't be late."

"There she is." Al pointed, and Vikki stood to greet her.

"Daisy! You look filthy—filthy rich, that is!" Polly gushed.

"Daisy?" Al's brows shot up.

"That's her front name. Daisy Gold. All madams have front names." She handed Vikki a calling card. "Here's the card you can show him. I had this printed up the other day. It's just like mine, only with your front name and a logo."

Admiring it, Vikki admitted, "Hey, if I ran a high-class brothel I'd use this card. I dig the gold-embossed daisy."

"I didn't have one made for you, Al." Polly turned to him. "Didn't know you'd be joinin' us. But I'm glad you are. Fact, it's a big relief. I wouldn't want Vikki alone with him."

"There was never a chance of Vikki being alone with that creepo," he snarled. "Do I need a front name, too?"

"Nah—just be your charmin' self." Polly straightened his tie, not that it needed straightening.

"Now I'm acting out every woman's fantasy." Vikki took out her sterling silver compact and touched up her lipstick.

"Just give a repeat performance of New Orleans when Rita showed up," Al said.

"But you said that was campy." Vikki pressed her lips together and blotted them with tissue.

"It was good enough to bamboozle Rita." A smile tugged at the corners of his mouth. "I can't imagine Bati being smarter than her."

"Smart?" Polly flicked her wrist. "Nah, he ain't smart the way Vikki is, education-wise. Calculating, biggity, yeah, but give him the comp'ny of a good woman, and he turns to cornmeal. But remember what I said, Vikki. He's a reptile."

"Good. No reptile ever graduated Georgetown,

either." Vikki took a deep breath and adjusted her wig one last time. "Let's go."

At the elevator bank, Vikki pushed the Up button. "Even though we're supposed to be talking business, I'm glad you told me how the company of a good woman affects him, Polly. It gave me a renewed confidence."

"Faster you git the blood out of his brain and somewhere else, the better, honey." Polly gave her a nudge.

They shared a laugh as they got onto the elevator. Al stayed stone-faced. Either he didn't appreciate the joke or he didn't get it.

They approached the double doors of Bati's suite. Polly rang the doorbell, and Vikki held her breath for the six seconds it took him to answer it. The door opened and there he stood—the bastard who'd plunged her into the agony of grief and changed her life.

"Hi, gang." His voice floated to her ears, smoother than Sinatra's. He didn't flaunt a greasy gangster look. His eyes weren't shifty or beady; his lips weren't fixed into a sneer. He was clean shaven, his shirt was crisp, his pants creased, his tie silk. Everything about his appearance reflected respectability and breeding. "Come in." He stepped aside and swept his hand through the air in a welcoming gesture.

Vikki hardly felt welcome. She tried to keep her hatred in check. It wasn't easy. This was an acting role in more ways than one.

"Hiya, *mon cher*," Polly greeted him, and Bati gave her a swat on the ass like they were an old married couple.

"You're lookin' good, vamp." After a quick scan

of Polly's upper anatomy, he turned to Vikki. "And this is Miz Daisy?" His eyes lingered on her décolletage. She tried not to let his gaze repulse her.

"Right you are, but just plain Daisy to you." Getting into character, she gracefully placed a cigarette in a diamond-inlaid holder and waited for him to light it. He plucked a lighter from his monogrammed shirt pocket. "Allow me. Hey, you're one right purty filly, dawlin'."

Al stepped between them and stuck out his hand. Vikki expected his fist. "Aldobrandi Po. I'll be a silent partner in our venture."

The men shook as Bati scrutinized Al's duds. The haircut didn't escape his inspection, either. "You look almost as rich as her," he remarked to Al as Vikki took a Garbo-like drag on her cigarette holder. She kept her gaze riveted on Bati as he headed for the bar.

"I'm even richer, but I don't flaunt it." Al affected a casual air. "It's my townhouse we're going to be using for this—this establishment. It's been sitting empty since I moved to Palm Beach. I figured my Paris pied-à-terre was too small. Too much competition, besides. Every other residence on the Left Bank's an upper-class brothel these days."

"Wouldn't know, never been there." Bati's left brow cocked. "How 'bout you give me the addresses of some of 'em?"

"My pleasure." Al's polite nod matched his tone. "If you tell them I sent you, they'll take good care of you. They only take clients by referral."

If Al isn't making this up, he knows too much about high-class brothels, Vikki thought with a twinge of that ugly jealousy.

As Bati gave them each a Jim Beam and water, Polly stood to leave. Vikki wanted to chain smoke, but it wasn't easy with a foot-long holder.

"I'll leave y'all alone to get acquainted and talk shop." Polly headed for the door.

"*Au revoir*, vamp." Bati swatted her rump again before he turned and cased Vikki as if searching for a dangling price tag.

As she fought down nausea, she silently vowed, *I'm doing this for you, Jack.*

"So—Ben—" She cleared her throat. "I hope this venture will be profitable for all of us. I purchased the personal telephone directory of a retiring Park Avenue madam for nine thousand dollars. I caught some high-powered names in there. You know, if this pans out the way I'm planning, I'd like to start a male escort service, too, eventually. There are quite a few wealthy, lonely women around."

"You plannin' to run that?" Bati directed the question to Al.

"Run it? I plan to *be* it." Al shot his cuffs.

"Well, you got yer work cut out fer ya." Bati held up his glass. "To your health, and a wonderful future as business pardners," he toasted her, sounding downright sincere.

"Why, thank you, sir." She forced a smile. *Stay in character!* she silently urged. They clinked glasses, and she made a sipping gesture but didn't drink. Bati lowered the television—of all ironies, NBS World News Tonight was on. He sank into an easy chair and took a leisurely sip of his drink, running his tongue over his lips. "Sounds like a noble way to make a living. But I'm hoping to make a hefty profit on this venture without having to do much physical labor."

"You will," Vikki assured him. "That's why Polly looked you up for this venture. Said you'd be a great asset to the business."

"Well, I always steered business Polly's way and never asked for a finder's fee." He stretched his legs out.

"You're very generous."

He looked down. "It's just the way I'm sitting."

"No, I mean—bringing her clients and not wanting to be compensated." She took another bogus sip. Al stood within shooting range of Bati's head.

"We were business pardners, till Pol got too big for her girdle and thought she was my boss, but if it wasn't for me, she'd've been on her own back fer the last ten years." He displayed an arrogant grin. "Now, with y'all as the major investors, that ain't gonna happen—is it?" He shot her a threatening glare.

"Of course not." She tensed every muscle in her body to keep from trembling. "It's equal through and through. And we'll make sure that's drawn up in the corporate documents."

"So—take a seat, Al, and Daisy, was it? Cute." He snickered. "Not too original, but cute. Polly always went in for the Great Gatsby. Always wanted to be Daisy herself. So drop the curtain and tell me your real name."

Gliding across the room, she flicked her ash into the nearest tray, eased onto the sofa with her knees together, swept off the hat, making sure the wig stayed on, and let the coat tumble from her shoulders. "My real name's Cynthia Van Meegeren. I'm a niece of Henricus Van Meegeren," she rattled on. "You do know who he was, don't you?"

"Should I?" Bati asked.

"One of the most notorious figures in the art world," she rattled off the Dutch rogue's biography. "He was an artist and a forger. He was accused of selling art to the Germans during the war, and to clear himself, he confessed to having forged the art. His fakes were subjected to scientific scrutiny, and he died a few weeks into a year-long sentence for forgery. He was a hero of sorts, but during that time I think the world needed all the heroes it could get. Even someone of his dubious character. He was a hero and an anti-hero at the same time. Shakespeare would've made a masterpiece writing about him. I have several of his paintings. I plan to hang them in our—our place of business."

"Hmmm." A spark of interest shone in Bati's beady eyes. "*Allors*, dubious character runs in your family, then."

"I like to think I inherited some of his talent. And not just in painting." She batted her painstakingly applied false lashes.

"Just the kind of gal I like." Bati stood, reached for her hand, and brought her to her feet. "You're a living doll."

Al patted the pistol under his jacket.

She gulped. *Stay in character!* "I wouldn't kick you out of the boudoir, either, Ben." She tapped the cigarette into the ashtray and placed the holder in her purse. She felt around until she touched the reassuring coolness of her .22. "You'd make a good male escort, too, if you're, uh, up to it."

"I'm up to more'n you can count on your purty

little fingers." His drawl carried a strangely soothing quality. Never mind singing, he could talk her to sleep. "I've wanted to change my line of work to something less strenuous."

He smiled, displaying straight teeth. Nope, they weren't crowns, either. She hated herself for thinking it, especially with Al standing there, but Ben Bati oozed sensuality.

Forgive me, she begged God—and Al.

Al spoke up. "I'd like to ask you a few questions about the business, if you don't mind."

"In a minute, boy." He turned back to Vikki. "Another drink, Miz, uh, Van—what was it?"

"Van Meegeren. Cynthia. But my friends call me Cissy." She rattled her six-carat diamond bracelet.

He moseyed over to the bar. "Right you are, sis."

She ignored that. "I don't like to mix business with cocktails."

"So, what brought you to this field of endeavor?" He refilled his glass.

"Well, I don't know if Polly told you, but I was a call girl a while back, in Washington, D.C." She recited her rehearsed lines. "Al has some contacts in Palm Beach who can get us started, with the view to opening another establishment down there eventually. I still maintain some contacts in Washington and entertain them when they come this way. I've always had an affinity for politicians. Never did get to meet the Kennedy brothers, though. Isn't it one of the blackest marks on our country's history the way Kennedy was killed, right there in the open, with his wife right next to him?" She forced nonchalance into her tone, when in reality the memories tore her heart apart.

"Depends on who you're askin'." Bati dropped ice cubes into his glass with tongs.

This segue into Jack's murder was easier than she'd rehearsed it. She pushed the excruciating memories away. *Stay in character!* "Jack Ward was far better than that youngster at the anchor desk now—what's his name, Peter something? Nobody will ever replace Ward. Isn't it terrible how he drowned?" Vikki sallied forth, in agony reciting these lines. Oh, God, she was no actress. *But it's all for you, Jack.*

Bati didn't respond, just unlaced his spit-shined shoes and slid out of them. *Like a snake*, she kept thinking. *A cold-blooded reptile.*

"Did you know Jack Ward at all, Ben?" she ventured, going for broke now.

"How would I know him?" Bati glanced at his watch.

"I thought you might've traveled in the same circles." She leveled her stare.

"They're pretty big circles." He went over and snapped the television off. "If you ask me, Ward was a nosy sumbitch. Did the world a favor by croaking." His tone remained detached, like he was talking about some historical figure he'd read about in *American Heritage.*

She wanted to choke him. Staying in character like this pushed her to the limit of human endurance. "I ask because Ward was one of my best clients. He told me he was onto the JFK plot. He told me a lot of things he probably shouldn't have."

Bati shot her a quizzical glance. Now he looked interested.

She ventured on. "Ward was on the inside of the whole thing. Do you think he was silenced because of what he knew? Like Dorothy Kilgallen and all those other poor victims?"

"Yeah, so were a few whores with big mouths. I knew a few of 'em personally: Kandi Kane from N'awlins, who threatened to write a book about it, and Theresa Norton, one of Ruby's gals." His answer tore through her like a bullet.

On one level, she reveled in self-satisfaction at how well she was pulling this off. On a deeper level, she shuddered in revulsion at who this man actually was. Goosebumps sprouted on her arms. The hairs stood out on the back of her neck. She fought the urge to shiver. Dear God, how did actors do it? *Stay in character!*

Bati strode up to her and stood so close, she could smell the booze on his breath, mingled with onions. "I hope you're not always all business, Cyn, or sis, or whoever you are." He bent his head over hers to kiss her. She couldn't stop him. His tongue darted out without warning. She tried to push him away, but it was like trying to move a rock.

Al yanked him off her, spun him around, and slugged him in the jaw. Knuckle cracked against bone.

"You flamin' asshole!" Bati held his jaw with one hand, reaching inside his jacket with the other. Faster than she could blink, he whipped out a gun and aimed it at Al's chest.

"No, don't shoot him, please!" Vikki pleaded.

"All right, let's have it." His voice grated like steel on concrete. "You might be a whore, but now I know"—he pointed at Al—"he's no goddamn pimp. You two and Polly are up to somethin' no good, and I wanna know what it is."

She released a ragged breath. *The jig is up.* "Put the

gun down, and I'll tell you."

His mirthless laugh made her skin crawl. "Nothin' doin'. I know you're both packin', Bonnie and Clyde. Now tell me what's goin' on, and if I don't believe it, he gets it first, then you."

"Tell him everything, Vikki," Al said as Bati raised his gun and aimed it at Al's head.

"All right, I'll tell you!" she shrieked, shaking so hard her jewelry rattled. "Just please don't shoot him!"

Bati kept a steady aim on Al as she trembled. "Having us followed, shooting at us in New Orleans..." She gulped air. "You killed the detective I hired and you drowned my husband. I had a lot of brushes with death finding out what happened. I want you to spare Al—please—he's just my bodyguard, doing his job. But you know what?" Her voice steadied. "Right now I don't give a damn if I die, because I'll be with Jack again. So kill me, and see if it gives you any satisfaction. But first just tell me why you killed him. Tell me!" Hands outstretched, she grasped Bati's lapels and shook him.

He didn't make a move to push her away. His hesitation unnerved her. She opened her palm and smacked him across the face. "You heartless, murdering bastard!"

He didn't recoil, didn't budge.

"It's over!" A flood of grief—over her own death—drowned her.

Bati stared her down without a blink. "What in the holy name of hell are you babbling about, woman?" His voice stayed calm and even.

"My husband, Jack Ward." She gritted her teeth. "Tell me what happened. For once, just find a shred of decency in that sick mind of yours and tell me why you had to drown Jack!" She raised her fists to pound at him. This time he caught them in one hand and threw them down.

"I didn't drown your husband, you fruitcake." His tone was as calm as if he were telling her the time.

"Stop denying it, you damn liar!" Her breaths came in gasps. "So it all backfired on me. I took a long time to track you down. I know who you are." She pumped her clenched fists, ready to pound him again. "You're Marc Antony of the Triumvirate. You followed my husband to Dallas and drowned him in that bathtub. Now, if you kill me, I can accept that. But just tell me why you killed Jack. Why? What did he have to do with all of it?" she shrieked, so desperate for the truth she was willing to die for it.

"I don't know what you're yip-yappin' about, and I didn't drown your husband in no bathtub." He looked down at her, shaking his head, as if she were insane. "I never even met your husband."

For a crazed instant, she almost believed him. His voice said it all.

"Just tell me the truth, please," she begged, hands clasped, ready to die and join Jack. "I give up. My plan failed. That's all I want. The truth. Don't lie to me, if you're going to kill me anyway. I know you were behind Jack's murder, because I know you're Marc Antony. Now—please, for the love of God, show me some mercy and just tell me what happened between you and Jack—then do whatever the hell you want to me." Her arms fell to her sides. She went limp. Her knees wobbled. She staggered over to Al and clung to his arm. "My life is over anyway. Do you know what

I've been through?" The tears came. "I'm a widow because of you. The least you can give me is the goddamned truth!" She sobbed.

"Okay, I'll tell you." His voice gentled, but his hand didn't waver. "Your husband started showing up at JFK rallies and things, and following me and my associates around. I figgered he was onto us. He was nosy, like I said. Typical vulture reporter. I am Marc Antony. I work for whoever'll hire me. For the Kennedy hit it was a branch of the CIA in cahoots with the New Orleans mob." He watched her as she leaned on Al, unable to stand straight. Al's arms held her up. Bati went on, "I never met your husband, never said hello or goodbye or a fuck-you to the guy, don't know how the hell he got into a bathtub and drowned or what happened to him, I swear it." He raised his right hand as if taking an oath on the witness stand.

"Look. Look at me!" Struggling to keep the trembling out of her voice, she tried to get him to take his attention off Al and onto her. Now she shook with fury, not fear. "Don't you know me? You've never seen me before?"

"Nope."

She yanked off the wig and her hair tumbled to her shoulders. "Now do you recognize me, Jack Ward's widow? You've never seen my picture?"

"You ever pose for Playboy?" He leered, his eyes lingering on her cleavage again.

"Certainly not! I was in *Look* magazine!"

"You kiddin' me?" He wrinkled his nose. "I don't read no goddamn *Look* magazine."

A wild, brash idea hit her like lightning. "Then maybe you'll recognize me from the photo you took out

363

of Jack's wallet." With one fluid motion, she ripped her blouse open and thrust out her bared breasts. Buttons flew across the room. "Now do you recognize me?"

He blinked, startled. His eyes bugged out. His mouth fell open—and at that moment Al lunged for him and knocked him off his feet with a karate kick. As Al grabbed Bati's gun, Vikki pulled out her .22, aimed, and fired. Her silenced gunshot pierced Bati's chest. He gurgled and gasped, eyes wide in surprise. Blood gushed from the wound. The metallic odor stung her nose and throat, and his lifeless body pitched forward. As he crumpled to the floor, she jumped aside and reached for Al. He wrapped her in his arms.

"My God, Vikki, you saved my life." His voice cracked.

"It's all right, Al. Let's just get out of here." Fumbling to pull her clothes back around her, she shook so hard she dropped her gun.

She swept it up and stuck it back into her purse.

"I knew I couldn't trust this S.O.B. when I first laid eyes on him, and then when he made a play for you—" His voice rose to a shout. "Filthy pig! To you, bum!" He kicked at Bati's corpse as he cursed. "*Va fa in culo!*" Kick. "*Figlio de puttana!*" Kick. "*Va a diablo!*" Kick.

Seething, his face crimson, he turned to her. "Wipe off everything you touched, and we'll get the hell out of here." He thrust a towel at her, and she wiped down her glass. It slipped from her shaking hands and shattered.

"Al, wh—what if the cops—" She couldn't finish.

He finished for her, like he always did these days. "They won't. It's just another mob hit. They won't knock themselves out investigating it."

"I'm glad you kept your wits about you when I yanked my dress open." She swept her bra, completely forgotten in the ordeal, off the floor.

He pulled her coat more tightly around her. "I'm more of an ass man, myself." He led her down the hall and into the elevator. She still shook so badly she stumbled most of the way. They crossed the Pierre's elegant lobby, glided through the revolving doors into a cab, and vanished into the night.

She didn't remember getting home. She passed out in the taxi and woke up on her father's couch, in Al's arms.

****

"Al!" A shot of fear pierced her like an arrow. She shivered. "Are they after us?" She searched frantically for her gun. "Where's my purse?"

"Your purse is here, and your piece is here. And I got his piece, too. I'm keeping it as a souvenir." He patted his pocket.

"Al—is Bati—" She stammered, unable to finish.

He stroked her cheek and brought her head to rest on his chest. "It's okay. Calm down. He's still dead."

"Are you sure?" She clamped her fingers around his arms, unable to let go.

"Yes, you hit the bull's eye."

"Al, he was Marc Antony! But he denied even knowing Jack. My God, what now?" She tried to sit up, but a wave of dizziness came over her. She held her head in her hands as he folded her into his arms.

"It's okay, he's on his way to hell, where he belongs. You want me to bring you a drink?"

"No. Where is everybody?" She glanced around the empty living room.

"I don't know. Nobody's home. Your father and Rosie are gonna drop their teeth when you tell them what we did there." She sensed the smile in his voice.

"They'll have to get over it." The scene began to replay through her mind. "It's like looking back on a bad dream." She focused on Al, a much more welcome sight.

"I thought I was numb to stuff like this, after seeing my old man shot in front of my eyes." He kissed the top of her head.

She snuggled up to him. "Thank God it's over."

As he stroked her hair, she remembered the wig. "Where's the wig? Oh, no, it's not still in that hotel suite, is it?"

"I hope you don't mind, but I chucked it. I didn't think you'd want to wear it again. I wasn't too crazy about it anyway. But—keep the dark one, okay?"

She managed a shaky smile.

"Just joshin'." He made a move to stand up. "Come on, let's eat. I'm starved. Let's go to Quaglia's, have a big Italian feast. Bring Polly. She's got something to celebrate, too."

She rubbed her head. "I'd rather not, Al. I'm not up to getting all dolled up and going to a five-star restaurant. I'm still shaking like a leaf here."

She heard his stomach grumble. "Okay." He held her close again. She raised her lips to his and they kissed. She melted into the comfort of his arms.

"What do you want? I think there's some gabagool and pastrami left." His stomach rumbled again.

"Just a bowl of soup." She moved over to let him stand. "I don't feel like being an adult of legal drinking age right now."

"You got it. I think I'll join you." He headed for the kitchen.

Polly called a minute later, and Al answered in the kitchen. "I'll let her tell you the good news," she heard him say, and she picked up the living room phone.

"I shot him, Polly. But half a heartbeat before he got Al," she gave her friend the good news, but all she wanted to do was forget it now.

"Bless your heart! You're his savior! Look, honey, I know you're shaken up ovah all this and need your rest. So I won't keep you. I just wanted to make sure you were okay and it all went to plan."

"Well, it didn't," Vikki corrected her. "We were plain lucky. Or someone was looking over us."

"I like to think the latter, too. Now y'all get some rest. I'll see you in the mornin'."

She sank into the sofa cushion, unable to sort everything out. It still went by in a blur, as if it had happened in her imagination, and not for real.

Relief mingled with the fury that tore at her heart. Benzo Bati was dead, but even though she knew the truth about what really happened—who killed President John F. Kennedy—the mystery of Jack's death went to the grave, too.

****

"Al, I'll never know who killed Jack now. Bati's dead, and he took his dying breath denying he had anything to do with Jack. I'll never know."

Al placed a steaming bowl of minestrone before her, Oysterette crackers floating at the top. "Here you go. There's an old saying in Southern Italy about soups: *Sette cose fa la zuppa*, which means soup does seven things: it relieves your hunger, quenches your thirst, fills your stomach, cleans your teeth, makes you sleep, helps you digest, and colors your cheeks." He counted on his fingers.

"Thanks, I'll try for all seven," she said as he tucked a napkin around her collar and sat down to eat his right out of the pot. She blew on hers and stirred it with her spoon.

"He had to be Jack's killer. It all pointed to him. You got him. What more can you do?" he asked her between soup slurps.

"I needed to know what really happened to Jack. But the bastard denied it. Even when he had a gun to your head, ready to kill you, and I knew I was next." The soup's warmth comforted her.

"What did you expect? A bended-knee confession? They're hired guns. They don't confess unless they're under serious torture. I told you that, so did your father and Rosie." He munched on a mouthful of Oysterettes.

"But he sounded so convincing, denying it. I almost believed him for a minute." She took a sip of water.

"So, maybe he was telling the truth." Al shrugged. "What matters is you did all you could, and I know Jack wouldn't want you to beat yourself up over it."

"But I have to believe he killed Jack, or I really will go insane." The bowl empty, she stood. "I have to lie down for a while. Thanks for the soup." She didn't know if it colored her cheeks, but it sure made her want to sleep. She stumbled up the stairs to her room, physically and emotionally exhausted.

"Then believe it," he said.

All she wanted to do was sleep for days and wake up with this nightmare behind her.

Lying in bed, she got out Jack's picture and caressed his image. "Jack, he's right. I did everything I could. I found JFK's assassins for you, and they got their justice, but I'll never know for certain who drowned you in that tub. I tried, Jack, I tried so hard." She kissed his image and held it to her heart.

****

A soft knock came through her sleep. Was it part of the dream? She wasn't sure; all she knew was that she wanted to keep dreaming. She didn't want this intrusion to disturb her and force reality back.

"Who is it?" Her voice rasped, harsh and hoarse with sleep.

"Me. Al."

That horrific scene rushed back to her uninvited.

She slid off the bed, smoothed her hair, and opened the door. He stepped into the shadows of her room. She didn't turn on the light.

"Just wanted to see if you were all right." He didn't take another step closer, although she stepped aside.

"You woke me up." That sounded more direct than "I was sleeping."

"I'm sorry. Can I come in?"

At the sight of him, a spark of arousal penetrated her dazed state. She fought back the raw desire.

He went straight over to her bed and sat down.

She snapped on the night light and looked into his eyes as she sat beside him. He wrapped the blanket around her. "You're right," she said softly. "I'll just have to believe Bati was Jack's killer and take it on faith. I did my best, and I hope I avenged Jack's death."

"That's the right thing to do, *cara*. But I didn't want to talk about that again—not right now." He reached into his wallet. "I have something for you. Here."

He handed her a bill folded into fourths and she waved it away. "I don't want any of your money."

"It's not me just giving you money. I want you to have this." He made the gesture again. She took it and absentmindedly unfolded it. It was a thousand-dollar bill.

"What's this for?"

"It's not meant to be a gift, Vikki. It's just something I want you to keep on you at all times. Just like mine. My emergency thousand. I want you to have one." He shut the wallet and slid it back into his pocket.

She nodded and tried to give it back, but he refused. "I appreciate the gesture, Al, but I have enough of my own money."

"No, I want you to have this one. My reason is kind of selfish. I want you to have this because—you might just have to save my life again someday, and it might not be this easy."

She smiled and moved close to embrace him, but first she tucked the bill into her bra.

"You're gonna keep it there?" His eyes played over her chest.

"Of course. If you lose your emergency thousand, you know where to reach for mine."

****

The thousand wasn't all he'd taken out of the bank. Sitting on the edge of his bed, he slid the velvet box out of his pocket and flipped it open. The diamond caught the light and dazzled in a rainbow of colors. It had cost him every penny he'd earned since starting this job, but she was worth much more.

The time was right. With the last suspect dead, she'd have to realize there was nothing more she could do, and they could concentrate on other things—like getting on with their life together.

The hunt for Jack's killer was over, and it was time to move on. If he couldn't convince her, this ring would. But for good measure, he'd stood before the mirror and rehearsed. "Mr. McGlory, I'd like your permission to ask for Vikki's hand…"

****

They all sat around the dining room table after a quiet dinner. No one seemed to want to gab. Rosie puffed on his cigar. Greta looked her age. Al toyed with his pudding. Polly fingered her bangle bracelets.

Billy stood and refilled everyone's glasses. "It's over, and the Triumvirate is dead now." He looked at Vikki. "Babe, you just have to realize you did your best to find Jack's killer. You couldn't have done any better, and even though I'd like to put you over my knee and spank you silly for those antics, it's over, and I pray God nothing like this ever happens to you again."

"I wasn't afraid, Dad. Not for one second. God was with me. Jack was looking over me." Her sprightly tone showed how well she'd recovered. "I've already moved on a great deal."

"Amen to that." Heads nodded, but still no one spoke.

Rosie took a sip of his coffee, lit a cigarette, took a drag, and looked around the table. "You guys can go back home. You did a great job. Thanks."

Vikki shot Al a questioning glance. But he stayed poker faced. He'd gotten good at it.

"We'll be hearin' about this JFK thing for the next

hundred years," Rosie said. "It'll never go away. There'll be conspiracy theories from here to kingdom come about it. But at least the gunmen are dead and there's some justice, but I have a hunch anybody else in the know will keep droppin' like flies. It always happens that way. Somethin' this big, it'll be even more obvious." He turned to Vikki. "But you did good, doll. And you know what? I'm damn proud of you."

Overwhelmed with love for her godfather, she wiped away tears. "Thanks, Rosie."

"So am I, babe," Billy volunteered.

"Me too, *cara mia*," and that was the first time Al called her that in front of other people. "You saved my life, and I'll be forever grateful. Mr. and Mrs. McGlory, your daughter is a true heroine."

Vikki blushed. Polly agreed. Angelo and Hilario nodded. Only Greta kept her eyes downcast. Vikki guessed memories of thirty years ago still haunted her.

"So—how did you distract Marc Antony enough in order to plug him when he had his gun aimed at Al?" Rosie wanted to know. She cast Al a wide-eyed "help me" expression. He shrugged, with a grin that said, "You're on your own with this one."

"Well, I, uh—" Her hand fluttered around her throat, and she grabbed her diamond cross for support. "I just—gosh, Rosie, it all happened so fast, I don't remember. I think he looked away for a split second, Al gave him a karate kick, and I took that opportunity to pull my gun out and fire. It all went by in a blur."

"So all that target practice paid off," Rosie boasted, chomping on his cigar. "I knew she could do it. Never doubted it for a minute."

"Then why were you so set against me meeting

these guys when you were looking for them?" she asked. "I don't want to rehash any of this, but I feel entitled to an explanation after all my—as you say— heroism."

"You wanted to go out on the front lines alone, and the front's no place for a lady alone," Rosie replied.

Yeah, well, *my* front saved the day, she wanted to retort as she bit her tongue. No way could any of them ever know what happened in that hotel suite to bring Benzo Battolini to his death.

"Well, I'm putting it behind me," she declared with a pump of her fist.

"And as long as Vikki's moving on, I'd like to join her." Al stood and turned to Billy. "Mr. McGlory, I'd like your permission to ask for Vikki's hand in marriage."

Before she could even gasp, she looked at her father as he winked. "Billy to you. But you don't have to ask me. You don't wanna marry me, you wanna marry her, right?"

"That's right. Thank you, Billy." Al cleared his throat. "*Cara mia*, will you marry me?"

Smiles, big and small, burst out around the table.

A rush of love overwhelmed her. "Of course," came out in a whisper.

He slid the velvet box out of his pocket, approached her, and dropped to one knee. "You want to hold out your hand for me to put the ring on?"

A vague memory returned to her. This was just how Jack had proposed, on bended knee. It seemed a lifetime ago now.

He slid a brilliant diamond solitaire onto her ring finger, brought it to his lips, and kissed it. "I love you with all my heart and want to spend the rest of my days with you." He stood and grabbed the wine bottle. "Now we toast and do the tarantella!"

One by one they came over and hugged and congratulated her. She still couldn't believe it was happening.

She remembered what her dad had said about her mother looking down upon him and saying, "It's about time." Now Vikki knew Jack looked down at her saying the same thing.

"Oh, Jack, I only hope you're up there dancing with Marilyn."

Chapter Twenty-Two

Her father's orchestra played late into the night at their engagement party. She couldn't imagine the wedding being a bigger celebration.

She tried to convince herself that she'd found Jack's killer and his death had been avenged. This engagement was the beginning of her new life, even though something still lingered, unfinished.

She chatted with Linc about his plans to travel the world as he took a piece of paper out of his jacket pocket. "Oh, and this is the key to my freedom. Whitefield's letter of recommendation. In a rare moment of benevolence, he wrote this and sent it to me. I ought to frame it."

She took it from him and began to read. "Very nice." She nodded. "He must've thought a lot of you, Linc."

"He might've, but he's still an insufferable prick, and I'm glad I escaped. When I get to Nepal—"

She didn't hear another word as her eyes froze on the signature. For one stunned moment, her breathing halted. Her heart stopped. She gasped for air as the letter slipped from her fingers.

Linc caught it as it fluttered to the floor. "Vikki, what's wrong?"

"The—letter—let me see that again, Linc."

He gave it back to her. She held it inches from her

eyes and examined the signature, like a bug under a microscope.

"Linc—the name. He signed it in—" She studied it for one more moment to make sure. "There's no mistaking it. That's Jack's pen he used."

Linc wet his lips. "You sure?" He barely spoke above a whisper.

"That ink. The blue-violet ink." She held the letter up to him. "I had it specially mixed for him by the stationers. And the width of the pen strokes, the—Linc, there's no mistaking it. This letter was signed with Jack's pen!"

He took it back and studied it in disbelief. "He had Jack's pen the whole time? Why? I asked around there a thousand ti—" He looked at her, his face drained of all color. "Oh, no, Vikki. You don't suppose—"

"No, I don't suppose. This time I know."

****

Vikki, Al, Billy, and Linc sat at the head table in the deserted banquet hall.

One thought haunted her: *The party's over.*

"Just because Whitefield signed a letter with Jack's pen doesn't mean he killed him." Al sat forward and folded his hands on the table. "You need to do some serious detective work here."

"The first thing we should do is find out if he was in the hotel with Jack that night." Linc slipped his tuxedo jacket off and undid his bow tie. "Tomorrow, Vikki, you and I will go to the NBS travel office, pore over the records, and see if Whitefield went to Dallas around November twenty-second."

"Won't they question why you're rooting through the files?" Vikki took the cigarette her father offered her.

"They won't know. We'll go after they're closed. I can still get in. I haven't quit working there yet."

****

Still juggling the emotional high of her engagement and the shock of seeing Whitefield's name signed with Jack's pen, she pulled herself together and slipped into NBS's travel office with Linc the next evening.

"It's not like we're breaking and entering," he rationalized, turning his key in the lock. "I still work here."

"I'm not worried, Linc." She gave his arm a reassuring squeeze. "After what happened with Bati, getting caught in here by a security guard would be like a skit on *The Red Skelton Hour*."

He flipped on the lights. They headed for the file cabinets in the eerie silence. "Here it is. The files for last November." He pulled out a manila folder. "Okay, Whitefield, you son of a bitch, where were you on the night of November twenty-first?" he muttered, flipping through the pile of receipts, boarding passes, and travel itineraries.

Peering over his shoulder, she clasped her hands. *God, please let something be here!*

"Here's all the receipts and stuff for that week—" He studied a few pieces of paper and boarding passes. She clutched his shoulder, breathing in short gasps. "Please let some evidence turn up," she prayed.

"Hey, wait." Linc turned and looked at her.

Her breath stopped.

"Remember when Jack tricked Whitefield into thinking he was getting an Emmy? Whitefield got all excited and bought a ticket to L.A. As he was about to get into the airport limo, Jack told him it was all a gag."

She nodded.

"Whitefield wants to follow Jack to Dallas on November twenty-first. He takes the L.A. ticket he didn't use for the Emmys, trades it in, and purchases a ticket to Dallas using an alias. The network already reimbursed him for the L.A. ticket. There's no chit to show Whitefield gave the L.A. ticket back or paid NBS for it. So what happened to the ticket?" He splayed his fingers.

"Let's place a telephone call to the airline and find out." She searched the paper-strewn desks for a phone.

"Use this one." He guided her to the nearest phone. She flipped through the Rolodex, found the airline's number, and dialed. "Hello, I'm an auditor at NBS. I have a ticket that NBS purchased, but it never got used." She gave them the information, and they put her on hold. She tapped her foot, took two paces each way, as far as the phone cord allowed. She watched the clock ticking on the wall. Finally, they told her what she needed to know. She hung up, her heart thumping. "The L.A. ticket was traded in for a ticket to Dallas for a Mr. Diamond."

A grin spread his lips. "Bingo. Diamond is the name Whitefield uses when he travels on business. Diamond—the NBS logo of three diamonds. Get it?" He pulled a phone directory off the shelf and flipped through it. He found the number he wanted and picked up the phone. "I'm calling the Dallas Hilton to see if a Mr. Diamond checked in that day."

Her heart leapt into her throat as she waited.

After he hung up, their eyes met behind both sets of glasses. Her pulse throbbed.

"Mr. Diamond checked into the Dallas Hilton on November twenty-first and out on the twenty-second."

Her jaw dropped. "Good God."

Linc continued, "That means Whitefield and Jack *were* in the Dallas Hilton at the same time." He made a fist and crumpled the file folder. "So he found out Jack went to Dallas and followed him there, the bastard."

"We got him, Linc. Just as good as red-handed." She leaned against the wall, unable to stand.

"But still—it doesn't prove he killed Jack. All it proves is that they were staying in the Hilton at the same time." He took his glasses off and polished them on his shirttail.

"Oh, I'll prove it, all right. This time I'm going to prove it beyond any doubt." She rubbed her hands together to warm them. She was ice cold all over. Her new diamond solitaire cut into her palm. "And I don't plan to use any jury, either."

Linc held up a hand. "Oh, no, Vikki, don't. Look what happened last time."

"There's no comparison. I wasn't afraid of Marc Antony, and I'm certainly not afraid of a weasel like Herbert Whitefield." She grabbed his sleeve. "Come on, let's get out of here. I'll buy you a drink. You look like you need one, and Lord knows I do."

****

After telling Al what they'd found, she collapsed in her father's lounge chair. A sip of chocolate milk gave her a shot of energy—and hope. "Okay, let's talk about something happy. The wedding."

Al sat across from her and gulped his own chocolatey drink. "I was going to marry Mona on Easter Sunday. I understand if you don't want to have it that soon, though."

She had a hunch what he was getting at. "Oh, your mama."

"No, she's happy." He shook his head, wiping his mouth with his hand. "After I broke it off with Mona, I talked to Mama. It was almost as hard to break it to her, but I told her it had a happy ending. I was getting married anyway, to the woman I love. She's happy now, and can't wait to meet you at the wedding."

She heaved a relieved sigh. "Oh, that's wonderful, Al. Of course I'd love to meet her. How about if I call her on the phone for a chat?"

"She only speaks Sicilian," he warned.

"Well…" She turned up her hands. "I can still call her. You can translate on the extension."

His eyes brightened. "That would be a very nice thing to do. She would love that."

"I just hope she doesn't resent me because I'm not Mona."

"She didn't really care if Mona was happy. It's me she cares about. I'm her little *bambino*." He gave her an embarrassed twist of his lips, eyes downcast.

"Every Italian boy is Mama's *bambino*." She told him what every Italian knew.

"Yeah, I should just let her enjoy it." He looked away. "But waiting isn't making it easy for me."

Her breath quickened. "Well, I can start by sketching a few designs for the wedding gown. But I don't want to get married before a year is up. I'm just— I don't think it would be right. I hope you'll understand."

"I *capisce*," he replied.

She put down the glass and clasped his hand. "I

know you're anxious. I'm pretty anxious myself. But, Al, you know—this isn't the fifties anymore. There are certain things we don't have to wait for."

She took his glass from him, put it down, and claimed his mouth with hers.

"Mmm, you taste like chocolate, so delicious." His hot breath in her ear made her tremble with desire. "You're sure you don't want to wait till it's legal and proper and blessed by the church?"

"What I'm thinking of doing to you right now is the farthest thing from legal or proper or blessed by the church," she whispered into his ear between nibbles.

He captured her lips in a lingering kiss.

They came up for air, and he pulled her to her feet. "Then let's go. The Plaza is waiting. And for once, that's not a gun in my pocket."

****

She turned away from the sweeping view of Central Park and faced her husband-to-be.

"Al, as much as I want..." What she really wanted was a cigarette to keep her hands busy. "Something's still bothering me."

"What? I love you, Vikki. You're going to be my wife."

Her inner voice told her to wait for the sacred wedding night. It wasn't Jack she was worried about any more. He had his standards. These were hers.

"I want you, Al." She flattened her palms on his chest. "I know it's not a sin to want you now. And it's not Jack. He wasn't the hero I made him out to be. He had affairs, and one in particular with a very public figure."

"Who?" he asked. "Jackie?"

She shook her head. "That I could've handled more easily. No, it was Marilyn Monroe."

He stood silent. Finally he uttered, "*Mama mia*," with raised brows, as if admiring a bragging friend. "I'm sorry you had to find that out about Jack, Vikki."

"I'm not. It made me see him in a whole different light. It made me realize much more, too." Jack's image formed in her mind. "I loved Jack, loved him fiercely, and he loved me. But it wasn't a nurturing marriage. We had such different interests, different passions. We loved each other, but we didn't *need* each other." She gazed into Al's eyes. "That's where it's different with you and me, Al. I'm not just in love with you. I need you."

"Then why are you so hesitant to let me make love to you?" He clasped her arms.

"My father, whom I respect and have always tried to model myself after, waited a year after my mother died."

"What good did it do him?" he prodded.

"None," she said. "He told me it was torture. Then Greta showed up."

"Then what happened?" he asked.

"I'll give you a hint," she said. "My half-sister Theresa was born nine months later."

Al laughed. "That's what you're afraid of?" He reached for his wallet and took out a foil wrapper.

That raised her left brow. "When did you get those?"

"Right after the engagement party." He held it between his fingers like a cigarette.

"From where?" She planted a fist on her hip.

He smiled. "They were an engagement gift—from

your father. Who doesn't want you to wait a year. *He* told me it was torture, too."

She felt her cheeks go hot.

"He gave me his blessing." Al cupped her cheeks. "And a lot of encouragement. So you've got his approval. And Jack's. Now give yourself yours."

It's all right, Vikki, she told herself. *He's yours. Love him.*

A delightful mixture of trepidation and excitement flooded her. "I'll be right back."

She dashed into the bathroom and brushed her hair around her shoulders the way he liked it. She wriggled out of her dress, tripping over it as she preened in front of the bathroom mirror, squirting perfume on her pulse points. An uninvited flashback to her wedding night with Jack came and went. She removed every stitch of clothing and wrapped herself in a towel.

She approached him, waiting for her in bed. The sight of him melted her. A soft glow floated through the picture window, moonlight mingled with twinkling city lights. He lowered the sheet to his waist as he lay bare-chested, his torso covered with a mat of dark curly hair. The thought of him pressed up against her, hard and wanting, heated her blood. She stepped closer. He learned forward, holding his arms out to her. The sheet fell away and revealed his nakedness underneath. She looked away, a sudden shyness overtaking her arousal. "It's all right, *cara mia*, you might as well get used to it. I'm going to be your husband," he said softly.

She managed a laugh. "My God, you'd think it was my first time."

"It is."

He reached forward to take her in his arms.

She lay beside him, and his mouth descended upon hers lightly, becoming more insistent, responding to her desire.

As her towel fell away, he broke their kiss. He traced a finger down her neck and over each breast in a slow circular motion. She sighed under his touch, hot liquid flames igniting deep within her. "Let me look at you." He half spoke, half growled. "You're gorgeous."

"Stop looking and start touching," she demanded. She stroked his chest, her lips upon his earlobe, her tongue darting out and flicking it playfully, her breath matching his with increasing intensity.

Fierce longing overtook her senses.

His lips and tongue moved down her body. She thrust her hips forward to meet his. She didn't want any more foreplay. She wanted him inside her—now.

But he stayed unbearably patient. "You're so beautiful, Vikki, I've been waiting so long for this," he whispered.

"Come here, Al." She pulled him on top of her. His body covered hers, and she clamped her thighs around his back. They gasped together as their bodies united.

She thrust forward to meet him, wanting him submerged in her. Arching her back, she invited him inside her, caught up in the feverish longing that only he could fulfill.

He pulled his hips away, and she moaned as an ache tore through her. "Am I too big for you?"

"Of course not!" she managed to gasp. He propped himself up on his arms, and she strained to join him again. "Come back here, you." She pulled him back down to her, and he filled her aching void. Her body pulsated in the midst of their riotous, desperate conjoining. She whimpered, she clawed, she surrendered. He belonged here, embedded within her. "I love you, I love you," he moaned, and how right it sounded coming from him.

She woke in the middle of the night. He lay next to her, his breathing deep and even. A fierce wave of desire shot through her, nestling in her thighs. She wanted this man who was soon to be her husband. With Jack it had been so different: passionate, fulfilling, but that grasping, possessive need had never controlled them.

"Al," she whispered into his ear, twirling his hair around her fingers. Through his sleep he heard her voice and realized it hadn't all been a dream. As he stirred, she took his hand and ran it over her soft curves. "I want you, Al." She yanked off his pajama bottoms, a little too fervently. "Take it all off."

"You nearly did!" But he was ready for her. He was already fully engorged as her thighs closed around him, squeezing him tormentingly in devilish agony. As his lips claimed hers, his hands wound through her hair, he crushed his body to hers, his tongue flicking over her neck, her earlobes, her eyes, murmuring all the time, "*Molta bella…*" He explored like he'd never touched her before.

She stroked and fondled him as he patiently tormented her, stoking the blazing fire for as long as possible. Her hand sought and grasped him, and she rasped, "I can't wait any longer," and guided him into her.

They moved together gently, then roughly, greedily, their raging fury and pent-up frustration released in fire and flood. She cried out as a blaze of spasms tore through her. Finally he grew soft and let his lips linger on her neck, bringing her face to his, teasing her lips with softened lazy kisses.

"We'd better save some for the honeymoon," he murmured as she heaved a serene sigh of release.

She didn't even have the energy to reach for a cigarette.

Chapter Twenty-Three

Al watched Vikki get dressed for her meeting with Whitefield. Sliding her nylons up her legs got an appreciative wolf whistle out of him.

"Save that whistle for when I take them off." She fastened her garters onto the stocking tops.

"I was surprised how calm your father took it when you told him about Bati. I thought he'd go through the roof." He watched her flick mascara on her lashes.

"Dad's an easygoing fellow, deep down. When it's after the fact, and there's nothing that can be done about it, he's cool with it. If I'd told him we were going to dress like a Park Avenue madam and a Cosa Nostra pimp and meet Benzo Battolini in a hotel suite, he'd have shackled me to the kitchen sink and never let me out of here. Besides—he always tells me he sees a lot of himself in me, and if you knew about his shenanigans when he was young—" She pumped the mascara wand inside the tube. "Just read the newspaper articles he saved. They'll turn your hair white."

"I heard a few of the stories from Rosie, and you're way more sensible than either of them were," he said.

"Most of the time. But I do have my moments." She finished with the mascara and opened a bottle of rouge. "But this isn't going to be confrontational. All I'm going to do is ask if he wants to host a tribute special to Jack on television. I'll play up the possibility of an Emmy for him." She swirled rouge onto the apples of her cheeks. "If the conversation goes the way I hope it goes, he'll slip and give himself away. Linc did say Whitefield has a huge ego and a lust for power—and an affinity for the hard stuff."

"Well, make sure power is all he lusts for. It killed me to see Bati making a pass at you." He made a fist and slammed it into his open palm.

"Well, in the end it killed him. And the end justifies the means in cases like that, doesn't it? Al, if our marriage is going to be a successful one, you'll have to realize I do get attention from men occasionally. As you do from women." She found her lipstick brush, swiped it over her peach lipstick and applied it to her lips. The brick red would be too dramatic.

"And that doesn't bother you?" He paced behind her.

"No, I'm flattered when a woman finds you attractive. It means I made a good choice. They can look all they want, they just can't touch." She blotted her lips and gave him the lipstick-imprinted tissue. "This should hold you till later."

He placed it on his crotch. "Doesn't come close."

"Oh, you're so crass!" She swatted him with her gloves. "Okay, here. This should really hold you." And she gave him her left glove.

****

"Vikki, it's so good to see you again." Herbert Whitefield stepped around from behind his desk and clasped her hand between his.

Where was the urge to choke him? For some reason she couldn't explain, she stayed calm, able to give him a smile. "Thank you, Herb."

He showed her to a seat. They exchanged a few ideas about the tribute show as she smoked and sipped coffee. She observed his body language, partially concealed behind his massive desk. He acted as natural as if he went out and killed colleagues every day.

She managed to steer the conversation off on a tangent. "Herb, I didn't tell anyone, and Jack probably didn't mention it to you, but we were having big problems and were separating at the time he died. I just couldn't put up with his philandering any more." *Stay in character*, that coach urged once again.

She waited for a reaction. He didn't show any.

"Vikki, I'm so sorry. I knew Jack was having affairs; everyone knew. I, uh—" He ran a finger inside his collar. "—thought you had an arrangement."

"We did, in a way. I was free to do whatever I wanted. I did—but that didn't include taking on lovers. Jack always told me about his indiscretions. He was very up-front about it." Once again, she waited for a reaction.

This time he nodded like he knew.

"I know about Marilyn and—the others," she went on. "At first, I looked the other way. I was in love with him, and we had the perfect life, otherwise. But eventually, I couldn't take any more, and we stopped living like man and wife. I was going to file papers after the first of the year. His lying to me about going to Chicago when he wound up in Dallas was the last straw. Maybe if he'd been honest with me, he'd be alive today." Her voice shook. This wasn't all an act.

"Everybody loved him, Vikki. I'm so sorry about the way it all turned out. But—how about the future?

Have you made any plans?"

"Well—" She kept her eyes downcast, then zeroed right in on his admiring gaze. "I'm going to design the costumes for my father's next musical. As for my personal life—I'm seeking romance again. I'm looking for a good single man, successful, handsome—someone like you, Herb. Do you—might you have any friends or colleagues who fit that description?" She moved closer and offered his roving eyes some cleavage.

Knowing he was single and on the make was her trump card. She knew a pass perched on the tip of his tongue.

"Well, heh, heh, I'm divorced, and I'd like to think I'm, well, all those things you said. Vikki—why not make a go of it?" He leaned forward, and his chair squeaked. "Let's have dinner together, a nice first date. I could never keep my eyes off you, especially on Emmy night last year. I was dying to ask you to dance, but you wouldn't leave Jack's side. I honestly never thought I'd have a chance with you. That's why I never pursued you." His smile bordered on a leer. "But I'll be honest, Vikki, and please don't take this any way except as the sincerest compliment—you've been my number one fantasy for a long time."

"Is that right?" Despite herself, she basked in the flattery. She was a female, after all. He was successful, single, handsome—everything he'd said. But the smile on her lips was one of smug satisfaction. He'd be putty in her hands.

"If you're not busy Saturday night, may I take you to dinner?" rolled off his tongue.

"Let's make it Sunday night." She needed more time to plan this.

"Sunday it is, then."

This is going to work, Jack, she vowed to her departed husband.

She finally had her man. She knew it.

****

"You're going out with this creep?" Al paced the room like a panther, his voice calm, even, and menacing. "Did you forget one thing? You're engaged to me."

A surge of desire shot through her as her gaze raked him up and down. She still wasn't off that high from the party yet, or from his proposal, or from the thrill of being his fiancée.

"Of course I didn't forget, and I appreciate your concern. But you have to understand I'm not going to give up now. It's not a real date. Well, he thinks it is. But you and I know why I'm really going out with him."

He stopped in his tracks and faced her. "Vikki, I hope you're not setting yourself up for a big disappointment here. Those other guys were trained assassins, and he's just a pen-snatching network executive who drinks too much."

"Who was also with Jack the night he was killed. This isn't something I'm going to let go by the wayside—or waste time calling the cops with more information they'll ignore." She sliced the air with her hand, just as he would. "No, Al, I have to do this and find out what went on there in the Dallas Hilton."

He approached her and clasped her hands. "But I don't want you in danger any more. I love you too much to lose you. Something might go wrong, he might have one too many and get violent, or—who knows."

Conflicting emotions tore at her—loyalty to Al, loyalty to Jack, and the ever-present need for revenge. She didn't want to feel this way now—this close to catching Jack's killer—again. "Al, please, we went through this before we went to see Bati. I love you too. But I need to know the truth, and despite what you think, I know I'm closer than I ever was. I can't let my love for you interfere with my need to do this. So don't make me feel guilty for going through with it."

"I wasn't trying to do that. I'm worried about you being alone with this crud." He tightened his grip on her hands.

"We won't be alone. We'll be in a restaurant. I'll be fine. I promise. Please, Al. I have to do this my way. I don't want to argue anymore. My nerves are raw, and so are yours, I'm sure." She pulled away, fumbled for a cigarette, and lit it, taking a long drag. She needed it.

"I saw the person I loved most in the world gunned down before my eyes, Vikki. When something like that happens to you, you vow it'll never happen again."

"I understand." She blew out a stream of smoke. "But giving up on this when I'm so close—put yourself in my place. Say you were married before and your wife got killed—"

"I have put myself in your place." He raised his voice. "Many times."

She stuck the cigarette into a groove in the ashtray and cracked her knuckles. "And?"

He looked away and threw his hands up. "I'd do the same thing. I wouldn't give up."

"There's your answer," she told him. "I can't give up either."

"I just don't think this will lead to anything." He

shook his head. "So they were both in Dallas to cover the president's visit there. It's a lot more logical one of those three Triumvirate guys did away with Jack. Probably Bati. Can't you leave it at that? Even you said you would."

She fixed her eyes on his. "Not with this new evidence."

"It's hardly evidence," he argued.

"All right, clue. Whatever you want to call it. I'd never forgive myself if I gave up now."

"Just promise me one thing." He followed her across the room to the closet. "If I get killed and nobody knows how it happened, don't go through all this for me."

She reached for his hand, and his fingers closed over her diamond. "I can't promise that. You just said you'd do the same thing if it were your wife who got killed."

"Of course, but that's 'cause I'm a crazy Sicilian."

She got her coat out. "Well, so am I. Partly, anyway. But it's enough."

He helped her on with her coat. "Where's this date?"

"It's not a date." She pulled a scarf from a hanger.

"Whatever the hell it is. Where is it?"

"LeCirque." She tied the scarf around her neck.

"And then?"

"Then nothing. I come home." She stepped into a pair of kitten heels.

"He's got a drinking problem, doesn't he?" Al badgered. "What if he's an abusive drunk?"

"From what Linc told me about him, he gets very honest when he's had too many. I'm going to play on his weakness. Like I did with Bati." She opened her purse to make sure she had everything. "Only this time, I know I've got the right one."

"Just promise me one thing. You'll only go to the restaurant with him and won't be anywhere with him alone. Even in a cab." He opened the front door for her.

"Okay, I promise." She peeked out to look for the taxi she'd called.

"And—" He watched her set her fox fur hat on her head. "Even if something does come out of this, don't do anything yourself. Call me first. Please."

"So now you're conceding that he might be the one I've been looking for?" She saw a pair of headlights light up the driveway.

"I'm just saying anything's possible, and don't fly off the handle and get emotionally wound up. Just stay calm, find a phone, and call me before you do anything. Please promise me that."

"All right, I promise, but like I said all along, I'm taking it one step at a time. It's like reading a book; you can only read one page at a time. Skipping ahead ruins the whole story. Now, step one is I'm going to meet with him and talk with him." She waved at the driver. "Be right out!"

"Why are you so orderly?" He pulled her back as she stepped onto the porch.

"Why are you so obstreperous?"

He didn't answer that. She didn't blame him. After all, English was his second language.

****

She had to admit the dinner at LeCirque was fabulous. The duck à l'orange was cooked to perfection, and Whitefield knew how to choose his wine, although she hardly took more than a sip. For this she needed all her faculties. She watched him polish it off himself.

"Herb, I'm sorry if I can't talk about anything but Jack. He was my whole life." She took a sip from her water glass.

"I understand. I'm a good listener." He lit both their cigarettes.

She excused herself, stopped at the bar, and ordered a bottle of Johnny Walker Black to be sent to the table.

She returned and cut to the chase. "Tell me, Herb, what was your relationship with Jack really like?"

"Well—" His eyes darted around, and he let out a small chuckle. "Jack and I might've had our differences, but he was a good guy. One of the best." He sniffed. Tears shone in his eyes. "I miss him."

The booze and two glasses arrived. She poured them each a neat one, hoping his recent tumble off the wagon was a permanent one.

"Did you ever have arguments?" she pressed on.

"Well, yeah, we all did—artistic differences, the usual." He took the initial slug of his Scotch. "Mmm. Nice and smooth."

She nodded with understanding. "You know, sometimes he got me so mad I'd say, 'I could kill you, Jack!' He used to get my blood boiling, some of the things he did. Did you ever get mad enough to actually want to kill him?" She took another sip of her water, watching him register a semblance of shock at this question.

"Hah? Oh—no. I never got that mad." He gulped another mouthful of Scotch.

"Well, you know what, Herb?" She flicked her ash.

"He came home a few times and told me you'd had some real knock-down, drag-out fights there at the network. There was a lot of back-stabbing, posturing, hostility—" She nodded. "Oh, yes. He came home with all the sordid details."

"Sure, but that comes with the territory. All those creative minds, all that power behind us—sometimes fuses get short."

"Oh, they got short, all right." She made her lips spread in a smile. "Jack had a temper on him. He smashed his share of breakables during his rants." She let out a low whistle. "Valuable ones, too, sometimes. Smashed our whole Lenox crystal collection we got as a wedding present from his own parents."

"Yeah, I saw him fly off the handle more than once. He was the wrong guy to cross." *Burp.* "'Scuse me." He held his hand to his mouth.

She topped off his drink. He was doing a good job of killing that bottle without noticing her giving him generous refills.

"He sure had his dark side," she agreed. "I'd say it was more of a sinister side."

He looked at her with raised brows, but she plowed on. "It seems you fought as much as we did. But we made up in a different way than you—I hope."

He tittered and took another pull on the drink.

"Herb, on one of his taped conversations with you, you tell him not to pursue something, I think it was the JFK plot." She stared him in the eye.

He nodded after a slight hesitation. "Well, he was onto something I thought was bigger than both of us."

"How did you know about it?" she prodded.

Whitefield wiped his brow. It was getting hot—for

him. "Jack told me about this because he figured I'd consider it a great idea of his and be his champion. Jack started tailing people he thought were the conspirators. He wanted to expose the assassination plot and become a big hero. I thought it was too dangerous. Jack didn't know who he was messing with." His cheeks grew red and blotchy.

"You'd rather have exposed it yourself, huh?" she probed, refilling his glass.

"Not expose it. Just leave it alone. Don't interfere with these guys, and stay the hell out of it." His fingers circled the glass.

"You knew the president was probably going to be assassinated and told Jack you should cover it, didn't you?" She sipped her water.

"I wanted us to cover it together. We're newscasters; our job is to report the news as it happens, not stop it from happening. I wanted us to, to…report it as it happened. I mean, if it happened…"

She broke in with, "So tell me again about these arguments you and Jack used to have. Did you ever fistfight?"

"Huh? Naah."

"Well, he used to beat me," she said, losing no momentum.

"No!" His bloodshot eyes bulged.

"Oh, yes. Gave me a black eye, bruises all over my body. I couldn't sit for days. Nobody knows about this." She lowered her voice. "I kept it quiet because I didn't want a scandal. He was too famous to go public with this; it would've ruined his career. Would've ruined the marriage, too. I didn't want to give up the house, the cars—you know, the whole little Camelot thing we had going."

"But he hit you?" His eyes bored into her.

"All the time. For the slightest things. I lost a sock in the dryer, he slugged me. I didn't have his favorite shirt ironed, he broke my wrist. He was very abusive." *Forgive me, Jack*, she pleaded silently.

"You never told your father?" he asked.

"God, no. Dad would've buried him alive." Before stubbing out her cigarette butt, she lit another off it.

"So you never really loved Jack?" He hunched forward, his glass in a white-knuckled grip.

"Love him?" *Sigh.* "At first I did, but after the wedding he started treating me like property. In the end, I didn't even like him. I was his trophy, his ornament. He was my security blanket, my meal ticket. My pot o' gold at the end of the rainbow. A little tarnished, but still a pot o' gold." She took a long thoughtful drag.

"So—are you relieved he's gone?" He drained his glass and refilled it.

"I have to admit I am, Herb. Much as I loved the lifestyle, I'm much better off without him, obviously. I'm sitting here breathing." She affected a relieved sigh, an amazing acting feat.

"That bastard!" His meaty fist pounded the table. "I never knew he had that side to him."

"Oh, yeah, he was a wild animal. Had a fit when I couldn't get pregnant, too." She forged on. "Wanted four kids. But I took precautions and didn't tell him." She fed him more. "Then he found my birth control and really beat up on me that time. That was the worst. Cracked ribs, dislocated jaw. He claimed I was dishonoring his right to reproduce."

"That selfish son of a—"

"Okay, I'll level with you, Herb." She folded her hands on the table. "As long as this conversation goes no further than this table."

He held up his hand and nearly knocked over the near-empty bottle. "Scout's honor."

"He tried to kill me. Tried to strangle me. Twice." She raised her hand to her throat and rolled her pearls between her fingers.

"Jesus, Vikki, why didn't you go to the cops?" His mouth hung open after he spoke. He shoved his glass between his lips and gulped.

"Oh, good heavens, I couldn't let a scandal like that loose." She toyed with an earring. "I couldn't see him go to jail. Imagine how that would've hurt the network's ratings, too."

"That rotten—you *are* better off without him!" Another fist pound. "We all are!"

Now something began to bubble to the surface. "What do you mean, Herb?"

"Oh, the network had their problems with him, too." It poured out of him. "He was difficult, to say the least. Kept demanding more money. Very demanding. Thought somebody died and made him king."

"Wouldn't it be ironic if someone had actually murdered him?" she intoned with a dramatic flair.

Whitefield nodded. "I must admit, plenty of people wouldn't 've minded seeing him out of the way, permanently. They weren't exactly crazed with grief when they heard—the news."

She zeroed in. "How about you?"

"Me? I—we were too much alike. I admired him, respected him, was even in awe of him, but we were such strong rivals, the competition was so fierce, we had each other in a headlock all the time. If we had horns, they'd 've always been locked. Now that I hear what he did to you—he tried to kill you! How could he!" Whitefield's hands clenched. "I despise him!"

"Enough to kill him?" She zeroed in closer.

"I could've pulverized him a few times," he admitted fast enough.

She asked, "How about that night in Dallas?"

"What?" He recoiled as if shocked with a cattle prod.

"Level with me here, Herb." Her eyes stabbed at his. "I know you were in the Dallas Hilton the same night Jack was. He didn't drown in that tub, did he? You killed him. But I'm not accusing you. Actually, I want to thank you. He would've murdered me sooner or later. I owe you my life. I want to make it up to you. I'm in your debt."

"Uh—" His face drained to sheet whiteness.

"It's okay, Herb." She sat back. "You did me a favor. Like you said before."

"So I did. He cheated on you, he tried to kill you, I got him out of the way. You'd be dead now if it wasn't for me. I saved your life. I did both of us a favor. He was going to be my boss, and I couldn't stomach that." On a rant now, he blathered, "Jack was going to expose the plot to kill JFK. I had to get him out of the way. I let him think I was with him on this all the way, and I—" He took a quick gulp of Scotch. "Double-crossed him."

"Oh, you did, did you?" *I'll show you a double-cross.* She fought her most primal urges to kill her prey where he sat. "How exactly did you kill him, Herb?"

He took a breath. "After Jack left for Fort Worth to cover JFK's Chamber of Commerce speech, a guy called the network for Jack. He gave some code name, TVC One-Five or some crap, and said if Jack's not there, to give the message to me, so I took the call. He said 'tell Jack they're gunning for him on Friday.' I said, 'Somebody's gunning for Jack?' He said, 'No, just tell Jack what I said—they're gunning for him on Friday.' I told him I'd make sure Jack got the message. Then I figured what it meant. My intention was to persuade Jack to get the JFK shooting all on film, once and for all." He pursed his lips. "That's how I knew the hit was going to be that day. Jack was already down there, still scouting around after these assassins. He flew his own plane because he was too impatient to wait for a scheduled flight. So I got on the next flight down there. I knew a live network pickup would be a nightmare for a local broadcaster. B'sides, an assassin wouldn't be too keen on carrying out a plan like that seeing television cameras all over the place." He took another gulp of Scotch.

"And the Secret Service would have some security questions for the broadcaster staging such coverage of an intended drive down a small stretch of a planned route. So live coverage was out. But I had to at least get it on film for broadcast later. And get Jack away from it all. So I—" He paused to take a ragged breath.

"I knocked on his hotel room door, he let me in, I smothered him with a chloroform-soaked rag, and submerged him in the tub." He shook his head, his face contorted with pain. "Th—the next morning, I sat through Kennedy's entire Chamber of Commerce speech at the Hotel Texas with one of the network's news film cameras running. When nothing happened there, I knew they were going to the Trade Mart after the motorcade tour through Dallas. So I planned to follow the motorcade to the Trade Mart, but it took a different route than the one in the newspaper I had. The papers published conflicting versions of the route. I was standing on Houston Street and saw the president's limo just before it slowed to make that sharp turn onto Elm." He gestured the curve with his hand. "He was shot before I got to the turn at Elm, and that's when all hell broke loose. I tried to get the camera running as I ran toward Elm, but it was over by then. I couldn't get through the crowds. The limo was already through the triple underpass and on the way to Parkland." His voice shook. "I heard the shots but couldn't film it. If I'd been just a hundred yards ahead of where I was, I'd 've got the whole thing on film. I'd 've got the gunman at the grassy knoll, and it would've been the biggest coup any network executive ever pulled off—in full view, the crime of the century. But that's just hindsight talking. It never occurred to me JFK would be shot that way—by a sniper, on a motorcade route. No president was ever shot by a sniper. It was always at close range, with a handgun. I thought it would be during one of his speeches, or when he was at the theater, even, like a grotesque copycat of the Lincoln assassination."

He wiped his sweaty brow and went on. "I saw a guy with a little Zoomatic as the last of the motorcade sped away. I asked him if he'd filmed any of it, and he said he did. I begged to buy it off him right then and there for ten thousand dollars. I wanted to bring him to the station and interview him. But he refused. He said he was going home to put it in his safe."

He swept away tears she knew were genuine, but it didn't appease her or give her any renewed respect for this bastard, even if he truly believed he'd done her a favor by slaying her dragon.

"Ward was always upstaging me, talked about owning the network someday. Then he planned to stop the JFK killing before they could carry it out. The men behind it wouldn't have liked that."

"He was doomed either way." She kept her tone neutral.

"Oh, what I could've accomplished if I'd filmed the whole thing! But the only person in the world with a movie camera on the motorcade route was Abraham Zapruder with his crappy Zoomatic. Nobody won that day. Nobody." Tears streamed down Whitefield's cheeks. "And I have something else to tell you." He covered his face with his hands.

"What?"

"I tried to have you killed when I heard you were trying to find Jack's killer. Frost told me. He was playing both sides. I thought you were onto me. I didn't want to get caught, so I tried to have you shot. I'm so sorry!"

Her heart surged. "When?"

"I had you followed, and in New Orleans it seemed like the best opportunity. I got my brother-in-law, a hunter, but he missed—shot at you and missed." Eyes downcast, he swiped at his tears.

"He shot Al, my bodyguard," she said. "But Al fired back."

Whitefield threw his head back and moaned.

"So why did you stop trying to have me killed?" she asked. "The bodyguards were finally a deterrent?"

"Not quite," he said. "I lost my hit man."

"What do you mean, lost him?"

"My brother-in-law died that night from gunshot wounds. He was bleeding to death in the car, trying to get away, and crashed into a utility pole. I didn't know anybody else willing to do something like that. I certainly couldn't. I'm no gunman. And you never came looking in my direction, so I figured it was safe enough to leave you alone." He drained his drink. She didn't bother refilling it.

She closed her eyes and digested all of that.

"I thought if you were out of the way, I—oh, God." He wiped his forehead with the linen napkin. She smelled his sweat from across the table. "But I was desperate. You hired Frost, and I thought you were on my tail—I was convinced I was going to get caught and go to jail and get the chair—"

"Well, it's all over now, Herb." He'd see the irony of that soon enough.

"I'm so sorry, Vikki. I always thought you were such a beautiful woman—another reason I was so jealous of Jack. He had this beautiful wife—"

"It's okay. I appreciate your honesty." She forced a soothing quality into her voice.

"Oh, Jesus." He swiped the napkin over his drooling chin. Sweat poured off him like a stuck pig. "It's such a relief to confess it. I've been carrying this around with me so long I started getting bleeding ulcers. I started treating the staff like dirt, and half of them quit—all because of me. I was in analysis, but couldn't tell the truth—I didn't want to go to jail. I had a nervous breakdown. I was in Sweet Hills, a mental institution on Long Island, for two weeks. I got out and tried committing suicide. I swallowed a bottle of pills." He picked up his empty glass and put it back down.

"But my brother found me, called an ambulance, and had my stomach pumped. I didn't want to live with this anymore. I started going to church again, became a born-again Christian. I thought religion could help me, could save me. I've been trying—begging God for my sanity back. I try to think of what good could've come out of it, grasping at straws for salvation. Please, Vikki—you got to realize, you'd be dead now if it wasn't for me. I saved your life. So it was a good thing I did. But I didn't want to hurt you. I was just—going crazy. Please, I'm begging you—"

"Herb, I think we'd better get the check and go." She signaled to the waiter. "I'll get this one." This was one "date" she didn't mind paying for. She reached in her bag for her wallet and patted her waiting gun.

****

She had nothing more to say to this man. She just wanted to make him pay for what he'd done to Jack.

They waited outside for a cab. Shivering, he wiped his sweaty brow. He stumbled into a passing couple. They brushed him off like an annoying fly.

"Herb, before we part company tonight, there's something I'd like from you." She shouted over the traffic noise.

"What?" He turned to her. "Anything."

"Jack's pen."

"Oh, yeah, of course." He nodded. "It's at my apartment."

"I'll come with you, you get it, and then we'll call it a night." She knew she'd promised Al she wouldn't go anywhere alone with him, but this risk was minimal. He was too drunk to make a lunge at anything except the floor.

A cab pulled up, he tumbled in, and they didn't talk till they got to his East 86th Street penthouse.

Knowing he'd been walking around with a cherished possession of Jack's blighted her with an added mix of pain and rage. But she'd finished pumping him with questions, hearing his confessions. All she wanted was Jack's pen, for now. She'd be back later.

They rode the elevator up in silence. Except for his hiccupping and belching.

He let them into his apartment and rummaged around on his desk. "Here, Vikki, I'm so sorry—" He hiccuped. "'Scuse me. Did a little too much imbibing tonight."

He handed her the pen. The sight of it brought forth a flood of tears. She held it and closed her fist around it tightly, a part of Jack for so long. "Why did you have to take this?" she demanded, fighting the urge to kill him right there. It was physically painful to refrain from firing a hole into his gut. "This was a prized possession of his!"

"I—I'm sorry, Vikki, it wa—was a trophy to me. Sometimes people kill people and keep things of theirs—jewelry, something they wore. I knew you gave it to Jack when he won the Emmy. Jack always carried it around, and I wanted something personal of his, to remind me of my triumph over him, my—it says 'to the Emmy winner' engraved on there, and—" He shook his head as if to shake something loose. "It would be as if I won the Emmy instead of him."

What a twisted mind. "Goodbye, Herb." She turned to leave, making a note of his penthouse number.

"Vikki, wait."

She stopped.

"I have something else you should have."

Thinking he was going to return her topless photo, she cringed. She turned and watched as he opened the desk drawer and took out a reel of tape.

"What's this?" she asked as he held it out to her.

"The—incident. Jack was dictating into his machine when I came to his hotel room, and the whole thing got recorded. Here—you should have it. Take it."

She stood, paralyzed. Finally, she shook her head. "No, I don't—" But something pushed her toward him, and he placed it in her hand.

She couldn't wait to get out of there.

"Vikki—can I see you again?"

What brass. "Oh, yes, you'll see me again."

"Sooner than you think," she added as she walked out.

****

Her clicking heels on the sidewalk echoed the slamming of her heart. "I'm going to kill him," she repeated like a mantra. She didn't even know where she was going. *Find a phone and call Al.*

Blind with rage, she stormed up East 86th Street, one thing on her mind—making this bastard pay for what he did. Her fists clenched inside her pockets, her purse with its weight of the gun banged against her side as she strode farther uptown.

She entered a restaurant on 89th Street and bolted for the pay phone across the carpeted entryway. She dialed "O" and called collect.

"Al, meet me at The King and Queen Restaurant, Eighty-Ninth and Park. It's urgent."

"Are you okay?" he asked. "What happened?"

"I'm fine. I'll tell you later. I just need you to get down here right now. I'll wait at the bar. Bring my portable recorder." She slammed the phone down, not wanting to talk any more about it over the phone.

She ordered a Scotch and water. It did nothing to calm her rage. No one in the elegant bistro gave her a passing glance. Dressed in furs and jewels, she blended right in, sitting at the bar looking like any other well-cared-for Upper East Side socialite with too much money and too many problems, including a propensity for the hard stuff.

She had to get out of public view and just be alone for a few minutes, so she drained her drink with a shaky hand, went into the spacious, well-mirrored ladies' lounge, locked herself in a stall, and wailed over and over, "I have to kill him! God, forgive me!" Her cries echoed and died in the depths of tile and marble. She was still trembling with fury when she crookedly applied lipstick. Her anger rumbled like a volcano building up to a violent explosion. *Come on, Al, hurry up so we can get back there and kill that sorry excuse for a human being!*

She waited at the restaurant entrance. The maitre d' asked her if anything was wrong. "Just waiting for my date." She surprised herself at how calm her voice sounded, when she really wanted to lash out at him, tell him to mind his own business, get out of her way. She paced around, then went outside and craned her neck up the street to see if Al was coming. No sign of him. She pressed her head against the glass door and pounded it with her fist. She'd give him five more minutes, then head back to Whitefield's alone.

This couldn't wait any longer.

As she turned to go back inside for the final five minutes, she heard the distinctive Cadillac horn. His car pulled up alongside the canopy.

She bolted for the door and threw it open. "Finally!"

"I drove like a madman to get here. What happened?"

She slid inside and pulled the door shut. "Head to Eighty-Sixth and we'll park there. Whitefield's the one, Al. He killed Jack."

"He confessed?" He turned to her. She saw the surprise in his eyes reflected in the traffic lights.

"Like Othello confessing to Desdemona's maid Emilia. That's not all." She took a deep breath and a trace of satisfaction fought through her gnarled knots of hatred. "You'll be happy to know that shot you gave the guy in New Orleans in the leg killed him. He bled to death. He was Whitefield's brother-in-law."

He blinked a few times, then a pleased grin curved his lips.

She held out the reel. "Whitefield gave me this."

"What is it?"

"It's the murder." Her stomach surged. "The tape machine was empty when they got Jack's things from the room, and this is why," she explained. "The whole thing got recorded. He gave it to me."

"Do you want to hear it?" he asked.

Holding the murder weapon itself couldn't have been worse. Instinct urged her to fling it into the street like it was something evil. But she wanted to hear it. She had to hear it. "Yes."

"Are you sure?" he asked.

"Yes, Al," she insisted. "Now."

He pointed to the glove compartment. "Your tape machine's in there."

She got it out, fed the tape through the empty reel, hit the Play button. She closed her eyes and held her breath.

Her heart slammed against her ribs. Nausea sickened her. This was something she wanted to do, and dreaded at the same time.

It began with Jack detailing his arrival in Fort Worth with his plane. *They changed the location of JFK's next visit to Dallas suddenly, and that made me suspicious. I flew my own plane down, not wanting to wait for a scheduled flight. I went to the Chamber of Commerce hall where JFK's giving his speech tomorrow, to see if anything looks suspicious, sniper nests, anything like that. It all checks out. I also got a map of the motorcade route in the paper. I can only hope he's keeping the bubble on the limo up. I heard Secret Service men in the bar talking about how they planned the parade route—the Dallas cops changed it at the last minute and published the wrong one in the paper. Then they started laughing about how the Hotel Texas, where the president and Jackie are staying, is being guarded by firemen. Firemen, for Christ's sakes...*

A knock at the door interrupted him.

Oh, hello, Jack said from a distance.

It's goodbye, you vulture, snarled Whitefield, followed by a loud thud.

Nothing more was audible. She hit the Stop button as Al squeezed the car into the only space on the street, next to a fire hydrant. He cut the engine and turned to her. "What do you want to do?"

With teeth and fists painfully clenched, she vowed, "I'm going to kill him. The same exact way he killed Jack."

Al nodded. "You got it."

Chapter Twenty-Four

Whitefield took a long time answering. He opened the door in his rumpled shirt and tie, looking like he'd been dragged through hell. His red-rimmed eyes and blotchy face told her he'd been either crying or drinking or both.

"Vikki—what—"

"Don't say anything, Herb." She gave him a shove, and he stumbled backwards. She entered and turned around. "Come on in, darling."

The door crashed against the wall and "darling" stomped in. Whitefield's face drained to dough-white.

They stood side by side, facing Whitefield. Al slid out his Colt and aimed it at Whitefield's heart.

"You double-crossed me!" Whitefield wailed at her, showering spittle.

"Just the way you double-crossed Jack," she replied with menacing calmness. "Now you're going to die just the way you murdered him."

"B-but..." He gulped. "How could you do this to me, after all I told you?" His eyes froze on Al. "Who are you?"

"Who wants to know?" Al answered back.

"Your time is up, Mr. Executive Producer," Vikki said.

Al headed out of the room. "I'll find the tub. And I'll make sure the water's good and scalding." He handed her his Colt. "Here, Vikki. Keep this on him. While you're at it, pop him one in the nuts so he can writhe in agony before we dunk him. It'll give me some satisfaction to know you got him with my gun."

She took the gun, warm from his body heat.

Whitefield stood there trembling, whimpering. His lack of dignity disgusted her. "Vikki, think this over. Killing me will accomplish nothing. It won't bring Jack back."

Water started running in the distance.

"Vikki—you'll go to prison for this!" He backed up against the wall.

The stench of feces wafted over to her. He'd certainly need a bath after this.

"Listen to me, Vikki," Whitefield pleaded. "I'm human. I made a mistake. We all make mistakes—" A dark stain spread over the front of his pants. "I'd bring Jack back if I could!"

Her eyes, narrowed slits of hate, bored into him. "Like hell you would. Now stop blubbering and start praying." Her finger steadied on the trigger.

She aimed the Colt at his wet crotch.

The water kept running.

Time halted.

She watched the figure before her, trembling, at her mercy. The running water stopped. The only sound was of his whimpering.

Al came back. "The tub's full. Let's go." He clamped his hand onto Whitefield's arm. "Come on, Vikki, the bathroom's down the hall here."

Whitefield grabbed onto the handrail. "Please, Vikki, think this over…" Stripped of self-respect, he sounded even more loathsome. "Don't kill me! I don't want to die!"

"Jack didn't want to die either, or did you even think of that, you selfish scumbag?" she spat.

"It ain't your choice, bub." Al jerked Whitefield toward the bathroom. Whitefield stayed quiet, tears streaming down his sweaty face. He bowed his head. It was then she saw the crucifix on the wall behind him, the figure of Christ facing straight at her. She heard His last words just as clearly as if He Himself were speaking to her: "Heavenly Father, please forgive those who stand before you, for they know not what they do."

"Al, wait."

"What for?" He tightened his grip on Whitefield's arm.

She took a breath and closed her eyes. A jumble of thoughts invaded her mind as a wave of emotions weighed down her heart—love, hate, grief, rage…

"Go call the cops."

Whitefield fell against the wall and collapsed in a heap of his own filth.

Al went to the phone. She lowered the Colt.

When the police arrived, Vikki handed the tape to one of them. "This is a murder the Dallas cops closed." She pointed to the crumpled figure. "He's the murderer. Now you not only have a case, you've got your proof."

As they cuffed him and took him out, she turned to Al. "You can still say we did it together."

"His fate was in your hands, Vikki."

"It's in the right hands now." She clasped hands with her future husband. "Let's go home. Topo Gigio's on *Ed Sullivan* tonight."

Epilogue

Vikki spoke softly, on her knees in the dark confessional, her hands clasped, her eyes closed.

"…and when the moment of truth arrived, Father, it was more scary than I'd ever expected. I had the life of this man in my hands. The killer of my husband. But when the moment came, I saw the crucifix and heard Christ's final words and knew I had to leave it up to God. He'll die in the electric chair. I can watch if I want. But I won't. I already saw him die a thousand deaths."

Heading out of the church, she took something out of her pocket and stuffed it into the poor box.

It was the thousand-dollar bill Al had given her. Maybe it would save a few lives.

****

Vikki and Al were married in 1965 and opened a private investigating firm together. Their first client was television station NBS.

Vikki's first anniversary present to Al was a nude sculpture of herself, by Franck LeJardin Jr. Franck made a copy, which now stands in the window of his gallery—and despite many offers from wealthy collectors and an ex-president, it is not for sale.

Linc Benjamin wrote a biography of Richard III after the king's remains were found in the Leicester car park, and claims to have seen Richard's ghost. But he only tells this to close friends.

Herbert J. Whitefield was convicted of first-degree murder and was given the death penalty. He hanged himself in his cell a week into his sentence.

~~

The above details are fiction. The following are from real life.

The man with the home movie camera who refused to sell his film to Whitefield was Abraham Zapruder, a Dallas dressmaker who filmed the only existing footage of John F. Kennedy's assassination as it happened. In 1999, the U.S. Government paid his heirs $16 million for the film.

In 1964, Guy Banister was found dead, some say with a bullet in his body, along with his partner Hugh Ward, within a few days of the Warren Commission's completion of its hearings. The killer was never found. I took creative license and changed the date of his death to December 31, 1963, to suit the story's timeline.

The reporter Dorothy Kilgallen was found dead in her apartment in 1965 "because she knew too much." The killer was never found. I changed the date of her death also to suit the timeline of this story.

David Ferrie, "the kook with the glued-on eyebrows," was a CIA contract agent who knew both Ruby and Oswald and also worked for Carlos Marcello, the Godfather of New Orleans. Ferrie suffered a "brain hemorrhage" and was found dead in his New Orleans apartment. The killer was never found.

Aladio del Valle, Ferrie's cohort, was killed in Miami the same hour that Ferrie died in New Orleans. He was shot in the heart and his skull split open with a machete. The killer was never found.

Jack Ruby was indicted by the Dallas County Grand Jury in 1963. Trial began in February 1964 and ended a month later with a verdict of guilty, with a sentence of death entered. In 1966, the Texas Court of Criminal Appeals reversed the conviction because of "irregularities" and a new trial was ordered. While awaiting retrial, Ruby died of cancer on January 3, 1967, in Parkland Hospital, where President Kennedy and Lee Harvey Oswald were pronounced dead after their murders. To his dying day, Ruby insisted he'd been injected with cancer cells in prison.

Hundreds of people supposedly connected to the Kennedy assassination plot died under mysterious circumstances in the following years. The odds against this happening are several trillion to one.

A word about the author...

Diana has written several historicals set in England and the U.S., and three time-travel romances.

She is a member of Romance Writers of America, the Richard III Society, and the Aaron Burr Association. In her spare time, she has been pursuing a Master's degree in archaeology and loves to visit historical sites all over the world. Diana and her husband own CostPro, Inc., an engineering business based in Cambridge, Massachusetts.

Visit Diana at:

www.dianarubino.com
www.DianaRubinoAuthor.blogspot.com
www.facebook.com/DianaRubinoAuthor
Twitter @DianaLRubino